D0397407

BRIGHT RAVEN SKIES

KRISTINA PÉREZ

〖Imprint〗
MAKE YOUR MARK

NEW YORK

[Imprint]
MAKE YOUR MARK

A part of Macmillan Publishing Group, LLC
120 Broadway, New York, NY 10271

Library of Congress Cataloging-in-Publication Data is available.

ISBN 978-1-250-13287-1 (hardcover) / ISBN 978-1-250-13288-8 (ebook)

Our books may be purchased in bulk for promotional, educational, or business use. Please
contact your local bookseller or the Macmillan Corporate and Premium Sales Department at
(800) 221-7945 ext. 5442 or by email at MacmillanSpecialMarkets@macmillan.com.

Series design by Ellen Duda

Map by Virginia Allen

Imprint logo designed by Amanda Spielman

First edition, 2020

1   3   5   7   9   10   8   6   4   2

fiercereads.com

An té a dhéanfadh cóip den leabhar seo, gan chead, gan chomhairle,
dhíbreodh é go Teach Dhuinn.

Sisters are made, not born.

For all of mine, on both sides of the Atlantic.

DRAMATIS PERSONÆ

IVERNIC ROYAL FAMILY

KING ÓENGUS, HIGH KING OF IVERIU—father of True Queen Eseult of Kernyv, uncle to Lady Branwen, holds his court at Castle Rigani in the Province of Rigani

QUEEN ESEULT OF IVERIU—mother of True Queen Eseult of Kernyv, aunt to Lady Branwen, sister to Lady Alana and Lord Morholt, originally from the Province of Laiginztir

IVERNIC NOBILITY

LADY BRANWEN CUALAND OF LAIGINZTIR—Royal Healer to King Marc of Kernyv, heir to Castle Bodwa, cousin to True Queen Eseult of Kernyv, niece of Queen Eseult and King Óengus of Iveriu, daughter of Lady Alana and Lord Caedmon

LORD DIARMUID PARTHALÁN OF ULADZTIR—heir to Talamu Castle, descendant of High King Eógan Mugmedón, son of Lord Rónán and Lady Fionnula, former love interest of True Queen Eseult of Kernyv

SIR BEARACH OF ULADZTIR—an Iverman in the service of Lord Diarmuid, a member of the Parthalán clan

LADY ALANA CUALAND OF LAIGINZTIR (*deceased*)—mother of

Branwen, Lady of Castle Bodwa, sister to Queen Eseult and Lord Morholt

LORD CAEDMON CUALAND OF LAIGINZTIR (*deceased*)—father of Branwen, Lord of Castle Bodwa

LORD MORHOLT LABRADA OF LAIGINZTIR (*deceased*)—uncle to Branwen, former King's Champion, brother to Queen Eseult and Lady Alana

MEMBERS OF THE ROYAL IVERNIC HOUSEHOLD

SIR FINTAN OF CASTLE RIGANI—member of the Royal Ivernic Guard and bodyguard to Queen Eseult

TREVA OF CASTLE RIGANI—head royal cook

DUBTHACH OF CASTLE RIGANI—servant at the castle, son of Noirín

NOIRÍN OF CASTLE RIGANI—castle seamstress, mother of Dubthach

MASTER BÉCC OF CASTLE RIGANI—former royal tutor to True Queen Eseult and Lady Branwen

SAOIRSE—from the coastal village of Doogort, an assistant to Queen Eseult in the infirmary at Castle Rigani

GRÁINNE—an orphan girl from the Rock Road befriended by True Queen Eseult

SIR KEANE OF CASTLE RIGANI (*deceased*)—member of the Royal Ivernic Guard and former bodyguard to True Queen Eseult, from a coastal village along the Rock Road

KERNYVAK ROYAL FAMILY

KING MARC OF KERNYV—husband of True Queen Eseult, uncle to

Prince Tristan of Kernyv, brother to Princess Gwynedd, son of King Merchion and Queen Verica of Kernyv

TRUE QUEEN ESEULT OF KERNYV—wife of King Marc of Kernyv, daughter to King Óengus and Queen Eseult of Iveriu, cousin of Lady Branwen, niece to Lord Morholt

PRINCE TRISTAN OF KERNYV—heir to Castle Wragh and the protectorate of Liones, nephew of King Marc of Kernyv, Queen's Champion to True Queen Eseult, son of Princess Gwynedd and Prince Hanno, grandson of King Merchion and Queen Verica of Kernyv, cousin to Ruan, Endelyn, and Andred

PRINCE RUAN OF KERNYV—son of Prince Edern and Countess Kensa, King's Champion and cousin to King Marc, heir to House Whel, older brother to Princess Endelyn and Prince Andred, cousin to Tristan

PRINCESS ENDELYN OF KERNYV—daughter of Prince Edern and Countess Kensa, lady-in-waiting to True Queen Eseult of Iveriu, sister to Prince Ruan and Prince Andred, cousin to King Marc and Prince Tristan

PRINCE ANDRED OF KERNYV—son of Prince Edern and Countess Kensa, king's cupbearer and cousin to King Marc, younger brother of Prince Ruan and Princess Endelyn, cousin to Tristan

COUNTESS KENSA WHEL OF ILLOGAN—head of House Whel, widow of Prince Edern, mother of Prince Ruan, Princess Endelyn, and Prince Andred, aunt to King Marc and Prince Tristan, sister-in-law of Queen Verica; Villa Illogan and the other lands belonging to House Whel are located on the south coast

DOWAGER QUEEN VERICA OF KERNYV (*deceased*)—mother of King Marc and Princess Gwynedd, grandmother of Prince Tristan, widow of King Merchion, originally from the Kingdom of Meonwara

KING MERCHION OF KERNYV (*deceased*)—father of King Marc and Princess Gwynedd, husband to Queen Verica, older brother to Prince Edern

PRINCE EDERN OF KERNYV (*deceased*)—younger brother of King Merchion, husband of Countess Kensa, father of Prince Ruan, Princess Endelyn, and Prince Andred

PRINCE HANNO OF LIONES (*deceased*)—father of Tristan, navigator with the Royal Kernyvak Fleet who became a prince through marriage to Princess Gwynedd of Kernyv; his ancestors came to Kernyv with the Aquilan legions from Kartago

PRINCESS GWYNEDD OF KERNYV (*deceased*)—mother of Tristan, older sister to King Marc, daughter of King Merchion and Queen Verica

GREAT KING KATWALADRUS (*deceased*)—king at the time the Aquilan Empire withdrew from the island of Albion to the southern continent; decreed that southerners could remain in Kernyv; started the raids on Iveriu that have persisted for a century

CONCHOBAR (*deceased*)—true father of Prince Ruan and Princess Endelyn, an Ivernic prisoner of war

KERNYVAK NOBILITY

BARON ANIUD CHYANHAL—head of House Chyanhal, one of the five largest baronies in Kernyv granted by Great King Katwaladrus; House Chyanhal's lands lie in the north, bordering on the Kingdom of Ordowik

BARON BRYTAEL DYNYON—head of House Dynyon, one of the five largest baronies in Kernyv granted by Great King Katwaladrus; House Dynyon's lands are adjacent to Liones and used to comprise some of Prince Tristan's territories

BARON CINGUR GWYK—head of House Gwyk, one of the five largest baronies in Kernyv granted by Great King Katwaladrus; House Gwyk's lands lie to the east, bordering the Kingdom of Meonwara

LORD DOANE GWYK—eldest son of Baron Gwyk

BARON MAELOC JULYAN—head of House Julyan, one of the five largest baronies in Kernyv granted by Great King Katwaladrus; House Julyan's lands are located close to Monwiku and the Port of Marghas

LADY NEALA JULYAN—eldest daughter of Baron Julyan

BARON RYD KERDU—head of House Kerdu, one of the five largest baronies in Kernyv granted by Great King Katwaladrus; House Kerdu's lands are located on the north coast

MEMBERS OF THE ROYAL KERNYVAK HOUSEHOLD

SEER CASEK—chief *kordweyd* of the temple in Marghas

SEER OGRIN—*kordweyd* who runs a rural temple on the moors

SIR GORON OF HEYL—former sword master to King Marc and Prince Tristan, King's Champion to the late King Merchion of Kernyv

MORGAWR—Captain of the *Dragon Rising*, member of the Royal Kernyvak Fleet

LOWENEK—an orphan girl rescued by Branwen from the mining disaster

TALORC—an Iverman who resides at Seer Ogrin's temple

MASSEN OF MONWIKU CASTLE—a stable boy

WENNA OF MONWIKU CASTLE—widow of Tutir

TUTIR OF MONWIKU CASTLE *(deceased)*—member of the Royal Kernyvak Guard

BLEDROS OF MONWIKU CASTLE (*deceased*)—member of the Royal Kernyvak Guard

FREOC OF MONWIKU CASTLE (*deceased*)—servant in the castle kitchens

ARMORICAN ROYAL FAMILY

KING FARAMON OF ARMORICA—father to Crown Prince Havelin, Prince Kahedrin, and Princess Eseult Alba

QUEEN YEDRA OF ARMORICA—mother of Princess Eseult Alba, stepmother of Crown Prince Havelin and Prince Kahedrin, originally from the Melita Isles and a distant cousin to Xandru Manduca

CROWN PRINCESS ESEULT ALBA OF ARMORICA—daughter of King Faramon, younger half-sister to Crown Prince Havelin and Prince Kahedrin

CROWN PRINCE HAVELIN OF ARMORICA (*deceased*)—son of King Faramon, older brother to Prince Kahedrin and half-brother to Princess Eseult Alba

PRINCE KAHEDRIN OF ARMORICA (*deceased*)—son of King Faramon, younger brother to Crown Prince Havelin, older half-brother to Princess Eseult Alba

QUEEN RIMOETE OF ARMORICA (*deceased*)—mother of Crown Prince Havelin and Prince Kahedrin

MEMBERS OF THE ROYAL ARMORICAN HOUSEHOLD

LADY SOFANA—head of the Queen's Guard and Queen's Champion to Queen Yedra of Armorica, a member of the Melitan Guardians

SIR YANNICK—a member of the Royal Armorican Fleet

CREW OF THE *MAWORT*

XANDRU MANDUCA—Captain of the *Mawort*, friend to King Marc of Kernyv, and a member of the powerful Manduca family, a mercantile dynasty from the Melita Isles; distant cousin to Queen Yedra of Armorica

CHERLES—crewmember of the *Mawort*, from the Melita Isles

DWARDU—crewmember of the *Mawort*, from the Kingdom of Míl

IERMU—crewmember of the *Mawort*, from the Melita Isles

SPIRU—crewmember of the *Mawort*, from the Melita Isles

OTHO—crewmember of the *Mawort*

PETRA—wife of Otho

PART I

THUNDER
WITHOUT RAIN

SMOKE AND ASH

MONWIKU CASTLE SMOLDERED. Kernyv was at war.

And so, too, was Iveriu.

Despite the mist from the moors, Branwen wiped hot sweat from her brow. Her mount thundered across the grass and her joints ached, unaccustomed to the stallion's gait.

When dawn had lit the carnage at the castle, the True Queen of Kernyv was nowhere to be found. Neither was her Champion.

The howl of a lonely wind rushed over Branwen, troubling the bushes of spiky yellow gorse scattered across the moorland. She pressed on.

Tristan and Eseult were missing, presumed kidnapped by the Armoricans.

Branwen urged her stallion faster, desperate, searching. King Marc judged that the Armoricans would try to abscond with his wife by sea. The Royal Guardsmen left standing after the attack had been scouring the northern coast all day for any sign of either the queen or the king's nephew.

Laughter like the sea's murkiest fathoms swelled in Branwen's mind. Deep down, she didn't believe that Queen Eseult had been taken by the Armoricans. Not least because the small boats and dinghies used to stage the attack had all been destroyed.

No, the truth was that her cousin, whom Branwen had once considered closer than a sister, had abandoned her husband. Her duty to Iveriu. Her honor. She had run away with Tristan—the first man Branwen had ever loved.

It wouldn't be long before Ivernic shores were once more razed, deluged with broken bodies. Branwen had failed in her most important mission. She'd traded her heart for peace but they had both turned to ash.

Dark fire simmered beneath her skin. The Old Ones, the Otherworld guardians of her island kingdom, had imbued Branwen with primordial magic to defend her cousin and her homeland.

But she was sick of saving Eseult and Tristan.

Dirt sprayed into the air from beneath her mount's hooves. In the distance, she spied the enormous arches of the Aquilan water bridge that hulked over the moors. Rubicund snakestone glistened in the late afternoon sun.

Branwen recalled her first day in Kernyv. There had been a disaster at the mine that lay in the shadow of the great arches. A burst floodgate had buried men alive; others were maimed by rubble, their limbs contorted.

She shivered. The disaster was nothing compared with the slaughter at the castle. When the Old Ones had refused to answer her pleas, Branwen bargained with Dhusnos instead—the Dark One who ruled the Sea of the Dead.

To save Monwiku, to save King Marc, Branwen had made a terrible choice.

She would have to live with the horror that she'd unleashed. The unnatural deaths wrought by the Shades.

"Branwen!" called Ruan from up ahead, interrupting her spiraling thoughts.

The King's Champion had brought his horse to a halt beside the Stone of Waiting. Visible for leagues in every direction, the emerald-colored longstone reminded Branwen of a crooked finger. Ruan claimed that if you waited here on a full moon night the face of your true love would be revealed.

The Kernyveu had a penchant for outlandish stories.

Branwen grunted and dug the heel of her boot into her stallion's flank. She no longer believed in true love, but there was a kernel of truth in the superstition. The Stone of Waiting marked a place of in-between. A place where the Veil between this world and the Otherworld thinned. A place that belonged wholly to neither realm.

As she drew closer to Ruan, his mane of dirty blond hair, sweat streaked, wavered in the breeze. He was not only the King's Champion but also the man who frequently shared Branwen's bed.

She still marveled that she knew what he looked like without his clothes.

Ruan rubbed his knuckle against his lower lip, brow crinkled in concern as Branwen approached. He'd objected to her joining the rescue party for fear of her safety, but King Marc overruled him. The king had witnessed Branwen's powers during the battle.

Ruan was dressed in the same clothes as yesterday, as was she. Clothes now stained with dirt and other people's blood. He scanned the flat moors around them and the Morrois Forest to the west, one hand tensed on the pommel of his sword.

"You look exhausted," he told her, face softening. When he smiled,

Ruan's eyes became a brilliant topaz and he developed a prominent dimple on his chin.

He spoke to Branwen in her own language, as he always did when they were alone. Branwen was the only person besides his mother and sister who knew that Ruan was not the heir to Prince Edern—King Marc's uncle—but the bastard son of an Ivernic prisoner of war.

With a mischievous tilt to her mouth, Branwen replied, "*Mormerkti*," in Kernyvak. *Thank you.* "As do you." But she was. She was so exhausted she felt nearly intoxicated.

Branwen sidled her mount next to Ruan's, and he stroked a hand over her long, tangled black locks. He lifted a small swath of her curls—they had turned whiter than a Death-Teller. A breath buckled in her throat as if she'd seen one of the Otherworld women who presaged your demise.

"Are you well, Branwen?" Ruan said, his voice low. "I didn't think fear could truly bleach someone's hair."

It wasn't fear that had whitened her curls. It was magic. Her life force was tied to her powers, and she'd used a tremendous amount fighting the Armoricans.

Branwen shrugged him off. "I'm as well as can be with my cousin missing."

Ruan held her gaze for a charged moment. Her statement was a challenge, a dare to see if he would tell her what he was really thinking. He'd long suspected Tristan and Eseult's relationship to be more than simply that of a queen and her Champion.

If her cousin's betrayals brought more war to Iveriu, perhaps Branwen should let her burn. The thought was treasonous, but then, the True Queen had already tried to assassinate *her*.

Coughing pointedly, Ruan offered Branwen the waterskin dangling from his saddle. "Here. Drink," he said. "With Lugmarch's blessing."

She accepted and drank thirstily. Lugmarch was reputedly made the first king of Kernyv after ridding the land of giants by serving them tainted mead.

Another ridiculous Kernyvak tale.

"Night approaches," Ruan noted offhandedly, watching the shifting clouds, their undersides painted with pink light. "We'll have to call a halt to the search." He may have affected a casual manner, but Branwen knew better.

As she returned the leather waterskin to him, his hand caught on hers; he removed the waterskin and turned her right palm skyward. Branwen gritted her teeth at the ache in her swollen wrist, which had deepened to a mottled purple from her struggle with the assassin.

Ruan's eyes widened. There was no ignoring the blackened scar in the center of her palm.

After her deal with Dhusnos, the Hand of Bríga had changed shape and darkened.

Branwen was grateful that Ruan wasn't versed in the ancient Ivernic language of trees. If he were, he'd be able to read exactly what Branwen had become:

Slayer. Killer.

"It's nothing," she said. Wind teased her cerulean cloak.

"Branwen." Frustration edged her name. "I saw those . . . those creatures. Did one of them hurt you?"

She shook her head. The Shades had defended Branwen because she'd allied herself with their master. Half man, half a carnivorous seabird known to the Kernyveu as a *kretarv*, the Shades were hideous to behold.

Their souls were condemned, indentured to Dhusnos for eternity. They sustained themselves by feasting on those with a beating heart, human or animal. Sucking the life from them, making their flesh wither. The Shades had laid waste to the Armoricans in stomach-turning fashion.

"Please, Branwen," Ruan said. "I can see the gears of your mind turning."

In exchange for their aid, Branwen had made a vow to the Dark One. By the New Year festival of Samonios, she would provide him with another wretched soul to crew his spectral ships. If she didn't, he would take the soul of someone she loved.

A fresh shiver racked her shoulders. Ruan traced his forefinger along the black stain, a tender yet demanding gesture.

"The creatures didn't touch me," she assured him. "I burned myself. It's not serious." Ruan parted his lips to protest and Branwen pressed a finger to them. "I'm the Royal Healer, and I would know."

She saw another rebuke in his eyes, but a shout rose from the forest. A man's voice. "Someone's been found," Ruan said, translating the Kernyvak.

She snatched back her hand. "Let's go," Branwen said, and kicked her stallion into a gallop. She reached the edge of the forest first, Ruan close behind, and entered a tunnel made from curved branches. Light fell across her in a lace-like pattern.

The day before the wedding, Branwen had taken part in a hunt for the *rixula*, a red-breasted bird whose name meant "little queen." Ruan had been the one to catch her. This time, Branwen needed to catch the True Queen first.

Another cry echoed through the trees. "False alarm," Ruan announced, aggravation clear. Hiding her relief, Branwen twisted in her saddle. "We should keep heading toward the castle. King Marc sustained injuries. I'll need to check them and change the bandages." This was true, of course, but Branwen also wanted Ruan to relinquish the hunt for the night, lest he find Tristan and Eseult in a compromising position.

Ruan worked his jaw. Marc's welfare was his paramount concern. Not solely because he was Ruan's king, but because he loved his cousin.

"You're right. We'll set out again at first light."

Branwen nodded, turning back around, and made a clicking noise from the side of her mouth. She bounced as the stallion trotted, every muscle in her body tight. Her eyelids fought against the pull of sleep. An hour passed as she and Ruan rode in silence, listening to the harmony of birdcalls, the sun hanging ever lower in the sky.

Suddenly a shrill whinny broke into the birds' evening song, discordant and nerve tingling. Branwen whipped her head toward the sound.

"Is that Senara?" Ruan said. Before she could respond, his mount was charging off the path. Branwen's tongue took on a metallic taste. She had no choice but to follow him into the copse.

Branwen's mare had bolted when she'd used the Hand of Bríga against the queen's assassins. Her fire magic had startled Senara.

The horse stomped a hoof, tossing her head, a slightly wild look in her eye. As if she'd been waiting, impatient. Perhaps she had scented Branwen in the forest. Branwen was fond of the high-spirited mare named for the hero Lugmarch's mother.

Ruan brought his mount alongside Senara. Her umber coat shone. He stretched a pacifying hand toward the mare and she allowed him to stroke her muzzle.

He looked to Branwen for an explanation. Her pulse raced.

"You said you'd been thrown from Senara. Not that you'd abandoned her in the forest," he said. That had indeed been the excuse Branwen had invented for her disheveled appearance the night before. "I'd wondered why you'd chosen a different mount today." A line appeared above Ruan's nose. "How did you get back to the castle?"

"I walked."

He screwed up his lips in annoyance. "*Bran*—" Ruan started and cut himself off. His eyes had latched onto something on the ground.

Bile rushed up Branwen's throat. On the tenebrous forest floor, between Senara's hooves, was something darker still.

A charred body.

Ruan leapt down from his horse, hand instinctively touching his sword. Branwen brushed her fingers over her mother's brooch, which clasped her cloak closed. It was all that she had left of Lady Alana.

Branwen slid out of the saddle, feigning confusion. Ruan led Senara away so that he could inspect the body—what was left of it. The corpse's mouth was frozen in a scream. Branwen suppressed one of her own, tasting her own disgust.

She had done that. The Hand of Bríga had burned him alive. She had defended herself with her most potent weapon when he attacked her. It was her life or his.

And yet, Branwen hoped her parents couldn't see her from the Otherworld—couldn't see the full brutality of her magic.

Ruan dropped to one knee beside the body. It was unidentifiable. His shoulders grew stiff as he withdrew a sword from beneath the corpse. Flakes of burned flesh clung to the steel. Revulsion passed over his features.

He didn't look at Branwen. She stood stock-still. Her heart pounded, yet she didn't tremble. Ruan pushed to the balls of his feet and stalked through the clearing. The air around them grew tauter than a bowstring just before an arrow is released.

Branwen knew what Ruan would find a few strides away. He knelt beside another body. She saw his chest rise and fall.

She felt as if she were stunned, caught in the lethal enchantment of a *kretarv*'s gaze. She could only watch as Ruan tried to unravel her lies.

Then something winked at Branwen. A flash of gold against the coming night. She staggered toward it, almost sleepwalking. The gold glinted again from a nest of leaves.

She didn't notice Ruan was behind her until his chest was pressed to her back, and he snatched the golden object from the low-lying branch.

He spun Branwen around violently to face him.

"My father's knife," he said. The lion emblazoned on its handle was the royal standard of Iveriu and it looked ferocious indeed. But not half as ferocious as Ruan's expression. "You told me you didn't know where it was." The knife was precious to Ruan and he had gifted it to Branwen. "You lied to me."

Branwen had told Ruan more lies than she could count. Lies to protect her cousin, lies to protect Tristan, lies to protect Iveriu. And yet she found solace in Ruan's arms. He knew parts of her nobody else did. He kissed her scars.

"Branwen, what happened here?" The words were rough.

As much as she wanted to punish her cousin for trying to have her killed, Iveriu needed Eseult to remain on the Kernyvak throne. Iveriu's needs mattered more than her own. When Branwen didn't reply, Ruan pressed her.

"The dead men were carrying swords forged from Kartagon steel," he said. "I recognize the blacksmith's mark. He makes the weapons for the Royal Guard. Tutir and Bledros never reported for their watch yesterday." Ruan drew in a long breath. "Tell me why there are two dead guardsmen, my father's knife, and your horse in the same copse, Branwen."

She wet her lips, crafting a plausible story.

"I was thrown by Senara, like I told you. The knife must have slipped from my boot when I fell." Branwen spoke slowly, deliberately. "I can't say why the guardsmen were here. I didn't see them."

Conflict brimmed in Ruan's eyes. He wanted to believe Branwen; she knew he did. He fidgeted the knife handle back and forth.

"Why did you *walk* back to the castle?" he asked.

"Night was falling and Senara had run off."

His gaze locked with Branwen's. "Why were you in the forest alone when we were on the brink of war?"

Because she'd wanted more than anything to make amends. Branwen had resolved to conjure an antidote to the Loving Cup—to release Tristan and Eseult from their false love, from the spell she had cast because she wanted her cousin to know happiness in her marriage to King Marc. The drink of peace that now promised more bloodshed.

But, why had Branwen cared so much for Eseult's happiness? Why had she risked her life time and again for a woman as selfish as the queen?

No answer came.

She swallowed several more times. It was wrong to use Ruan's feelings for her against him, but she saw no other option. Yet another thing her cousin had stolen from her. Softly, she said, "Remember when I told you I had a favorite cave in Iveriu where I liked to escape?"

Ruan nodded. "I know it was foolish, but I—sometimes I feel caged on Monwiku," she continued. "I wanted to feel free. For an hour or two. Can you understand that?"

Ruan's jaw slackened. "I can. But, Branwen, something grisly happened here. And I think Senara returned to the last place she knew you were."

Branwen took a large step backward. "Is this when you accuse me of treason again, Prince Ruan?"

He inhaled shortly. She had intended to wound him with the use of his title—his fake title.

"Ruan!"

It was King Marc. Panic streaked across his Champion's face. He tucked the knife into his waistband.

Branwen prayed the king wasn't in danger but she couldn't be more appreciative for the distraction.

"You take Senara," Ruan barked at her. "We'll come back for the stallion." In a blur of motion, Ruan tied the reins of the horse Branwen had been riding to a branch.

"Don't leave my sight," he said as Branwen flung a leg over her mare. Senara neighed.

"Treason it is, then," Branwen concluded.

Ruan growled something that might have been her name or maybe a curse. He slapped Senara into a canter and jumped back into his own saddle. He kept Branwen's mount in front of his, driving them both hard toward the direction where Marc's voice had originated.

In a matter of minutes they joined a group of Royal Guardsmen, dressed in the black and white that indicated the king's service, clustered around a tree.

Could it be Tristan or Eseult?

Marc stood with his guards, sword at his side. Normally the king didn't bear arms, trusting his retainers to protect him. But Marc no longer knew whom he could trust.

Someone had provoked the war with Armorica—and it wasn't the king.

"Ruan," Marc said, glancing toward his Champion. He was a young king, only twenty-seven, but he looked completely haggard. His silver eyes were dull, and he tugged at his beard. He said something to Ruan rapidly in Kernyvak, and then switched to Aquilan for Branwen's benefit. The Aquilan Empire had ruled the island of Albion, as well as much of the southern continent, until a century ago, and its language was still the common tongue among the nobility of many kingdoms.

"We've found an Armorican," he told her. "We need a translator."

Branwen released a heavy breath. Did the Armorican know where the True Queen was? Doubtful. But at least the discovery of her cousin's betrayal had been delayed for another day.

Branwen dismounted and came to stand beside Marc. She heard Ruan grunt but he shouldn't complain. She hadn't left his sight. Branwen tilted her head at the king, asking for permission to approach the prisoner. He stepped aside, letting her into the circle.

The prisoner was slim. His knees were tucked into his chest, head bowed, leaning against the trunk of a tree. Eight sword tips were pointed at him.

Branwen's eyes were drawn to the prisoner's hands, folded over his knees. The fingers were tapered, his skin golden-brown. Elegant. She slid her gaze upward to the yellow knit cap on the Armorican's head, then darted it back down to his hands.

Branwen stepped toward the prisoner. "Don't get too close," Ruan cautioned from behind her. She snorted.

"Sister," King Marc said. Branwen's heart clenched. He genuinely regarded her as such. She crouched in front of the prisoner. Gently, she touched a hand to the Armorican's scraped knuckles.

The prisoner snapped his head up and Branwen saw that his nose was broken.

She also realized that the prisoner was a woman.

"I'm a healer. Are you in pain?" Branwen said in Ivernic, reaching toward her nose. She repeated the question in Aquilan, and recognition blazed in the woman's eyes.

The captive had understood Branwen, which meant she was no common sailor. And there was no need for a translator.

The woman flinched as Branwen leaned closer and her cap skewed to one side, a messy braid falling against her shoulder. A few gasps rose up from the Royal Guardsmen.

Hatred shone in the woman's eyes as she watched Branwen watching her.

Frenzied memories from last night rushed through Branwen. The lithe Armorican who had assaulted King Marc, the woman's scream when Crown Prince Kahedrin was felled, and Kahedrin's final words.

Now . . . you'll deal . . .

"Princess Alba?" Branwen said.

The other woman bared her teeth and spat in Branwen's face.

"Onward, Armorica."

LAMENTS OF THE SEA

AN EERIE QUIET SETTLED OVER the rescue party as they returned to Monwiku, not with the True Queen or Prince Tristan, but with the Armorican princess.

Branwen watched Alba closely, wiping the spit from her cheek as Ruan bound the princess's hands and saddled her on his mount, seating her in front of him as the stallion carried them along the coast.

Kernyv comprised the southwestern peninsula of the island of Albion, and they rode directly into the setting sun. As Branwen squinted, she could almost make herself believe that she glimpsed Iveriu's silhouette across the water.

Alba rankled at Ruan's touch, chafed against the ropes around her wrists. Branwen didn't know whether women in Armorica could inherit the throne, but it didn't matter. She was King Faramon's last living child. Faramon would want—*need* Alba back. Branwen's own mother had killed herself rather than give the late King of Kernyv a highborn hostage, and Lady Alana was the only sister to the Queen of Iveriu.

Branwen stayed close to King Marc throughout the journey, as vigilant as any of the Royal Guard. The wound on his thigh that he'd received from Prince Kahedrin leaked blood as dark as mead. She wanted to examine it as soon as they reached the castle, but Marc bade her attend Princess Alba's injuries first. He was too noble to speak aloud what they both knew to be true: If Alba died, Kernyv lost significant leverage in any negotiations with Armorica.

Marc was perhaps too noble to be king.

The tide was out when Monwiku Castle came into view. Both the last rays of sunset and the first pale moonglow shimmered on the sand as the horses traversed the causeway. The rescue party left iridescent hoof-prints behind them.

Kernyvak legend recounted how the small island had been carved by rampaging giants, and perhaps it had. When Branwen arrived in Kernyv a few months ago, she'd been awestruck at the castle rising from the sum-mit of a hill upon an island, its five rounded towers scraping the sky. In the gloaming, the first precocious leaves now quivered on the trees that sprouted from its bedrock, heralding spring.

Monwiku seemed strangely like home to Branwen, even with the smoke billowing from King Marc's savaged gardens.

Round stone dwellings were sprinkled along the shoreline, half of their thatched roofs charred. Anger scalded Branwen anew. Monwiku boasted its own brewery, granary, barracks, stables, and the hundreds of servants required to manage them—hundreds of innocents attacked while asleep in their beds. How many of the castle servants had perished in the assault?

Branwen guided Senara past the docks, up a cobblestone path that zigzagged the hill toward the castle. They passed beneath a foreboding granite archway guarded by two marble sea-wolves, jowls opened wide, baying at the tide. Chest tightening, Branwen blinked away the image of the assassin's tortured corpse. The rescue party reached the stables, halfway up the hill, and only one stable hand was there to greet them.

She dearly hoped he wasn't the only one left.

Princess Alba was to be confined, under armed guard, in the apartment in the West Tower just above Branwen's own. The five towers of the castle where the royal family resided ringed the inner bailey, almost like a rose. Branwen retreated to her room first to collect her healing supplies. The bed was unmade, several garments tossed on the floor. She remembered Ruan beneath the sheets and shook her head, dismissing the thought.

Four Royal Guardsmen were posted outside the apartment that until recently had been occupied by Dowager Queen Verica, Marc's mother and Tristan's grandmother. Branwen ardently wished the old queen were here to offer sage counsel. Before she died, she'd asked Branwen to watch over her son and grandson, but last night Tristan had told Branwen she was nothing to him. And he was nothing to her but an obstacle to peace.

"*Nosmatis*," said the guardsman closest to the door, and Branwen wished him a good evening in return. Her boots resounded against the polished stone.

Alba stood by the window, gazing down at the circular courtyard, cracking her knuckles. She was tall for a woman and she held herself with poise.

Wind chimes rang out from below. At a lower pitch, Branwen detected the surf crashing against the base of the island. The Kernyveu believed that the laments of the sea must be answered lest the lonely sea deluge the land. The Veneti Isles had once formed part of the Kernyvak peninsula, Marc had told her. Now they were a refuge for pirates.

Alba pivoted to face Branwen as the door clicked shut. Branwen didn't expect a warm welcome, and she didn't receive one.

"What do you want?" the princess demanded in Aquilan. She spoke brusquely, yet there was a melodic cadence to her voice. It rose toward the high ceiling.

"I am the Royal Healer," Branwen said. "My name is Branwen. I'm here to treat your wounds."

Alba canted her head, gaze shrewd. "You're not from Kernyv."

Branwen walked toward her slowly. She could almost hear the *plink-plink* of Queen Verica's dice. The elderly queen had loved games of chance, and Branwen was playing one right now.

"No, Lady Princess. I'm from Iveriu."

"Lady Princess?" Alba snorted. Candlelight accentuated her wry expression. "I prefer *Captain*."

Branwen stopped when there were a few handsbreadths between them. She gestured at an armchair beside the hearth.

"Won't you be seated so I can examine you?" she said matter-of-factly. Branwen surmised that this princess wasn't partial to flattery, and she was in no mood to do any flattering. Alba folded one arm over the other.

"The sooner the nose is set after it's broken, the better it will heal," Branwen said.

"I'm not vain. My brother Havelin had a crooked nose, and it suited him."

She believed Alba cared little for her looks, although not even the swelling around her nose could disguise the beautiful lines of her face. She was also younger than she'd appeared in the forest. Branwen recalled that King Faramon's daughter had seen one summer less than

Eseult. Tomorrow was Eseult's birthday, she remembered with a start. Her cousin would be eighteen.

Alba set her teeth at Branwen's scrutiny.

"There are other complications from a broken nose," she informed the princess.

"Such as?"

"Would you like to be able to breathe properly or not? I've had a long day." Her tone was tart and it required substantial willpower not to teeter on her feet.

Alba made a noise in the back of her throat, then showed herself to the armchair. Branwen was aware of the other woman's gaze following her movements as she filled a shallow basin with water from a pitcher on the court cupboard and laid it on a small table near the hearth. She dipped a linen cloth into the water and raised it toward Alba's face.

She jerked back. "What are you doing?"

"I need to clean the wounds. If I were going to kill you, I'd have done it in the forest."

"You're not going to kill me." Enmity glittered in her sable brown eyes. The princess knew her own value.

"Glad we're in agreement," Branwen said, and began wiping the grime and soot from Alba's forehead. The princess closed her eyes. Branwen noticed faint tracks through the dirt on her cheeks, tracks left by tears.

Alba hissed when Branwen dabbed around the fracture. "I saw your brother Havelin last year," she said to distract her. "At Castle Rigani, during the Champions Tournament."

The princess curled her lip. "I'm glad he didn't win. The Iverni are too eager to lie down with sea-wolves."

Branwen forced her hand not to slap the other woman. For years she'd also thought of the Kernyveu as the wolves of the sea, the sea-wolf

18

being the royal insignia, but King Marc had sacrificed much for a chance at peace. The part of Branwen's heart that was not yet shadow-stung told her that Alba was only a girl of sixteen or seventeen who had just lost her brother, and she was a hostage in a hostile land. But that part of her heart was diminishing.

"I'm sorry for the loss of your brothers." Branwen's tone was formal, distant. "My own parents were killed in a raid." She didn't mention that, as a boy, Marc had taken part in that raid.

"Then what would your parents think of you now?" Alba sneered. "At the beck and call of a pirate?"

Rage spiked inside Branwen, her heartbeat deafening. *She would make an excellent Shade*, said a teasing voice. Branwen struggled to catch her breath. Marc needed the Princess of Armorica alive.

Blood dripped from Alba's nostril. She wiped it away, muttering what Branwen presumed was an Armorican curse.

"May I?" she asked. The princess nodded. Dusky smudges were forming beneath both of Alba's eyes. Branwen pinched the bridge of her nose, testing the bone. She heard a crackling sound. "Is your vision at all blurry?" Branwen said, sensing that her own fatigue would soon hamper her eyesight.

"No."

She clucked her tongue at Alba's half-spat response. "Take a deep breath through your nose." Alba did as she was bade. "Now, exhale." The princess's breath was harsh. "Any difficulties?" Branwen asked.

"No."

Branwen turned to the leather satchel containing her supplies, rummaging around until her hand grasped a jar of lichen and garlic paste. Andred, her apprentice, and Ruan's younger brother, was very skilled at making salves.

"This is to prevent infection," she explained to Alba who eyed the ceramic pot askance. She rubbed it into the cuts on Alba's nose and cheek. "Any other sword wounds?" Branwen said mildly. Alba shook her head.

"Only a few pulled muscles."

"Fine. After I leave, wash yourself thoroughly and I'll have clean clothes sent." Branwen scanned the twigs in Alba's haphazard plaits. "And a comb."

"I don't like dresses." Alba's chest lifted, imperious. For a moment, she reminded Branwen of her cousin. She noted Alba's calfskin trousers and filthy yellow tunic—deep Armorican yellow. "No use for dresses on a ship," Alba said. "They only slow you down when you need to make a quick escape." Defiance lit her eyes and her mouth hinted at a smirk.

Branwen heard the threat, but she didn't take the bait. "I'll let the laundress know." She retrieved a glass vial from her satchel and held it out to the princess. "A few drops in water will relieve any discomfort from your injury. Sleep upright, propped against the pillows. If you develop a fever or begin to bleed profusely from your nose, tell the guards to send for me."

Alba narrowed her eyes. "You're quite comfortable giving commands to royalty."

"I am the *Royal* Healer."

The princess released a reluctant laugh that became a grimace. "Keep the vial. I won't lose my wits around my enemies."

"As you like." Branwen dropped the vial back into her bag. "You're lucky, the bone isn't fractured too badly. It should heal of its own accord."

"If I were *lucky*, Kahedrin would be alive and you'd be mourning your king."

"Rest well, Lady Princess." Branwen enunciated each syllable crisply as she slung the satchel over her shoulder and proceeded toward the door.

"How did you know?" Alba called from the other end of the room. "How did you know who I was?"

Branwen turned. "Kahedrin told me his sister Alba preferred sailing to parties. And that you had the attitude of a giantess."

Her lower lip trembled once, a sheen to her eyes.

"He didn't deserve to die," she said. Guilt flooded Branwen. She had been the one to heft the ax. But then she imagined blood trickling from Marc's mouth.

"Neither did my king."

Branwen exited. The sound of the porcelain pitcher smashing against the stone floor echoed down the corridor.

✠ ✠ ✠

Branwen's gaze strayed to the Queen's Tower as she crossed the inner bailey. Torchlight illuminated the granite and malice surged in her chest.

Where were Tristan and Eseult tonight?

The only occupant of the tower at present was Endelyn, Ruan's younger sister and the queen's lady's maid. Branwen's knowledge of how Prince Edern had terrorized his household made her sympathetic to Endelyn, especially since she knew that Endelyn was also the daughter of the Ivernic prisoner.

Andred was the sole natural son of Prince Edern, his hair dark and curly, whereas Endelyn and Ruan were fair like their mother Countess Kensa. Branwen circled her injured wrist. She'd ask Andred to help her wrap it later.

Andred and Endelyn had spent all day tending to the wounded in the barracks and servants' quarters. Branwen could barely conceal her surprise that the snobbish princess—who wasn't truly a princess at all—was willing to get her hands dirty. Perhaps Branwen should be more charitable. She knew how hard it was to live a lie.

The smell of smoke lingered in the air. Smoke and death.

Fire and sea and fighting men. Branwen's childhood nightmares were made manifest last night.

She exchanged a *nosmatis* with the guard at the entrance to the King's Tower. There was a haunted look in his eyes. How many of his friends had died in the attack? How would he explain the appearance of the Shades to himself?

Branwen followed the twisty staircase to the second landing. Her thighs ached, her legs growing weak beneath her, as she fought her dizziness. She heard the rumble of Marc's and Ruan's voices from behind the door to the king's study.

She knocked once as she entered. "Branwen, please, join us," said Marc.

He offered her a worn smile. By the light of the Aquilan oil lamps, the few red bristles in his beard were more pronounced against the brown. He sat at the head of the large, oblong table used for council meetings.

Branwen's gaze swept around the room, skimming the *fidkwelsa* board in the far corner. She and Marc had yet to play her favorite game of strategy.

Ruan was seated to his right, and he greeted Branwen with considerably more apprehension. "Lady Branwen," he said.

"Prince Ruan."

Marc's eyebrows lifted. Branwen pulled out the chair on the opposite side of the table from Ruan and rested her leather satchel atop it like a barricade. Ignoring the tension, the king angled his shoulders toward her.

"How is Princess Alba?" he asked.

"Furious." Ruan made a scoffing noise. "But her nose will heal," Branwen said, directing her answer at Marc. "Her other wounds are superficial. She'll make a full recovery."

"Good. That's very good. *Mormerkti*."

Marc touched the antler shard that Branwen knew lay beneath his tunic. The king was a follower of the Horned One: Carnonos was a man from the Aquilan Empire who had given his life to save his father, was impaled on the antlers of a great stag, and reborn as a god. His followers wore the antler to honor his sacrifice.

But neither the Horned One nor the Old Ones had intervened to save the king last night.

Only the Dark One.

"I am sending a messenger to King Faramon with news that his daughter is our guest at Monwiku," Marc said. "I trust that if he has knowledge of my wife's whereabouts he'll divulge it." Steel tipped his diplomatic words.

As part of the Seal of Alliance with Iveriu, Marc had agreed to make Eseult not merely his Queen Consort but a True Queen: a full sovereign in her own right. She would continue to rule in the event of his death. The possibility that she had fallen into enemy hands was intolerable.

Branwen and Ruan shared an involuntary glance. The suspicion in his eyes sent her heart reeling, her mind scrambling. Neither of them believed that King Faramon had the slightest inkling where the True Queen was to be found. But, for Iveriu, Branwen needed to maintain the fiction.

Desperation parted her lips. "We could interrogate Alba," she suggested to Marc, hating herself a little bit more.

Ruan shifted uncomfortably in his seat. "She's a woman, and a princess." His tone was indignant. Ruan had confided in Branwen that he'd killed his own father when he'd changed the target of his beatings from Ruan to Endelyn. He would never lift a hand against a woman.

"She's an enemy warrior," Branwen countered, shocked by her own vehemence. "And a skilled one."

True, very true, teased a scornful voice in her mind. She rubbed her brow, nearly scratching herself. *When you stop lying to yourself, it's my voice you hear*, the Dark One had told her.

Marc leaned over the table, placing a hand on Branwen's shoulder. "I know how much you want your cousin back," he said gently. He looked worried—for her. "I do, too. But we must treat Alba as her rank demands and trust that Faramon will do the same for Eseult."

Her cheeks flamed. "Certainly." Branwen flattened her right hand against the table, quelling her lethal impulses.

The king returned his attention to Ruan. "What news of Captain Morgawr?"

Morgawr had captained the *Dragon Rising* that brought Branwen and Eseult from Iveriu. They had fought the Shades together.

"I sent my fastest rider to Captain Bryok at Illogan. When Morgawr reaches him, he has orders to return his convoy to Monwiku," Ruan reported. The morning before the attack, Morgawr had sailed a contingent of the Royal Fleet southward to form a defensive ring around the peninsula, to guard it from an Armorican offensive. The shallow waters around Monwiku had always protected it from an assault by sea. No one had anticipated a stealth attack from fishing boats.

The king nodded at Ruan. "A message was also sent to my mother and the other barons to come to the castle as soon as they are able—and to bring soldiers to supplement the Royal Guard." Another nod.

"And *Xan*—Captain Xandru?" There was an almost undetectable catch in Marc's voice. He darted a sideways glance at Branwen. Xandru

Manduca came from a prominent mercantile family in the Melita Isles. But he wasn't merely a merchant. He was a spy, and the king's former lover.

Ruan shook his head. "The scouts couldn't sight his ship from land. He must have caught a good wind."

Marc ground his teeth. Xandru was a distant cousin to Queen Yedra of Armorica and he'd volunteered to act as Kernyv's ambassador. He'd also set out from Monwiku immediately after Queen Verica's funeral. His attempts to persuade King Faramon that Marc hadn't authorized the pirate attack that killed his eldest son, Havelin, would come too late, however.

"I pray he won't become another hostage when he lands in Karaez." The king touched the antler shard again.

"He's a Manduca," Branwen said. "And he's very capable of taking care of himself." Xandru was both charming and skilled with a blade. She'd already found herself on the wrong end of it.

Marc inhaled, attempting another smile, but there was no crinkling at the corners of his eyes. The stained glass rattled in its casing as a gale blew off the sea.

Sliding her gaze to Ruan, Branwen said, "Have you sent riders to Liones? When I last saw Tristan he told me he'd be heading there in the morning. Perhaps he left early?"

Liones was a protectorate of Kernyv, located on the peninsula's southern tip. Queen Verica had gifted the land to Tristan's mother. Tristan could be its king if he hadn't pledged fealty to Marc. Save for the Loving Cup, Tristan had always been loyal to his uncle, but his status posed the threat of civil war.

"I have sent a messenger to Castle Wragh, yes. If that's indeed where he went." Doubt dripped from Ruan's response. "My Lord King," he began, choosing his words carefully, and Branwen felt a snake coil around her heart. Marc lifted his chin.

"My Lord King, Tristan's horse is missing from the stables. As is the True Queen's."

Branwen skewered him with a look. "And what of it?"

"It would suggest that the True Queen was not taken from the castle against her will."

Branwen felt as if she were being tossed overboard into a sea of nightmares.

"Are any other horses missing?" King Marc asked, detached.

"No, sire."

Marc tugged at his beard. "There are many reasons why that might be, Ruan," Branwen said. Her agitation bled through her voice.

"There are," Ruan agreed. "But I discovered something else in the Morrois Forest."

"Go on," said the king.

"Tutir and Bledros. They didn't report for watch before the attack. I found their bodies in the wood. They'd been burned—to disguise their identities, almost as if it was premeditated. But I recognized their weapons."

King Marc's shoulders grew taut, the muscle in his jaw flickered.

"What do you suspect, Ruan?" he said in a level tone.

"My Lord King, the evidence indicates that neither Tristan nor Eseult were present at the time of the attack. Why would they leave the castle in the middle of the night? It suggests foreknowledge." Ruan cleared his throat. "We have to at least entertain the possibility that Tristan delivered Queen Eseult to the Armoricans. Or that he wanted to keep her safe because he's planning on claiming the throne and making her his bride."

Marc's fist hammered the table. The wood reverberated like a thunderclap.

"I will entertain no such thing!" The king rarely lost his temper, and Branwen held her breath. "Tristan is my blood. My *brother* in the truest sense. I know you see each other as rivals, but to accuse him of treason? I didn't think your jealousy ran so deep."

Ruan blanched; his nostrils flared. "Tristan is your brother, but *I* am your Champion. I defend your crown first. My duty is to keep you on the throne." He leaned forward, pleading, avoiding Branwen's glare. "If Tristan isn't working with the Armoricans, then why else would he and the queen disappear together?"

Branwen held on to the table as phantom waves buffeted her.

"Unless it was because they'd arranged a tryst," charged the King's Champion.

"That's enough, Ruan." Marc pounded the table again. "I won't sit here and listen to you slander my queen."

"I'm not the only one at the castle who's noticed how much time Tristan and Eseult have been spending together since her accident. How many serenades he gives her. How many harp lessons."

"Leave me," Marc snarled. "I refuse to discuss this further. You're dismissed."

Exasperation gripping Ruan's face, the chair skidded against the stone as he pushed to his feet. He bowed from the waist.

"*Nosmatis*, my Lord King."

Marc didn't reply. Ruan shot Branwen a pained glance. She too remained silent. When Ruan strode from the room, back as straight as he could manage, King Marc hung his head in his hands.

Branwen said nothing. She listened to the king's steadying breaths and the laments of the sea. His hands still blinkered his eyes and his head remained bowed as he said, "Ruan won't be the only one to harbor such suspicions. Many nobles seek to discredit Tristan after the alliance with Iveriu, but they won't be honest enough to tell me to my face."

Unfortunately, Marc spoke the truth. Several of the barons looked down on Tristan because his father had been a commoner and his ancestors had come to Kernyv from Kartago with the Aquilan legions. They also bore a grudge against King Marc and the High King of Iveriu for agreeing to free the prisoners of war from both kingdoms. The Kernyvak nobility had grown used to free labor for their fields and mines.

Marc gave his head a shake. "Besides you and Ruan, I don't know who I can trust." He lifted his gaze at last to meet Branwen's.

"I'm sorry, brother."

Marc trusted her implicitly, and yet she had used magic on him, on Tristan and Eseult. Her throat grew scratchy. Branwen didn't deserve Marc's trust, or his love, but she took it greedily.

"May I inspect your wound?" she said, trying to rein in her emotions. "I noticed you beginning to limp."

Marc released a soft laugh. "I can't hide anything from you."

"It's my healer's eye."

The king pushed his chair back from the table. Branwen stood and pressed her fingers around the wound. The tan material of his left trouser was stained nearly black. Kahedrin's sword had pierced Marc just above the knee.

"I need to remove the pant leg," she said. Marc nodded. Branwen retrieved a scalpel and cut away the fabric. The gash was the length of her forefinger.

"It's barely a scratch," Marc said.

"If you don't want to lose the use of your leg, you'll follow my instructions." He laughed again at the severity of Branwen's tone. "This *scratch* needs stitches."

"You keep me honest, sister."

With a gulp, Branwen filched a decanter of Mílesian spirits from a sideboard at the far end of the room. She splashed some on Marc's thigh to cleanse the wound.

"Either I'll have to ask the King of Míl to send me another bottle of his finest spirits or I'll have to stop being shot with arrows and stuck by swords."

The king was attempting a joke but it was no laughing matter. Shortly after the royal wedding, an Armorican assassin had attacked King Marc in the forest. Branwen had never been convinced that he'd been sent by King Faramon, but nobody would share her doubts after the siege of Monwiku. The assassin had been poisoned in the castle dungeons before he could reveal who'd hired him.

"Branwen," Marc said more seriously, as she returned to his side. "The magic you used last night. Are you . . . do you need anything? To recover?"

"I'm tired, but we all are." In truth, Branwen didn't know if she'd ever recover.

"I'm in your debt. Again. As is my kingdom." He paused. "I'd like to know more about your magic." His silver eyes were kind, yet Branwen's stomach pinched. "When you're ready," Marc added.

She nodded, although she didn't understand her magic herself.

Branwen poured a few drops from the vial Alba had rejected into a goblet of wine for the king.

"We call this Clíodhna's dust in Iveriu," she said. "She's an Otherworld queen whose song heals the sick. Andred found it for me in the forest. It will ease your pain as I sew you up."

The Kernyveu added a spice to their wine that never failed to tickle her nose. She sneezed as she handed Marc the goblet.

"*Mormerkti.*" He took a long sip. "Would you consider asking Andred to be your apprentice full time? I fear that being the king's cupbearer is putting him in too much danger. I know he thinks he's a man, but he's only fourteen."

Branwen heated the tip of a needle with the flame of the oil lamp.

"I think he would be devastated," she said. "And I don't know who else you could trust so completely?" She shook her head to clear the fog of exhaustion.

Marc pursed his lips. The king's cupbearer was his only defense against poisons.

"You may be right." He hissed as Branwen slid the needle through the flesh. Despite her weariness, she worked quickly and deftly. "Someone paid the pirates to make the attack on Karaez look like I'd sanctioned it. But who stands the most to gain?" Marc mused.

"Some would say Tristan," Branwen said quietly.

The king glanced up. "Do you believe him capable?"

She pulled a stitch through and his flesh whimpered. "I don't, Marc. I don't think he'd betray you." *On purpose*, Branwen added in her mind.

"*Mormerkti.* I value your opinion. If Tristan has spent more time with Eseult since the miscarriage than I have, then that is entirely my fault."

The king didn't know that the child his wife had lost wasn't his, and Branwen could never tell him. She loved him as a brother, had forgiven him for his part in her parents' deaths, and yet she couldn't test their bond that far.

"I pray they're together tonight," he said. "Tristan would defend his queen to the death." Marc swallowed. "I also pray it hasn't come to that."

His eyelids fluttered from the Clíodhna's dust. "When you stepped off the ship from Iveriu, I thought that you and Tristan might be well suited," said the king, and Branwen felt as if the needle in her hand were piercing her own heart. "But I can see why you and Ruan found each other. You both like to be right."

"Courtship is hardly the most pressing subject at hand."

Marc laughed, a tad more dreamily. "Fair enough. I'll apologize to Ruan for shouting at him. He's only trying to protect me."

"A king doesn't need to apologize."

"No, but he should. When he's in the wrong." Marc sighed. "Your cousin told me something her father said—that a king's subjects keep him in power. King Óengus is a wise man."

Branwen nearly missed a stitch. It was Lord Caedmon, Branwen's father, who had said that, and it had been Branwen who relayed his counsel to Marc when she came to his marriage bed disguised as her cousin.

To prevent the *kordweyd* from discovering Eseult was no longer a maiden—that she'd lain with Tristan on the voyage from Iveriu—Branwen had taken her cousin's place on the wedding night. To keep the peace, Branwen had resolved to give the king her virginity instead. And yet, lying next to Marc who was good and kind, she couldn't betray him so grievously.

Branwen had tricked him, Tristan, Eseult, the *kordweyd*—everyone—into believing the deed had taken place. She offered her blood to the Old Ones, bartering. Praying they would be appeased, satisfied. That her gods wouldn't let war come to Iveriu because Branwen had been foolhardy enough to conjure the Loving Cup.

The weight of her many deceptions pressed more heavily than a mountain on Branwen's chest.

"Tomorrow is Eseult's birthday," she said.

Marc scrubbed a hand over his face. "I won't rest until she's found.

Until they're both found." He took Branwen's hand, his movements less precise than normal. "When Eseult is back at Monwiku, I'll fill her bedroom with every honeysuckle in Kernyv."

"Why honeysuckle?" Branwen said. She finished suturing the wound and smeared some of Andred's salve over the stitches.

"You said it was your cousin's favorite flower."

"Ah, of course. I must be more tired than I realized."

"We both should rest." Marc kissed Branwen on the cheek. "Sleep well, sister."

"*Nosmatís.*"

Branwen collected her things and tidied them into her satchel, but she had no recollection of Eseult's favorite flower or why her cousin might have chosen it.

WHITE RAVEN

A BROODING PRESENCE FILLED THE HALLWAY.
Ruan leaned against a tapestry that depicted the burning of Isca. When the Aquilan Empire had retreated from the island of Albion, Meonwara—Kernyv's neighboring kingdom to the east—staged an invasion. The king known as Great King Katwaladrus repelled the Meonwarans from Kernyv's borders, and then followed them home, setting their capital city of Isca alight.

Queen Verica had come from Meonwara. Branwen wondered what she'd thought every time she'd spied the destruction of her homeland preserved in silken thread. Wrath? Humiliation? Queens were taught to endure their resentments quietly. Branwen had been taught to endure. Her heart no longer wanted to be quiet.

"Are you spying on me, Prince Ruan?" she demanded.

He pushed away from the wall. "I was *waiting* for you, Lady Branwen. We need to talk."

"We have nothing to talk about. You've made your suspicions plain to the king."

Ruan reached for Branwen. "What we haven't talked about could fill the Dreaming Sea." He took her right hand in his, and she winced. He gentled his grip and stroked her swollen wrist with his other hand.

"Ruan, I'm ready to collapse," she said, letting her weariness bleed into her voice. "Can your accusations wait until the morning?"

He clenched his jaw. "You're infuriating, Branwen," he said, and she wished the mellow candlelight didn't make his features so appealing. His shoulders heaved as he let out a breath, but he didn't let go of her hand.

"I'm the King's Champion," Ruan said low. "It's my duty to see the threats to his crown that Marc doesn't see. Either because he can't see them, or because he refuses to see them."

He was right. Of course Ruan was right. Branwen's stomach tightened. "I've never questioned your loyalty to the king," she said. "But mine is to the True Queen. To Iveriu above all." Branwen should be out looking for her cousin right now, in fact, but she didn't know where to start or how much longer she could remain upright.

"Our loyalties are only in conflict if those we serve are in conflict," he said steadily, holding her gaze until it was nearly too much. Branwen didn't dare look away.

Dim light undulated between them. Her hand grew clammy in his.

"Last night," Ruan began. "I saw Tristan running from the Queen's Tower. Moments later, I found you crying. Why were you fighting?"

Why were they fighting? Because after suffering alone with the burden of the Loving Cup for so long, Branwen had finally decided that the lovers should suffer with her.

Branwen snorted at Ruan, choking on a bitter laugh. "Do you think that I uncovered Tristan's plot with Armoricans but failed to alert anyone?"

"No." He stood close enough that his breath tickled the tiny hairs above her top lip. "But I think you *are* protecting someone."

When had he learned to read her so well? Branwen had been foolish to let the King's Champion past her barriers.

She offered Ruan a scrap of truth. "Tristan was angry with me. He shouted at me. That's why I was crying."

But Branwen had enjoyed his anger—her *own* anger. She had delighted in telling her cousin that Tristan's love was the result of Branwen's magic. Nothing more; nothing less. The Queen of Iveriu was insistent that no one could ever know of the existence of the Loving Cup. Especially not the lovers who imbibed it.

Branwen had been eager for Eseult to find happiness, but more than Eseult's happiness, the Queen of Iveriu had wanted to ensure King Marc made her daughter a True Queen. Her aunt believed love would be stronger than any treaty.

This was the first promise to her aunt that Branwen had ever broken. It no longer seemed to matter. The Loving Cup had gone horribly wrong and Branwen wanted the lovers to know that their pain, their passion was nothing but an illusion.

Ruan studied Branwen hard, waiting for her to continue. Tears of loathing stung her eyes. She could tell him none of those things.

"Why was Tristan angry with you?" he prompted.

"Because of Queen Verica." Another scrap. "Because I knew she was dying, but I didn't tell him." Ruan shifted his weight, interlaced the fingers of their right hands. "Tristan blames me for his goodbye being so brief."

Ruan's voice was soft as he asked, "Why didn't you tell him?"

"Queen Verica didn't want anyone to know. I'm a healer, and a healer must keep her patients' confidences." It had been the first rule of healing that her aunt had instilled in Branwen. "If they don't trust me, I can't help them."

"I know how much you care for your patients. You treat them equally regardless of their station. It's one of the things I admire most about you." An almost wistful expression came over Ruan. "But, Branwen—" He took a breath, inhaling her name. "I still think there's something you're hiding from me. Someone you're trying to shield. What really happened yesterday in the Morrois Forest?"

She stiffened. "If you think *I'm* one of the threats to Marc that he can't see, why didn't you tell him about Senara? Or the knife?"

Ruan shook his head. "Isn't it obvious?" he said. "Because you're my *karid*, Branwen."

She took a small step backward. *Karid*. It was a Kernyvak word. King Marc had described Xandru that way. *Beloved*. Branwen and Ruan had shared their bodies, but not their feelings.

"Ruan." She swallowed.

"You don't have to say it back." He lifted her injured hand to his lips. "I know you don't think you can fall in love."

Branwen's knuckles were scraped, scabbed. He kissed them. "Is there a similar word in Ivernic?" Ruan asked in a hush. "My father never taught me."

Branwen swallowed again. His true father had died badly when Prince Edern discovered the countess's affair, but he'd given Ruan his language and he'd given him his knife.

"*Kridyom*," she rasped. "Heart-companion."

Ruan placed his left hand flush against Branwen's heart.

"*Kridyom*," he repeated.

She shivered. For a moment, she wanted to do nothing but melt into Ruan. To forget everyone and everything else—every vow she had ever made, every time she'd prayed that one day she'd make Lady Alana and Lord Caedmon proud.

"They attacked me," Branwen told Ruan. "Tutir and Bledros."

Alarm rounded his eyes. "Why would the Royal Guard attack you?" He dropped his hand from her chest. "What cause would they have?"

"What do men most often want when they attack women?" A coppery tang filled her mouth as she bit the inside of her cheek. She would not feel guilty for allowing Ruan to draw a false conclusion about men intent on murdering her.

Ruan swung his gaze up and down the corridor. "I've known them both for years, Branwen," he said. "Bledros was first commissioned by House Whel, and I recommended Tutir for the Guard. His wife just had their second child. I was a witness at his daughter's Anointment at the temple in Marghas."

Branwen suppressed a pang of grief for Tutir's children. Fathers could be murderers, too. She stared at Ruan blankly.

"Men don't always see the same side of other men that women do. I feared for my life." Her words were hard. "Do you doubt *me*?"

The grinding of his teeth said that he did. "You killed them?" Even though they were alone, Ruan spoke so that only Branwen could hear.

"I had your knife. It was self-defense." She crossed her arms. His tormented gaze anchored her to the spot.

"Why wouldn't you report the attack?" he said.

"Maybe I was terrified. Afraid of an interrogation like this one?" Branwen said, the pitch of her voice rising. "I'm still a foreigner here. And let's not forget that your mother and Seer Casek accused me of murdering the Armorican assassin not so long ago!" Countess Kensa had deemed Branwen a threat from the moment she'd laid eyes on her, although Branwen couldn't ascertain why. Seer Casek was the chief *kordweyd*—seer of the Horned One—and he disdained Branwen for her Ivernic gods.

Yet none of those were the reasons she'd hidden her crime. Although they were good ones. Branwen hugged herself against the changing winds.

Ruan worried his lower lip. "I can understand your fears," he said. "But Tutir and Bledros weren't stabbed, Branwen. They were burned. If they attacked you randomly, how were you able to burn their bodies? *Why* would you?" Each question became more urgent, more labored, as if Ruan didn't want to ask it, but felt compelled by duty.

"It doesn't make sense, and believe me I want it to make sense," he told her, but the man who called Branwen his beloved might pose a greater danger to Iveriu than the Loving Cup ever had.

"Why don't you tell me what *you* think happened?" Her words were vengeful darts.

"I think someone lured Tutir and Bledros to the forest, and that someone was lying in wait. That the murders were premeditated."

"What reason could I have for wanting the guardsmen dead?"

"I don't think you had motive, Branwen. Tutir was on duty when the Armorican assassin was found dead in the dungeon. Perhaps he was involved, and someone was covering their tracks."

"Someone like Tristan, you mean."

"*Krídyom*," Ruan said. The word crashed over Branwen. "The only person you would lie to my face to protect is your cousin. Tell me what happened, and I promise to stand by you."

Panic lanced her. He was close, so close, too close to the truth—to ruining the peace. She only had one choice.

Ruan took a step forward. "Stop," Branwen said. "You can stop your wild conjecture. I need to show you something—in your room." She would give him a truth. Just not the one he was expecting.

"Branwen, I don't think we should let ourselves get distracted . . ." He trailed off.

"I'm not trying to *distract* you." She laughed haughtily. "But I need total privacy."

Ruan nodded, his neck glowing faintly red. Branwen followed him to the floor below, where the King's Champion resided. The layout of each tower was identical and Tristan's empty apartment occupied the same location in the Queen's Tower.

Ruan allowed Branwen to enter first. The oil lamps on the walls were already lit. The lamps were fueled by nuts foraged from the wood, and a heady aroma suffused the chamber. Ruan was habitually untidy. Tunics and britches were strewn over the backs of chairs, and a plate of half-eaten pickles lay next to a pile of maps. The servants had graver concerns today than cleaning up after the prince.

"Lock the door," Branwen said. Ruan huffed a small breath. The latch clicked. He turned around to face her.

She pressed the Hand of Bríga to her middle. When the alarm was sounded last night, King Marc had sent Ruan to secure the True Queen. Ruan had seen the Shades prowling through the castle, but he hadn't seen Branwen fight.

"Ruan, I lied to you about the mark on my hand. But not about killing the guardsmen. I know that you follow the Horned One and that you think little of gifted women," she said. His lips parted at her statement but the intensity of her stare made him close them again. The *kordweyd* were exclusively men, and women were barred from the Mysteries of the New Religion.

"In Iveriu, we follow the Old Ways. Our gods, and the Otherworld-dwellers we call Old Ones wield tremendous power."

Branwen lifted her right hand, palm upward.

"They gave me magic," she said. The Hand of Bríga was composed of three aspects: the Fire of the Hearth, the Fire of Inspiration, and the Fire of the Forge. No woman had wielded it since the legendary Queen Medhua.

A wisp of midnight danced above Branwen's palm. Liquid, beautiful, dangerous. A dark flame with a golden silhouette.

Before her deal with Dhusnos, the flame had been blue.

Ruan looked at Branwen, stunned. He didn't make a sound.

"I summoned the creatures you saw. Shades, we call them. We were losing and we needed more . . . warriors to protect the castle." The flame seemed to grow animated at her words. "I ended Tutir and Bledros when they attacked me. It wasn't premeditated. *Me*. Not Tristan. Not the True Queen. *I* burned those men alive."

Ruan took a shallow breath. For once, the rakish King's Champion was speechless.

Branwen closed her fist to squelch the flame. When she'd arrived in Kernyv, she'd known she would have to become someone new. *Slayer*. She never would have imagined who that would be. *Killer*.

Or maybe it was who she'd been all along.

She unlocked the door and left her lover where he stood.

✵ ✵ ✵

Branwen woke at daybreak from a fitful sleep. King Marc often paced the castle gardens when sleep eluded him, but the gardens were watered with blood. The Kernyveu would be returned to their families for burial; the Armoricans would be burned in accordance with their traditions.

Rustling could be heard from Alba's suite on the floor above hers, and from the inner bailey below. No one at the castle had slept well.

Branwen stretched her arms above her head, the muscles of her back and shoulders sore, complaining. She had scarcely treated her own cuts and bruises last night before stripping down to her shift and collapsing into the bed. She cursed the stiffness in her injured wrist. What would Ruan do with the knowledge she'd given him? Exhaustion had only blanketed her mind with calm for a few bittersweet hours.

Sighing, Branwen padded to the window, surveying her quarters. Eseult had exiled Branwen from the Queen's Tower after Countess Kensa accused her of inducing the queen's miscarriage. At the time, Branwen had been shocked that her cousin could give any credence to the countess's malicious words. Her cousin's mistrust had been a soul-deep wound. Now she marveled at her shock. Eseult had been selfish and prone to tantrums since before she could walk.

Branwen was thankful to have a room to call her own.

The sky was a painful blue this morning, so clear it threatened to unveil her secrets. She poured water from a pitcher into a shallow basin that lay on the table beside the window. The basin was glazed red, most likely imported from the southern continent.

Branwen should hurry. Ruan and Marc would be at the stables preparing for another day of searching. Where would Tristan and Eseult go? Liones was the logical choice—Tristan must have loyal retainers there—but it was also the first place the king would look after he'd scoured every corner of the northern coast.

Her cousin never thought much for consequences. She lived in the moment, and Branwen had once envied her ability to enjoy herself—to truly feel joy without worrying that it was about to slip from her fingertips.

But Tristan should know better. The lovers couldn't hide forever.

Branwen dipped a linen cloth into the basin and washed her face as she'd done for Alba. Sunlight glimmered on the water. Branwen's reflection stared back at her as the ripples stilled.

The swath of curls that rested against her left temple was ash-white. No wonder Ruan had been alarmed. Her copper-colored eyes, which she'd inherited from Lord Caedmon, gleamed brighter, almost fiery. The girl in the water did not resemble the girl who'd stepped aboard the *Dragon Rising* in Iveriu.

She wasn't a girl at all. Branwen had celebrated twenty summers the day after Long Night. In the three months since, she felt as if she'd survived another twenty. She pulled out the chair beside the table and slid her body into it. The wood creaked.

If Branwen couldn't find Tristan and Eseult before the King's Champion did, all of her sacrifices, all of the blood she'd spilled, would be meaningless.

Her gaze was attracted by the sunlight that skipped along the surface of the basin. Yesterday, she'd been spurred on by fear. Delirium had stretched her mind so thin she'd actually forgotten she possessed another way to find the lovers.

The second aspect of the Hand of Bríga was the Fire of Inspiration, and water was a place of in-between, neither earth nor air: a conduit between this world and the Otherworld. The Old Ones had been sending Branwen dreams and visions since she was a child, although she had not yet mastered how to summon the visions, to control them.

Using her magic would drain Branwen further. She saw no other choice.

She inhaled deeply and let her gaze merge with her reflection until the planes of Branwen's face ceased to be distinct. She was both at Monwiku and outside it.

Where is my cousin? she asked the Old Ones.

The cliffs along the Rock Road surged up from the Ivernic Sea. Branwen could smell the rosemary she always associated with Lady Alana. In the distance, she spied the top of a burnished head. *Essy!* someone cried.

The queen's childhood name sounded alien. Wrong. It reminded Branwen of tinkling icicles.

This was the past.

Show me where the True Queen is this very moment, she clarified.

Branwen's gaze caught on a raven, black as night, soaring upward from the branches of a hazel tree. The raven spotted Branwen as well. It began flying straight toward her. Cunning radiated from its eyes—eyes like rubies.

The creature swooped low, flying in a circle around Branwen. Its caw chilled her blood. A warning? An invitation? The bird was smaller than one of the Dark One's *kretarvs*, but it scared Branwen more. It scared Branwen because she felt the sea breeze on her face and the flapping of wings. The exhilaration of flying coursed through her.

As she watched, the black leeched from the raven's wings like dye. Obsidian raindrops landed at Branwen's feet. Around and around the bird flew until its feathers were all the color of bone.

One by one, the feathers, too, fell to the ground. A shower of white scattered among the black rain.

The raven continued to fly: a skeleton with fire-bright eyes against a painful blue sky. Then its bones turned to smoke.

The plume swirled around Branwen. She gasped, lungs clamoring for air, as the vision broke. Her heart slammed against her rib cage. Sweat dripped down her cheeks.

She was cast out.

The Old Ones would provide her no answers.

THE TIES THAT BIND

EXCITED YAPPING BOUNCED AROUND THE inner bailey as Branwen exited the West Tower. The queen's dog scrabbled over the cobblestones, pawing at Endelyn's skirts. Her sandy-brown hair was lank and her gown rumpled. There was no berry tint to her cheeks or jewels around her neck. The princess was usually immaculately presented.

"Good morning, Endelyn," Branwen said in Aquilan. The dog barked and scurried toward her. He'd been a puppy when the queen adopted him, but he was growing fast.

"Arthek keeps looking for his mistress," said Endelyn. "He wouldn't stop yowling or whimpering all night." Arthek breathed noisily through his flat nose, his wrinkled face and floppy ears charmingly ugly. He barked again.

Endelyn crouched down and scooped the dog into her arms. She hadn't been overly fond of the little beast when the queen brought him home from Seer Ogrin's temple, but this morning she clung to his wriggling body. Ogrin was the only *kordweyd* that Branwen liked, however begrudgingly.

"Ruan said there's no sign of Tristan. Or the queen." The tenderness in Endelyn's voice when she spoke Tristan's name was unconcealed. He viewed her as a younger sister, but that wasn't the role she wanted. Tristan was handsome and brave, and a simpler version of Branwen had wanted him to sing her to sleep, too.

"I'm heading to the stables," Branwen said. "We'll find the True Queen and her Champion." *I'll find them.* She had one more idea of how to contact the Otherworld for help.

Endelyn scratched Arthek behind the ears. Her blue eyes were misty, haunted.

"I held Freoc's hand as he died," she said. "He worked in the kitchens. I didn't know his name before yesterday. He must have prepared many of my meals, and I didn't even know his name." Endelyn's voice grew thick. "I didn't know his name, and he died holding my hand." She squeezed the dog more tightly.

The princess's display of emotion left Branwen at a loss. A breeze rustled the ivy that had rooted itself stubbornly into the cracks between the stone tower walls.

"Was it always like this in Iveriu?" Endelyn said.

"Always like what?"

"The fear." Her lips trembled. "The death."

"Yes." The word was clipped.

The tears on Endelyn's cheeks glittered in the sunlight. Branwen fought the impulse to comfort her. They weren't friends and Endelyn had provided the countess with evidence for her false allegations against Branwen. The princess sniffled.

"I'm sorry," Endelyn said. Branwen sucked in her cheeks. "I never thought about what it was like for the . . . Iverni." Did she wonder what it was like when her own father was stolen from his home? Endelyn was too young when he was killed to remember him, Ruan had said. Despite their previous history, the princess's admission stirred something in Branwen.

"You know Freoc's name now," she told the princess. "Honor his memory." Branwen saw herself on the beach below Castle Rigani, her aunt delivering the news that shattered her world. "The fear never leaves you," she admitted. "But you can go on with honor."

Endelyn dried her eyes with one hand, still gripping Arthek.

"*Mormerkti.* I'll see if Andred could use my help today." She showed Branwen a meek smile. "I hadn't thought I'd take orders from my baby brother, but you've trained him well."

"I take very little credit."

"*Bran—*" Endelyn stopped at her own informality. "Lady Branwen, my brother—Ruan, I mean, he was . . . during the attack he couldn't stop worrying about you." She compressed her lips. "I know he has a reputation as a flirt—"

"A reputation you informed me about," Branwen reminded her.

"Yes." The princess stroked Arthek. "But I wanted to say . . ." She delayed again, eyes shifting around the courtyard, and Branwen's patience wore thin.

"I really must get to the king," Branwen said.

"Of course." She inhaled. "Lady Branwen, I have given you no cause to like me, but when Ruan loves, he loves deeply. He pretends he's impervious to everything, but he's not."

Branwen couldn't begin to formulate a response. "Have a good day, Princess Endelyn," she said, and picked up her pace toward the stables.

Death unmasked everyone in different ways. For Endelyn, her distress betrayed a kindness that Ruan had hinted at, but which Branwen had thus far failed to see. She was right that she'd given Branwen no

47

reason to like her, but she clearly loved her brother and she'd been moved by the pain of her countrymen.

The princess would not be the only of the Kernyveu to taste true fear for the first time. Cornered animals were the most ferocious. Branwen had to prevent them from lashing out at the True Queen. At Iveriu.

Chimes clanged from the branches of trees with spear-shaped leaves and long, spindly trunks. Branwen rushed halfway down the hill of Monwiku, the wind teasing wisps from her firmly plaited hair, arranged to disguise the bleached curls as best she could.

"*Dymatis*," King Marc said, manner harried, when Branwen found him in the stables. The wind had blown open her cloak, which she'd fastened closed with her mother's brooch as she echoed his "good morning."

The king's gaze fell to the thistle-like needle of the round, enamel brooch, and his jaw tensed. Lady Alana had been wearing the ornament when she died—when a young Marc had watched her die. Branwen had forgiven him, yet his guilt endured.

On the silver underside of the brooch, engraved in the Ivernic language of trees, was Branwen's family motto: *The right fight*. She had once believed that fight to be as black and white as the Kernyvak flag. Her stomach churned.

Marc coughed. "You almost missed us," he said, checking the bit on his stallion's bridle. "We're about to set out."

Ruan stood a short distance away, leading his mount from its stall. His eyes on Branwen were questioning, searching. Did he think her more or less of a threat to his king now? She slipped her gaze past his and leaned into Marc. He hadn't shaven.

"Brother," she began. Ruan's horse clip-clopped on the hay and stone, and Branwen's throat swelled. "Brother, I need to go to the White Moor. Alone." The White Moor was known to belong to the Old Ones, although those who followed the Horned One avoided the place.

"With your permission," Branwen said. Discreetly, she turned her right palm upward. The blackened scar was camouflaged beneath a hastily wrapped bandage. "I need to pray to my gods for Tristan's and Eseult's safe return."

Marc flicked a glance at Ruan. Ruan canted his head. Neither man was certain if the other knew about Branwen's magic.

"Yes, of course," the king agreed after a moment's hesitation. "Appeal to your gods to bring them home."

"*Mormerkti.* I'll be back by sunset."

"Be safe."

"And you," Branwen said. She lifted her gaze to Ruan. "Both of you."

As she brushed by Ruan in the direction of Senara's stall, he whispered in her ear.

Kridyom.

✠ ✠ ✠

The palfrey stomped her hoof as she neared the White Moor. Animals were particularly sensitive to the proximity of Old Ones, and Senara didn't hesitate to make her displeasure known. Old Ones were neither good nor bad—they were something other. The Iverni considered the most powerful of the Old Ones to be gods. Although Branwen had never heard of a human becoming a god or being transformed into an Old One in the manner that the Horned One's followers believed Carnonos was.

Sunlight failed to fully penetrate the fog, and it was as if Branwen were riding through the clouds. She quaked, recalling the white raven of her vision.

She glimpsed a doe weaving between the trees as the moor gave way to forest. The day was relatively mild and early spring buds blossomed beneath Senara's hooves. The urgent beat of Branwen's heart prevented her from enjoying the scenery. She sensed the Otherworld tugging her closer, claiming her.

Branwen dismounted in a copse where all of the branches were adorned with tiny bells, colored pieces of string, and other mementos. The horse neighed. Each length of fabric was a wish, an offering to the spirits of the healing well nearby.

She tied up Senara's reins with the promise of extra oats when they returned to the castle. Her mount nickered, uneasy. Mist enveloped Branwen as she walked farther into the thicket.

The Kernyveu had been coming to the well since ancient times. Since before the Aquilan Empire had set its sights on the island of Albion. Those who remained faithful to the Old Ways still did. Branwen had come seeking the well's guardian.

A path of moss-covered stones led her across a small stream. Water splashed Branwen's boots. She rubbed her thumb against the inside of her right palm, relishing the friction from the bandage. The faint line made by the blade of binding at the royal wedding peeked out from beneath the cotton.

At the Champions Tournament in Iveriu, Goddess Ériu had selected Kernyv as her Consort. The Iverni believed that when the goddess lay with her chosen king, they renewed the Land together, brought prosperity to their subjects. But the marriage of King Marc and Queen Eseult had not been consummated in accordance with the Old Ways.

Through the mists, a hut made from snakestone appeared. Beside it stood the sacred well.

Could one physical act truly mean the difference between peace and war? If it did, how were the Ivernic gods any better than Seer Casek demanding a bloodied Mantle of Maidenhood?

The Old Ones are never satisfied, hissed a voice beneath her skin.

From the corner of Branwen's eye, she spied the doe again, drinking from the bubbling waters. The tip of its right ear was missing and its coat was reddish umber, flecked with bright white spots. Unusual. The hairs on her arms stood on end.

The door to the cottage was wrenched open. "Branwen," the Wise Damsel greeted her, expression wary. Her hair was loose around her shoulders, deep garnet streaked with gray. Crow's-feet had gathered around her eyes, but not from smiling. She looked to be fifty summers. Branwen suspected her to be much older.

"Ailleann," Branwen replied. The Wise Damsel had once told Branwen to call her by her given name. She pressed her palm against her abdomen, feeling distinctly unwelcome. "Good morning."

"Is it?" The older woman didn't move from the threshold. "Death has walked on Kernyvak soil, *enigena*." *Daughter*, she called Branwen in Ivernic. There was no affection in the term. Branwen had yet to discover how Ailleann had come to speak her language.

"I need your help," she told Ailleann. Impatience sheared the ends of her words. "The True Queen is missing."

The Wise Damsel showed no reaction. She continued to flay Branwen with her gaze. Faster than she could blink, the other woman had seized Branwen's wrist and ripped off the bandage. Her eyes flashed, such a dark brown they appeared black.

"Death crossed the Veil at your invitation."

"Yes." Branwen lifted her chin. "Monwiku nearly fell. I had to—it was the only way to save the kingdom."

Ailleann shrugged. "Kingdoms rise and fall."

"You're a healer. You can't care so little for the lives of innocents!" Branwen shot back, cheeks heating.

"I tend the well, and I help those I can. What they call themselves or who rules them is not my concern."

"We can't all hide in the mists." Branwen yanked back her hand. The heat spread down her neck, across her chest. "I couldn't watch people dying around me and do nothing!" Her shout was rough, echoing through the forest.

"It is a dangerous thing to act like a god, *enigena*. To decide who is innocent and who merits death."

"I did what I had to do. Only Dhusnos was listening!"

Branwen had chosen Marc when she raised the ax against Kahedrin. Maybe she had acted like a god but so did all men in battle. Branwen had chosen Kernyv and Iveriu when she unleashed the Shades on the Armoricans.

"I would do it again," she told the Wise Damsel.

The wind stirred around them. "Then why are you here asking for my help?" the other woman said. "If the one you call Dhusnos has already taken you by the hand?" She gestured pointedly at the nightlike mark.

"I told you, the queen is missing. I need you to scry for her location."

"You cannot find her yourself." It wasn't a question.

"No." Branwen's voice was tight. She stroked the ebony scar. "The Old Ones are no longer speaking to me."

"No," the Wise Damsel repeated. "It is not the Old Ones who have stopped speaking to you. You cannot walk with death—with the Dark One, and remain unchanged." Branwen's eyes dropped to the mark. *Slayer. Killer.*

"But you were changed even before, *enigena*."

52

She glanced up. "I don't know what you mean."

"The memory you sacrificed to ease the True Queen's pain, I warned you that it would alter the fabric of your very self. Whatever you lost opened you to the dark."

The ties that bound you are gone, Dhusnos had told Branwen beneath the waves. He had already sensed it, too.

"But I didn't complete the spell," Branwen protested. "The queen didn't ingest the ashes." She had burned her mother's harp for nothing. The jar containing the antidote was smashed when the queen's assassins ambushed Branwen in the forest, its contents scattered far and wide.

Yet another sacrifice made in vain for her cousin.

If the spell had been successful, Tristan and Eseult wouldn't have run away.

The Wise Damsel crossed her arms. "You offered the memory and it was accepted. If you did not use the magic that was your choice."

"It wasn't my *choice*!" Branwen burst out. "I was attacked in the woods. The ashes scattered to the winds."

"Then perhaps Dhusnos is not the only one watching over you."

"I don't have time for riddles!"

Ailleann turned on her heel, retreating into her cottage. Branwen hooked her elbow. "Wait. Stop! *Please*, Wise Damsel," she begged. "Please help me find the queen before it's too late."

A long moment passed. Branwen swallowed a sob. In her mind she saw fields smoldering—fields that she had set on fire.

The Wise Damsel jerked from her grip. "Come," she barked. Branwen followed before she could change her mind.

Kindling crackled in the hearth. Ailleann filled a shallow bowl from a bucket as Branwen hovered. Firelight gleamed on the surface of the water. Ailleann set the bowl upon a wooden table and seated herself.

"*Sit*," she commanded Branwen. She did. "What did you see in the water, *enigena*?" the Wise Damsel asked.

"Nothing. It was meaningless." The other woman held her gaze. "A white raven," Branwen revealed. "Its feathers fell as it flew, until it was nothing but bone. And then smoke."

"Primordial magic is both creation and destruction," said the Wise Damsel, which Branwen well knew. "The Iverni have their names for the Old Ones and the Dark One, but those are unimportant. The gods of light and darkness have always coexisted."

Branwen resisted the urge to interrupt. "Your magic is out of balance," the other woman continued. "When you called on the god of death, the world of the living was put beyond your reach. You cannot search the water for those still on this side of the Veil."

Branwen's pulse pounded in her throat.

"What did the Dark One want in exchange for his aid?" the Wise Damsel demanded.

"A life," she forced out. "One life for many. By next Samonios."

You will kill of your own volition. She shuddered as the words ricocheted around her skull. *Not in self-defense, not in the defense of another—but because you want to, Branwen of Iveriu.*

"The Branwen I met a few months ago would not have made that bargain," Ailleann remarked.

"Much has happened since I arrived in Kernyv." The older woman remained unmoved at her explanation. Leaning closer, Branwen asked, "Is there a way to void the bargain?"

"Double-cross a god?" The Wise Damsel's laugh was abrupt. "I wouldn't."

Branwen's flesh tingled; the scar grew hot. She hadn't really believed there would be. She folded her hands together. The other woman peered down at the water, eyes becoming unfocused. Her breathing deepened. Branwen studied each wrinkle on the other woman's pale face as she went into a trance.

Branwen tapped one thumb against the other.

Outside, the stream gurgled. A log shifted in the hearth, startling Branwen.

At last the Wise Damsel opened her sea-dark eyes. "Your cousin is alive," she pronounced.

Branwen exhaled, although her relief was tempered. "Where is she?" The words came out in a rush. If Eseult had been killed by the Armoricans at least it would not turn Kernyv against Iveriu.

"I saw a crown by a river."

"*Which* river?" she asked, and Ailleann replied with a shrug. "But what use is that? How am I supposed to find her?" Branwen exclaimed.

The older woman narrowed her eyes. "I asked the question and received the answer the Otherworld saw fit to provide. Gods don't exist to serve mortals."

"No, they exist to play with us!" Venom coursed through Branwen's words, her heart.

"Don't be naïve," scolded the Wise Damsel. "You have asked and received much of your gods. You have dealt willingly in primordial magic."

Branwen thrust out her hand. "I didn't ask for the Hand of Bríga!"

"Didn't you?" A snort. "I offered to help you tame your magic, Branwen of Iveriu. You let it wield you instead. And now it is no longer the Hand of Bríga you possess."

"Death saved my life."

"Once your magic is gone, death won't be able to save you. If you burn yourself out, there will not even be enough left of you to enter the Land of Youth."

Fury made Branwen's lips quiver. She pictured the white raven. The possibility of never rejoining Lady Alana and Lord Caedmon in the Otherworld—of never being reborn together—was a worse punishment than any she'd foreseen. It was cruel. She slammed her palm on the table.

"All I've ever wanted was to protect the people I love, and this is how the gods repay me? Why give me magic, then?"

"If a hungry man eats until he is sick, he cannot blame the cook."

"He can if the cook starved him first." Rancor rattled Branwen's teeth.

The Wise Damsel pushed to her feet. "It is time for you to leave. There is nothing more I can do for you, *enigena*. You must regain your own balance. Until you do, don't come back." She swung her arm toward the door.

Branwen's mouth fell open. She stood, hands curled into fists.

"I told you that the Old Ones could not bear the consequences of your magic for you, Branwen of Iveriu."

"You did." She took a step toward the door. Dhusnos had been cast out by the Old Ones for insulting the Goddess Ériu: she who embodied the island of Iveriu itself. Ériu *was* the Land, and she had thrust Dhusnos into the sea. Now Branwen had been cut adrift, too.

"Find the part of yourself you lost," said the Wise Damsel.

Branwen shook her head. "Whoever that girl was—I'm glad she's gone."

A LOVE SONG

THE KING'S FACE WAS DRAWN as Branwen entered his study. She was the first to arrive for what was bound to be a tense occasion.

Platters of cured meats and cheeses had been laid on the table in the center of the room. Flames flickered above candelabras set on either side of a silver bowl of apples. King Marc was intent on adhering to the rules of hospitality even if his dinner guest had attacked his castle.

"*Nosmatís*, sister," Marc told her. The corner of his mouth lifted, but his posture remained taut. Branwen heard the hope and question in his greeting. Her own nerves were frayed after her encounter with the Wise Damsel.

Branwen walked toward the king, placing a hand on his arm, and answered in low tones. "The queen is alive." Marc's eyes brightened instantly. "I don't know where," she said. "Only that she is near a river."

He cut the air with two fingers, as followers of the Horned One did to invoke their god. Then he clasped Branwen's shoulders and drew her into an embrace.

"*Mormerkti*," the king said in a deep voice. "Thank all the gods."

"I'm sorry I can't be of more help."

Marc drew back, still holding her shoulders. "Knowing she's alive gives me courage. You are a blessing to me, Branwen."

Her stomach roiled. She'd brought far more curses than blessings down upon the king.

"Your gods spoke to you at the White Moor?" he said. He squeezed Branwen's shoulders and dropped his hands. Branwen didn't know which gods the Wise Damsel had consulted. She wondered if Ailleann might be an Old One herself—or whatever Old Ones called themselves.

"Yes," Branwen said simply.

"We'll ford every river in Kernyv. In Albion." Determination underscored the king's statement. But, then what? What chaos would ensue? She didn't need to ask whether the Royal Guard's search had borne any fruit today. If a trace of either Tristan or Eseult had been found, the entire castle would be buzzing with it.

A knock came at the door. "Enter," said Marc, and Andred's face lit when he saw Branwen. Behind her brother, Endelyn chewed her lips together.

Branwen's apprentice moved swiftly, hobbling slightly, and gave her a hug. His left foot was curved partially inward, yet Andred never let it stop him from doing anything he wanted to do.

"It's good to see you, Lady Branwen," he said. Less than two days had passed since she'd said goodbye to the boy in the stairwell of the King's Tower as the Armoricans attacked. It felt like a lifetime.

"And you." Branwen hugged him back, mussed his hair. Andred resembled Prince Edern in coloring, but their hearts were nothing alike.

"Thank you for taking charge of the wounded today, Andred. You've done well. I'm proud of you."

He blushed. "Endelyn makes a good assistant," Andred teased his older sister. She lingered a few paces away from the group. Branwen expected a snide rejoinder but the Kernyvak princess merely lifted her eyebrows, continuing to chew her lips. She had changed into a gown of heavy crimson linen that served to make her complexion more wan. Branwen was also dressed for the occasion—she had rearranged her hair and chosen a laurel green gown with embroidered trim for the king's dinner.

"Lowenek has been helping, too," said Andred, his voice brimming with warmth for the orphaned Kernyvak girl whom Branwen had rescued from the mining disaster.

"I'm glad she's well." Branwen smiled.

"I am obliged for everyone's aid," King Marc said, looking from Andred to Endelyn, then Branwen. "This tragedy will unite Kernyv, not destroy us."

"*Kernyv bosta vyken*," Andred declared. His expression was deadly earnest. *Kernyv forever.* Sometimes when Branwen looked at her apprentice, she saw a seasoned old man rather than a boy of fourteen. "Let me pour you some wine, my king," he suggested.

"Pour us all some wine!" Ruan's voice boomed from the doorway.

On his arm, Princess Alba stood, nose tilted upward, proud. Her hands were no longer bound but Ruan's grip on her elbow was iron tight.

Ruan grazed Branwen with a glance. She looked away.

King Marc took a step forward. As far as Branwen was aware, he hadn't visited the Armorican princess since her capture in the Morrois Forest.

"Good evening, Princess Alba," the king said to her in Aquilan. "Thank you for accepting my invitation to dine together."

"How could I refuse?" Her words were a blade.

The swelling around Alba's nose was diminishing slowly, and the skin was purpling like ripe elderberries. Otherwise, she appeared in good health.

"Come, sit by me," King Marc entreated, strolling toward the head of the table. He motioned at the chair to his right. The seat usually occupied by Ruan. "I trust you're acquainted with my other guests," he said to Alba as if this were any other formal dinner. Marc's ability to control his demeanor was truly remarkable.

Alba nodded. "Hello, Endelyn. Andred." The Armorican royal family was old friends with House Whel, trading with them for the white lead from their mines. At the wedding, Kahedrin had told Branwen that they used to visit Villa Illogan often. Alba was a couple of years older than Andred, and a few younger than Endelyn. They must have all played together as children.

"Hello," Andred replied uncertainly. Endelyn sneered.

Ruan escorted Alba to the table, seating himself next to her. She had been provided with a light blue blouse and beige leather trousers that hung loose on her hips. Her dark brown hair was coiled into several neat plaits atop her head. The princess looked ready to flee at the slightest opportunity, and Branwen wondered at the wisdom of letting her eat with a knife in such proximity to the king.

Branwen chose the seat opposite Alba, stroking the fresh bandage she'd tied around her blackened scar. She would let no further harm come to Marc.

Andred poured the wine for everyone at the table, testing the king's cup before letting him drink.

"To the fallen," King Marc said, raising his goblet. He spoke directly to Alba. Branwen and the others echoed him somberly.

Alba gritted her teeth. "To the fallen."

A fraught silence descended over the dinner table.

Avoiding Ruan's attempts to catch her gaze, Branwen remarked to Alba, "I trust you haven't been feeling feverish."

"No. But thank you for your concern, Branwen." The princess's tone contradicted her polite smile.

"*Lady* Branwen," Ruan corrected Alba. "She is Queen Eseult's first cousin." He finally succeeded in drawing Branwen's attention. "She is also a most talented healer. You're in the best possible hands, Lady Princess. We're blessed she came to Kernyv."

Branwen sipped her wine. She recognized the apology beneath the compliment, but her feelings for Ruan were more knotted than the roots of a tree. Alba looked between her and Ruan, calculating, too canny for Branwen's liking.

"Ruan has always been the most charming of House Whel," said Alba. She smiled at him pertly.

"I wouldn't say that," replied Branwen, patting her apprentice on the shoulder. Endelyn afforded Branwen a chiding glance. Until this morning, Branwen hadn't realized that the protectiveness between the siblings ran both ways.

"I once fancied myself in love with him, too," Alba mused. "Like every other noblewoman along the western seas." She snorted. "Ruan was even my first kiss."

Branwen's eyebrows lifted skyward. He was at least seven years Alba's senior.

"A *stolen* kiss, Lady Princess," Ruan said, his discomfort clear. He appealed to Branwen with a glance. Turning his shoulders toward Alba, he said, "Which as you recall, I put a stop to immediately—you were only thirteen!"

Alba shrugged. "I was curious what all the fuss was about." To Branwen, she said, "I can't fathom the trail of broken hearts that Ruan has littered across Albion. Can you, Lady Branwen?"

"Better to litter hearts than bodies!" Endelyn retorted. Branwen was taken aback at the vehemence of her defense.

Alba clenched the table violently and hot wax spilled from the candelabra to the wood. "If you hadn't sent pirates to kill Havelin, I wouldn't be here!" she said, raising her voice.

"Princess Alba," King Marc began firmly. "I deeply regret Havelin's death—but I did not sanction the raid. In fact, your cousin, Captain Xandru Manduca, was already on his way to Karaez to parlay with King Faramon on my behalf before you besieged my castle."

Branwen noticed Alba's knuckles flex on the tabletop.

"I don't believe you."

"It's the truth," Ruan told her in a tone of flint. "Despite the assassin you sent to kill my king in the forest after Long Night."

Alba gasped. "Assassin? What assassin?"

"Too late to play the innocent, Lady Princess."

Several emotions washed over Alba's face before she rinsed them clean. To King Marc, she said, "You may well regret Havelin's death, but you don't regret Kahedrin's." Swiveling in her chair, Alba stared down Ruan.

"Did you know that Lady Branwen is a killer as well as a healer?"

Alarm rippled across Ruan's features. His gaze pierced Branwen once more and she saw his confusion, his trying to puzzle out whether Alba knew about Tutir and Bledros.

"That's right," Alba said. "Lady Branwen killed Kahedrin. I saw it with my own eyes." She turned on Branwen. "You drove an ax into his back like a coward. You didn't have the guts to fight him with honor. You *have* no honor!"

"I defended my king, as anyone would do!" Branwen countered even as her chest hollowed out. She darted her eyes back to Ruan, and his lips were parted in surprise, perhaps relief.

"Is that why you took Eseult?" Marc pressed in close, wrapping his hand lightly around Alba's wrist. "Because Kahedrin is dead?" His grip was light but it was threat enough.

"Eseult?" Shock splayed on Alba's face. "The True Queen is missing?" She circled her gaze around the table. If her shock was feigned, then the princess was an exceptional actress.

"Why else wouldn't she be at dinner?" Endelyn sniped.

Alba's jaw tensed.

"If any harm comes to her," Marc began, letting a thread of menace into his voice, "your father will be very sorry." He released her hand.

"No, *no*. We didn't take her," Alba protested. Panic raised the pitch of her voice. "We never intended to kidnap the queen."

"Just to kill the king," said Ruan, rife with disgust.

Her nostrils flared. "We're at war."

"Why should we believe you?" Andred said to Alba. Branwen snapped her head toward her apprentice. "Why should we believe you *don't* have the queen?" the boy persisted.

"Because I'm the only one left!" Alba told Andred hotly. "My men are dead. My boats are destroyed." She looked at Branwen. "My *brothers* are dead." Directing a jagged glance at King Marc, she yelled, "There is no one left to kidnap Queen Eseult—even if I wanted to!"

Angry tears glistened in Alba's eyes; Branwen saw her fighting them.

Marc and Ruan exchanged a heavy look. Alba had merely confirmed what Branwen and Ruan already knew to be true. What Marc must now suspect: Tristan and Eseult had left the castle of their own accord.

Tannins and acid from the wine rose back up Branwen's throat. She flattened her lips to stop from vomiting onto her dinner.

"This morning I sent another messenger to King Faramon," Marc told Alba. "I informed him that you are to be our guest here in Monwiku until Kernyv and Armorica can settle our differences." The princess visibly swallowed.

"I have no desire to prolong this misunderstanding, Lady Princess." Alba made a disbelieving noise, and Marc pressed a hand to his heart. "I swear it on my life."

The princess folded her arms, leaning back in her chair, staring at her untouched food.

"My father didn't authorize the assault, King Marc. Kahedrin and I . . . we wanted revenge for Havelin. My eldest brother died a hero, defending our shores against pirates—his death warranted more than *diplomacy*." Her eyes remained pinned to her plate. "King Faramon didn't agree. You may find that my father doesn't want me back."

King Marc had called the siege brazen. Apparently it was even more brazen than any of the Kernyveu had realized. Branwen felt a grudging admiration for Alba despite the cost of her actions. Admiration and sympathy. Alba had tried to avenge one brother and lost another. Branwen pushed away the guilt, knowing it would return as sure as the tide.

"Princess Alba, I am confident that you will be sailing home to Karaez in no time," said the king.

Her mouth pinched. "You don't know my father." She blinked and a single tear slid down her cheek. No one spoke. Then Alba inhaled, tilting her head at Marc.

"In Armorica," she said, "the rites of the dead are performed within seven days to honor the seven Old Ones of Armorica." The king nodded. "Would you permit me to prepare Kahedrin's body for the pyre?"

"Of course. You may honor your brother however you wish."

"Thank you, my Lord King."

The meal was finished quickly, in silence, and Ruan returned Alba to her luxurious prison. Branwen accompanied Andred to the barracks to help him set one of the guardsmen's broken arms. When at last she'd retired to her own chamber, she scrubbed her hands and face, muscles aching as she pulled on a nightgown. She'd just slipped into bed when she heard a soft rapping at the door.

With a sigh, Branwen scrambled to her feet. "May I come in?" Ruan asked as she levered open the door. Warm light from the corridor glowed on his weary face.

She stepped aside to let him enter and clicked the door firmly shut behind him. Whatever Ruan wanted to discuss, Branwen was certain she didn't want them being overheard.

Only a single candle flickered on the bedside table. Before the room had been given to Branwen, King Marc had stored his excess maps and books here—the ones that overflowed from his substantial study. Shadows wavered across shelves upon shelves of weighty tomes that lined the walls.

Ruan canted his head at one of the shelves and plucked a wooden sword, child-size, from atop a collection of Aquilan treatises.

Examining the paltry weapon, he turned to Branwen and said, "I don't think this blade is terribly sharp." Teasingly, he brandished it at her.

"My uncle gave it to me when I was a girl," Branwen explained. "He wanted me to learn to defend myself. He said he wouldn't always be around to protect me."

"King Óengus," Ruan surmised.

"No. Lord Morholt. The King's Champion."

"The one who dueled with Tristan?"

Branwen nodded, taking the sword back from Ruan. She twirled its blunt tip against her forefinger. "When Morholt was denounced as a traitor, all of his possessions were destroyed. I couldn't part with it."

She drilled the tip harder against the grain of her skin. "It was dishonorable what he did—coating his spear in poison before the Final Combat, and yet—"

"You loved him," Ruan interjected.

"No." Morholt had always been a joyless man and Branwen couldn't honestly say that she'd ever loved him. "My uncle died fighting for what he believed in, even if it was treason and I—I suppose I understand that."

"Branwen." Her name was full of yearning. Ruan put a hand on the sword to stop its twirling. "Branwen, I'm sorry I didn't know what to say . . . to *think* last night."

"And you know now?"

"I'm here because I want to understand." He pried the sword from her grasp and replaced it on the shelf. His face was half-shrouded by night. "If you say you killed Tutir and Bledros in self-defense, I believe you. I confessed my greatest shame to you. I killed my own father." The word was brittle. "The man who raised me," Ruan corrected himself. "And you didn't spurn me." He took her right hand in his. She'd removed the bandage for sleep and the scar glimmered midnight in the candlelight.

"I want to understand your magic, Branwen."

"So do I."

Her shoulders deflated. She walked over to the bed, smoothing out the velvet coverlet, and perched atop it. Ruan followed, waiting, still standing. She stared at Dhusnos's mark. The Wise Damsel said she no longer possessed the Hand of Bríga. The proof was tattooed on her skin.

Every letter in the Ivernic language of trees had two meanings. The first was a tree or a plant. The lines imprinted on Branwen's palm formed the symbol for a fern. A flowerless plant. It was a fitting description of death.

Ruan lowered himself next to her on the bed. "Have you always had magic?" he asked quietly. He stroked her cheek, coaxing, his touch tender.

She shook her head, then, "Perhaps," Branwen said. "The women in my family have always been healers." Peering sideways at Ruan, she said, "When Tristan was poisoned at the Champions Tournament only magic could save him. I offered the Old Ones my blood for magic."

"Why?" The word came from low in Ruan's throat.

"If Tristan had died in Iveriu, Marc would have had no choice but to invade."

"True enough." He sighed. "The bond I've always sensed between you and Tristan. Is it because of the magic?"

Branwen couldn't answer that question. "Magic changes many things," she said.

"I'm not jealous," Ruan said. "I'm not. I'm glad you saved Tristan." She lifted an eyebrow. "If you hadn't, we'd have never met."

Her heart warped. She placed her hand above Ruan's. His beat rapidly too. Branwen would never be able to feed him more than crumbs of truth. To keep Eseult on the throne, to keep the peace, she would always have to lie to the man beside her.

Ruan lifted her hand and kissed her palm. "And the fire?" he whispered against Branwen's skin.

"We Iverni believe that creation and destruction come from the same source."

Ruan intertwined their fingers. "Love is both."

"Love is dangerous." It had been Branwen's love of Eseult that brought forth the darker side of her power—that summoned the fire to kill Keane and condemned him to be a Shade. Yet Branwen felt no such love for her cousin now. It was as if all the years they had shared together were behind a pane of glass.

"When Monwiku was attacked," she continued, "I made my gods another offering. But no power comes without cost."

He watched her intently. "What kind of cost?"

"Every time I use magic—" She pulled loose a white strand from her plaits. "I die a little." Spoken so plainly, she understood its full truth. Of course Dhusnos had always been drawn to her, and she to him.

Ruan's chest expanded as he drew in a long breath. "Please don't tell the *kordweyd*," Branwen begged him. "Otherworld knows what Seer Casek—or your mother—might do. I'm sure they'd consider me unnatural."

"I've never believed in the Horned One, Branwen. I didn't see any mercy in my father or in his god." He traced the length of her scar. "I didn't believe in *any* of the gods until I saw the flame rise from your hand last night."

As if in response, the candle on the bedside table flickered wildly.

"You have the power to ruin me now, too," Branwen told him.

"Your secret is safe with me." Ruan tugged her nearer, kissing her brow so she could feel his breath on her eyelids. "*You* are safe with me."

Branwen suppressed a whimper. She didn't know if he could ever be safe with her. She gripped the bedspread with one hand.

"Then you no longer see me as a threat?" she said.

Ruan laughed. "Oh, you're definitely a threat. But not to Marc. I'm losing count of how many times you've saved his life." He sobered. "It should have been me to defend him against Kahedrin."

"You were where the king needed you."

"And yet Tristan and the queen are still gone."

Branwen pulled back, scooting a handsbreadth away from him. The wind moaned from the garden. Ruan gazed into her eyes, gliding his thumb along her knuckles.

"Armorica didn't kidnap your cousin," he said.

"Alba could be lying."

"*Kerdyom.*"

"When we find the True Queen, there will be an explanation. The kingdom will be overjoyed at the queen's return, and the peace will be restored." Branwen spoke with lethal calm. "We must maintain the peace, Ruan."

"I wish I were a bard like Tristan so I could compose a love song about Branwen of Iveriu, fierce and true." He let out a strained laugh, shifting closer along the edge of the bed. "At least I can rhyme."

"I never asked for a love song."

"You never ask for anything." Ruan rested his forehead against hers. "Maybe that's why I want to give you everything."

Branwen stroked Ruan's back and the bristles on his jaw. Desire spread from deep in her body, erasing any drowsiness.

"If it were up to me, Branwen, we would be the only two people in the world." Ruan dropped a kiss onto the crook of her neck.

"Right here, right now, there's only us," Branwen whispered and blew out the candle.

She threw her nightgown over her head and let the moonlight glisten on the scars the Shades had given her aboard the *Dragon Rising*. The monsters who were once her enemies but were now, if not her friends, then her allies.

What did that make Branwen? If she no longer possessed the Hand of Bríga, what did she possess?

Right now, she didn't care. Ruan buried his face in her curls, fingers teasing and demanding as they explored her flesh. She undressed him with purpose, a new hunger in her kisses. Craving. She wanted everything that Ruan had to give.

Branwen might be aligned with death, but for the few hours between night and day, she was so, *so* alive.

WAITING GAME

BRANWEN TOOK HER PLACE AT the King's Council meeting but she couldn't shake the feeling of drowning. The room seemed at once too vast and too crowded. Her dreams had plunged her deep beneath the starless tide. Chaos incited the waves. As the heads of the Kernyvak noble Houses filed into the king's study, Branwen heard her own greetings as if they came from underwater.

She stared down the length of the table, surveying the councillors, their features stark in the vivid sun that streamed from the windows, waiting for King Marc to begin. He stood at the head of the table. This afternoon Ruan occupied his usual place next to the king. Ruan had kissed Branwen with the dawn, but dread oozed beneath her skin for what the day might bring.

"Thank you all for coming," King Marc said to the room. "We have much to discuss." He spoke in Aquilan for Branwen's benefit. Kernyvak was the native tongue of everyone else assembled.

Countess Kensa flicked Branwen a barbed glance. The countess had seated herself opposite her son, at the left hand of the king. Kensa was scarcely more than forty summers, and quite beautiful. The way she carried herself reminded Branwen of a viper poised to strike.

"We are grateful to be here," said Baron Julyan. "This is a dire moment in the history of our kingdom, but we thank the Horned One to see you hearty and hale, my Lord King." He drew an X in the air.

The head of House Julyan was the most elderly of the barons. His beard was long and white, his hands liver-spotted, and his bones creaked as he moved. But his affection for his young king was genuine.

"*Mormerkti,*" Marc replied. "Have there been any reports of raids on your lands?"

The old man shook his head. The territory belonging to House Julyan lay on the southeast coast, closer to Armorica.

"No, sire. And no sightings of the True Queen. Or Tristan."

The absence of Queen Eseult and her Champion was a crater at the far end of the table that could not be ignored. Even awake, Branwen could barely catch her breath. She eyed Ruan sidelong. Between keeping Branwen safe and doing his duty to Marc, she didn't know which the King's Champion would choose.

Marc glanced at Baron Kerdu who sat between Ruan and Baron Julyan. The head of House Kerdu was of Kartagon heritage, like Tristan, and laugh lines creased his dark brown skin.

"Nothing to report, sire." House Kerdu's lands were bounded by Meonwara to the east and Ordowik to the north, but it had no sea borders.

King Marc turned to Baron Gwyk and Baron Dynyon, whose territories both lay in the southwest. They also shook their heads. House Dynyon had once controlled most of Liones before the tip of Kernyv was gifted to Tristan's mother. The mustached baron made no attempt to disguise his longstanding bitterness.

Baron Chyanhal frowned in apology when Marc's gaze landed on him. His lands lay a day's ride farther up the north coast from the Morrois Forest. Branwen wasn't surprised. The Royal Guard had found no evidence of the pair in the forest.

The five great baronies of Kernyv had been carved out by King Katwaladrus to reward the men who had helped him repel the Meonwaran invasion. House Whel was the newest, an upstart, owing its status to mineral wealth. They claimed only a small cape on the south coast, and Countess Kensa was hungry for more land.

"Villa Illogan is secure," the countess informed King Marc.

Prince Edern had married Kensa for her gold, but the older noble families sneered at the Whels' origins as wreckers. Ruan had explained that his maternal ancestors first built their fortune luring Aquilan ships onto the rocks, plundering them, and trading their wares with the Aquilan legions whose supply ships had never arrived.

Inhaling a heavy breath, King Marc nodded at his councillors.

"I am gladdened that our losses haven't extended beyond Monwiku," he said. "It is some good news among much bad."

"The temples are sending more *kordweyd* from across the kingdom to care for the wounded," Seer Casek announced. He had selected the seat between Countess Kensa and Baron Dynyon. Sunlight winked off the diamond-encrusted antler shard that dangled around his neck, and his pale, shaven head.

"Lady Branwen does an admirable job as Royal Healer," he continued. He peered across the table at her. "But she is only one woman." The seer's smile was full of teeth.

Late Queen Verica had warned Branwen that Casek loved power more than he loved the Horned One, and he saw Branwen as his opponent.

"Sadly the Royal Infirmary does not yet exist," he added.

King Marc cleared his throat. "The temples are very generous, Seer Casek."

The king's support for his queen's project to build a Royal Infirmary—headed by Branwen—had brought him into direct conflict with the *kordweyd*. In Kernyv, the temples cared for the sick and they did not train women as healers. But King Marc needed the support of the seers to rule. Now, perhaps, more than ever.

"We do no more than honor the Horned One," replied Seer Casek, touching the fragment that rested against his chest.

Branwen seethed in silence, not wanting to make Marc's situation more difficult.

"Has the Royal Guard made no progress in locating the route Queen Eseult might have taken?" Countess Kensa demanded of her son, and icy-hot waves of fury deluged Branwen. "She couldn't have simply vanished."

"No, Countess," Ruan replied. "Captain Morgawr will establish a naval perimeter along the northern coast, and Captain Bryok will remain positioned near Illogan. If any Armorican ships try to flee with the queen—" He dashed a sidelong glance at Branwen. "They will be stopped."

Branwen expelled a breath, curving her lips in gratitude. He rubbed a knuckle against his eyebrow, uncomfortable.

"Should we not be sending the Royal Fleet to raze Karaez to the ground?" said Baron Dynyon, puffing out his chest. His fiery mustache twitched as he spoke and he had a tendency to fleck it with spittle. "The Armoricans besieged our capital and took our queen hostage! Or, for all we know, both she and Tristan are dead!"

Baron Dynyon was pugnacious and arrogant by nature, and Branwen liked him not at all. Beside him, the head of House Gwyk grunted in agreement. Baron Gwyk had lost an eye raiding Iveriu, but his glass one was the warmer of the two.

The divisions between the noble Houses were enacted in the seating arrangements, with Barons Kerdu, Julyan, and Chyanhal positioned on Branwen's side of the table, opposite Kensa and the others. And yet, despite their differences and grievances, all of the barons nodded at Baron Dynyon's outburst.

"My trusted retainers," said King Marc. "There is other news." He waited a beat. "We have captured Princess Alba." Scattered intakes of breath were heard from around the table. Countess Kensa glared at her son, undoubtedly angered that he hadn't told her in advance.

"I intend to sue King Faramon for peace, for a ransom and reparations," the king announced.

"Ah, that changes the situation," said Baron Julyan.

"Does it?" Baron Chyanhal said. He was a slim but well-muscled man with tawny-brown skin, younger than the other barons. "A direct attack on our court cannot go unanswered."

Branwen pulled at her bandage. The head of House Chyanhal was usually prone to caution, but even he wanted blood.

"We agreed to support one last diplomatic mission," said Baron Kerdu to King Marc. "But that was before the Armoricans sailed warships into Monwiku. Has there been any word from Captain Manduca?"

Marc shook his head. "He may not yet have reached Karaez." The king stroked his beard, which was becoming unruly. The night before his departure, Xandru had teased Marc about his needing Xandru to shave him. Branwen didn't think the king had slept since the attack.

"When Captain Manduca does arrive in Armorica," said Baron

Gwyk, "he will discover that King Faramon sent Crown Prince Kahedrin and Princess Alba to avenge the death of his eldest son."

"King Faramon didn't send them," Branwen said, speaking for the first time.

Countess Kensa arched an eyebrow. "What are you talking about, Lady Branwen?"

Ruan answered his mother. "Princess Alba claims that she and Kahedrin led the assault without her father's permission."

Kensa scoffed, waving a dismissive hand. "A clever gambit. She failed. What else would she say?"

"I believe her," Branwen said. Her anger stirred. Her power.

"You've made clear to this council on numerous occasions that your priority is to keep Iveriu out of a war, Lady Branwen—even with your own queen missing. You do not care what is best for Kernyv, and what is best for Kernyv is to wreak such havoc on Armorican coasts that no one dares attack us again!"

"I killed Crown Prince Kahedrin." Branwen laid her right hand flat on the wooden table. It took all of her self-control not to set it on fire.

"You weren't here when the Armoricans attacked, Countess. Don't tell me what I wouldn't do to protect Kernyv—and Iveriu. We're bound now."

A stunned silence fell over the councillors.

"Branwen saved my life," affirmed the king. "She is as much my Champion as Ruan." Ruan's jaw tightened and Branwen wished that Marc had chosen his words more judiciously. After a moment, Baron Julyan banged his finely whittled cane against the stone floor.

"We thank you, Lady Branwen," said the elderly baron. "You're a Kernyvwoman now, as far as I'm concerned."

Countess Kensa puckered her mouth. The others clapped. "Here, here," Baron Kerdu echoed. Branwen's pulse didn't slow.

"*Mormerkti*," she said to the room.

"Princess Alba also claims that kidnapping the True Queen wasn't part of her plan," Ruan said, and Branwen tensed further. "Nor, she says, did Armorica send the assassin who attacked King Marc in the forest."

"I am not in the habit of taking my enemy at his word," Baron Gwyk retorted.

"*Her* word," said Branwen.

He sniffed. To the king, he said, "Armorica has been threatening us—threatening *you* for months. It's time to act."

King Marc folded his arms. Branwen noticed him discreetly support the shoulder that had been struck by the Armorican's arrow.

"Princess Alba and her father remain under the impression that we sent the pirates to attack their capital first. Faramon has now lost both his sons," said the king. "I want to end this vendetta while we still can."

"It doesn't matter who sent the pirates," said Ruan. "If we don't respond with force now, then other kingdoms—like Ordowik—will see us as easy prey. They will circle us like vultures."

"I agree with my son," said Kensa.

"As do I," said Baron Chyanhal.

"We can't afford to act while the True Queen might be aboard a ship bound for the Armorican capital of Karaez," King Marc stated in a controlled roar.

"We can't afford *not* to act, my Lord King," Countess Kensa told him. "We have Faramon's last surviving heir. He won't risk hurting the True Queen."

"Lady Branwen," the king appealed. "What is your counsel?"

Kensa and Seer Casek exchanged a look. The other barons directed their attention to Branwen as well. It was quiet enough to hear the pounding of feet on stone. Agitated knocking followed a few seconds later.

"Come in!" growled King Marc, composure dissolving.

Andred's face appeared in the doorway. "Someone's here—I was helping a guard at the gatehouse, and he . . . he says he brings news of Tristan. And the queen."

"Bring him here. *Now*."

The boy hurried away. It was as if Branwen's breaths were laced with broken glass. She felt Ruan's gaze on her but she couldn't look at him.

More footsteps. Heavier. Methodical.

The door was pushed all the way open.

A man of sixty summers, dressed in traveling clothes, filled the doorframe. His shoulders were broad and his bulk solid, reminding Branwen of Sir Fintan, her aunt's bodyguard at Castle Rigani. This man had light brown skin, a graying beard, and an impressive sword of Kartagon steel at his hip.

"Sir Goron?" said King Marc.

The other man bowed deeply. "My Lord King."

One of Marc's rare smiles graced his face which, given the circumstances, left Branwen befuddled. "It's been years."

"It has." Sir Goron didn't smile but there was warmth to his severity. "Tristan told me of the attack. He sent me to find out what happened. I'm glad the castle hasn't fallen."

"So are we," replied Marc, and when he spoke to this man, it was with great respect. "Tristan was with you?"

Sir Goron nodded. "He and the True Queen are safe at my cottage."

Whispers of thanks to the Horned One rose to the ceiling. Branwen's emotions swirled. "Where?" the king asked.

"A hard day's ride. Beside the River Heyl."

Marc dashed his gaze to Branwen. A crown by a river. The Wise Damsel had been right. "Branwen," he said. "Sir Goron was the sword master who trained me and Tristan. Your cousin is safe. Tristan took her where he knew she'd be safe." To his former teacher, Marc said, "Retreat before you attack." His smile broadened.

"Glad you boys were listening," Goron replied, gruff.

"Get a hot meal and a few hours' sleep, and we'll leave before sunset," King Marc told the sword master.

"But we haven't settled on a plan for Armorica," countered Baron Dynyon.

The king glowered. "I'm going to get my queen. Everything else can wait."

"Praise the Old Ones," Branwen said.

The words were empty.

A SWORD
BETWEEN THEM

THEY SET OUT AT DUSK, riding into the night. This time when Branwen insisted on accompanying the king, Ruan raised no objection. Sir Goron rode in front, Branwen and Marc behind, and Ruan in the rear. The king was adamant that the traveling party should be kept small so as not to be slowed down.

Burning pinks and oranges striated the sky as they skirted around the Morrois Forest and followed a road with which Branwen was unfamiliar. The River Heyl ran through the moorland and emptied into an estuary on House Whel territory. Sir Goron's cottage was located to the north, in a most deserted spot along the river. He said he preferred fish to people, and Branwen didn't think he was jesting.

Marc wore a plain cloak of black wool. If there were any raiders roaming the countryside, or common thieves, the king didn't want to attract any attention. Branwen kept her eyes peeled for Death-Tellers. All she heard were hooves beating earth.

"Why did Sir Goron leave court?" Branwen asked Marc in a hush, after an hour had passed in silence. The moon was starting to rise.

He fidgeted with his reins, considering. "Sir Goron served my father faithfully for many years. He was his Champion before he was entrusted with training me to fight like a king. From the time I was seven years old, we practiced together every day. I spent more of my childhood with Goron than either of my parents."

The king paused and Branwen sensed reluctance in him to continue. He drew his mount closer to Senara, and Branwen's palfrey threw back her head. The mare never liked for other horses to get too close.

Marc rested a hand on Branwen's shoulder. "Goron took me on my first raid," he said, and she went rigid. The sword master had led the ambush that killed her parents. Blind rage made Branwen dizzy. She clutched the front of her saddle.

"I'm sorry, sister. I owe you the full truth after all you've done for me."

Branwen gulped, unable to speak. "When my father died, Sir Goron asked me to release him from his oaths of service to the crown. He said he'd passed on all he could to me and Tristan, and that he had no more appetite for battle. He wanted a quiet life—to atone for the blood he'd spilled." King Marc sighed. "I couldn't refuse his request. Although I've missed him."

"Thank you for telling me," she said tightly.

Marc nodded, putting space between their mounts. "It was clever of Tristan to seek Goron out. He's the best swordsman Kernyv has ever seen. I should have thought of it myself."

"We've all been panicked, brother."

"We have." He looked up at the stars beginning to prick the sky. The ancient Kernyveu had believed they were gods. "The council wants a war," said the king.

Marc returned his eyes from the stars to Branwen.

"You never gave me your opinion."

Branwen pressed her tongue against the back of her teeth. She breathed in and out. "I am not unbiased."

"Nobody is. Be honest with me," he said. "What advice would you give me if I weren't a king?"

Empathy engulfed her. Marc wanted so much to be a good man. Not for the first time Branwen wondered if a good man could not be a good king.

She shifted in her saddle. "Countess Kensa is right that I want to keep Iveriu out of a war. I also want to prevent more slaughter on Kernyvak shores," she stated. "When King Óengus declared the Champions Tournament it was because Iveriu needs allies. No kingdom can stand alone."

"Your uncle and I agree on many things," said Marc.

Branwen lowered her voice further. "You know I've never been convinced that Kahedrin hired the assassin. And we still don't know who sent the pirates to Armorica flying a Kernyvak flag. But, I imagine it's the same person. Someone who wants this war very badly."

"On that we are also in agreement," the king ground out.

"However, I also fear the truth of Ruan's words that if we do nothing, we invite another challenge."

"So you would counsel war?" Marc's chest lifted with a surprised intake of breath. "I am loath to reward treachery."

"We still have Princess Alba. And Armorica does not have Queen Eseult." Branwen canted her head. "Is there something we can demand for Alba's return that will be regarded as a victory?"

The king touched his beard. "You pose an interesting question," he said. "I will think on it."

The conversation dwindled as the moon rose to its apex. Branwen's entire body was sore when they stopped to water the horses just after midnight. King Marc wanted to reach his queen before morning. Ruan approached Branwen as their mounts drank from the river. He massaged her shoulders and she let out a soft moan.

"You're good at that," she said.

Ruan wrapped his arms around her, drawing Branwen's back against his chest.

"I do my best." He kissed her discreetly on the temple, yet her body couldn't entirely relax into him. "You must be relieved your cousin is safe," he said. They hadn't been alone since Sir Goron walked into the council meeting.

"Of course." But the True Queen had still tried to murder her, and Branwen didn't relish the prospect of spending the rest of her life trying to keep the lovers apart.

"It seems your cousin was never in any true danger," Ruan remarked.

Except from me. Branwen spun around in his arms to face him.

"Thank the gods," she said. Moonlight made Ruan's hair appear silvery-white. She toyed with a strand.

Ruan frowned. "Sir Goron also tells me that Tristan and the queen arrived mid-afternoon the day after the attack," he said, and Branwen's mind raced. The journey took twelve hours, which meant that Tristan and Eseult would have had to leave before the assault began.

"Their horses must have traveled like the wind," he noted.

"They must have." Branwen's look could turn lesser men to stone.

"*Bran—*"

She shrugged off Ruan's embrace and rejoined the others. The traveling party followed the riverbank until the promise of daybreak began diluting the murk. Physical exhaustion distracted Branwen from the many worries taking root in her mind like flowering thorns. King Marc might be willing to overlook discrepancies in the timing of Tristan and Eseult's departure from Monwiku, but his Champion was not.

With the sun still below the horizon, a small stone house with a thatched roof came into view. As they drew nearer, Branwen spied the silhouette of Lí Ban, the queen's stark-white mare. Beside her, Tristan's dappled gray stallion grazed on grasses and wild mushrooms. Eseult had named her mount for an Ivernic sea goddess, a mermaid whose ballad Tristan had serenaded her with aboard the *Dragon Rising*.

Marc pulled back his reins, halting his own steed. He put his lips together in a whistle, mimicking a birdcall. Branwen recognized it as the signal he and Tristan had devised as boys. No noise came from within the cottage.

Above the doorway hung a pair of antlers. Sir Goron must be a devotee of the Horned One. Marc dismounted immediately. He entered the cottage first, Branwen half a step behind. Embers glowed in a fire pit that had been dug into the dirt floor, casting a faint light on the sleeping alcove in the corner. Only a tapestry separated it from the main space of the one-room dwelling.

Sweat beaded on Branwen's brow despite the fresh air.

In what state would King Marc find Tristan and Eseult when he drew back the curtain?

Blood and bone, forged by fire, we beseech you for the truest of desires.

Branwen had cast the spell in Kerwindos's Cauldron. She knew its power. Could the lovers resist the temptation of a whole night alone together? Ruan followed at Branwen's heels and she didn't dare glance backward.

Marc began drawing the tapestry—which depicted the Horned One saving his father—to one side. Branwen couldn't breathe. One simple motion could unveil the secrets Branwen had been keeping for months. Bring her kingdom to its knees.

Swish.

The lovers were asleep, a sword between them. Fully clothed.

Tristan woke in an instant, hand gripping the hilt of his weapon before he even opened his eyes. The edges of Marc's mouth twitched in a smile, relief smoothing his brow. Evidently he wasn't completely immune to Ruan's accusations that Tristan and Eseult had run off together.

The Queen's Champion slept closest to the door, and he heaved the sword toward whoever had disturbed him in one fluid motion as he sat up.

He stopped himself. "Marc?" Tristan said as his eyes focused.

"Brother." Love brimmed from the word. The king loved his nephew perhaps too well, but Branwen could only be thankful for it.

Tristan's eyes skipped from Marc to Branwen, then behind them to Ruan.

Eseult stirred, scrubbing a hand over her face. She always was a heavy sleeper.

"You're here," she said.

"I am," answered the king, but the queen's gaze was fixed squarely on Branwen. Sitting up beside Tristan, Eseult hugged herself closer. Her flaxen tresses fell past her shoulders, unplaited.

Fear in his voice, "The castle?" Tristan asked.

"We held it," Marc said, with a meaningful glance at Branwen.

"What happened?" Tristan looked to his king, then Ruan. Not at Branwen. "Who attacked us?"

"Armorica," replied Ruan from behind Branwen. She slanted her gaze his way. The King's Champion's hand also rested against his sword.

Tristan cursed at the response.

"Didn't you see their colors?" Ruan's question was far from casual.

Had Ruan also noted that both Tristan and Eseult were dressed in day clothes? The queen wore the same deep indigo gown as the night before the attack. If she'd been roused in the early hours of the morning, shouldn't she be in a nightgown?

"I was more concerned with getting the queen to safety," Tristan told his cousin, "than checking the banners of our assailants."

"Marc sent me to assist you at the Queen's Tower," Ruan said. "But you were already gone."

"I'm fast on my feet. A reason you've never bested me in a fight."

"And I'm indebted, Tristan," said King Marc. Authority rang from his voice. Tristan and Ruan had always chafed at each other, but their antipathy was something more now.

"I'm only sorry I wasn't there to defend Monwiku with you, brother," Tristan told Marc. Devastation roughened his voice.

"You have nothing to be sorry for." The king turned the focus of his attention to his wife. "My queen—*Eseult*. I can't tell you how overjoyed I am to see you unharmed." Marc took a step toward the cot.

Tristan swung his legs beneath him and moved out of the way. The cot dipped as King Marc lowered himself onto the edge, taking Eseult's hands in his and kissing them.

"I give thanks to your gods and mine that we're reunited."

Eseult sought Branwen with her eyes, and they were wisely filled with apprehension. "As do I," the queen told her husband, head bowed, shy.

Tristan came toe-to-toe with Branwen as he exited the sleeping nook.

His warm brown skin and pronounced cheekbones were as attractive as they'd always been, but the hazel flecks in his dark eyes were cold. He returned his sword to its sheath.

"Branwen," he greeted her.

Your heart isn't noble. Tristan's angry words from their last encounter rattled in her skull. Branwen, too, had promised to destroy him if he further threatened the peace.

"You've escaped death again," she said. Her voice was as frosty as his eyes.

Tristan brushed past her, knocking her shoulder more than necessary. Branwen glared after him and found Ruan watching their exchange. He raised his eyebrows.

Tristan crouched beside Goron, who stoked the embers, adding another log. He'd entered his own home unnoticed. Tristan murmured something to him in Kernyvak that Branwen didn't understand.

"Sister," said Marc. Branwen twisted back toward the king. "I haven't let you say hello to your cousin properly." He pushed to his feet. Eseult wrapped a blond strand around her pinkie, taut.

"Branny," she said. "The Old Ones are watching over you. I'm so grateful." The queen's gaze darted toward Branwen's hand. The one she now knew could produce fire.

"As am I, Lady Queen." She embraced her cousin because she knew it was what Marc would expect, but her hold was limp.

"Branwen told me that your birthday was this week," King Marc said to his wife.

"She did?"

"When we return to Monwiku we can celebrate however you wish."

"Thank you," the queen said in a small voice.

Walking over to the fire pit, Marc said, "We left the castle at sunset. Let us sleep awhile before we return. It's not quite light yet."

"An excellent idea, sire," Ruan enthused. "Cousin," he said to Tristan.

"You won't mind giving the king your place in the bed?" His smile was halfway between vicious and rakish.

"Of course not." Tristan exhaled through his nose. "I've had more than enough rest. I'll stand watch."

"Ah well, you were sleeping on duty when we arrived."

"*Ruan*," King Marc barked. Ruan's shoulder blades snapped together. "Your lack of sleep has sharpened your tongue too much."

The King's Champion worked his jaw; Branwen saw a true wound in his expression.

"Branwen will share the bed with her cousin. Ruan, you will share the floor with me." Marc tugged at his beard. "Goron, I hate to put you out of your own bed," he said to his former teacher.

"Nonsense. Hay makes a man go soft." Again, Goron didn't smile, yet Branwen heard a grin in his voice.

"Are you certain?" Branwen said to the king. Lying next to her cousin would be the furthest thing from restful.

"Quite certain."

She nodded. "*Mormerkti.*"

Tristan retreated outside the cottage and the other men lay down beside the fire pit. Ruan and Sir Goron positioned themselves defensively on either side of the king.

Eseult pulled the curtain closed, giving her and Branwen privacy that Branwen didn't want. Nevertheless, fatigue overwhelmed her and she flopped against the hay-filled mattress. The queen lay down next to her, draping a coarse woolen blanket on top of them. Sir Goron had served King Merchion for years. Branwen wondered why his home was so modest, his belongings utilitarian.

Her eyelids drooped. Eseult pressed in closer, whispering, "I would never hurt you, Branny. I *wouldn't*. No matter what else you think of me, I didn't send those men after you. Somehow I'm going to prove it."

Branwen turned onto her side, facing her cousin. Eseult possessed the same Rigani-stone green eyes as Branwen's mother. They used to fill her with affection—now nothing remained but scorn, hot and desperate.

"Nobody is worth a war," Branwen told the queen low. Vindictive. "Including you. Including me. I'll keep your secrets for that reason—and that reason only."

Eseult grabbed her hand. "I won't let you forget." She traced her finger atop Branwen's bandage. Angry strokes. Frantic. "Not you without me, not me—"

"*Stop it.*" Branwen yanked her hand away. "I don't know why you keep doing that—it means nothing to me."

She rolled over, showing the queen her back. She blocked out her cousin's sniveling.

Maybe Eseult regretted her actions. Branwen didn't care. Her cousin had always placed her own heart above all others.

Marc was too selfless to be king, and Eseult was too selfish to be queen.

Branwen bit down on her fist and released a silent scream.

THE DIFFICULT KIND

THE SCENT OF SMOKE STILL clung to the salty breeze at Monwiku. Branwen wended her way down the hill to the castle cellars, late afternoon light illuminating the canopy of leaves. She carried a lacquered box filled with oils to clean and anoint the body of the man she'd killed. A tally that was steadily increasing.

Slayer.

Who would be next? Who would Branwen sacrifice to the Dark One?

Lanterns creaked from the spike-leafed trees. She heard other signs of bustling. The residents of Monwiku were starting to resume their regular duties. It had been a week since the attack, and the cows needed to be milked, chickens fed, weapons forged. Duty didn't wait on grief. Branwen had learned when her parents died that sometimes duty was the only way through it.

Since they'd returned from Sir Goron's cottage, she'd spent the past few days tending to the wounded with Andred, avoiding Tristan, Eseult, and Ruan. Weariness had kept conversation to a minimum on the homeward journey. Branwen could tell that Marc was sad to have said goodbye to his former sword master.

Much to Branwen's astonishment, Endelyn had been visiting injured servants whenever her duties as the queen's lady's maid allowed. Branwen taught her how to change a bandage and to check for signs of infection. The attack seemed to have shifted something profound in the Kernyvak princess.

As the trail led Branwen closer to the Royal Guards' barracks, she spotted the face she'd once dreamed about. Her grip tightened on the box in her arms.

The white sash that cut a diagonal against Tristan's black tunic was too bright. Because he was the Queen's Champion, the silk was embroidered with the insignias of both Kernyv and Iveriu. He pulled at it when he saw Branwen, equally awkward.

"*Dymatis*, Lady Branwen," Tristan said as he stepped onto the flagstone path.

Her gaze caught on the small scar above his right eyebrow. When he'd first washed up on the beach below Castle Rigani, Branwen had found the imperfection endearing. Later, she'd learned that he'd received the scar from Ruan. Tristan had witnessed Prince Edern whipping Ruan as a boy, and Ruan had convinced him to stay quiet.

Branwen flicked her eyes to the ground. "*Dymatis*, Prince Tristan." She continued past him.

"Marc told me," Tristan said. Branwen stopped, turning on her heel to face him. "Marc told me you killed Kahedrin to save him."

Their eyes locked. Branwen made no reply.

"Thank you," he told her. "I should have been here."

"Yes. You should have." Branwen stepped in closer; Tristan flinched. "Where *were* you? What happened?" she demanded.

He raked a hand through his mop of inky curls. She'd once found that irritated gesture endearing, too. Tristan exhaled a hot breath and Branwen felt it on her brow.

"After our . . . argument, I set off for Liones. I needed to be alone," he began. "Eventually, I realized I was being followed."

"Eseult." Branwen made her cousin's name a hiss. Tristan ducked his head.

"I insisted we return to the castle but as we rounded the bend on the coastal path from Marghas, we saw Monwiku in flames." He swallowed, thumb circling the pommel of the sword at his waist. "I knew Marc would want me to get Eseult—the True Queen—somewhere safe."

He lifted his gaze to meet Branwen's. "Not returning to fight for my king was the hardest thing I've ever done," Tristan said.

"Also the most suspicious," Branwen retorted. "Don't underestimate Ruan. He sees far too much."

"You certainly don't underestimate him."

"You have no right to jealousy."

"Don't I?" Tristan's eyes narrowed. "I have no idea what to feel— how I *really* feel about anyone. Anything. *You* took that away from me, Branwen." He gripped his sword. "When I look at the queen, when I look at you . . . all I see are lies!"

I'm sorry. But Branwen couldn't say the words aloud. She had once loved this man enough to siphon the poison from his body into hers. Tristan had been the first man to capture Branwen's heart, and to show her the starless tide.

"I've been protecting both of you as best I can," she said instead. "You don't make it easy!"

His posture straightened. "I won't fail Marc again. I'd exile myself to Liones if I could and never come back. He wants me here."

Branwen raised her chin. "I'll do my utmost to stay out of your way, Tristan. Just keep your queen out of mine."

"You don't really believe she sent the guardsmen after you?" he whispered, glancing around them.

"Who else?"

"She loves you, Branwen." Tristan paused. "Still."

"Not as much as she loves herself."

"She's not capable of murder!"

"I've known Eseult my whole life. She's capable of more than you think."

Tristan's expression darkened. "As are you." He pointed at Branwen's bandaged hand. She had no injury; she just wanted to avoid questions.

"I'm told Shades landed at Monwiku. That they fought for *us*." He leaned in closer. "What did you do?"

"What no one else could." Branwen clutched the box between them like a shield.

Worry rearranged his features. "What did it cost you?" He tilted his chin at the white curls tucked behind her ears. She'd given up trying to disguise them.

"I am nothing to you, Tristan—that's what you said. Don't show me false concern."

Branwen barged past him and practically ran the rest of the way to the cellars. He didn't call after her.

Two guardsmen were posted outside the entrance. Princess Alba was a royal hostage, but she was still a hostage. She was the only bargaining chip that King Marc had left. After the barons and Countess Kensa had welcomed the True Queen back to court, they had gone home disgruntled that the king had yet to make a decision about Armorica.

Oil lamps hung from the walls. The last time Branwen had been in the castle cellars was to prepare Queen Verica for burial. They were cool enough to delay the body's decomposition. All of the rulers of Kernyv were interred in a tomb on the northern coast. One day, Tristan and Eseult would lie there side by side. But not Branwen.

Alba swung around at the sound of Branwen's footsteps, reaching instinctively for a weapon at her hip that wasn't there.

Her movements were liquid, nearly as startling as the Wise Damsel's. The princess wrinkled her nose at Branwen. Lamplight revealed her golden-brown cheeks were damp with tears.

"You," Alba practically spat. "Have you come to gloat?"

She thrust an angry hand at the body of Prince Kahedrin who'd been laid out on a stone table behind her.

The words landed like a punch. The guilt Branwen had been denying ate at her ironclad heart.

"No, Lady Princess. In Iveriu we prepare our dead for the journey to the Otherworld as you do in Armorica." Although the Iverni did not burn their bodies. Branwen extended the lacquered box toward Alba. "I have brought the Oils of Passage."

The princess's bottom lip quivered. "I told you I prefer *Captain*."

Her voice cracked, and Branwen felt her own throat constrict. Branwen had killed Keane. She had killed Tutir and Bledros. As well as other Armoricans in battle whose names she'd never know. Those deaths were justified. As was Prince Kahedrin's.

And yet, Branwen had never been confronted by the grief-stricken loved one of a man she'd felled. She recognized the other woman's pain, felt it keenly—the same pain she'd been forced to nurse when she was six years old.

"I'll leave the oils here," Branwen said, taking a step toward the stone slab. "Captain," she added. She would afford Alba the respect of calling her by her chosen title. There was little else she could do for her.

Alba regarded Branwen warily. She set the box beside Prince Kahedrin's head. His eyes had been open when he died. Summer blue. Someone had closed them. The prince's build was stocky and his skin pale. He and Alba were half siblings but that clearly mattered not at all.

"He doesn't look like himself," said Alba, coming to stand next to Branwen. She touched a hand to the crown of Kahedrin's flaming red hair. It had grown dull.

The first time Branwen had met Kahedrin, they'd been hunting the *rixula* before the wedding. Whoever caught the red-feathered bird was meant to be gifted a year without death. Branwen glanced at his sister.

"Kahedrin saw Ankou. Right before he died."

Armoricans believed that Ankou was the Old One who trafficked in death. She shepherded souls to the Otherworld. They burned their dead to make their souls easier for her to collect. Branwen had intended to console Alba with the knowledge, but the other woman recoiled.

"You shouldn't have been with him—it should have been me!" Alba shouted as a sob racked her body. Without thinking, Branwen wrapped an arm around Alba as she began to weep. After a minute, she pushed Branwen away violently.

"I understand why you hate me," Branwen said. "I've spent most of my life hating the Kernyveu who killed my parents."

"I will never stop hating you." Alba wiped her nose with the sleeve of her tunic. Branwen was glad there was no knife attached to her breeches.

"But I hate myself more," said the captain. Misery stained her tongue. "Kahedrin wasn't even supposed to be here." She choked back another sob.

"He thought my plan was reckless." Her gaze swept over her brother's waxy visage. "Impulsive." She laid her hand atop his lifeless one. "He refused to back me, and I gathered my most loyal men anyway." Alba snorted in disgust. "At the last minute, just as we were pushing from the dock, Kahedrin jumped in my boat. He said he was coming along to make sure his little sister didn't get herself killed."

Branwen clasped her hands together.

"Kahedrin always said I'd grow up to be the difficult kind of woman—he meant it as a compliment." Alba pierced Branwen with a look. "And I got him killed." Her lips curled. "I have no more right to prepare his body than you do. We both killed him."

The younger woman's chest heaved. Branwen remained quiet as Alba struggled to regain her composure.

"It would be my honor to assist you, Captain," Branwen said. "If you would permit me."

Alba inhaled a long breath through her nose.

"Now that the True Queen has been found alive—and *not* kidnapped by Armoricans," she said, "will King Marc let me go home?"

"I don't know." Branwen turned to leave.

"Yes," Alba said tentatively. "Yes, I would like your help."

With a minuscule smile, Branwen removed the oils and linen cloths from the lacquered box. Alba murmured something in Armorican, perhaps a prayer to Ankou, as they began. Working together in silence, the two women cleansed Kahedrin's body with wild mint and garlic, masked the stench of death with lavender.

Branwen would not ask forgiveness from the sister of the man before her, and she would not receive it. Yet Branwen felt unforeseen affinity with the Armorican captain. Both she and Alba had chosen what they thought was the right fight.

And both of them had failed.

Still, a strange warmth spread through Branwen. For a fleeting moment, she felt something akin to peace.

✣ ✣ ✣

Crickets filled the castle gardens with their night song as Crown Prince Kahedrin's body was carried down to the pyre.

Alba followed behind her brother to the first level of the terraced gardens. More blood than petals had now showered the earth.

Branwen lingered on the terrace above, watching Tristan, Ruan, Endelyn, and Andred stand solemnly around the pyre. They had all known Kahedrin for years. They had been friends once. Childhood playmates.

Someone wanted them to become enemies. Someone had succeeded.

Above the Dreaming Sea, westward toward Iveriu, the sun sank into the depths. Golden highlights streaked somber clouds. Branwen smelled rain in the air.

Marc noticed her lurking at the edge of the second terrace as he escorted Queen Eseult down the stone steps that led to the bottom of the garden. He bade his wife continue without him.

"Sister," he said to Branwen. "I've been looking for you." The king's eyes were tired and the circles beneath them distinct.

"I was helping Alba prepare Kahedrin's body."

Lips pursed, Marc nodded. "I hope this is the last funeral we attend for a long time," he said. Branwen drew in a breath, raising her brow in agreement.

"Sister," he said again. "I remember this day every year. I remember what I did."

Today was the anniversary of her parents' deaths. Fourteen years ago, and a year to the day that Branwen had rescued Tristan. There was a terrible symmetry to it all. As if she were a puppet and the Old Ones were pulling her strings.

Marc reached a hand toward the brooch on Branwen's cloak. Her mother's brooch.

"Every year, I pray at the temple. I ask mercy from my god." He met Branwen's stare. "Is there a tradition you keep?"

Involuntarily, her gaze sought the queen. Her cousin had always been the one to soothe Branwen, with her silliness and her love stories and her elderberry wine. This Branwen knew. But she could no more grasp the memories than shadows upon a wall. They had no warmth. No substance.

Branwen shook her head. "I've always felt closest to my parents by the sea," she said.

Marc offered her a hand. "Join me." He indicated the mourners below.

"I'll stay here." She inhaled. "I have no right to mourn the man I murdered."

He embraced her and kissed Branwen's brow. "I love you because you mourn him, sister."

She let a tear glide down her cheek as King Marc took his place beside his wife.

Alba sang a lament. Branwen didn't understand the words but she felt the other woman's heart-wound. Alba's voice was a sweet alto. Raw. Branwen could hear Lady Alana's harp accompanying her on the wind.

The sweetness of Alba's voice would seem at odds with the young, brazen captain who had defied her father and besieged a castle thought to be impermeable.

When the song was finished, a torch was lit.

Branwen stayed and watched the bonfire from her perch until long after the others had left. Wood and bone crackled. Orange and copper sparks drifted up toward the wandering stars. The soles of Branwen's feet began to ache yet she scarcely noticed.

"You're still here."

The moon was waning and the light on Ruan's face dim. He treaded softly on the scorched grasses. "I checked your room after I escorted Alba back to hers."

"How is she?" Branwen asked, although she knew it to be a useless question. One designed to make the asker feel better.

"She adored Kahedrin. And Havelin," Ruan replied. "Her loss is great. But Alba's resilient. I remember once, when she was visiting Villa Illogan, she fell from a pony and broke her arm. She was too embarrassed to tell anyone."

He laughed. "It took two days before anyone realized—and she was only eight. Seer Casek was barely able to set it."

"Seer Casek?"

"He used to be the *kordweyd* at the temple in Illogan." Ruan sighed. "Anyway, Alba will recover." He stopped beside Branwen, raising a hand to her jaw and stroking its length.

"Maybe she will. She won't be the same."

"I know you're feeling guilty, Branwen. But I wouldn't trade Kahedrin for Marc."

"Neither would I." And that was perhaps the true source of her guilt.

"I regret that Kahedrin put me in the position to choose," Branwen said. Or maybe she had set herself on that course exactly one year ago today when she pulled Tristan from the raft?

"I don't want to have to choose," she said. There was a hitch in her voice.

Ruan took her bandaged hand in his, placing it against his cheek. "*Krídyom.*"

"Please, Ruan. Don't make me."

Regret fractured his face. "We both know that Tristan is lying about what happened on the night of the attack."

"If he and my cousin had decided to flee together, why would he send Sir Goron to tell Marc where to find them?" Ruan frowned at her words. "You know I'm right," she pressed him.

"I don't know what I know, Branwen."

"No, you don't." She placed her other hand on his cheek, framing his face. "The queen is back. Marc believes Tristan. Keeping the peace is what he wants."

"What do *you* believe?" Ruan asked. "Truly?"

Branwen's stomach flipped over several times. "*I*—I believe that my kingdom needs peace. My parents were murdered fourteen years ago today by Kernyvak raiders."

"You never told me."

"I'm telling you now." Branwen's chest expanded. "Marc was on that raid. As was Xandru. And Sir Goron."

"*Branwen.*" Her name became an exclamation. Ruan's eyes rounded. "If he weren't my king, I would avenge your family." He shook his head. "But you've saved Marc's life. His kingdom."

"That is how much I believe in peace, Ruan. Enough to forgive the man who killed my mother."

Ruan stared at Branwen dumbfounded. "I didn't think I could be in more awe of you."

She made a noise at the back of her throat. "I'm a killer, Ruan. A cheat. A liar. I'm not selfless like your Horned One. What I know—what I *believe* is that no one needs to die if Tristan and Eseult have committed an indiscretion."

Ruan's mouth became a tight line. "But, Branwen—"

"*No*." She cut him off, fury mounting. "Eseult is back at Marc's side, which is where she'll stay. We're at war with Armorica. Do you want to resume war with Iveriu as well? With your father's people? *Your* people?"

Ruan opened his mouth to speak, and Branwen silenced him with a finger across his lips.

"If you implicate my queen in treason, you implicate me as well. If you endanger Iveriu, you make me your enemy."

Her breath came in pants. "Do you love me, Ruan? Or do you want to be *right*?"

He stepped back from her embrace, dragging his hands through the hair that hung about his shoulders.

What would Branwen do if Ruan chose to pursue his suspicions? What wouldn't Branwen do to keep the peace?

Ruan dropped to his knees before her.

"I love you, Branwen. *Karid. Kridyom*." He stared up at her. He withdrew his father's knife and offered it to her in supplication. "I believe in *you*."

Relief was intoxicating. Branwen fell to her knees beside him. She wrapped her hands around his neck, bit his lower lip, and kissed him as if she were the one who'd been rescued from a life raft.

The bonfire continued to lick the sky.

"Make love to me," she told him.

Ruan pulled back. "Here? In the garden?"

"Here."

Starlight glimmered off her mother's brooch. *The right fight.*

For tonight, Branwen had won.

DEATH STALKS US ALL

W HENEVER BRANWEN ENTERED ALBA'S APARTMENT in the West Tower, she still half expected to find Queen Verica casting her dice. In the week since Kahedrin's funeral, the southerly wind from the Mílesian peninsula had deepened the spring and Branwen hardly needed her cloak. This time last year, she'd been nursing Tristan back to health in her cave; this year she had a different royal patient in her care.

"You seem distracted today," Alba noted as Branwen dabbed a disinfectant ointment along the scab on the other woman's cheek. Her gaze had strayed through the west-facing window to the gardens below. The only time she saw King Marc look at all peaceful was when he worked with Andred and Lowenek to clear the wreckage and begin to replant.

Ignoring the remark, Branwen said, "Your nose is almost fully healed." She finished applying the ointment. "You may have a scar here."

Alba shrugged. "The sea doesn't care if I have scars."

"I suppose it doesn't." Branwen resealed the jar and placed it in her satchel.

"My muscles are growing tight from being confined to my rooms. I need to exercise the ones I pulled during the . . . a couple of weeks ago." The captain leaned forward in the armchair. "As Royal Healer, might you give me permission to train outside?"

Branwen gave her a cagey look. "You expect me to put a sword in your hand?"

"I don't need a sword," Alba replied, shaking her head. "My brothers taught me how to box and wrestle like they do in the Aquilan military." With a wry smile, she added, "You could be my sparring partner."

Branwen snorted. From a healer's perspective, she could see the benefit of allowing the other woman to exercise her muscles lest they atrophy. She was less enthusiastic about the prospect of being punched in the face. Still, the memory of Alba's lament over Kahedrin's pyre clung to her.

"I will have to ask the king's permission," said Branwen.

"I would appreciate that." A pause. "Thank you."

Sunlight winked off a silver chain around the captain's neck, a small charm dangling from it. Branwen squinted. It was a skeleton with its arms outstretched. Following Branwen's gaze, Alba said, "This is Ankou."

"Does everyone in Armorica still practice the Old Ways?" she asked.

"The Cult of the Horned One has its temples, but we Armoricans are stubborn." Alba plucked the charm from her tunic and ran her forefinger along the skeleton's silhouette. "On our thirteenth birthdays, we choose which of the seven Old Ones to make our patron."

Lowering an eyebrow, Branwen said, "And you chose your death goddess?"

"Death stalks us all—I prefer to think of her as a friend."

Gooseflesh broke out across Branwen's arms at her words. She suspected that if Alba came face-to-face with the Dark One, she might feel differently.

"We embrace death so that we enjoy life more," Alba continued. "Most Armorican warriors worship Ankou."

"Did Kahedrin feel the same?" Branwen asked. Alba balked and she shot her a dirty look. "I-I didn't mean to offend you." The other woman exhaled a harsh breath. "It's only that in Iveriu we believe Dhusnos rules the Sea of the Dead, and we fear him," Branwen said.

Alba lowered her gaze to her talisman. "That seems strange to me. In Armorica, we believe that Ankou was the first of the Old Ones to be born from Kerwindos's Cauldron. The mother of creation knew that all life must end—eventually," she said. "If we spend our lives fearing death, we spend them fearing ourselves."

Branwen stroked the bandage wrapped around her right hand. She feared death and she feared herself, and she had good reason for both. But hadn't Goddess Ériu banished Dhusnos to the waters that surrounded their island? Was his insult so grave? Branwen swallowed. Was not the Land also responsible for the starless tide?

"Who is your patron?" Alba asked her, breaking into Branwen's thoughts.

"Bríga," she replied after a moment, her voice near a whisper. Although she no longer knew if that was true.

The captain nodded. "Our healers worship Bríga, too."

A knock came as a member of the Royal Guard opened the door. Branwen nearly jumped. "Pardon the intrusion, Lady Branwen," said a young man with freckled skin. "The king is requesting your presence in his study."

"I'll come right away." She rummaged in her satchel and presented

Alba with a jar of blue glass. "Massage the arnica paste into your sore muscles. I'll ask the king about letting you train outside."

Alba accepted the jar. "Might I beg you another favor?" Branwen made an *mmm* noise as she slung the satchel over her shoulder. "A book?" Catching her eye, the other woman said, "I'm excellent company but there's a limit to how entertaining I find myself."

Branwen couldn't help but laugh. "Any subject in particular?"

"History. If you can manage it?"

The light filling her eyes reminded Branwen of Master Bécc, the royal tutor at Castle Rigani, and his enthusiasm as he regaled her and Eseult about ancient kings.

"I'll see what I can do," she said.

As Branwen reached the doorway, Alba called out, "And find yourself some trousers—I can teach you a thing or two about fighting."

Of that, Branwen had absolutely no doubt.

✢ ✢ ✢

A scroll lay before King Marc on the table.

"You four are my family and my most trusted friends," he began. Ruan, Tristan, and the queen had also been summoned. Branwen sat beside the King's Champion, body tensed. "We have received a response from King Faramon, and before I assemble my council I want to know your thoughts."

"What does Faramon say?" asked Tristan. He sat opposite from Branwen, and they avoided eye contact. Eseult was seated beside him, at the left hand of the king. She held herself like a deer with an arrow aimed at its throat.

"He has offered a ransom for Princess Alba." Marc looked from

Tristan to Ruan. "Gold," he elaborated. He tugged at his beard, which had grown even longer, the reddish bristles more prominent. "Faramon is aware that our treasury has been depleted by the fall in exports of our white lead."

Ruan cursed. "He's aware because Armorica has started importing from the Kingdom of Míl instead!"

Branwen shifted in her seat, feeling her lover's restless energy. The mining disaster last year had been caused by pressuring the miners to dig faster. Before her arrival in Kernyv, she hadn't realized how dependent the kingdom was on trading their minerals. House Whel had been most affected by the lack of demand for white lead.

"Gold isn't enough," the king agreed.

"We should demand land on Armorica's northern coast. Perhaps a port," suggested Ruan.

"Has Xandru reached Karaez safely?" Branwen asked Marc. "Does King Faramon know you didn't send the pirates?"

The king lifted a leather pouch from beside the scroll, the size of a fist.

"Seeds," he replied. Xandru always sent Marc seeds for his garden. "He's there—and safe. For now." Branwen nodded, glad, as Marc took in another breath. "Faramon also knows that Kahedrin died in the assault on Monwiku."

Beneath the table, Ruan put a hand on Branwen's knee. "Then I'm surprised he's not offering more for Alba's release," said the King's Champion.

Marc squeezed the pouch. "I've been pondering what I can demand in exchange for the princess that will bring the hostilities to a swift conclusion." He looked around the table, the corner of his mouth lifting as his gaze met Branwen's.

"What I want," said the king, "is an alliance. A *permanent* alliance."

"What do you propose?" Tristan asked.

"That we fight the pirates together. Take back control of the Veneti Isles once and for all. Bring them law and order, subjects of the Kernyvak crown."

Branwen had learned that the Aquilan Empire seized the islands and used them as a penal colony when they ruled Albion. The prisoners were abandoned when the Aquilan legions retreated to the southern continent. Those remaining had turned to piracy to survive.

The afternoon grew unnaturally still. Then Ruan exclaimed, "You can't be serious. The other councillors will never support your plan."

"I am very serious, Ruan. I am the king, and this is what I want." An unusual roughness clipped the king's words. "What I believe is best for my people."

"You also said you wanted our opinions," his Champion countered. "And my opinion is that your proposal will make Kernyv seem weak to the rest of Albion. It will make *you* seem weak to the rest of the kingdom."

Marc slammed the bag of seeds on the table. "Thank you for your frankness." To Eseult, he said, "What is your opinion, my queen? What would you counsel? This should be our decision."

The True Queen wet her lips. She looked pale in the afternoon light. Tristan had succeeded in keeping Eseult from Branwen's path since her return. Or, perhaps, the queen had made herself invisible. Only now did Branwen notice her cousin's sunken cheeks and how the bodice of her dress fit more loosely. A shadow of her former self.

"I think we should do whatever will end the war," said Eseult, hesitant. She dashed a glance at Branwen. "Before Armorica decides to attack Iveriu."

Marc nodded, his expression softening as he looked at his wife.

"Thank you for your support. The True Queen and I are in agreement." Shifting his gaze from Eseult to Branwen, he said, "I will also write to King Óengus. I fear that if the pirates were bold enough to attack Armorica, it won't be long before they resume their raids on Iveriu."

Branwen's stomach lurched at the possibility.

"My intention is to propose a three-kingdom alliance," Marc continued. "I will ask Óengus to send any ships he can spare to join our campaign against the pirates."

It was an ambitious plan. Branwen had never heard of a treaty between three kingdoms where each was on equal footing.

"Ridding the Southern Channel and the Dreaming Sea of pirates will benefit us all," Tristan said. Except for whoever sent the pirates to Karaez in the first place, thought Branwen.

King Marc glowered at his Champion. "Do I have everyone's support?"

"You always have my support, Marc," answered Ruan. "But I feel compelled to tell you that the barons and my mother won't be happy."

"Then you will convince the countess to make her *king* happy."

The threat hung in the air. Ruan noticeably swallowed.

"My Lord King," said Eseult, regaining his focus. "I have been visiting the wounded with Endelyn." Branwen coughed. That was news to her.

"I'm sure your presence heartens them," Marc told his wife.

"*Mormerkti.*" Eseult's lips curved into an uncertain smile. "The servants' quarters are cramped. I was—I was hoping we could break ground on the Royal Infirmary immediately. We need more space to care for *our*—" She paused. "Our people. It's the only birthday present I need."

Marc took his wife's hand. Branwen slid her finger against the grain of the wooden table. "Of course," he said. "Our people are fortunate to have you as their queen."

The door squeaked open as Endelyn appeared. "Forgive me," she said. "A woman is here for Ruan." Branwen canted her head at her lover. "She says her business is urgent," Endelyn told her brother.

Almost snarling, he demanded, "Who is it?"

"The wife of Tutir."

Ruan's hand tightened around Branwen's knee. They exchanged a panicked glance.

"Show her to my rooms. Tell her I'll be there soon."

"I'm not *your* lady's maid, Ruan."

"*Endelyn.*"

"Go," said King Marc to his Champion. "Our discussion is at an end."

Ruan sketched a frustrated circle on Branwen's thigh, then pushed to his feet. He darted her a backward glance before exiting. To the king, Branwen said, "Princess Alba asked if she might be able to exercise outdoors."

"Is that wise?" said Tristan, crossing his arms.

Branwen afforded him a glare. "It would help her recover from her injuries."

"The injuries she sustained besieging the castle?"

"Yes."

More than that, though, Branwen remembered how being outdoors had provided a respite from her own grief. Remaining cloistered in the West Tower would only serve to make Alba's fester.

Marc let out a sigh. "Very well," he said. "These negotiations may take some time and if they're successful, Alba will be our ally once more."

"Thank you, brother," said Branwen.

"Just be certain she's well guarded."

The meeting at a close, Branwen was eager to excuse herself from her cousin's presence. She found Andred skulking in the hallway.

Suppressing her fear about what Tutir's wife might want with Ruan, she greeted her apprentice.

A grin spread over his face. "I did it!" Andred told Branwen excitedly. "The gods' blood—I made it flower!" He beckoned her. "Let me show you."

Andred's bedchamber was located down the corridor from the king's study. Despite her nerves, she followed. At the far end of his room, beside the window, a translucent stone box glimmered. Basking in the rays of the sun, it reminded Branwen of snow. The stone was hot to the touch, however.

Leaning some of his weight against the tabletop, Andred removed the lid of the rectangular box with great care. The flowering box was Aquilan technology, heating the plants inside by trapping the sunlight in the stone. Ingenious. Almost like magic.

"I finally figured out the right amount of sun exposure," Branwen's apprentice explained. He'd been experimenting with this particular plant for months, trying to make it bloom. "I want to see if the oil from its petals can really cure a blood infection like the Treatise of Hepius claims."

Andred plucked a delicate blue flower from within the box.

"It's beautiful," said Branwen. The color was the precise shade of the tide just after sunset.

"I can't wait to show Xandru," said the boy. "When he returns to Monwiku." Xandru had brought Andred the box from abroad, and the captain was well loved by Branwen's apprentice.

Grinning from ear to ear, Andred placed the blossom in the center of Branwen's right palm. As she admired the vibrant cobalt petals, she began to feel light-headed, as if she'd imbibed too much elderberry wine. Euphoria rushed through her.

Immediately, the gods' blood started to wither.

The petals faded to a sickly hue, then gray, then white, as they curled in on themselves. Andred's face fell.

The euphoria dispersed, leaving dread in its wake. "I'm so sorry," Branwen told the boy. Acid sloshed in her gut.

"It's not your fault." Andred twisted his mouth to one side. "The air must be too cool for the blossom to survive outside the box. It thrives in a hot climate." He tapped his chin. "I'll try again."

Her apprentice plucked the dead flower from Branwen's hand.

The petals had already desiccated.

"I-I need to check on Princess Alba," Branwen lied. "I'll see you at dinner." She wouldn't be able to swallow a morsel.

Rushing from Andred's quarters, she caught her own reflection in one of the weathered mirrors that lined the hallway.

Her copper eyes glinted red. And the white streaks in her hair were gone.

Something was very, very wrong.

HAND OF DHUSNOS

THE TIDE WAS LOW ENOUGH to traverse the causeway on foot, and Alba insisted on training in wet sand. Four guardsmen formed a loose perimeter around Branwen and the royal hostage. From the bottom of the hill, Monwiku Castle loomed above them, its towers scraping the sky.

Sand tickled between Branwen's toes. She ran side by side with Alba around the circumference of the island. Armorican warriors ran barefoot on the beach to build speed and endurance, Alba had explained. Branwen's thighs burned, her calves ached, but over the past week she'd started looking forward to their daily training sessions.

Ruan assured Branwen that Tutir's wife posed no threat to her. Still, doubts remained. Except for now, for this hour pushing her body to its limits. She could almost forget everything save the pounding of her feet.

A warm wind teased Branwen's curls loose from her plaits. The white strands had returned the morning after she'd caused Andred's flower to wither.

Alba caught her eye, cracked a grin, and broke into a sprint. Breath straining in her lungs, Branwen chased after the other woman. Ruan had laughed at first when she'd asked to borrow a tunic and breeches; when he met Branwen returning to the West Tower hot and sweaty, however, he'd decided she looked better in his trousers than he did.

Branwen loped clumsily, the sand resisting her. Up ahead, Alba moved like an acrobat: spine erect yet fluid, every muscle under her control. On the night of the attack, Alba's lithe form had been distinct among so many fighting men. Her grace lethal.

Despite all the reasons they had to hate each other, Branwen had begun to enjoy the other woman's company—to wonder if forgiveness might one day be possible.

The sun was at its peak and perspiration dripped from Branwen's brow, stinging her eyes, salty on her lips. Alba let out a whoop and dropped, laughing, onto the sand. Her plum-colored tunic was stained black with sweat. Branwen crashed down next to her.

"Beat you again," Alba declared, triumphant.

Gasping for air, "Next time," Branwen said between pants. The captain snorted. Unlike her childhood horse races with her cousin, Branwen would never let Alba win on purpose, and she felt sure the princess wouldn't let her, either.

Wiping sweat from her hairline, Alba said, "Have you been practicing the stances I taught you?"

Branwen nodded. She found tremendous relief in punching her bed cushions when she couldn't sleep. "Give me a minute," she said, still trying to catch her breath. To her astonishment, the captain had demonstrated the basic techniques of Aquilan boxing and had yet to break Branwen's jaw.

Alba laughed. "I meant to thank you for the books. I'm enjoying

Cornelius's annals of the Western Isles. Although the Aquilan opinion of the Iverni isn't very high."

"Oh?"

"Cornelius is under the impression that you commit human sacrifice to ensure a plentiful harvest because the Iverni don't know how to plow properly."

"Human sacrifice? We certainly do not!" Branwen bristled. "My tutor in Iveriu said that Aquilan histories of other kingdoms serve only to justify their invasions of them."

"He sounds like a smart man." Alba jumped to her feet, spraying Branwen with sand. "Ready?" She extended a hand, her grip tight as she pulled Branwen up after her.

Branwen raised her fists. Alba held up her hands, palms flat, facing Branwen.

"Left foot forward," Alba said, correcting her position. "Knees softly bent." The captain spoke like someone accustomed to being obeyed. Branwen shifted her feet.

"Good. Now cross punch."

Branwen double-checked that the bandage was tightly wrapped around her right fist before making contact with Alba's left palm. Branwen's knuckles were battered and raw from training. The slap as she made contact with Alba's skin was satisfying.

"Again," the captain ordered. Branwen complied. Alba watched her attentively. "Do Ivernic women not learn to fight?"

Keane's face surfaced in Branwen's mind. She missed a punch. "I learned a little self-defense," she said. But her lessons had been focused on evading raiders, getting away, and waiting to be rescued. "Nothing like this." Alba was a woman used to rescuing herself. In another life, she's someone Branwen would want to call a friend.

The captain grunted. "Now the left." Branwen punched. "Use your hip. Hit with your whole body."

"Do all Armorican women fight like you?" she asked, the small bones in her left hand starting to complain.

"Not many. My mother insisted I train with my brothers." Sadness passed over Alba's face. "In the Melita Isles, my mother's homeland, noblewomen have always hired female bodyguards. The Melita Guardians are famous from Kartago to the Sea of Light."

Branwen knew nothing about these Guardians, but they made her think of ancient Queen Medhua. "We have many stories of warrior queens in Iveriu. My aunt doesn't bear arms, but she's a master of the Old Ways."

Alba swept a hand toward Branwen's head from the right, forcing her to duck.

"Good. Now punch." She did. Alba swept her hand from the other direction. "Duck, punch. Duck, punch," she commanded.

Branwen's heartbeat accelerated. "King Marc informed me that my cousin Xandru arrived in Karaez," Alba said as Branwen found her rhythm. "He and Xandru have always been close. I remember when I was a little girl they sailed together, sometimes coming to visit us at Castle Arausio." *Duck. Punch.* "Xandru must esteem the king highly to take up his cause against his own family."

Duck. "I believe the Manduca family also has an interest in *ensur—*" Branwen gulped down a breath. "Ensuring their merchant vessels can safely travel through *th—*" Another breath. "The Southern Channel." *Punch.*

"Perhaps," said Alba. The muscles in Branwen's back began to mutiny. She would need a bath of arnica milk this evening. "It seems I'm to be stuck on this island until my father offers sufficient ransom," the captain mused. "King Marc will find that my father's anger doesn't easily ebb. I deceived him and weakened his bargaining position."

"You're his heir," Branwen forced out between punches. "He needs you back—no matter how angry he is."

Alba raised her fists. "My turn," she said. Branwen held up her hands. Her palms weren't as callused as the other woman's, and the impact made her wince.

"I never wanted to rule." *Punch.* "With two older brothers it wasn't a possibility, anyway. All I've ever wanted was the open sea." *Punch.* "My father let me sail because I was expendable." *Punch; cross punch.* "Now even if I'm ransomed, my life will never be my own again."

Punch. Punch. Punch.

Branwen stumbled backward. Alba kept coming, driving Branwen closer to a pier where dinghies were moored. From the corner of her eye, she spotted something entirely out of place. She blinked.

At the end of the pier stood a fox with a red-currant coat and snow-tipped ears.

Punch; cross punch. As the fox turned around to face her, Branwen gasped.

The creature had two black craters where its eyes should be, and the flesh had been stripped from its jowls. It was more skeleton than fox.

Just as the hideous beast released a bloodcurdling howl, Branwen doubled over in pain. Alba drove a punch upward into her chest. Before she could recover, the captain landed another blow to Branwen's left cheek. She toppled into the sand.

"Did you think I'd befriend my brother's murderer so easily?" Alba fumed. "The Aquilans were right about the ignorance of the Iverni." She kicked sand into Branwen's face and sprinted toward the pier. The grains scratched Branwen's eyes.

Still in shock, she reached for Ruan's knife, which she'd kept strapped to her thigh beneath her breeches. Branwen wasn't nearly as naïve as Alba believed, but she'd let her guilt cloud her judgment and the princess had used it to her advantage.

"Stop!" Branwen screamed. "Stop her!" She wouldn't make that mistake again.

The Royal Guardsmen snapped their gaze to Branwen, alarmed. They hadn't realized the game had turned deadly. If Alba escaped, King Faramon would no longer be forced to negotiate with Kernyv.

The skeletal fox shrieked and charged toward Branwen. Blood trickling from her mouth, she pursued the other woman, wielding her knife. When the fox brushed against Branwen's ankles, ice solidified in her veins. The creature spurred her on.

Staggering through the pain, Branwen caught up to Alba, grasping the tail of her tunic. She yanked as hard as she could. The captain wheeled around, sneering at the blade in Branwen's hand.

"Would you stick a knife in my back, too?" Alba taunted her.

Branwen licked the blood coating her teeth. "We need you alive."

The guardsmen were closing in. Alba saw them as well. She hooked Branwen's ankle, and Branwen fell sideways, landing hard on her left shoulder. Branwen cried out. Alba launched herself on top of her, straddling her with her knees.

She wrested the knife from Branwen's hand and pressed it to her throat.

"Come any closer," Alba shouted at the guards, "and I'll slit the Royal Healer's throat!"

The men stopped in their tracks, swords drawn, uncertain how to proceed.

Branwen ripped the bandage from her right hand. "I would advise you to let me go, Captain."

"Or what?"

Branwen squirmed beneath the knife. It was true that she couldn't burn the Crown Princess of Armorica alive—with so many witnesses—despite how much her power was singing, yearning for release.

"How far do you think you can get?" Branwen said through clenched teeth. "Planning to swim to Armorica?"

"Maybe I don't plan on escaping. Maybe I just want you dead."

"You've had plenty of other opportunities." To the guards, Branwen yelled, "Arrest her! King Marc needs her more than me!"

Alba's brow furrowed in disgust. "You're so ready to die for the king of your enemies?"

"He's *my* brother."

Branwen shoved her right hand against the other woman's sternum with all her might. The blade bit deeper into Branwen's throat.

Suddenly, Alba convulsed. The knife dropped into the sand, and Alba fell atop Branwen's chest. Delirious energy surged through her. The beach began to spin. She felt as if she were back on the *Dragon Rising*, being pitched to and fro by the waves.

The fox scurried around Branwen, its void-like eyes burning coals.

The Armorican captain was heavy on Branwen's chest, yet her own body was weightless. In her mind's eye, she saw Kahedrin. He was younger than when Branwen had met him. He sat on the deck of a ship, tying an intricate knot with a length of rope. He held it out to Branwen, and she felt both irritation that she hadn't been able to tie the knot and the desire to make him proud.

Kahedrin ruffled her hair, his smile warm.

This wasn't Branwen's memory.

It was Alba's.

She rolled the other woman's body off her, terror pulsing in every nerve ending. The fox yowled again. Branwen lowered her face close to Alba's. *Thank the gods.* She was still breathing.

The Royal Guardsmen surrounded them. Branwen had no idea what exactly they had seen transpire between the two women.

"The princess is alive," she told them. "Return her to the West Tower." Branwen retrieved Ruan's knife from the sand. "I'll find the King's Champion."

Branwen rose to standing, still unsteady on her feet. As she gripped the knife, she noticed that her bruised knuckles were healed. Soft.

She touched her lips. The bottom one was no longer split.

She cupped her jaw. It didn't ache.

Two of the guardsmen lifted Alba from the beach. Her braid fell to one side.

It contained one thick swath of gray.

The skeletal fox met Branwen's eye, opened its mouth of bones and shrieked.

Branwen ran, sprinting ahead of the guards, away from the gravelly laughter of the Sea of the Dead. She had offered herself to them. *Slayer. Killer.*

Branwen buzzed with energy that wasn't hers. Life that wasn't hers. Just as she had made the flower wither, she had stolen life from Alba. Just like the Shades consumed the living. And the stolen energy had healed Branwen's wounds.

It was no longer the Hand of Bríga she possessed.

It was the Hand of Dhusnos.

120

YOU NEVER SAW ME

BRANWEN'S FEET POUNDED THE COBBLESTONES as she ran up the hill to the castle and through the courtyard to the King's Tower. She didn't feel the ground beneath her. Her leg muscles quivered but panic made her fly.

"Ruan!" she called. She hammered a fist against the door to his chamber and barged in. There was no sign of her lover besides an unmade bed and an apple core on a side table. Rushing back into the hallway, she collided with Andred.

"Lady Branwen, is something wrong?" the boy asked as he recovered his footing. Worry creased his forehead.

Everything is wrong. "I need to find your brother."

"I saw him on his way to the Queen's Tower."

"When?"

"Half an hour ago, or so." Her apprentice touched a hand to Branwen's elbow. "Can I help you with something?"

She cringed, afraid to leech life from him, too. "No," she told him, tone curt. His face crumpled. "Thank you, Andred."

Branwen bolted down the corridor. Fresh perspiration drenched the front of her tunic. A sultry breeze teased the wisps along her brow as she dashed across the courtyard, yet Branwen's blood remained chilled.

Why would Ruan be heading to the Queen's Tower at this time of day? Perhaps he had business with Tristan. She scraped her teeth together as she ran.

When Branwen reached the entrance to Tristan's chamber on the ground floor of the tower, she was scant of breath. She knocked more hesitantly on the door of the Queen's Champion. Hers, she knew, would be an unwelcome face.

No answer.

She knocked again. Foreboding clawed at Branwen's senses. She lifted the latch and pushed open the door, calling out, "Prince Tristan?"

Empty.

Her shoulders caved as she exhaled. The last time she'd entered Tristan's chamber uninvited on the *Dragon Rising*, Branwen had discovered her cousin in his bed. But Tristan's bed was neatly made; a woolen blanket folded in a square rested atop the sheets.

She'd never been inside his room at the castle, and she couldn't prevent her eyes from roving over his living quarters. Sunlight glowed on a desk by the window that overlooked the sea. An inkwell and a quill cast shadows on a piece of parchment.

Curiosity lured Branwen closer.

It was music. Notations dotted the pale vellum like black stars: an inverted night sky. *The Dreaming Sea* was scrawled across the top of the page in Ivernic.

Branwen's heart cramped. She'd heard the song in a dream, an

Otherworld melody, before Tristan had even told her he was composing it. Maybe the Old Ones sung to him, too. The ballad was still only half finished.

She rubbed her jet-black scar. Shaking her head, Branwen turned her back on the music. The past was long finished.

Boots tromped on stone. "*Dymatis*, Lady Branwen," said a member of the Royal Guard as he proceeded past Tristan's door and up the stairwell. Branwen's smoldering dread flamed to life.

Pushing past the barrel-chested man, she raced up the twisting stairs to the third landing. Five other guardsmen loitered in the hallway that led to the True Queen's suite. Their hands rested on the hilts of their swords, posture stiff, greetings circumspect.

The drumming of Branwen's heart reached her temples.

At the end of the corridor stood Endelyn. The Kernyvak princess twisted her skirts so tightly between her hands as Branwen approached that the knuckles turned white. "Lady Branwen," she said. "Did you need me in the infirmary?"

Endelyn's smile was fixed, her blue eyes apprehensive.

"I was looking for your brother," Branwen replied, as calmly as she could manage.

"I haven't seen him this afternoon."

"No?" She took another step forward. "Andred said he was here."

Endelyn's smile faltered. "He's mistaken."

Gesturing at the half dozen guards, Branwen said, "Why are there so many guardsmen?"

"King Marc's orders. To protect the True Queen."

Ruan had mentioned no such increase in protection to Branwen. "Where's Tristan?" she asked. She leaned into Endelyn and the other woman's face pinched.

Endelyn wasn't nearly as practiced a liar as her mother.

"No matter," said Branwen. "There's something else I need to discuss with my cousin." She reached for the door latch, and Endelyn grabbed her wrist.

"The True Queen said she's not to be disturbed."

Branwen's temples throbbed as she ripped her wrist from the princess's grasp.

"No! You can't!" Endelyn shouted from behind her, pitch high and frantic, as Branwen swung open the door.

She stopped on the threshold and relived her nightmare.

Tristan embraced Eseult as she wept. They perched together at the edge of the canopy bed, Eseult half on his lap, her head on his shoulder. He stroked her flaxen hair.

Branwen seemed condemned to relive her pain, her humiliation again and again. Except this time, she wasn't the only witness.

Peering over Branwen's shoulder, Endelyn gasped.

Tristan shot to his feet. "This isn't what you think." His gaze skipped from Branwen to Endelyn, who followed her into the bedchamber.

"Unfortunately, cousin, it's exactly what Lady Branwen thinks," said Ruan as he emerged from the space between the walls. The secret chamber designed for the queen to hide in during an attack. Where Branwen had waited to take her cousin's place on the wedding night.

Rage flashed through Branwen, white and blinding. Her lover was a liar, and now everything was coming undone.

"What do you think you're doing?" Tristan spat at Ruan. "Spying on the queen!"

The King's Champion strode toward the bed, which was located in the middle of the room, but his eyes were locked on Branwen's.

"The queen sent Tutir and Bledros to kill you," he told her.

Branwen stiffened. "I did not!" Eseult protested. She rushed from the bed toward Branwen, grabbing her forearms and shaking her. "By the Old Ones," the queen said in Ivernic. "I swear I didn't!"

"It wasn't a random attack," Ruan said, speaking directly to Branwen. "I have proof!"

Proof? She stared at him, stunned. *What proof?* Then she realized, "Tutir's wife." Ruan nodded. Her lover said Tutir's wife didn't pose a threat to Branwen. He'd said nothing about the queen.

All-encompassing rage burned through Branwen until she was nothing but a husk.

"When you found the message on your pillow," Endelyn said to Eseult, "you immediately sent me to fetch Tristan." She stepped in closer to her queen.

Eseult released her hold on Branwen, whirling on her heel, jabbing her lady's maid in the chest with her forefinger.

"You? *You* sent the note? You two-faced—"

"It was me," said Ruan.

Finding her voice again, Branwen asked, "What note?" The words were hard, and the look she gave her lover was harder still.

Tristan was the one to answer her. "Blackmail. A message that accused the queen of trying to have you killed because . . ." He swallowed. "It also accused the queen of having an affair—with me." His eyes pleaded with Branwen. "The note said to dismiss me as Queen's Champion or suffer the consequences."

"And what did she do?" said Ruan, callous and mocking. "She called you to her side, said you were the only one in Kernyv who cared for her, and lamented that Branwen would never believe her lies. She admitted it!"

"You're twisting the queen's words," Tristan growled. "Threatening, entrapping, and spying on the queen is treason, cousin!" His chest heaved, trembled with fury.

"We'll see who the king believes, *cousin*. I have other evidence. Other witnesses."

Panic sliced Branwen deep. Other witnesses besides Tutir's wife?

Ruan walked confidently toward Eseult.

"By my authority as King's Champion, I am placing you under arrest on charges of adultery, treason, and conspiracy to commit murder. Please come with me, Lady Queen."

"Tristan!" she screeched.

The starless tide deluged the bedchamber. Branwen could taste it. The tang was familiar. She was drowning in it. The call of a Death-Teller traveled beneath the waves.

Tristan unsheathed his sword. "Don't touch the queen." He sheared the space between Ruan and Eseult with his blade.

"*Do not touch the queen*," he repeated, each word a thrust.

The King's Champion stepped back, and drew his own sword. The Sea of the Dead was everywhere, Branwen realized, as Ruan laid his blade flat atop Tristan's. *Branwen* was part of it, would never be free of it.

Tristan threw off Ruan's sword and the cousins began to fight in earnest.

Instinct, or habit, propelled Branwen to grab Eseult by the shoulders and thrust her out of the way. The moment Branwen had sacrificed so much to avoid had finally arrived. The sunless part of her heart was relieved.

The Old Ones had warned Branwen with the vision of Eseult tied to a pyre the night she'd removed Uncle Morholt's finger from his corpse. The air had been steadily squeezed from her lungs for months.

Steel rang against steel. The cousins clashed swords, their footwork quick, dancing around the furniture.

"Stay back!" Ruan hollered at the guardsmen filling the doorframe. The King's Champion wanted to best his cousin. Grunts accompanied the thrusts and parries.

The table by the window crashed onto its side. One of the armchairs sailed toward the hearth.

"Marc loves you most of all," Ruan said with disgust, crossing Tristan's sword. "And you betrayed him!"

He backed Tristan against one of the pillars of the canopy bed. "You ran off with his wife!" Ruan angled the tip of his blade against Tristan's jugular. "You want his crown!"

"You're wrong."

"I'm not." He nicked the skin of Tristan's throat. Blood welled to the surface.

"Ruan, don't!" Endelyn screamed. She ran over to her brother, pulling back on the shoulder of his sword hand. She might believe Tristan to be a traitor, but Branwen could read the yearning on the other woman's face.

Ruan glanced back at his sister, and his momentary distraction was the opening Tristan needed.

He kicked his cousin's ankle, an underhanded move, and Ruan's body swayed to the left. With a shout, Ruan swiped at Tristan. Tristan twirled on the spot.

His blade arced through the air with tremendous force.

"No!" cried Endelyn. She pushed Ruan to the floor.

Tristan's sword bit deep into flesh. The squelching sound was like nothing else.

Eseult screamed.

Blood began to gush from a line across Endelyn's stomach.

The world grew eerily still. Branwen would have sworn that even the waves outside had ceased to churn.

Tristan threw down his sword. Metal clanged against stone. He lunged toward Endelyn, catching the princess as she began to fall.

"Branwen!" he shouted, hoarse, jolting her back from outside herself.

Ruan released a roar that wasn't even close to human. He targeted his sword once more at Tristan, his entire body quaking.

With his arms around Endelyn, Tristan lowered himself to the floor. He cradled her like a babe, with her back pressed to his chest. "What did I do?" Revulsion contorted his features. "Help me!" he yelled again at Branwen.

"Curse you, Tristan!" Ruan shouted at his cousin. He lowered his weapon and crawled over to his sister on his hands and knees.

Endelyn's eyelids fluttered. She was in too much shock to scream. All color had leached from her face.

The marigold bodice of her gown was soaked crimson, a horrifying sunset spreading from her middle.

Branwen crouched beside the princess knowing there was no medicine that could heal her. She would be dead before Branwen could even fetch her satchel.

She shook her head at Tristan. Tears streamed down his face.

"I'm sorry," she said.

Ruan tore at his hair. "Branwen?" he croaked. Eseult had started kneeling beside them, and the King's Champion snarled at her like a rabid dog.

"Seize the queen!" he shouted at the guardsmen. Instantly, they sprang into action. Two burly men clamped a hand on either of the queen's arms.

"Tristan," Endelyn murmured, gazing up at him, affection unguarded. Blood leaked from her mouth.

"Help her," Tristan begged Branwen. "Please—like on the ship."

"I can't," she whispered. Branwen didn't know what would happen if she tried.

Endelyn lifted her arm to Tristan's cheek. He intertwined their hands.

"Stay with us," he said, a ragged request.

"It was always you," Endelyn told him. She coughed, spraying him with blood. "But you never saw me."

"*Please*," Tristan groaned. Piercing Branwen with his gaze, he said, "Do whatever you want with me, just save her!"

Branwen looked from Tristan to Ruan. Ruan's eyes were bloodshot. He loved Branwen. He'd lied to her. He'd already killed his father to protect Endelyn.

She lowered her gaze back to the mark of Dhusnos. Endelyn was on the brink of death. Branwen didn't think she could wound her any further.

"Order the guards to leave," she told Ruan.

A question on his face, he commanded the guards holding Eseult, "Take the queen to the King's Tower—and shut the door behind you!"

The True Queen began to sob as they dragged her from the room. Endelyn's breathing slowed, scarcely a rattle. The door slammed closed.

Branwen ripped the fabric of Endelyn's dress to reveal her abdomen. The sword had cut deeply enough to expose her intestines, which poked through the flesh. Tristan made a retching sound and swallowed back his vomit.

Ruan took his sister's other hand, and began whispering to her in Kernyvak. Tears dripped from his cheeks to hers as he leaned over her.

"Give me space," Branwen said, pity muting her anger.

She closed her eyes and summoned her fire. She recalled the Wise Damsel's lessons about control.

An obsidian flame appeared above her palm as her eyes opened. She pressed her hand to Endelyn's stomach as she'd done with Eseult on the *Dragon Rising*, with Talorc at the mining disaster. Blood spread between Branwen's fingers.

Sparks of night made contact with Endelyn's flesh, but the flesh did not stitch itself back together. Everywhere the sparks landed, the skin began to darken. To die.

Decay spread through Endelyn's bloodstream. The stench was putrid.

Branwen whipped her hand back, horror surging through her together with a wintry euphoria.

Ruan's name was on Endelyn's lips as she drew her last breath.

Trembling, "I-I'm sorry," Branwen stuttered. To Ruan she said, "I'm so sorry. She's gone. Your sister is beyond the reach of my magic."

Tristan looked at Branwen with disbelief, and fear.

"Guards!" Ruan shouted. The door opened immediately. "Take Prince Tristan to the dungeon."

Tristan laid Endelyn's body gently on the floor and rose to standing.

"Shackle him!" Ruan said. "Don't trust anything he says."

Tristan let himself be arrested without a fight. He let his hands be bound in silence.

When Ruan and Branwen were alone, sobs racked Ruan's body. He closed Endelyn's eyes and kissed the lids.

"Why did you do it?" Branwen asked.

"To protect you, Branwen. To protect the people I love from a murderous queen!"

She stared down at her palm. Her healing magic was gone. All that remained was written on Branwen's flesh.

"Maybe we have the queen we deserve."

Nothing But Cinders

BRANWEN COULDN'T SLEEP. IN A few short hours, the fate of Iveriu would be decided. Countess Kensa and the other barons were assembling for the trial of Tristan and Eseult.

The chimes in the trees answered the waves as Branwen wandered the gardens. A half-moon lit her path. Not all of the flower beds had been destroyed in the assault. The sturdier plants survived. Moonglow on the white bushes made Branwen shiver.

She skimmed her hand over the blossoms and pricked her finger on a thorn. Her blood looked the same as everyone else's, but it wasn't. When she'd first been imbued with the Hand of Bríga, Branwen had feared it would make her less human. Now there was no doubt she was part monster.

Alba had been sleeping for the better part of the past two days. Sapped of strength, she hadn't roused when Branwen visited. How much of her life had Branwen thieved—a month? A year? All she knew was that the scars she'd received from the Shades aboard the *Dragon Rising* were gone. Her skin was unblemished.

The Crown Princess of Armorica wasn't the only royalty sleeping under armed guard. Queen Eseult had been sequestered in Ruan's quarters. The King's Champion didn't trust the queen to be alone in her own tower, although Branwen knew her cousin wasn't as capable of an escape attempt as Alba had been. Tristan remained locked in the dungeon beneath the Royal Guard's barracks. Both of them were forbidden visitors.

A rabbit darted out from beneath the rosebushes. It stared at Branwen, twitching its whiskers. She thought of Arthek, Eseult's ugly mutt. Branwen had brought the dog to Andred to look after, hoping to cheer him. The boy was inconsolable at the loss of his sister, although Lowenek was trying her best.

Branwen meandered toward the secluded part of the garden where she'd spied on Tristan and Eseult kissing the night of Queen Verica's funeral. How many times had she saved the lovers? Would she save them again? *Could* she?

A lone figure rested on the bench in the predawn, half shrouded in shadows.

"Sister," said King Marc as she neared. His visage was paler than the moonlight. "Sit with me?"

Branwen smoothed her hands over her skirt. She hadn't seen the king since the arrests. Joining him on the stone bench, her pulse grew erratic.

"Neither of us sleeps well," she said.

"No." Marc's shoulders were hunched, his head bowed. He was the portrait of a man defeated. "Even I hadn't anticipated another funeral so soon."

Scarcely more than two weeks had passed since they'd burned Prince Kahedrin's body. This evening, Branwen had prepared Endelyn to be viewed by her family. She'd stitched up the mortal wound and rubbed lavender oil into the dark, necrotic flesh. She couldn't completely disguise the odor. Then Branwen dressed Endelyn's body in a clean gown embroidered with ivy leaves that the princess had favored.

Slanting his gaze at Branwen, the king said, "I'm sorry you've been unable to see your cousin."

"I-I understand."

"A king shouldn't miss his mother." Marc gave a sad laugh. "But I wish Queen Verica were here to tell me what to do."

Branwen laid her left hand atop his. "In this moment, you can just be a man."

He shuddered a breath. Quiet and starlight filled the space between them.

Finally, Marc said, "I broke my promise to my sister. As Gwynedd lay dying, I swore I'd always protect Tristan." Grief shaded his voice. "And tomorrow, I have to decide his fate. What if I love him more than my kingdom?"

Sorrow welled inside Branwen. She had conjured the Loving Cup because she'd once loved Eseult more than Iveriu. When she reached for that love, however, she tasted nothing but cinders.

"You haven't failed," Branwen said, gripping the king's hand.

"If your cousin loves Tristan, perhaps it is because my own heart wasn't sufficiently open." Marc's tortured whisper affected Branwen deeply. It wasn't his love for Xandru that had led Tristan and Eseult into treason.

She had never wanted to tell Marc the truth about the Loving Cup more than she did right now. Except the truth wouldn't change the outcome of the trial. Revealing that Iveriu had intended to bespell the king would only guarantee a war. All Branwen could do was keep lying.

"Brother," she said. "I don't believe the charges against the queen."

"She would never harm you," Marc agreed, and Branwen swallowed.

"But Ruan has sufficient evidence to be heard by the King's Council. And Tristan admitted to drawing his sword first against Ruan."

"I'm sorry I couldn't save Endelyn," she said in a weighted hush. And she was. Since the Armorican attack, Branwen had seen a different facet of the princess, and Endelyn had loved her brother enough to take the sword meant for him. She had loved Tristan, too, in silence, and now she would never get the chance to be loved by someone in return.

"I'm afraid not even my magic was enough," Branwen said.

Marc leaned back, meeting her eyes. "When the Horned One calls for us, we must go. You did everything you could."

"You know I don't believe in the Horned One."

The king pulled the antler shard from beneath his tunic. "It gives me comfort, sister." He sighed. "It gives me comfort to believe in order."

"I'm glad." Branwen had seen too much, knew too much about the whims of the gods to still believe in order.

"Your magic—" Marc pointed at her right hand; she turned the palm upward, revealing the scar. "Will you tell me about it?"

A knot formed in her chest. The king waited.

"The women in my family have always practiced the Old Ways. I—" Branwen hesitated. "I asked the Old Ones for power to protect Iveriu."

On Whitethorn Mound, she'd offered herself in exchange for Tristan. When Keane had threatened to expose Eseult, she'd beseeched them for help.

The Wise Damsel was right. "I asked for power," she repeated. "And they gave it to me." Branwen had asked for the Hand of Bríga.

"And the . . . warrior creatures who saved us from the Armoricans?" Marc said, eyes intent. He held his pendant taut.

"Shades, we call them. They belong to Dhusnos, the Dark One." And now, so did Branwen. "He rules the Sea of the Dead."

The king started to trace the raised flesh on her palm. "*Don't,*" Branwen said. She jerked back. "It's a weapon like any other. *I* am a weapon."

"You are much more than that." She frowned. "To me you are." Marc tucked an errant curl behind Branwen's ear. "I promised you that Iveriu would know no more violence from me, sister. I will do everything in my power to protect Eseult."

"*Mormerkti.*" Yet Branwen feared that the more Marc did to protect the peace, the less power he had.

He kissed Branwen on the crown of the head.

"I'm going to close my eyes and pretend to sleep." The king rose to his feet. "Thank you for letting me lay down my crown for a little while."

Branwen nodded. "*Sekrev.*"

Marc showed a sliver of a smile, tugging on his beard, and disappeared into the gardens.

Branwen sat alone and she shivered. She turned to the rosebush behind her. Cupping one of the blooms, she pictured Castle Rigani under siege, the bodies of her friends strewn over the ramparts.

The rosebuds began to wither.

As Branwen's fear spread, heart thumping, so did the decay. The promise of springtime flooded her, made her giddy, and the entire rosebush shriveled. Petal by petal, thorn by thorn.

Branwen could take life and give death. Fear was the key. She'd feared Alba escaping, and she'd feared what Tutir's wife wanted with Ruan.

Fear was the Dark One's greatest weapon.

And now it was hers.

BLOOD PRICE

MIDDAY SUN STREAMED THROUGH THE windows of the Great Hall, glinting off King Marc's crown. It was a simple gold torque. The only other time Branwen had seen him wear it was at the wedding.

Two thrones had been placed on the raised dais at the far end of the feasting hall.

One of them was empty.

Everyone stood except for the king.

Marc wasn't in the habit of making his courtiers bow and scrape, preferring to hold council meetings in his study. Today was different.

His wife and his nephew stood before him accused of treason, adultery, murder, and conspiracy.

The snakestone that comprised the Great Hall's vaulted ceiling undulated in the sunlight like a shimmering wave of blood. Dread slithered through Branwen's being.

Baron Julyan began the proceedings. As the most senior of the king's advisers, it fell to him to officiate the trial. He leaned on his expertly crafted alabaster cane.

"We will first hear the case against Prince Tristan of Liones and Kernyv," he said. He did not speak loudly, but the acoustics carried the baron's voice to the back of the hall.

Branwen tossed Queen Verica's dice inside the pocket of her dress. The trial was a gamble, and she hoped the old queen was watching over her grandson from the Otherworld.

The baron lifted his chin at Ruan. The King's Champion stood on the dais, at the king's right hand. He wore his all-black Royal Guard uniform and the white sash that denoted his status. His complexion was grayed.

Branwen knew Ruan's despair at Endelyn's death was profound. Yet she couldn't forgive him for his betrayal. Perhaps all of her forgiveness was already spent.

"Prince Tristan," Ruan said, aiming a heated gaze at his cousin. "You are charged with murder and treason against the crown. The punishment for which is death by burning. What say you?"

Tristan cleared his throat and fingered the collar of his tunic. He'd been provided with fresh clothes during his imprisonment to replace those covered with Endelyn's blood. The turquoise of his shirt reminded Branwen of the seaweed called mermaid's hair that she'd been collecting on the beach when his raft washed ashore.

Tristan stood at the edge of the dais, hands shackled, facing the trial's audience. All of the barons were assembled, as were some of the Royal Guard and a few servants.

Queen Eseult stood beside her Champion, her eyes pinned to the floor. Lowenek had been assigned to the queen's service during her confinement. The nimble fingers, which Queen Verica had thought would make the girl a skilled surgeon, had deftly gathered Eseult's wheat-colored tresses into a crown of braids.

Looking from Ruan to Countess Kensa, Tristan said, "I am responsible for Princess Endelyn's death. But it was not murder. It was an accident."

The countess inhaled sharply, nostrils flaring. She was dressed in a gown of black satin. Her only adornment was a pair of ruby combs on either side of her face, shaped like a hand, which held back her dark blond plaits. A red hand was the sigil of House Whel.

Andred stood beside his mother, also donning a white sash, and the misery etched into his face made him look far older than his fourteen years.

Tristan caught Branwen's eye where she stood beside Baron Chyanhal before angling his body toward the king.

"On the charge of treason," he said. "I believe my uncle knows that I would never willingly betray him."

Willingly. Branwen squeezed the dice in her pocket hard enough to make herself grimace.

King Marc kept his expression neutral, although his gaze drifted to his wife. Eseult's complexion was Death-Teller white, and blue veins were visible beneath the back of her hands, folded primly together at her waist. Her lips were compressed, one corner of her mouth twitching.

"What compensation does House Whel seek from Prince Tristan for the loss of your daughter?" Baron Julyan asked Countess Kensa somberly.

"His head."

A small breath escaped from Eseult, but she didn't look up. When they were children, Branwen's cousin had never been one to take her punishment without protest. Since returning from Sir Goron's cottage, the queen had grown so quiet it was unsettling.

Branwen peered sidelong at Baron Gwyk and Baron Dynyon. They stood just behind the countess, and it was no surprise that they muttered their support. Baron Kerdu and Baron Chyanhal, however, looked at Kensa with contempt.

For once Branwen couldn't begrudge the countess her spite. The pain of losing a child was unimaginable. Especially when Ruan and Endelyn were all she had left of the Iverman who was killed for loving her.

King Marc inhaled. "Countess, I have known Endelyn since her birth and my heart breaks for you. However, Tristan has stated that her death was unintentional. Is there no other compensation that you will accept?"

"Why should I?" Kensa retorted. "Prince Tristan unintentionally killed my daughter while trying to kill my son!"

The king flinched at her furor. He directed a glance at Baron Julyan.

"I believe that Lady Branwen, the Royal Healer, was a witness to the circumstances that precipitated Princess Endelyn's death," said the old man. "I call upon her to give testimony."

Branwen clenched the dice. No one had suggested she would be testifying. She wanted to dive into the darkest heart of the sea.

Her cousin's green eyes gleamed with fear as she finally raised them from the ground.

Branwen had the power to condemn her, and she knew it. But Branwen would never condemn Iveriu.

"I have already recounted the events to the king," Ruan protested. "As have members of the Royal Guard."

"Yes, and the other guardsmen have sworn that they saw Endelyn push you from Tristan's path," replied Baron Julyan. "She was not the intended target."

He rapped his cane on the ground. The baron was generally a jovial man, and his grandfatherly appearance cloaked the steel Branwen now saw in his eyes. To attain eighty winters in this world required not only luck, but mettle.

The tendons in Ruan's neck protruded from his skin. He dared a glance at Branwen for the first time. His anguish was tangible.

"Lady Branwen?" prompted the baron. All eyes shifted to her.

She coughed. "Prince Tristan drew his sword in defense of his queen."

"His treasonous, adulterous queen!" interrupted Countess Kensa, raising her voice.

Eseult shrank backward, retreating further into herself.

King Marc lifted a single hand. "That has yet to be proved, Countess. I will pardon your slander because I know how grief-stricken you are."

Her eyes blazed, the same sapphire color as her daughter's had been.

"Thank you, my Lord King," she said tightly.

"What led Prince Tristan to draw his sword?" the head of House Julyan questioned Branwen.

"Ruan had been spying on them," she answered. A grunt of disapproval emanated from Baron Kerdu.

"And how did you come to be present in the queen's bedchamber?" Baron Julyan pressed her.

"I was looking for Ruan." Branwen panned her gaze over the rapt faces of the audience. This part of the story she could relay more easily. "Princess Alba had made an escape attempt—I went to the King's Tower to alert him."

A few shocked intakes of breath resounded through the hall.

"Andred told me he'd seen his brother on his way to the Queen's Tower," she said.

"Is this true?" Ruan asked his younger brother.

Andred nodded. "Yes." He could barely form the word.

Branwen read the self-loathing in the set of the boy's shoulders. *If only.* If only he hadn't told her where Ruan was headed, perhaps Endelyn would still be alive. Branwen had collected enough of her own *if onlys* to know it was a pit with no bottom.

"I searched the Queen's Tower for Ruan," she continued. "When I reached the third floor, I found Endelyn waiting outside the entrance to the queen's suite with half a dozen guards."

Baron Julyan stroked his wizened cheeks. "Did this seem strange to you, Lady Branwen?"

"It did." She fidgeted with the dice. "Endelyn tried to prevent me from entering, but I pushed her out of the way. Inside, I found Prince Tristan and the True Queen. Ruan had been hiding in the space between the walls."

King Marc shot his Champion an outraged look.

"*Branwen*," Ruan said rough and low. "You saw Tristan and Eseult embracing!" His wounded expression was unbearable. "As did Endelyn— only she can no longer speak for herself!"

"I saw the Queen's Champion consoling his queen because of the note *you* had Endelyn deliver," she countered. "Tristan never intended to harm Endelyn, and you know it."

Shaking his head, Ruan stepped back a pace.

"I have heard enough on this topic," King Marc declared. "Countess Kensa, name a blood price in accordance with Princess Endelyn's station."

The countess curved her hands into talons.

"Endelyn is worth more than *gold*." She prowled toward the dais, stopping just before Tristan, close enough to spit.

Countess Kensa wasn't a warm or maternal woman, but her grief seemed real. "You took my child from me," she told Tristan. A solitary tear slid down her cheek. "Endelyn can never be replaced."

Tristan hung his head in shame. "I would take something from you as well," said the countess.

"Name it."

She waited a beat. "Liones."

"Liones is Tristan's birthright," King Marc said, leaning forward on his throne. "It was gifted to my sister."

"Liones is what I want." The look Kensa afforded the king could cut glass.

Tristan inhaled a breath through his teeth. His curls bounced as he nodded.

"Liones is yours—all except for the lands bestowed upon Lady Branwen."

King Marc stroked his beard, unable to keep regret from staining his features. He would see Tristan's loss as another broken promise to his sister, another personal failure.

Kensa's lips quivered as she announced, "I accept the blood price."

Branwen recalled Ruan telling her that his mother had long wanted Liones because the soil was mineral rich. Acid coated her throat. She didn't believe even the countess would have wished her daughter's death, but she had turned Endelyn's death to her advantage.

As Countess Kensa strode back toward Baron Dynyon, who appeared nonplussed, Branwen couldn't help wondering whether the countess had only demanded Tristan's head because her true objective was his land.

Baron Julyan banged his cane again.

"On the charge of treason against Prince Tristan, what evidence is there?" he said, turning to the King's Champion.

"If you would indulge me, Baron Julyan, I would like to present the evidence of Prince Tristan and Queen Eseult's treason simultaneously."

Branwen's heartbeat thrummed through her entire body. She noticed the queen's shoulders jerk, lifting toward her ears.

"I will permit it," replied the baron. "Proceed."

The wooden dais creaked as Ruan crossed toward his cousin and the True Queen.

Peering down at Branwen, the man who knew her more intimately than any other said, "Lady Branwen. What was the content of the letter I had Endelyn deliver?"

"Accusations."

"What *specific* accusations?"

Branwen took a step toward the dais. She barely resisted the desire to chuck the dice at Ruan's head.

"The letter accused the queen of trying to have me killed."

"Yes." To the king, he said, "I sent the True Queen the letter to see how she would respond. She sent for Tristan—her lover—and lamented that Branwen would never believe she was innocent."

"You entrapped the queen and now you're manipulating her words for your own purposes!" Tristan roared. Even with his hands bound, he seemed dangerous.

Ruan ignored his cousin. "Lady Branwen, were you not attacked by two members of the Royal Guard on the afternoon before the Armorican assault?"

"Yes," Branwen ground out.

"Where are these men?" King Marc thundered, furious, and Branwen met his gaze. "They're dead," she said.

Another ripple of gasps spread through the hall.

Branwen could see the calculations taking place in the king's mind. The charred remains that Ruan had found in the Morrois Forest. The flame he'd seen Branwen use to defend the castle.

"Lady Branwen is very handy with a blade," said the king.

"That she is," agreed Ruan. Branwen held her breath. "And why did the queen send the guards to kill you?"

She allowed herself one second of relief that he hadn't mentioned the bodies were burned.

"The note *you* sent the queen *alleges* that she ordered my death because I had discovered an affair between Tristan and Eseult," she told the man who had called Branwen his beloved.

Unable to look at either the queen or her Champion, Branwen said to King Marc, "But I discovered no such thing, and I do not believe my cousin wishes me ill."

Both lies tasted brackish in her mouth. The king inclined his head.

"And on the night of the assault," continued Ruan, "when King Marc sent me to protect the queen, is it not true that Prince Tristan and Queen Eseult were already gone when I arrived?"

Branwen folded her arms. "We know that Prince Tristan took the queen to safety at Sir Goron's cottage."

"And yet, by Sir Goron's own admission, their arrival time indicates that they must have left before the castle was attacked."

Baron Julyan's lips parted, inhaling at the revelation.

"You have no idea when Tristan or Eseult left the castle, Ruan," Branwen said, storming toward him, "because you were in *my* bed!" His face smoothed in surprise. "The court already knows we're lovers." She whirled toward the other nobles; Countess Kensa's face was flushed. "I see no reason to be coy."

Ruan ran a hand through his hair. "You're right, Branwen. I don't know when they left." He paused and she felt short-lived triumph. "But I have a witness who does."

Her breath buckled as she forced herself not to react.

"Massen?" called Ruan, signaling with his arm.

A boy of ten years, cheeks heavily freckled, walked with trepidation toward the dais from the back of the crowd.

"Massen is a stable hand," Ruan explained. Branwen exchanged one discreet sideways glance with Eseult. Her cousin looked as if she'd just seen her own death.

Ruan spoke to the boy in Kernyvak. There was silence before the boy replied. Tristan gritted his teeth at the words that neither of the Iverwomen understood.

"The boy says he saw Queen Eseult leave the castle on her mare, Lí Ban, almost two hours before the attack began," Ruan translated. "Tristan's mount was also missing from its stall." Appealing to the barons, he said, "Why would the True Queen leave the castle in the middle of the night if not for a tryst?"

Eseult opened her mouth to speak, and Branwen silenced her with a glare.

"That proves nothing," Branwen retorted.

"No, but this does." Ruan extracted a small scroll from his pocket. "Tutir's wife brought it to me when he never returned home."

He motioned at a woman with fair skin and chestnut hair. She stepped to the front of the crowd, a babe in her arms and a daughter at her side who only just reached her knees. Both of her children had brown skin and dark hair like their father. Branwen's heart seized with guilt, her mouth growing dry.

Tutir's wife was named Wenna, but that was all Branwen could make out from what she told King Marc in Kernyvak. Again, she saw Tristan's complexion grow ashen.

Baron Julyan took the scroll from Ruan.

"This is the queen's seal," the elderly baron confirmed, tapping the maroon wax.

"It was delivered the morning of the attack," said Ruan. "Clearly the queen sent the Royal Guard to do her dirty work while she intended to flee with her lover."

"But they came back!" Branwen exclaimed. "Why would they do that?" When Ruan didn't have an immediate response, she said, "May I see the message?"

"I have already verified the queen's handwriting. Wenna brought the letter to me because she does not read Aquilan."

"All the same, if my cousin tried to have me murdered, I'd like to see the order for myself." She appealed to King Marc with her eyes.

"I see no reason to deny the request," he said.

Baron Julyan handed the scroll to Branwen. She scanned it, stalling for time.

Lady Branwen has imperiled the life of the True Queen. She must die.

Her eyes raced across the words several times. There was nothing unambiguous. Nothing left open to interpretation.

Then Branwen noticed something she hadn't expected.

The Great Hall spun around her. She was hardly able to mask her own surprise.

"Queen Eseult did not write this letter," Branwen declared.

Ruan pivoted toward King Marc. "I compared the hand to other documents."

"Yes, and the forgery is very good. But I know something that the forger doesn't."

"And that is?"

Branwen dashed a glance at the queen. "My cousin's Aquilan grammar is appalling," she replied. She turned her eyes to the king, and then the barons. "Our tutor at Castle Rigani despaired of Eseult." She held up the letter. "And yet the declensions here are perfect."

Exasperated, Ruan shouted, "You would defend your cousin with your life—even when she tried to murder you!"

"But she didn't!" Tears stung Branwen's eyes. "She didn't." Eseult had been telling the truth, after all. The knowledge was heady. Branwen's body felt boneless.

"Ruan?" Andred said in a small voice. He took a step toward the dais.

"Yes?" he snapped.

Pulling at his sash, Branwen's apprentice said, "My Lord King. On the night of the attack, when you sent me to protect Endelyn, I—"

"Yes, Andred?" Marc's tone was leery, yet kind.

"I saw the queen's seal ring in Endelyn's chambers. I didn't think anything of it at the time."

"That doesn't mean anything!" Countess Kensa rounded on her youngest son. "How dare you cast suspicion on your sister! Your *dead* sister!"

"I owe the king the truth." He raised his chin.

"Endelyn had no reason for wanting Lady Branwen dead!"

"*Someone* wanted Branwen dead," Ruan said, pleading with Marc. "Only Tristan and Eseult make sense!"

"I believe it was House Whel that most recently accused me of treason," Branwen reminded him, breath coming short and furious. "Who accused me of harming the queen! In fact, I believe it was Endelyn!"

Ruan just gaped at her. "You don't mean that."

King Marc rose from his throne. "The evidence against Tristan and Eseult on the charges of treason, adultery, and conspiracy is circumstantial at best. Slanderous at worst."

"You're blinded by love, my Lord King. And your desire to see the best in people!" cried Ruan.

"You, too, have benefited from that love, Ruan." He leveled his Champion with a glacial stare, then turned it on Countess Kensa.

Besides the three of them, only Branwen knew that Ruan had confessed his murder of Prince Edern to the king.

"Sire," said Baron Julyan. "The evidence against Prince Tristan and Queen Eseult is circumstantial, but it cannot be denied."

"Then what would you have me do?" demanded King Marc.

Holding himself very straight, he said, "As Head of House Julyan, I invoke the ancient rite of Honor by Combat. Let the Horned One decide the truth on the field of battle."

"I will fight for the True Queen's honor," Tristan said immediately, charging toward his cousin. "As well as my own."

Ruan lunged forward to meet him, teeth bared.

"And I will fight for the crown."

Not Just Magic

ANOTHER SLEEPLESS NIGHT SAW BRANWEN roaming the castle. King Marc had allowed three days for the preparations to be made for the Honor by Combat. Anticipation held Monwiku tight.

As dawn approached, Branwen found herself at the entrance to the Queen's Tower. Eseult remained in the King's Tower, sharing Marc's suite of rooms until the conclusion of the trial. After the trial, her cousin would either be vindicated or burned as a traitor.

Branwen greeted the guardsmen posted outside Tristan's chamber, to which the king had allowed him to return.

"King Marc sent me to evaluate Prince Tristan's health before the combat in the morning," she lied.

They let her pass, eyes wary. Castle gossip would have already informed them that the Royal Healer had felled their comrades. She had asked King Marc for permission to award Tutir's wife part of the incomes from her lands in Liones—anonymously, and he'd agreed. The guardsman had tried to kill Branwen, but he believed he was acting on the orders of his queen, and Branwen had done worse things for her rulers.

Candlelight streamed from beneath Tristan's door as she knocked.

A puzzled expression gripped his face when he saw Branwen standing before him. Without speaking, he motioned for her to come in and closed the door behind them.

The candle guttered on his desk. Fresh ink dripped from the quill. On Tristan's bed lay a sword and a whetting stone.

He stared at Branwen, waiting for her to explain the reason for her visit, but she couldn't explain it to herself.

Hovering beside the desk, she touched a finger to the wet parchment. "*The Dreaming Sea*," she said.

Tristan scratched the scar above his eyebrow. "I'm trying to finish the ballad before . . . in case tonight is my last chance." He paused. "But I have no harp."

Branwen gulped. Her aunt had gifted Tristan the *krotto* that had belonged to Lady Alana when she believed Branwen and Tristan would be wed.

"I burned it," she told him.

The hazel flecks in his eyes sparked. "Why would you do that?"

"To undo what I'd done. The pain I'd caused. To create an antidote for you and Eseult."

Drawing down a ragged breath, Tristan stepped closer. She could feel his body heat. "Why are you telling me this, Branwen?"

"You were right, Tristan. My heart isn't noble." She held out her right palm. "This is the mark of Dhusnos. I couldn't save Endelyn because my healing magic is gone. I offered my blood to the Dark One to save the castle. My magic is death magic now." Branwen lifted her eyes to Tristan, blinking away tears.

"Please don't die tomorrow, because I won't be able to bring you back."

The truth tumbled out of her, and it was not what she'd expected to say. Tristan cursed in Kernyvak. "I wish it were easier to hate you," he said.

"I'm sorry, Tristan. I'm sorry for what I did to you." Branwen clenched her hands into fists. "For not trusting you."

"You must really be afraid I'm going to lose."

He cocked half a grin, and Branwen couldn't remember the last time she'd seen him do that. Her shoulders began to shake in a laugh that became a sob.

"Maybe I am," she mumbled. Concern replaced his grin. Tristan took her hand and guided her to the bed, sitting down beside her. His touch still provoked a rush of warmth that Branwen couldn't control.

"I don't want to die with you hating me, either," Tristan said, casting her a sidelong look.

"I hated you because your love wasn't stronger than my magic." He winced at Branwen's honesty. "That was wrong," she said. "I've done so much wrong."

She bit her lip to suppress another sob. "I wanted peace for Iveriu and I wanted my cousin to be happy—and now . . . now you have to win, or the queen will be executed and the peace shattered."

"I intend to win." Determination filled his voice, and her heart skittered. Iveriu needed Tristan to win, but Branwen couldn't bring Ruan back from the dead, either.

Tristan sighed. "I only wish you'd created the antidote sooner," he said. "It seems particularly unjust that we should be entrapped now. When everything has changed."

Branwen's head snapped up. "What do you mean?"

"Since the night of the attack, it's . . . it's as if a fog is lifting." Brow puckered, Tristan raked a hand through his messy curls. "I don't know how else to describe it, but . . . but when I look at Eseult—I don't feel that same pull, like I can't breathe unless I'm near her."

"That's not possible." Her stomach lurched. "I didn't complete the spell because I was attacked by the guardsmen."

"Eseult says the same is happening for her."

"But the other day, you were embracing in the queen's chamber!"

Tristan scowled. "You told Baron Julyan I was consoling the queen—and that's exactly what it was. Although apparently *you* thought you were lying!"

"I'm very adept at lying," said Branwen, slipping back into her invisible armor.

"Listen." He sighed. "I will always care for Eseult. Magic or no, we've shared something and we . . . we lost a child." Regret weighted his words. "But I—both of us—our feelings are shifting. If I survive tomorrow, I'm going to ask to be released from the queen's service. I want to cause her no more grief."

Branwen nodded, but she couldn't believe what she was hearing. Had the power of the Loving Cup started to wane on its own? The Queen of Iveriu had been so insistent that the lovers never discover its existence.

Could it be? Surely it couldn't be that knowing you were under a spell was enough to unravel it? Half of Branwen was on fire; the other half was solid ice.

"Branwen, you've gone pale," said Tristan.

Had the truth been the antidote all along? Was truth stronger than magic?

Branwen pressed a hand to her chest, trying to catch her breath.

"I wish I had told you the truth sooner," she managed.

Tristan draped an arm loosely around Branwen's shoulders.

"We've both hurt each other very much," he said.

"Yes."

"And Eseult. She's been devastated."

"I know." It was a rasp.

"If I win tomorrow, can we begin again?" Tristan met Branwen's eye. "As allies," he clarified. "Someone forged the queen's handwriting, stole her seal, and ordered your death, Branwen. Someone wants both of you dead."

"Do you really think it was Endelyn?"

"No. At least, if she stole the queen's seal, I don't think it was her idea." Sadness swept over him. "She loved her family to a fault."

"It wasn't Ruan."

Tristan frowned. "It's clear he's in love with you." He spoke without inflection. "Which leaves the countess."

"She is my least favorite person at court," Branwen said. "But how would my death benefit her?"

"I don't know. If I win tomorrow, I'm going to find out." Tristan clutched a strand of her hair out of habit. He dropped it, embarrassed. Then he said, "The white streaks are gone. Did you dye it?"

Branwen's instinct was to lie. And yet Tristan was the first person besides her aunt whom she'd told about her magic.

"When I bargained with Dhusnos, he took my healing magic. And he . . . he made me more like a Shade. I—" She dared to meet the dark eyes that she had once lost herself in. "I can steal life now."

Tristan opened and closed his mouth.

"I am the monster you think I am."

"No, Branwen. *No.*" He took her hands in his. "There have been moments when I hated you as much as I ever loved you—but I've never thought you were a monster. If anything, you are more than human, not less."

This time she couldn't stop herself from crying. "I should let you finish your ballad," she said.

Tristan lifted her hands to his mouth and kissed her knuckles.

"Thank you for—" He audibly swallowed. "For coming to see me."

"I look forward to hearing how your ballad ends after you win."

Branwen left before she could spill any more of her secrets.

Crossing the courtyard, a shadow interrupted her path.

Ruan's expression was grim, his pain unmasked as he said, "I won't ask you who you'll be supporting."

"What did you expect? I serve Iveriu first."

A shaft of light fell upon them as the sun crested the horizon.

"If I should die, will you mourn me, Branwen?"

The question brought her up short. Tangled, thorny emotions pricked her beneath her skin.

"I love you," Ruan told her, reaching a hand to her cheek. "I would have given you everything I have, everything I am." His touch was tender, longing. Branwen fought the familiarity, the rush of memories.

"All I wanted was for you to look at me and see all that you ever wanted," he said more urgently, cupping her cheek. "But I don't know if you'll mourn me."

"I begged you, Ruan." Her throat was raw. "I *begged* you to maintain the peace. You broke your promise. You lied to me."

"I broke my promise because I wanted to *protect you!*" he exclaimed. "I was willing to let go of my suspicions until Tutir's wife brought me the queen's order to kill you."

Branwen stepped back, out of his reach. "It wasn't her!"

"I feared for your life. I feared she might try again." Ruan thrust an angry hand in the air. "She *still* might."

Branwen shook her head. "Someone wants me dead, but it's not the queen. More likely it's your mother. Or Seer Casek!"

"Don't be ridiculous!" Ruan's chest heaved. "I know you despise Casek, but he's the one who cared for me after my whippings. He's a better man than you think." Leaning into Branwen, he said, "When I told you that the queen sent Tutir and Bledros after you, you didn't look shocked. Or outraged."

"Because I didn't believe you, Ruan!"

He closed his eyes, exhaling through his nostrils, and gave one shake of the head. "You knew," he said, almost to himself. "You already knew."

Branwen clenched her jaw, afraid to speak, angry tears streaming down her cheeks.

"What a thing it must be to be truly loved by you," Ruan said, deep sadness in his voice.

"I warned you not to make me your enemy."

He glanced back at the Queen's Tower. Sun burnished his blond hair like a lion's mane. "It's not just magic between you and Tristan," said Ruan. "I'll never forgive him for killing Endelyn."

"Endelyn died because you had to be right!"

Ruan lurched back as if Branwen had punched him. The words had left her mouth before she could stop them, and yet she wouldn't take them back.

Ruan blinked as they both released several harsh breaths. Finally, he said more softly, "If I die today, promise me you'll look out for Andred. My mother has always resented him for being his father's son."

"I will," Branwen promised. Ruan nodded and turned to leave. "And

I *would* mourn you," she said. He flattened his lips. "But you could choose dishonor. You could live with being wrong."

"Except I'm not. I'm not wrong."

Ruan stalked from the courtyard.

Branwen closed her eyes for a moment to feel the sun on her face.

ÉTAÍN'S SONG

THE SKY HAD BECOME A wash of gray above the beach where the combat would take place.

Just on the other side of the causeway from Monwiku, sand had been cleared, battle lines drawn, and several tents erected on the mainland. In accordance with Kernyvak tradition, all of the king's subjects were welcome to witness the Honor by Combat. Walking among the fishermen and farmers, Branwen could feel the apprehension webbing through the crowd. She heard both Ivernic and Kernyvak being spoken.

When word reached her aunt and uncle at Castle Rigani of Eseult's trial, the Queen of Iveriu would know that Branwen had failed in her duty to protect the Loving Cup—and her homeland. She deserved the recriminations of the woman who raised her. The cowardly part of Branwen's heart was glad she didn't have to witness her disappointment in the flesh.

Wet sand stuck to her boots as she made her way toward King Marc's tent; the others were occupied by the noble Houses. All of the king's councillors had sent for their families. Branwen hadn't seen this much of the nobility assembled since the royal wedding. Even if Tristan prevailed today, would rumors regarding the True Queen's honor ever cease? The Ivernic queen that half of the Kernyvak Houses already detested?

And if Tristan didn't prevail, could Branwen let her cousin burn? She glanced down at the mark of Dhusnos. The power to rescue Eseult—to kill anyone who tried to stop her—lay in the palm of Branwen's hand.

Would she use it?

In her peripheral vision, she spotted Ruan standing at the edge of House Whel's tent, speaking with his mother. She refused to turn her head or meet his gaze.

Distracted, Branwen smacked into a solid shoulder. "Excuse me," she muttered in Ivernic.

"In a hurry, Lady Branwen?" replied a snide, unwelcome voice. Seer Casek raised a supercilious eyebrow, showing her one of his terribly pleasant smiles.

Branwen regretted not having elbowed the *kordweyd* harder, but, "Yes, pardon me," she repeated in Aquilan. She started moving past him when he asked, "Have you heard of the hero Enkidu on the island of Iveriu?"

She stopped, pivoting to meet his eye, a knot forming in her belly.

"Enkidu was born in the Desert of Thorns, at the time the Aquilan Empire began to rise," Seer Casek informed her. "The Horned One granted him supernatural strength to defeat a monster—half man, half leopard—that had been set upon his people by their enemies."

Branwen went very still. This Enkidu sounded like Iveriu's legendary Hound of Uladztir, but she very much doubted that the *kordweyd* merely wanted to regale her with heroic exploits.

"At an oasis in the Desert of Thorns, Enkidu came upon Artume, who was as beautiful a woman as he had ever seen," Casek went on. "He fell madly in love." A pause. "But Artume was the daughter of the king of Enkidu's enemies. She had been sent by her people to discover what made him so strong."

Branwen narrowed her eyes. "And did he tell her?" she asked.

"He did. Enkidu confided in Artume that the Horned One had shaken his right hand, and that was the source of his strength."

"His right hand?" Swallowing, Branwen pressed her own flat against her thigh as dark susurrations stirred inside her.

"Yes. And while Enkidu slept, Artume cut it off. He lost his divine strength and died battling the next monster sent by Artume's father." Seer Casek tilted his head. "That is why women do not partake in the Mysteries of the Horned One."

"I don't see why the actions of one woman should preclude all women from your Mysteries, Seer Casek."

"It wasn't her actions, my lady." Casek wagged his finger at her. "Enkidu broke his faith with the Horned One because of Artume. He promised the Horned One never to reveal the secret of his strength, but he loved Artume more than his god. Artume was Enkidu's temptation—his weakness."

"It seems to me that Enkidu's weakness was his own."

A hollow chuckle. "Perhaps you are right, Lady Branwen." Casek clasped the jewel-encrusted antler shard with one hand, lifting it to his lips and nodding at something over Branwen's shoulder. She followed his gaze.

Tristan.

"We'll know soon enough," said the seer and he turned on his heel, proceeding toward House Whel's tent.

Forcing her hands not to tremble, forcing herself not to steal Casek's life in front of the entire court, Branwen sought out King Marc's tent.

The heat from her nostrils as she exhaled nearly made her believe in dragons.

The tide was starting to come in. Tristan stood at the waterline between the mainland and the causeway, surrounded by at least a dozen Royal Guards. Since the attack their ranks had been bolstered with men from House Whel and House Kerdu. The presence at the castle of soldiers loyal to the countess unnerved Branwen.

She directed a glance at Tristan but he didn't notice; he appeared entirely focused on the cliffs that towered above the beach.

When Branwen reached the king's tent, she startled.

She did not find Eseult sitting beside Marc. Instead, the chair to his right was occupied by Princess Alba.

And to his left, sat Xandru.

"*Dymatis*, my Lord King," said Branwen. As this was a formal occasion, she curtsied. Purple smudges were smeared beneath Marc's eyes, but his beard had been closely shaved for the first time in weeks.

Branwen shifted her gaze to Xandru, who lounged in his chair, long black hair pulled back by a leather tie, golden-brown skin wind-chapped from days at sea.

"Welcome back to Monwiku," she said. "I'm glad to see you safely arrived. When did you land?"

"Thank you, Lady Branwen. King Faramon is always a gracious host. The *Mawort* put into port a few hours ago." Peering across the king to Alba, Xandru said, "My little cousin has always been a difficult houseguest."

There was a vague family resemblance between the pair, something in the tilt of their mouths.

Princess Alba gripped the armrests of her chair. She was dressed in a gown of wild Armorican yellow, a citrine-studded tiara atop her head. Branwen sucked her teeth. What was the meaning of this?

"Perhaps the accommodation isn't to my liking," said Alba, glaring at Xandru. Then she flicked an irate look at Branwen. The women hadn't spoken since their boxing match, and Branwen didn't know what Alba remembered of her escape attempt.

Before she could articulate any of the many questions buzzing around her brain, Branwen heard King Marc say, "We are about to begin. Queen Eseult has been allocated her own tent for the duration of the trial." He couldn't conceal the worry in his eyes. "Would you sit with her?" Motioning at the last tent along the beach, he added, "She shouldn't be alone."

"Of course." Curtsying once more, Branwen forced down her misgivings.

She hurried along the beach. Two guardsmen stood on either side of the opening to the queen's tent; the flaps were pulled back to allow a full view of the combat pitch.

"The king sent me," said Branwen. The guards nodded brusquely.

Stepping inside the tent, she met her cousin's look of surprise. The crown of diamonds and onyx that Marc had bestowed upon his wife at her coronation graced her brow. She embodied a True Queen. But, for how much longer?

"May I watch with you?" Branwen asked her cousin.

"Yes." A nervous smile. "Yes, I'd like that." Eseult patted the seat of the chair next to hers. Both were upholstered with plush cushions of black damask.

Branwen perched on the end. The muscles of her upper back were so taut that a headache was forming behind her eyes. She hadn't been completely alone with her cousin since the night of Queen Verica's funeral. Wind rustled the flaps of the tent, and the hum of the crowd pulsed around them.

Neither of the cousins spoke.

There had been a time, not much more than a year ago, when Branwen had thought there would never be anything she and her cousin wouldn't tell each other. She glanced at Eseult, who offered her another painful smile, and tried to recall that intimacy.

"Thank you for defending me—" Eseult began at the same time Branwen asked, "Did you know Captain Xandru had returned?"

After a fraught moment, Eseult nodded, saying, "He came to the king's suite early this morning. Then Marc excused himself. I don't know what they discussed."

Branwen clumped the material of her skirt between her hands.

"Princess Alba is sitting with the king in his tent," she informed the queen. From the fact that Alba was wearing a crown, she no longer seemed to be a prisoner. Although Branwen doubted the princess could get very far from Xandru's sights if she tried.

Eseult screwed up her nose. "Maybe King Faramon agreed to the alliance?" she said. Branwen didn't reply. Something had changed—that much was certain. And life had taught Branwen to loathe surprises. She forced out a somewhat calming breath.

"Branny," her cousin started again. "Thank you for taking my side against Ruan."

"You didn't send the order to kill me." Branwen's reply was crisp.

"No, I didn't. But I'm—I'm sorry that I've made you think I could." The queen's chin trembled. "I can see why you did." She pulled a golden strand from one of her plaits, wrapped it around her forefinger and yanked.

"I was a fool to ever want to be Étaín," she said.

Branwen's chest constricted. Étaín's song had always been her cousin's favorite. The ballad of a woman married to one brother but in love with the other. Eseult had asked Tristan to perform it on the night of the Farewell Feast in Iveriu.

I did not ask for the love I was given; the love for which I must be forgiven.

It was Branwen's magic that had made her cousin into Étaín. Too much had passed between them for simple words of apology. She took Eseult's hand and unwound the strand of hair from her finger.

"I'm scared, Branny. I'm so scared."

A horn sounded, setting Branwen's nerves alight. She dropped the queen's hand.

Baron Julyan processed from his tent to the pitch, stopping in the center, opposite the king's tent. He leant on his alabaster cane as he bowed. He spoke in Kernyvak, then Aquilan. King Marc must have asked the elderly baron to ensure that the True Queen understood what was happening. His heart was the noblest of them all, and Branwen's magic had endangered everyone he loved.

"The trial of Honor by Combat is older than the Kingdom of Kernyv itself," Baron Julyan announced to all those within earshot. A thrumming hush emanated from the spectators.

"Our ancestors trusted in their gods to settle their differences, and so do we. Prince Ruan. Prince Tristan!" He summoned them forward.

Ruan walked from the east, Tristan from the west. Both the King's Champion and the Queen's Champion were dressed in black and white. The hazy light shimmered around them. Branwen had witnessed this scene before; when she blinked she could see Uncle Morholt and Tristan preparing for the Final Combat.

"I'm scared, too," Branwen admitted to Eseult.

"I wish it were me instead of Tristan," said her cousin. "He doesn't deserve this." Branwen canted her head; the look in Eseult's eye was fierce.

"I think maybe I do," said the queen, and the confession stole Branwen's breath away.

"Prince Ruan has accused Prince Tristan and True Queen Eseult of treason," Baron Julyan proclaimed. As if anyone present were unaware. When the two Champions reached the center of the pitch, the head of House Julyan said, "Before we commence with the combat, Prince Ruan, would you like to withdraw the charge?"

Branwen clamped her lips together. Ruan had never bested Tristan in a fight. In fact, he'd once conceded to Branwen that his cousin was the better swordsman. And yet his loathing, his sheer stubbornness, forced him to declare, "I do not withdraw the charge."

Eseult covered Branwen's hand where it rested on her lap.

"I'm sorry," she said. "I don't want Tristan to lose, and I don't want Ruan to die. Anyone can see how much he loves you."

"Love isn't enough."

"I know," whispered her cousin, holding her stare. "I know it isn't." Branwen swallowed a lump in her throat and it tasted of blood. The tears she fought were scalding.

To the Champions, Baron Julyan said, "You are each allowed one weapon only. Have you chosen?"

Ruan unsheathed a broad *fálkr* sword, its blade gently curved. Branwen had tucked his father's knife into her boot.

Tristan drew a *kladíwos*: a long, thin Ivernic weapon. It was hard to ascertain from this distance, but Branwen thought it might be the same sword she'd purloined from the armory at Castle Rigani when King Marc had sent a search party for Tristan last spring.

"The rules of Honor by Combat are simple," said Baron Julyan. He stroked his substantial white beard. "The contest is concluded when one fighter disarms the other. Mortal wounds are allowed, but the gods will only be seen to have passed judgment if one of the combatants loses his weapon."

Branwen and Eseult traded a terrified glance. If both men died without being disarmed, what would that mean for the True Queen? The rules of men, written by men, yet again disregarded the women.

"He who loses his weapon loses his honor, and the gods will have affirmed the honor of the victor." The baron's voice boomed over the silent crowd. "When the horn blows again," he said, swinging his gaze between Ruan and Tristan, "you may begin. Starting positions at three paces."

Baron Julyan waited until the Champions had retreated the appropriate distance. As the baron returned to his tent, Branwen spied Andred exiting House Whel's. Her eyes followed the boy as he joined Lowenek, who stood together with Talorc and Seer Ogrin. Either Andred would lose his remaining sibling, or Tristan and Eseult would burn.

Branwen nearly missed the blare of the horn for the pounding of her heart.

Eseult gasped as the Champions raced toward each other. The sea rushed closer to the land. From the first day Ruan had met the *Dragon Rising* at the port of Marghas, he and Tristan had been careening headlong into this moment, their childhood animosity turned deadly.

The clang of steel on steel shredded the humid breeze. Unbidden, Branwen recalled the heat of Ruan's breath and lips as he kissed the space between her breasts. He hadn't challenged Tristan for Branwen, and yet his disdain for their bond was one of the many reasons he wouldn't back down.

Étaín—in jealousy was I born and named. Traipsing through the tide, trotting atop the water, Branwen glimpsed the skeletal fox. There, and gone. *Étaín—destined to bring my lovers pain.* The Otherworld sang to her; taunted her.

Tristan leapt high in the air, tucking his knees tight to his chest, as Ruan swept the *fálkr* at his ankles. It was a move King Marc had used when he'd dueled with Prince Kahedrin, and which both had learned from Sir Goron. Who had instructed Ruan? Branwen doubted it was the father who beat him.

"Oh, Branny!" Eseult exclaimed. Ruan had landed a blow on Tristan's left arm. Blood welled where the sleeve of his tunic gaped open. "I don't think I can watch." She gripped Branwen's hand tighter. "But I must."

Branwen interlocked their fingers. Tristan shouted, spitting at the surging tide, and rounded on his cousin.

At the Champions Tournament, the Iverni believed their goddess Ériu would choose the victor. Today, the Kernyveu believed that their gods would pass judgment by confiscating the weapon of the man without honor. Some of the spectators on the beach followed the Horned One; others the Old Ones. Or, perhaps, gods whose names Branwen didn't even know.

Which god, then, was determining the outcome of the contest? Branwen had to hope it was a trickster god, because Ruan was right about Tristan and Eseult's adultery despite being wrong about the reason. Branwen had stolen Tristan's honor, and if Ruan lost today, she would have stolen his as well.

The Champions clashed blades, Tristan driving Ruan closer inland. Branwen could hear the men trading insults. She couldn't decipher the Kernyvak words but their facial expressions were enough.

Blood spurted from Ruan's right calf, just below the knee. He staggered sideways, the tip of his *fálkr* grazing the sand, before recovering. The crowd roared as Tristan also sustained another wound on his thigh.

Eseult's complexion went whiter than lace.

"Branny, I need you to know I don't blame you. For the baby—I didn't mean what I said. I was angry and I wanted to blame someone for what happened." She gazed at Branwen, a sheen to her eyes. "It felt better to hate you than myself."

"I won't let you die," Branwen told her, and she realized it was true. If Eseult were found guilty, it would mean war. Branwen would smuggle her queen back to Iveriu, no matter the cost.

"I'm not saying this because I'm afraid of dying!" Eseult's reply was urgent, with a hint of irritation that was almost reassuring. "Do you remember when I made you fetch me that apple?"

"What?"

"When we were girls. I forced you to scale that tree in the garden. You fell and sprained your ankle, but you never told Mother on me."

Branwen's eyes followed Tristan and Ruan as they danced through sand and surf.

"Yes, I remember," she said distractedly.

"You've always kept my secrets," said Eseult. "I'm sorry for making you. I'm sorry I wasn't worthy of yours."

Branwen inhaled shortly. "You weren't wrong when you said I'm no longer who I was," she told her cousin. "Your miscarriage was an accident—but I've taken other lives."

A scream tore from Ruan's throat. Tristan had sliced his sword arm, right near the elbow. His grip around the hilt of the *fálkr* slackened. Eseult rose halfway out of her seat.

Tristan pursued the King's Champion with two thrusts. He ducked as Ruan arced his blade too widely. Twirling in the sea foam that now lapped his boots, Tristan elbowed his cousin once in the face and once in the gut.

Ruan's sword fell to the ground.

He dove for it. Blood painted the sand.

Tristan kicked the *fálkr* out of the other man's reach.

With what seemed like Otherworldly speed, Tristan lunged for the fallen weapon. A raven cawed as Tristan brandished both weapons above his head.

Branwen slammed back in her seat. The raven gliding above the Champions was black. Black, not white.

Ruan scrambled to his feet and sprinted for his cousin when the horn sounded.

Eseult let out a yelp. "He's won?" Hope strained her voice. "Tristan's won—hasn't he?"

The look on Ruan's face was utterly bleak. He cursed and tore at his hair, matting it with his own blood.

Tristan had won. Tristan had won, but Branwen didn't thank the Old Ones. She didn't thank any of the gods.

Dull light gleamed off both of the blades in his hands. His shoulders rose and fell, sweat pouring from his brow as he held them aloft.

King Marc emerged from his tent. He strode toward the two Champions. He carried himself with confidence but without joy.

Surveying his nephew and his cousin, he pivoted toward the crowd.

"The Honor by Combat has been decided," the king declared. "Prince Tristan has upheld his honor and that of the True Queen." He maintained a neutral countenance.

"Queen Eseult," said King Marc, beckoning her from the tent. "Please join me."

Eseult stared, dazed, paralyzed by relief. "*Get up*," whispered

Branwen. Her cousin tugged on their joined hands. "Come with me," she said.

Branwen escorted her cousin toward the king. She met Marc's gaze, and she saw grief there.

Taking the *fálkr* blade from Tristan, the king said to Ruan, "Your charges against Prince Tristan and True Queen Eseult have been proven false."

He paused, and Branwen saw the cords in Ruan's neck tighten.

"Do you choose death or dishonor?" King Marc asked his cousin.

Ruan inhaled through his nose. He looked at his king, and then at Branwen. Her bottom lip quivered. She had warned him, she had shared her body with him, and she didn't want to attend his funeral.

The sea also waited for his answer. Ruan searched the crowd, and Branwen saw his gaze land on Andred.

"Dishonor," he said after several long moments.

King Marc nodded. Branwen spied the muscles in his jaw relax a fraction. He would not be forced to play the part of executioner today. The king lifted the *fálkr* to Ruan's sash, the white now speckled with furious crimson.

"Prince Ruan of House Whel, you are stripped of your status as King's Champion. Henceforth, you will hold no official position at court. You will return immediately to your family estates at Illogan where you will remain unless I send for you."

The blade made a smooth sound as it cut through silk. The sash fell onto his boots.

Ruan bowed from the waist. Murmurs swept through the crowd. Given the severity of the allegations that he'd brought against the True Queen, the punishment was light indeed. Neither Tristan nor Eseult protested, but Branwen worried what the other courtiers might think.

"Lady Branwen," said the king. "You will see to Prince Ruan's wounds before his departure."

"Yes, my Lord King." With a curtsy, Branwen sidled next to Ruan. She suspected that Marc wanted to give them the chance to say goodbye.

"Don't pretend you're sorry I lost," Ruan said to Branwen under his breath.

"I won't."

Goodbyes wouldn't be necessary.

King Marc plunged the tip of the *fálkr* into the sand, deep enough for it to stand on its own, and extended his hand to Eseult.

When she accepted, he raised hers to his lips and kissed it.

"Prince Tristan," the king began. "You have served your queen and your kingdom faithfully. The Horned One and the Old Ones have shown us all the truth."

Tristan bowed deeply. "Thank you, my Lord King."

A few hisses rose from the crowd as Captain Xandru escorted Princess Alba in the direction of the king. Ruan and Branwen exchanged a sideways glance. He seemed as curious as she was. The king had apparently confided in no one but Xandru about the terms of Alba's elevated status.

"My friends and subjects," said King Marc. Branwen saw Countess Kensa and the other barons step out from the shadows of their tents.

"King Faramon and I have reached an accord. Together with Iveriu, we will sign a mutual defense treaty and fight off the pirates who plague all of our shores."

Marc paused to let the news sink in. Branwen saw outrage on some faces, fear on others. A satisfied nod from Baron Julyan. Ruan ground his teeth. He believed this was a sign of weakness, but he no longer held any authority to speak on the matter.

Looking from his wife to his nephew, King Marc went on.

"King Faramon believes that the best way to ensure this alliance is with a blood tie, and he has offered the hand of his sole heir, Crown Princess Alba, in marriage."

At Xandru's side, Alba made a face like she was chewing needles.

"Prince Tristan," said the king. "I must ask you to perform one last service for me and for your kingdom."

Dark laughter filled Branwen's mind.

"Will you consent to marry Princess Alba?" King Marc asked his nephew.

Tristan lowered the *kladíwos* to the sand as he got down on one knee.

"I pledged my fealty to you, my Lord King, upon becoming a man. I am yours to command."

Do not believe this life is what I wished. Tristan dashed his eyes toward Branwen; the hazel flecks were so many falling stars. *A thousand years, sealed with a kiss.*

Pressing a fist to his chest, he pronounced, "Peace above all."

PART II

THE BURNING TIDE

TOO BOLD TO BE WISE

PREPARATIONS FOR THE SECOND ROYAL wedding within the year and the campaign against the pirates in the Veneti Isles had consumed Monwiku Castle for the past month. The smell of roasted meats for the wedding feast this evening wafted through the courtyard as Branwen walked by the kitchens. Spring had passed in the blink of an eye and now the air was pure summer.

The lace covering Branwen's right palm itched in the heat. Eseult had surprised her by crocheting a fingerless glove. The stitches were sloppy but the intent, she believed, was sincere. Most people assumed that Branwen's hand had been disfigured during the Armorican attack, and she let them believe it was vanity that led her to conceal her flesh.

Tonight the fires of Belotnia, the Festival of Lovers, would be lit along the coasts of Iveriu and Kernyv. Armorica, as well. Master Bécc had taught his charges that the three peoples had once been a sole tribe before they left the Mílesian peninsula thousands of years ago. Tomorrow morning, the combined fleets of Kernyv, Armorica, and Iveriu would launch their joint assault, bringing the fight directly to the pirates on the Veneti Isles. The islands would provide the pirates a refuge no longer.

Taking the stairs up the King's Tower, Branwen hoped there was enough shared culture, enough shared purpose for the Three Kingdom Alliance to hold.

She knocked on the door to the king's study, her gaze landing first on Xandru. He showed Branwen a careless smile, which she knew to be well practiced. King Marc had yet to appoint himself a new Champion, although Xandru had scarcely left Marc's side as he negotiated the details of the treaty and Tristan's marriage contract.

Branwen pushed thoughts of the former King's Champion from her mind. Sometimes she missed him—the feel of him—in the night. Perhaps it was always this way with lovers. Ruan had been her first, and her desire was a field of briars.

Stepping farther into the study, Branwen's attention was drawn to an almost familiar face.

"Diarmuid?" she said.

"Lady Branwen," he replied in Ivernic. "It's good to see you again." Lord Diarmuid inclined his head. He tapped the pale blue patch covering his left eye. "With my good eye, that is," he added. Blue was the color of Uladztir, the province of Iveriu governed by his clan. Diarmuid gave a rueful laugh.

Branwen stared blankly. Not because of the missing eye, but because the Lord Diarmuid she knew wasn't prone to self-deprecation. Sunlight winked off the Rigani stone on the hilt of his *kladiwos*. Eseult had been willing to throw away the peace with Kernyv for this man, and he'd lost interest when she could no longer offer him a crown. She'd swooned over Diarmuid's pleasing face, and the eye patch made him no less handsome, yet there was a careworn aspect to him now. His head, too, had been shorn of the golden curls that once ringed his face.

Diarmuid's square jaw tensed at Branwen's silence. King Marc, who stood beside the Ivernic lord, darted her a look of confusion.

"I bring gifts from home," Diarmuid hastened to say, gesturing at the end of the table. "Elderberry wine from Treva. A new shawl from Dubthach's mother."

"Thank you," Branwen said at last. "That's very kind. What news of Castle Rigani?"

"Dubthach and Saoirse were handfasted after Samonios," Diarmuid replied. "I believe they're expecting their first child at the end of the summer."

The news provoked a genuine smile. When the villagers had brought Saoirse to Castle Rigani following a Kernyvak raid, her leg was shadow-stung, and she was close to death. The Queen of Iveriu had guided Branwen through purging the rotted flesh. After Saoirse recovered, she'd stayed on at the castle in the queen's service.

"And your parents," Branwen said, stilted. "I trust Lord Rónán and Lady Fionnula are well." Again, King Marc's eyes widened in curiosity. Switching to Aquilan, she told him, "Lord Diarmuid's father is the head of the Parthalán clan in the north of Iveriu."

"*Was* the head," Lord Diarmuid corrected her, expression clouding. He also switched to Aquilan for the king's benefit. "Talamu Castle—my family stronghold—was attacked just before Imbolgos. Lord Rónán was killed and I—" He pointed at the eye patch. "The north is mine to protect now."

Shock drenched Branwen. "Pirates have never sailed that far up the coast."

"Not pirates." Diarmuid gave one shake of the head. "Reykir Islanders."

She was stunned. Reykir Island lay in the middle of the Winter Sea, far to the north, and they'd never had a quarrel with Iveriu.

"I'm sorry," she said, forgetting for a moment how much animosity she harbored toward the northern lord. "Truly sorry for your loss."

King Marc put a firm hand on Diarmuid's shoulder. "My deepest condolences," he said. "With the signing of this treaty, we will face our enemies together."

Diarmuid gave a half bow. "King Óengus is glad to contribute our best warships to the campaign, and I am honored to be leading the Ivernic forces."

"We are grateful for your aid," said King Marc. "No one besides the pirates has set foot on the Veneti Isles for a hundred years. They won't be expecting a direct assault."

Branwen would never condone the actions of the pirates, but if she'd been a prisoner abandoned to her fate, left stranded on a tiny island in the middle of the sea, she could no longer doubt she would have found a way—*any* way—to survive.

Footsteps approached from down the corridor, and Diarmuid's gaze fixed on something over Branwen's shoulder.

"One Iveriu," he said solemnly, in Ivernic, and bowed from the waist.

She turned as her cousin entered, followed by Sir Goron. With Tristan's engagement to Alba, the old sword master had been convinced to temporarily serve as Queen's Champion.

Eseult's lips parted at the sight of Diarmuid. Several emotions swept over her face. She had cried for weeks aboard the *Dragon Rising* when the arrogant lord had failed to even bid her farewell.

"Lord Diarmuid," said the True Queen. "I . . . I didn't know you were coming." Unconsciously, she lifted a hand to the base of her skull, fidgeting one of her plaits.

"Your father sent me as emissary with his seal." He indicated three sheaves of parchment in the center of the long table. Each of the three kingdoms would keep a copy of the treaty so that the terms could not be disputed.

Eseult nodded. "Of course," she said uncertainly. Branwen noticed Xandru observing the queen closely.

"Saoirse and Dubthach are having a baby," Branwen announced, in Aquilan, to dispel the tension. To King Marc, she explained, "Dubthach is the son of the head seamstress at Castle Rigani. We spent our child-hoods together."

The queen's eyes lit. "How wonderful."

She crossed toward her husband, touching the antler shard that she had recently started wearing. Branwen didn't know why and she hadn't asked. "We should send Dubthach's baby a gift, my Lord King," said Eseult with genuine excitement.

"Send whatever you wish." Marc gave her a kiss on the cheek in greeting. "How is the construction progressing?" he asked.

"Well." A satisfied smile curved her lips. "Very well."

The foundation stone for the Royal Infirmary had been laid after the Honor by Combat, and Eseult spent the majority of her time on the moor with Seer Ogrin and the builders. "Andred is a great help with the translation."

The king answered her smile. "Where is he this afternoon?"

"I told him and Lowenek to enjoy themselves before the wedding."

"Just so," agreed her husband. Andred had retreated into himself since his sister's death, although Lowenek was his constant companion. Endelyn's funeral had been held at Villa Illogan—a private family affair to which Branwen was not invited. Countess Kensa said she wanted to keep her daughter close, on family land, rather than in the royal tomb.

Xandru exchanged a charged look with Marc. How did he feel watching his former lover and his wife? The king and queen didn't act like a couple in love, but their interactions had grown less uncomfortable. On occasion, Branwen glimpsed the charm and mischief that her cousin had used to beguile so many.

"Excuse our tardiness," said Tristan, nearly out of breath, as he and Alba strode into the study.

Branwen's stomach clenched. For months she'd willed away any tender feelings she might have for him. Tomorrow, Tristan would leave for Armorica and she might never lay eyes on him again. Even when seeing his untouchable face tormented Branwen beyond measure, it hadn't occurred to her she might spend her life without him.

Alba surveyed the room as if assessing a battlefield. Following the betrothal announcement, she had lopped off all of her hair. Her smooth locks bobbed around her chin. Perhaps it was an act of rebellion, but the style flattered the Armorican princess.

She tucked the gray streak behind her ear as she said, "*Dymatis*, King Marc. Tristan and I went for a ride."

"I will miss the view of Monwiku from the cliffs," said Tristan. Longing thinned his voice.

Branwen toyed with her glove. Tristan had once promised to show her his favorite vistas in Kernyv. Tristan and Alba made a most attractive pair, it was undeniable, and they'd spent the last few weeks getting to know each other. Regret gnawing at her, Branwen, like Eseult, had found reason to be everywhere but where they were. She didn't let her thoughts linger on how her cousin felt seeing Tristan and Alba together; the newfound peace between her and Eseult was already as fragile as morning dew.

"The final amendments to the marriage contract have been implemented," Xandru informed Tristan, then turned his eyes toward Alba.

Branwen's gaze slid to the spy. King Marc had managed to simultaneously achieve the alliance he wanted and quiet the rumormongering as to the nature of Tristan and Eseult's relationship. It was an unofficial exile. Instinct told Branwen it had been Xandru's suggestion.

"Excellent," Tristan replied. He set his jaw. His eyes momentarily met Branwen's before noticing Lord Diarmuid's presence, surprise creasing his brow.

"Hello, Prince Tristan. Congratulations on your wedding," said Diarmuid. He extended a hand. "It seems the best man won our match at the Champions Tournament, after all. The Old Ones have brought us peace."

"Thank you," Tristan replied with a swallow, and shook the Iverman's hand. Branwen had divulged the truth about Eseult's affair with Diarmuid to Tristan in anger. Now he glanced at Eseult, stance wary. The awkwardness of the reunion for all of them was palpable.

King Marc cleared his throat. "Let us commence with signing the treaties so that the bride and groom may prepare for the ceremony—and the rest of us can begin celebrating!" His smile was mirthful, if contrived.

"First, the marriage contract," said Xandru. A smaller scroll lay beside the treaties on the table, as well as a pot of indigo ink and two quills.

Alba nibbled her lip once before approaching the table. She lifted the quill as if it might bite her. Tristan placed a hand lightly on the shoulder of his betrothed. Branwen's stomach turned over again.

"Lady Branwen, Lord Diarmuid," said Xandru. "Since you are both disinterested parties, I would ask you to witness the contract." He held Branwen's gaze, and she swore the spy could divine truths about her that she didn't want to know. Or, more likely, his network of informants was vast.

"It would be my honor to witness the marriage," said Diarmuid without hesitation. The mantle of leadership had transformed his demeanor and, for once, Branwen thought it entirely for the better.

Alba signed the contract first, and Branwen respected the other woman's steely resolve. Tristan looked at Marc as he signed his name next to that of his future wife.

"*Kernyv bosta vyken*," he vowed. His uncle nodded.

Diarmuid scrawled his name beneath the two future monarchs', affirming their validity. Tristan's stare bored into Branwen's cheek as she wrote *Lady Branwen Cualand of Laíginztír* beside his name, but she couldn't look at him. The ink blurred in her vision; she scrubbed her eye as if troubled by a speck of dust.

Xandru clapped first, followed by King Marc. Diarmuid gave a hearty whoop. The ceremony was a public declaration, but Tristan and Alba were now legally bound.

They couldn't be unbound without a war.

"Crown Princess Alba," said Xandru. "As his sole heir, your father has authorized you to sign the Three Kingdom Alliance in his stead." She visibly swallowed. If not for her brazen siege, this alliance would never have come to pass.

Was it fate, her goddess Ankou, or something else completely that had guided her hand?

Alba signed her name three times on each of the three copies of the treaty. Then Diarmuid handed King Óengus's seal to Eseult.

"You should be the one to act for Iveriu," he said.

Hesitant, the True Queen gripped the wooden handle. The rounded seal at the end was crafted from gold.

Xandru retrieved an oil lamp from the sideboard at the other end of the study, and lit the wick. Diarmuid held a stick of green wax to the flame. He dripped a thumb-size dollop onto the vellum.

"One Iveriu," said Eseult as she pressed the seal into the sticky substance. Three times she imprinted the lion of Iveriu onto parchment, cementing the alliance.

King Marc was the last to sign. He raised his own seal. He admired the peace that had been won with so much blood, so much loss.

"A new era begins for all of our kingdoms," King Marc declared as he stamped a sea-wolf into wax.

Applause followed and Xandru poured everyone a glass of Mílesian spirits. The spy drank from the king's cup in Andred's absence. Branwen trusted Xandru to protect Marc with his life—even if she trusted him in nothing else.

She swallowed her spirits in one gulp and made her excuses, claiming she needed to tend to a patient. King Marc had asked Branwen to assist Alba before the ceremony, and she needed half an hour to herself. Overwrought, she collected the shawl and the elderberry wine, and hurried from the study.

"Branwen! Lady Branwen!" called Diarmuid, chasing her down the stairwell.

She stopped, inhaling an annoyed breath. Pivoting to face him, "Yes?" Branwen demanded.

"I have a letter." He reached into the pocket of his breeches. "Queen Eseult—that is, your aunt, asked that you open it in private."

Branwen's pulse rose skyward. On today of all days, she didn't know that she could bear to read her aunt's words of reproach. What else could the letter say? Branwen deserved the censure, she knew she did. The Loving Cup, the trial—all of it was her fault.

But she could not read it today.

Diarmuid handed her the scroll, its seal unbroken: a *krotto*. A golden harp with silver strings was the symbol of Laiginztir. Her aunt would always be a proud Laiginztir woman, like Lady Alana. Her throat went dry.

"Thank you, Diarmuid."

He rubbed a hand over his shaven head. "Branwen—"

"Is there something else?"

"I need to thank you and . . . to apologize." Branwen held herself very straight, waiting. Diarmuid's chest lifted as he said, "A lot has changed since you left for Kernyv." He frowned. "I've been a horse's ass. Thank you for not betraying my treason to King Óengus."

Branwen's jaw dropped. "I may only have one eye now, but I see more clearly," Diarmuid went on. "I see what you always did . . . that peace is more important than one man's desire." He touched his eye patch. "I am truly sorry for making you complicit in my treason."

She made a choking sound. She had perpetrated so many of her own betrayals since their last encounter that Branwen could only say, "The past is in the past. I offer you my friendship, Lord Diarmuid."

"I accept it heartily."

"Tomorrow we will fight for Iveriu together."

His brow puckered in surprise. "You're coming with us?"

"There will be many wounded. I will be needed."

"I've always admired your conviction, Lady Branwen—even when we were adversaries." Diarmuid gave her a chagrined smile. "I don't think peace will ever be a constant, but it's still worth fighting for."

She listed her head to one side. "I used to think you were too bold to be wise."

"And now?"

"Sometimes the wise must also be bold."

ALL THAT REMAINS

AS PRINCESS ALBA WAS NO longer a hostage but an honored guest, Branwen had to be announced before she was given permission to enter Queen Verica's former apartment. Alba stood as Branwen crossed the threshold, raising an eyebrow. Mauve light glowed around the princess, the days stretching further and further each eventide.

"King Marc asked if I would assist you with preparations for the ceremony," Branwen explained. She tapped her leather satchel, which she'd filled with berry tints and lip stains instead of medicines.

"Unless you intend to injure me before the wedding, I don't require the assistance of the Royal Healer." Alba folded her arms across her chest.

"I was my cousin's lady's maid for years."

A line formed above Alba's nose. "I can't picture it," she said. Branwen made no comment; she lifted a stubborn chin. Exhaling languidly, Alba relented. "If you insist. I've never had patience for cosmetics."

No, thought Branwen, *only for planning naval assaults.*

She bid the princess to be seated at the table where Queen Verica had played so many games of dice. Glancing at the bright yellow draperies, Branwen said, "This room belonged to Princess Gwynedd—Tristan's mother—when she was a girl." The old queen had told Branwen that her daughter had requested curtains the color of sunshine.

Branwen retrieved a delicately carved comb of ivory from the depths of her satchel.

"You saved Tristan at the Champions Tournament," said Alba, giving her a crafty look. "He said you became friends after you saved his life."

She nodded, running the teeth of the comb through Alba's short locks, which were knotted from her earlier ride.

"He's a good man," Branwen said. Tristan obviously hadn't told the princess that the Champions Tournament was the second time she'd saved his life. "He'll be a kind husband."

"It doesn't matter. I never wanted to marry, but I put my kingdom in this mess and I must bear the consequences." Alba's jaw clenched as she spoke. "My father always says that to those who much is given, much is expected."

Rigor spread outward from Branwen's belly. She had asked much from the Old Ones and yet she only knew what the Dark One expected. A life. Tonight was Belotnia. Seven months remained to deliver Dhusnos his Shade.

Finished with the combing, Branwen used beeswax to smooth the ends of Alba's hair. "I like it short," she told the princess.

Alba shrugged, dismissive. "I was fed up with braiding it. My mother will have a fit. She says Manduca women are famed for their dark tresses."

"Are you close?" asked Branwen, and the other woman speared her with a glare.

"Close enough. She doesn't understand why the sea calls to me."

Branwen did, even now, despite the danger that lurked beneath. She still saw the beauty. "I'm sorry your mother isn't here for your wedding day."

"King Marc was adamant that the wedding take place before the campaign against the Veneti Isles, and my father refused to send any more royal hostages to Kernyv until the treaty had been signed. He always uses an abundance of caution." Alba met Branwen's gaze. "Unlike me."

Branwen didn't respond to the threat. She selected a cheek stain the color of wild raspberries. Holding it out, she said, "This will suit your complexion."

"If you say so." Alba watched as Branwen used her thumb to apply the waxy substance to her cheekbones. The knife wound from the siege had faded to a pink line.

"Tristan is a man of two peoples, like me," said the princess, after a minute, as if edging toward a question. "He's had as little choice in this marriage as I did . . . I hope we can learn to live with each other."

"He's an easy man to live with." Branwen blended the rouge into Alba's golden-brown skin.

"My father required Tristan to renounce any claim to the throne of Armorica. And King Marc also stipulated that he renounce any claim on the Kernyvak throne to preclude any possibility of foreign rule." Alba inhaled a shallow breath. "Tristan will never be king. I will become queen upon my father's death, but Tristan will remain a prince. I don't know many men who could live with that."

Branwen stopped for a moment, considering her words. She hadn't been made aware of all the terms of the marriage contract.

Then, with confidence, she said, "Tristan can. He's never wanted to rule. He only wants to serve his kingdom."

Alba leaned forward in her chair. "How is it that you know Tristan so well? I thought it was Queen Eseult he was supposed to be in love with."

The surf roared from below the window.

"*He's not*," said Branwen, terse. "He's not in love with the queen." She shook her head. Finally, maybe, it was actually true—might become true.

"He's a fine warrior at least." Alba made an approving face. "He'll make a better sparring partner for me than you did."

"I'm glad." Branwen could imagine it: Alba and Tristan finding common ground, fighting for a common purpose. Her stomach pinched.

"I don't regret trying to escape," said the princess.

"I wouldn't believe you if you said you did."

She stared at Branwen dead on. "I still can't fathom how you subdued me. I'm faster. A superior fighter."

"Luck," Branwen lied without hesitation. "You hit your head on a rock."

"I don't remember any rock."

"That's usual with a concussion." She turned to pluck a horsehair brush from beside the rouge on the table.

"And is bleached hair a symptom of a concussion, too?" Alba twirled the gray streak in her short hair around her pinkie, undoing Branwen's careful arrangement.

"I have no explanation for that, Captain."

The Armorican princess latched onto Branwen's elbow, forcing her to turn back toward her. "We who follow Ankou believe that when she touches you, she leaves a sign. If she touches you three times, when you cross the Veil you'll become one of her maidservants."

Branwen shivered. "Death-Tellers, I think you Iverni call them," said Alba.

"Yes."

She yanked her elbow from the princess's grasp and chose a paint that resembled liquid gold to accentuate the other woman's sable eyes.

Alba continued to watch her keenly as she dipped the tip of the horsehair brush into the mixture. When Branwen leaned forward to outline Alba's eyes, Alba said, "Kahedrin liked you." She paused the brush midair. "He came home from King Marc's wedding saying he'd met an Ivernic healer with nerve."

"I liked him, too."

"But you killed him."

"Yes, I did." A drop of gold fell to the floor. "I mourn for your loss, but I don't regret my actions."

"No," Alba said, echoing Branwen's words, "I wouldn't believe you if you said you did." Her smile was baleful. Although Branwen's guilt persisted, despite Alba's escape attempt.

Drawing in a breath, Branwen commanded, "Close your eyes," as she lifted the brush to the other woman's eyelids.

Alba wriggled her nose as she complied. With her eyes closed, the princess looked no older than her seventeen years. She approached her marriage like a soldier and she wasn't someone to court sympathy—yet she had Branwen's all the same.

"I wish I were coming with you tomorrow," Alba admitted. Branwen applied another layer of gold.

"There are many ways to fight," she replied.

The princess opened her eyes; they reminded Branwen of the sea at midnight. "I will honor my brothers by ruling as they would have. My mother is a foreign queen—their stepmother, but they embraced her. They embraced me." Alba touched the medallion of Ankou that hung between her breasts. "I will embrace Kernyv. And Iveriu." She blinked. "It's what Kahedrin would have wanted."

Branwen used the edge of her sleeve to dab the golden tears that had pooled beneath Alba's eyes.

"You will make an excellent queen."

Alba swallowed. And in that moment, another queen was announced. Eseult walked toward them dressed in a gown of Rigani green silk, with lace trim.

"You look beautiful," the True Queen said to Alba.

"Thank you, Lady Queen."

"Branwen always works magic with a brush," she said. Eseult winked at Branwen, and she saw no guile there. It was a compliment, not a barb, despite the chaos that Branwen's magic had unleashed.

"We're nearly finished," Branwen told her cousin. "Then you can change into your bridal gown," she said to Alba, who sat in a simple cotton shift.

Wetting her lips, Branwen asked, "Is there—do you need me to lay out a First Night dress for . . . after the ceremony?"

Branwen had embroidered her cousin's First Night dress, although they had both worn it to complete their deception of the king.

"There will be no Mantle of Maidenhood," the True Queen declared.

Alba showed Eseult a small smile. "I appreciate your intervention on my behalf," the princess said. "I do not like Seer Casek at all."

Branwen whipped her head toward her cousin, overcome with many unnamable emotions. She hadn't known the *kordweyd* had made such a demand, but it came as no surprise that he would try to exert his influence.

"The marriage contract is signed," said the queen. "The alliance is sealed. What happens in your bedroom is of no concern to the seers." She looked at Alba with a wistful expression. "I have been where you are . . . and your relationship with your husband is yours. It's how you define it."

Without thinking, Branwen took Eseult's hand and squeezed. Tears beaded her cousin's lashes; her own throat grew tight. As if sensing Branwen's discomfort, Eseult said, "I can help Alba into her bridal dress and escort her to the Great Hall. Why don't you change into your feasting gown?"

Grateful, she nodded. To Alba, she said, "Good luck," and it was all Branwen could do not to sprint from the room.

She retreated down the stairs with as much poise as she could muster before flinging herself onto her bed and sobbing into her pillow.

Night had fallen when Branwen dried her face and changed into the same turquoise gown she'd worn for Marc and Eseult's wedding. She glimpsed her reflection in the looking glass. She was pale, her freckles more pronounced, yet her coppery eyes still held a hint of fire. She had left her pastes and powders in Alba's suite. It seemed fitting. Her skin was as naked as she felt.

Branwen was halfway through plaiting her black curls when a knock jolted her from her thoughts. Maybe Alba was right. Maybe shorter hair would be more convenient.

She slipped the letter from her aunt into the pocket of her gown. She was both afraid to read it and afraid to be without it. Branwen loved her aunt intensely, wanted to keep a piece of her close, even if it was an emblem of her own shame—even if her aunt didn't know what she'd become.

"I leave in the morning," said Tristan as Branwen opened the door.

A beat passed before she answered. "As do I."

"I know." He tugged at his own curls, which he'd also tamed with beeswax. "I know, and I won't ask you not to go. You wouldn't listen, anyway." He half smiled.

Tristan was dressed in a tunic of white satin and black velvet trousers. The material must have been hot in the summer air, but he looked extraordinary.

"Shouldn't you be at the Great Hall?" Branwen said, afraid that she might not be able to keep a leash on her feelings, desires that had been leashed for far too long.

He withdrew a sheaf of parchment from behind his back.

"*The Dreaming Sea*," he said. "I wrote it for you."

"But I thought—"

"I know what you thought." Tristan sighed. "Or, I can imagine."

Branwen took the vellum from him, not entirely sure she wasn't dreaming now. She began to scan the words that accompanied the music. It was the ballad of Emer and Tantris. She gaped at him.

"*Tristan.*"

He raised a hand to stroke her cheek. "I can't blame you for everything." His knuckles were rough, yet soft against Branwen's skin. "I don't. Not anymore."

"I'm so sorry. I robbed you of your honor . . ." Her voice broke. "I wish I could give it back."

Tristan shook his head. "I will earn back my own honor. I will make my vows to Alba, and I will live by them. I will honor her and Kernyv until the day I die."

"I know you will."

"I understand why you did what you did, Branwen. To marry for peace is a hard thing. I know why you wanted to give Eseult love."

"A hero's sacrifice, you told my cousin." Branwen trembled. "You were right."

His eyes gleamed. "I will give Alba all the love I can—all that remains."

Branwen gripped the music in her hand. "At the Champions

Tournament," she said. "I knew one day you'd want a princess for your-self." She tried to laugh but it creaked like warped wood.

"When I returned to Iveriu, you were the only woman I wanted, Branwen," Tristan told her. "The only woman I thought I could ever want."

He pressed his lips to hers, only for a second, and their hearts beat as one.

"In my dreams, Tantris and Emer will always find each other," he whispered against Branwen's mouth. "That will have to be enough."

Dreams were never enough, but they were all Branwen would ever have.

"You'll be late," she forced out.

A lifetime passed in the look they shared, as if they were in the in-between. A lifetime together that Branwen and Tristan would never know. Then he nodded and vanished through the doorway.

Branwen opened the drawer containing the strand of mermaid's hair she'd been saving since the day they'd met. It was time. Time to release the dream.

She pulled off her glove and summoned her black flame. She burned the seaweed to dust, then licked her palm.

It was salty and sweet and gone.

DANCE WITH ME

BRANWEN WITNESSED TRISTAN'S MARRIAGE TO Alba in a daze. Candlelight from the chandeliers wavered around the couple. Alba stood regally in her gown of Armorican yellow, the color of the sun in late afternoon, and she was nearly as tall as her husband.

Branwen watched from the audience, just before the raised dais, close enough to listen to every word of their vows. And yet she heard none of them.

King Marc cut himself with the couple's blade of binding, offering his blood into the chalice for Tristan. He handed the blade to Xandru, who offered his blood for Alba on behalf of Armorica and the Manduca family.

A heated look passed between the men. Sorrow formed like a pebble in Branwen's throat and she swallowed it down. If Marc hadn't been born a king, he could have performed this ceremony for himself with the man he loved. She peered sidelong at the True Queen who stood next to her, almost protective. Their eyes met. Could her cousin guess the truth of Marc's heart?

There were no ballads sung like at Ivernic weddings, but Branwen could hear Tristan's dulcet baritone all the same.

Odai eti ama.

After Seer Casek had anointed the bride and groom with the blood of the witnesses in the Kernyvak tradition, a rite of Ankou was celebrated. Armoricans paid homage to the Old One they'd chosen as their patron on their wedding day. Alba offered Tristan a cake served at Armorican funerals to symbolize the death of the life he had known before their marriage. He took one bite, and Alba took another.

When they kissed, the married couple was born into their new life together. Branwen cast her eyes to her feet. She had once kissed Tristan back to life, too.

Eseult took Branwen's hand and drew the symbol on her palm that she knew was meant to be comforting, although its meaning still eluded her.

This time she didn't pull away.

✝ ✝ ✝

The feast was lavish but Branwen barely touched the freshly baked fish or candied fruits. Eseult had made certain that Branwen was seated beside her at the king's table. She flashed her worried smiles throughout the meal.

King Marc was seated in the center of the table, with Tristan and Alba to his left. Although this was their wedding feast, Marc was still the King of Kernyv. His place was at the center of the table—and the kingdom, lest anyone forget.

All of the barons and their families offered their congratulations to the newlyweds in turn. Branwen was surprised to see Countess Kensa in attendance. She sat with Seer Casek at one of the lower tables, dressed in all black except for the hand-shaped combs that adorned her hair, rubies glittering like hate. Branwen recalled what Ruan had told her about Casek caring for him after his beatings. Perhaps that was why the seer and the countess were thick as thieves.

When it was time to offer House Whel's wishes to the bride and groom, Countess Kensa didn't smile, and she didn't so much as glance in Tristan's direction.

King Marc entreated all of the wedding guests to dance as the musicians began to play. Branwen remained seated, feeling as if she were already spinning. A smile pulled at her lips when she spotted Lowenek dancing with Andred. He was cautious at first, but he soon forgot his self-consciousness as the girl beamed at him.

Eseult wandered back to Branwen's side, leaving the king on the dance floor to make conversation with a young Armorican lord who had been sent by King Faramon to witness the marriage.

"You don't fancy dancing?" said her cousin, taking a seat.

"Not tonight."

Twisting her mouth into a sly smile, Eseult said, "Diarmuid tells me that Treva sent you elderberry wine. We could escape to drink it in secret like we used to?"

"Doesn't it taste better when it's been pilfered from the kitchens?"

Eseult laughed. "Probably." She worried the antler shard.

Eyeing the pendant, Branwen said, "Did King Marc gift that to you?" Something stirred in her core, something that wanted a fight.

"Seer Ogrin."

"So you're a follower of the Horned One now?"

"I don't know, Branny," her cousin replied, not reacting to Branwen's vinegar tone. "The craftsmen are carving a statue of Matrona for the portico. Seer Ogrin has been telling me about her." Her voice drifted off.

Carnonos was the name of the Horned One before he became a god, and Matrona had been his mother. Queen Verica had been a great devotee, and since she'd provided the financing for the Royal Infirmary she requested that it be dedicated to Matrona. Although the seers barred women from the Mysteries of the New Religion, in some places in Albion there were temples and shrines devoted to the worship of the Horned One's mother.

Branwen refilled her goblet with spiced wine.

Fidgeting with the pendant, Eseult said, "I like the idea of Matrona, of her love for her son. A mother for us all."

"Your mother loves you," Branwen countered.

"She's loved me as best she could." Her cousin's eyes glinted. "She always had to be my queen first."

Branwen's eyes caught on Tristan as he twirled Alba, and he was laughing. Alba was a graceful dancer, which was unsurprising given how talented a fighter she was. Branwen took a gulp of wine.

"I know how hard this must be for you," said Eseult, following her line of sight. "My love for Tristan feels as distant as if it happened to someone else." She spoke in a whisper, yet Branwen shot her a panicked look. "It wasn't real. I understand that now, I—I *feel* it. But the love you shared with Tristan . . . that was earned."

Branwen was at a loss for words. She still didn't understand how the spell had been broken. Unless it was similar to the binding spell her aunt had used to trap Lord Morholt's soul in his body. Queen Eseult couldn't retrieve the traitor's finger because if she touched his body the spell would be undone.

"I've rebuilt my heart without Tristan," Branwen told the queen, daring her to contradict her. "I've already let him go."

Eseult glanced at her with skepticism. "Have you heard from Ruan?" she asked. "If he's in your heart now, then I . . . I want you to be happy."

"I was never able to let him in," she said, and she knew it to be the truth.

The Wise Damsel had told Branwen that we all build the houses we live in, but Branwen had built hers without any doors.

The queen nodded, sadness rinsing her face.

"I never let Diarmuid in, either. Not really." She drew down a long breath. "Seeing him today, it—I was surprised by how little I feel. I didn't love *him*. I loved the idea of freedom."

"I understand that," Branwen admitted. She laid her hand palm up on the table. "The symbol you've been drawing. What is its meaning?"

Eseult's eyes rounded. "You really don't remember, do you?" Branwen shook her head. "How is that possible?"

"I worked a spell," she said. "I wanted to take away your pain—over Tristan, over the baby." Branwen licked her lips, which tasted of spice. "But I had to trade a memory to the Old Ones. I didn't know which they would take."

"The Old Ones do as they please." Eseult gripped the antler shard.

"Maybe they do." Branwen sighed. "Why should they be any different from us?"

Her cousin traced the first stroke, featherlight. "Honeysuckle," she said. "Remember when Master Bécc taught us the language of trees?"

"I remember the letters. Nothing else."

Frowning, Eseult added the second mark. "Hazel," she said. "The honeysuckle vine wraps itself around the hazel tree, and if one is separated from the other, they both wither." Her cousin paused, voice growing hoarse. "We made the vow on Belotnia Eve, when you were twelve, and carved our names into the hazel tree beneath the South Tower: *Not you without me, not me without you.*"

It was a lovely story. "I'm sorry I don't remember," said Branwen.

"I am, too, Branny. But I will remember for both of us."

King Marc approached the table with Xandru. "The two most beautiful women at the feast should be dancing," said the king. He extended a hand to Eseult. It was paramount that the entire court of Kernyv and the visiting Armorican nobility see King Marc and Queen Eseult enjoying each other's company.

Xandru tilted his chin at Branwen. "May I have the pleasure?"

From the corner of her eye, she spied Tristan and Alba holding hands, exiting through a side door of the hall.

"Another time. After the battle." Branwen stood. "I want to ready my surgical tools and supplies. I'll see you at the dock."

"After the battle," said Xandru with one of his facile smiles.

Branwen fled in the direction of the gardens, afraid that she might run into Tristan and Alba headed to the West Tower. Whether they consummated their marriage tonight or a year from tonight, Branwen didn't want to know—had no right to know. She trailed her gloved hand over a bush of fragrant lilacs and watched them wither in the starlight.

"I knew if I waited here long enough, you'd find me."

Ruan stepped out from the cover of a spear-leafed tree. "You hate crowds," he went on. "And polite conversation." He stepped closer. "You can't make it through an entire feast without needing to run away."

Branwen froze. "I know you, *karid*," Ruan told her.

"Are you drunk?"

"I've never been more sober."

"What are you doing here?" She scowled.

Ruan showed her his fake, roguish smile. "I was invited. I may have been dishonored, but the rest of the world still thinks I'm a prince." The squeaking of the lantern overhead underscored his bitter laugh. "Are you glad I'm not dead, Branwen?"

Fury ignited inside her. "You know I am, Ruan."

"Do I?" They stared at each other, breathing hard. "We buried Endelyn next to our father. Our *real* father. I wanted you there," he said. "But I didn't think you'd come."

"I would have come if you'd asked," she said, softening her tone.

"You could have revealed my lineage at the trial, discredited my mother's claims for a blood price. You could have ruined me."

"I never wanted to ruin you."

"No," he said sadly. "I did that." Strains of music carried from the Great Hall on the sultry breeze. "Dance with me," Ruan said.

"Here?"

"As I remember, you have a fondness for gardens."

Branwen flushed. Low in her body desire awoke, like a dragon. "Everything is broken between us," she said.

"I know," Ruan replied, and slipped his arm around her waist, drawing her in close. They joined hands. "But it's our tradition. We always dance at weddings."

He pressed a cheek to hers. Tiny bristles that she hadn't noticed in the dim light tickled her skin.

"I don't regret choosing you as my first lover," Branwen told him as they swayed. He twirled her in the moonlight. When she spun back against Ruan's chest, he said, "Since it couldn't be Tristan?"

Outrage shot through her and before she realized what she was doing, her left palm had connected with his cheek.

Rubbing his jaw, Ruan said, "Having you train with Alba was a mistake."

Branwen didn't apologize, although he wasn't wrong. She had dreamed of her First Night being with Tristan—or Emer had dreamed of it with Tantris. Alba would, she suspected, know Tristan in a way Branwen never could. Love wasn't needed between lovers, and Tristan was an easy man to desire.

Branwen plunged her hands through Ruan's long, untamed hair and dragged his mouth to hers. She bit him and she kissed him, and his hands roamed her body. Ruan's caresses were frantic, impassioned. She lost herself in his need, in her own.

She pushed him off the path, behind the lilac bush. She forced him to his knees, and he kissed the bodice of her gown, just below her belly button. Branwen dropped down into the grass, pushing Ruan onto his back, tugging at the waistband of his breeches.

"I'm just using you," she told him.

"You always were. But I don't care."

Branwen pulled away. She crawled backward in the grass.

"You should care, Ruan."

He sat up, reaching for her. "I'll take what you give me," he said.

She glanced at her gloved hand. She had taken too much from Ruan already. It would be so simple for Branwen to become a Shade herself.

"You deserve more."

Ruan cocked his head. "You still believe that?" He stared in disbelief. As Branwen lifted herself from the ground, he retied the drawstring of his trousers. "Well, I'll see you in Marghas."

"You're coming on the raid?"

"The countess doesn't want me to," he said, chagrined. "After Marc stripped me of my position at court, she tried to forbid me like I'm still a child." He laughed. "But I will always protect the king. Marc has asked me to act as translator for the Ivernic ships."

Ruan rose to his feet as well. "I love my kingdom, Branwen. Everything I did was in service to the crown."

"That's why I believe you deserve better than me," Branwen said.

"At least tomorrow we'll be fighting on the same side."

Perhaps for the first time. "*Nosmatis*, Ruan."

TRUTH TO TELL

THE MORNING WAS BRIGHT AND unforgiving.

Dawn tasted acrid and Branwen had slept scarcely more than an hour. She left the letter from the Queen of Iveriu under her pillow, still unread. If she survived the campaign against the pirates, she would read her aunt's admonishments. Not before. Better to die without knowing.

Her cousin, never an early riser, had surprised Branwen by meeting her at the stables as she readied Senara for the ride to Marghas.

"Branny," she had said. "I still love you more than any kingdom—even if I haven't shown it. Please come back, and I promise you I will do better."

Branwen had embraced her cousin, holding her tight. She smelled like honeysuckle. But Branwen had made no promises of her own.

Her magic was desperate for release, for an enemy she could fight head on. And if she burned herself out in service of peace, so be it.

Now she stood on the dock where she'd taken her first steps onto Kernyvak soil.

"*Dymatis*, Lady Branwen," said Captain Morgawr. She smiled at the captain whom she now regarded as an old friend, although they'd known each other less than a year.

He tugged at his bushy mustache, sun warming his dark brown skin, and pointed at the *Dragon Rising*. "The old girl is ready for another battle," he said.

The sail that Branwen had once repaired with one of Eseult's dresses had been replaced, as had the mast that snapped in two during the battle with the Shades.

"Why is it that sailors insist ships are women, Captain?" she said.

"Because they're stronger and more stalwart than men." He winked, but he meant what he said. Branwen laughed. "The *Dragon Rising* will lead the assault. I'd feel better with you aboard my ship."

Morgawr gave her a knowing look. He'd seen her fire magic burn the Shades from the inside out. Would her magic still work against them, she wondered, now that she was also tethered to Dhusnos?

"The king has assigned me to the *Mawort*," Branwen informed Captain Morgawr. At the end of the dock, King Marc was performing a blessing, asking the Horned One to watch over the Royal Fleet by tossing several pairs of antlers into the surf. Branwen couldn't stop her nose from twisting as she noticed Seer Casek's silhouette beside the king's.

"Just as well," said the veteran captain. "If we run into any trouble, we'll need a healer. Better to have you farther behind in the convoy."

The journey to the Veneti Isles would take nearly a full day's sail and many dangers lay in the open sea, both natural and supernatural. Thirty ships were setting out from the Port of Marghas with the aim of seizing the former Aquilan fortress that the pirates used as a stronghold.

"I'll ask my gods to watch over you," Branwen told Morgawr.

"And mine you." He kissed his antler shard and cut the air with two fingers. "See you once we've taken the fort."

Captain Morgawr strode toward the *Dragon Rising*, and Branwen meandered toward the *Mawort*, catching a glimpse of Ruan at the helm of Lord Diarmuid's ship. She nodded in acknowledgment and kept walking. A year ago, the notion that those two men would be sailing into battle together would have been inconceivable.

Fate was unpredictable, sometimes wondrous, and could not be controlled. Even though Branwen had traded her heart, and perhaps her soul, in trying to control it.

The ships began to cast off.

King Marc lingered at the end of the *Mawort*'s gangway, alone, waiting for Branwen.

"Sister," he said. His voice was leaden. He clasped both of her shoulders. "Thank you for taking part in this raid."

"I wouldn't be anywhere else."

He nodded. "Your mother would be proud of the woman you've become."

"I hope so," Branwen said, emotion swelling, sharp and unexpected. She didn't dare hope the same of her aunt.

"I must beg a favor," the king said. She waited. "Stay close to Xandru."

"I can take care of myself."

Marc's eyes dropped to Branwen's gloved hand. "That's what I'm counting on."

Oh. *Oh.* He wanted Branwen to protect his *karid.*

In an ominous voice he said, "I have not forgotten that someone tried to murder you, sister. Neither has Tristan. There is more than one mission taking place." Marc glanced around them. "Please, stay with Xandru. You will need each other."

"You have my word," she said, giving him a confused look.

"Good." He kissed her forehead. "I won't lose another sister."

✚ ✚ ✚

The cliffs seemed to rise higher the farther south along the coast they sailed.

The *Mawort* was a sleek vessel, narrower and lighter in the water than the ships of any of the royal fleets. Xandru had explained that the Manduca mercantile dynasty was so successful because they had the fastest ships in the known world—the design of which was a closely guarded secret.

The waters surrounding the Veneti Isles were treacherous, requiring a special skill to navigate, especially at night, which was why the fleets had waited for a full moon to attack. Xandru had also mentioned, in his habitual nonchalant manner, that he had made further improvements and modifications to the design of the *Mawort*. His vessel, he claimed, could navigate the islands with ease under any conditions.

Belying the captain's characteristic indifference, the genuine enthusiasm that lit Xandru's eyes as he spoke about engineering reminded Branwen of Andred and his flowering box experiments. Because the hull of the *Mawort* was shallower, however, it was impossible to stand up belowdecks without stooping. Branwen found a wooden crate on the bow to use as a stool instead. She scanned the clouds for any sign of *kretarvs* and circumspectly observed the mercurial captain interacting with his crew.

The men were all handpicked by Xandru, mostly from the Melita Isles, some from the Kingdom of Míl, and they'd been sailing together for years. Xandru was fluent in at least four languages by Branwen's count, a useful skill for a spy, and his crew followed his orders immediately and efficiently. Though his manner was mild, he brooked no compromise. Branwen began to see more readily what might have drawn Marc to the captain.

When they reached Liones, Xandru pointed out Castle Wragh. It was impressive even at a distance, constructed from pearlescent stone. The lands that Tristan had gifted to Branwen lay nearby, although the castle itself had been forfeited to Countess Kensa together with Liones.

Would Ruan take up residence at Castle Wragh if he survived the coming battle? she wondered idly. Everything that had come before Branwen stepped aboard the *Mawort*, and everything that would come after the battle, seemed at a very far remove.

Twilight seeped through the sky, a maelstrom of fiery pinks. It might be the last sunset she'd ever see. Branwen had lived her whole life with the threat of violence, constantly vigilant against raids, swift and barbaric, that came without warning. This was different. A strange sort of anticipation.

No one knew precisely where the Veil between this world and the Otherworld lay in the sea, but Branwen sensed the Sea of the Dead. She heard the Dark One's whispers. Or maybe it was only the whitecaps frothing.

Xandru dragged another crate beside Branwen's, sitting down and offering her a waterskin and strips of salted pork.

"It's hard to eat before a raid," he said. "But you should."

Branwen accepted the waterskin, throat suddenly parched. When the Wise Damsel was teaching her to scry, Branwen had asked the Old Ones who was the greatest threat to peace. They'd sent her a vision of herself aboard a ship, pirates pursuing, her hands covered with blood.

As she drank, Xandru said, "Marc told me to keep you close when we reach the Veneti Isles." He broke off a piece of salted pork and tossed it into his mouth.

"He told me the same thing."

Xandru laughed. "Yes, he would have." Leaning in closer, the captain said, "Despite your talent as a healer, most men who are injured in battle won't survive the voyage home. I didn't want you on the mission."

His gaze became intent. "You mean too much to Marc," he said.

Branwen startled at the seriousness in his voice. She choked on the water, starting to cough. Glancing around the deck, she realized the rest of the crew was keeping their distance.

"I know it was your mother," Xandru continued. Branwen coughed harder. "Her death has haunted Marc our entire lives. He's craved peace since we were fourteen years old."

"I've forgiven him," she managed.

"Yes, that's why I didn't want you to come. I don't put much credence in the gods, but I'm thankful you came to Marc's court." He paused, looking back at the coast as it slipped from view. "The recent . . . upheaval notwithstanding, a burden has lifted from Marc's shoulders. He didn't believe he could ever be a good man."

Xandru swallowed. "You don't know the hope you've given him."

Branwen fought the hot sting of tears. "He is—he is a good man."

"Far too good to be king."

"But you love him for it."

The captain lurched back on the crate. His shoulders snapped together, jaw tight. The look he gave Branwen put all her senses on high alert.

Xandru's lips twitched. Waves lapped against the hull. She held his stare even as instinct told her to dive overboard.

"We don't always get to spend our lives with the people we love," he said. The statement was too cavalier, and it fell flat.

"No, we don't." Branwen knew that only too well.

"Marc wants peace, and I want what he wants." Dusk had faded to blue, casting a cool light on Xandru's face. "I am not a selfless man. Marc is the one person who comes before me in my own heart." He paused. "Why didn't you tell your cousin when you saw us together at Queen Verica's funeral?"

There were many reasons, far more than Branwen could disclose.

"It was not my truth to tell," she settled on.

"You wanted to come on this raid. I've seen men before who hunger for battle," he said. "Why?"

"I want peace. It's all I've wanted since my parents died." Branwen drained the remainder of the water. "I also have things for which I need to be forgiven."

Xandru tapped his chin, lifting one corner of his mouth.

"Many rumors abound about how Monwiku Castle was saved," he said. "Some say the ancient Kernyveu rose from their graves to defend their homeland."

"Is that so?"

"Is there anything you want to tell me, Lady Branwen? Such as why Marc assured me you'd be an asset to my mission and not a liability?"

"Healing is not my only skill," Branwen replied.

Xandru threw his head back in amusement. "I think you're more like me than Marc, my lady."

Just then a shout came from belowdecks.

Xandru leapt to his feet.

A second later, a lithe figure raced up the ladder, emerging onto the deck, and strutted toward the captain.

Looking from Xandru to Branwen, Alba put her hands on her hips. "You didn't think I would sit out this fight, did you, cousin?"

Xandru sighed. "Your father will have my head."

"Only if the pirates don't take it first." Alba gave Branwen a cursory glance, noting, "I see you took my advice about finding yourself some trousers." And she had.

"Where does Tristan think you are?" Branwen demanded.

Alba shrugged. "He'll need to learn to keep up."

Branwen almost laughed; then she looked at Xandru. This wasn't part of the plan.

"It's too late to turn back," he declared. "We must reach the Veneti Isles before dawn."

Alba's smile was triumphant.

"Could I trouble you for a sword?" she said.

WHEEL OF FORTUNE

THE NIGHT SEEMED AN ETERNITY until it was nearly over. One by one, lanterns that swung from riggings across the fleet, a second canopy of stars, were snuffed out.

The Veneti Isles were clustered together west of Liones, like four petals on a clover. The fortress for the former Aquilan penal colony had been built on a promontory of the most southerly island, overlooking a sheltered harbor. By the light of the full moon, the convoy of royal forces had sailed south around the islands, bearing east to avoid being spotted, and then switched to a northern tack.

Alba sat cross-legged on the deck beside Branwen's crate, sharpening the blade of her *kladiwos*. Branwen gritted her teeth against the sound, which rang out over the waves.

King Marc had received intelligence, most likely from Xandru, that the majority of the pirate ships would be moored in the harbor so the men could celebrate Belotnia, and Branwen found it unsettling that the pirates enjoyed the same festivals as she did. The other three islands were sparsely populated. If the combined fleet could seize the main island, it would bring them all to heel. The plan was to swoop up from below, launching a frontal assault on the pirates' safe harbor before they could rise from their beds.

It amazed Branwen how quiet a fleet of ships could be. Silent and as lethal as a shark. Captain Morgawr had once told her that sharks presaged a storm. The pirates had no inkling that a storm was driving straight at them, brutal and voracious. The fleet's orders were to burn all of the pirate ships where they were docked so there would be no escape.

For over a hundred years, no lone kingdom had possessed the maritime power to challenge the pirates. They could never have foreseen the Three Kingdom Alliance, or a king with the will to bring it to fruition.

In the first glimmer of dawn, the rocky coastline of the southernmost island became visible beyond the front of the convoy. The ships started to arrange themselves into a diamond pattern. Small roars erupted as ropes were loosened and sails swung into position. Alba continued to sharpen her sword.

Kernyvak and Armorican vessels took their places side by side. Black sea-wolves on blinding white sails were interspersed with red owls against yellow—the royal standard of Armorica. The Kernyvak and Armorican fleets had more experience of naval warfare and therefore comprised the first four rows of the diamond with the *Dragon Rising* at the very front, like the tip of a spear.

The five ships King Óengus had contributed were positioned in the center, toward the back, with three further Kernyvak ships bringing up the rear. Scanning the golden lions set against sails of Rigani green, Branwen felt a swell of pride.

"Shouldn't we be getting into formation?" Alba called out, walking over to Xandru at the helm of the ship.

The *Mawort* skimmed the outside of the diamond configuration, just beside Lord Diarmuid's ship. Branwen followed Alba with her gaze.

"I am the captain of this ship," Xandru told his cousin, and then ignored her. She continued to stare at him to no avail. Finally, she stalked off.

The princess wasn't the only restless member of the crew as the waves faded from black to gray. They should make landfall at daybreak.

Branwen withdrew the knife Ruan had given her from her boot, rolling the handle back and forth between her gloved fingers. Frigid sweat itched beneath her tunic. She'd forced down a few pieces of salted pork, which she now regretted, as bile rose in her throat.

"Take this," said Alba, reappearing from behind Branwen, pointing a sword at her throat. Branwen jumped. Alba scoffed at the knife. "You need a bigger blade," she said.

"Thank you."

Alba kept the *kladiwos* aimed at Branwen for another breath, then laughed and handed it over. "Try not to stab me in the back," said the princess. Branwen didn't reply. She accepted the sword, admiring the owl engraved on its hilt. "Owls are sacred to Ankou," Alba explained. "Armorican weapons often bear her mark."

Her dark eyes scoured Branwen, trying to provoke a response.

"Thank you," she repeated. She shoved the knife back into her boot.

The sun crept closer to the horizon, and Branwen noticed a faint outline of gold lingering on Alba's eyelids from the wedding feast. The princess seemed far more comfortable on the brink of war than she had on her wedding night.

Branwen stood and crossed the deck toward Xandru. In a low voice she said, "Marc told me there was more than one mission taking place in the Veneti Isles. What is yours?"

Xandru's hand was steady on the wheel of the ship.

"Have you not wondered who controls the pirates?"

"I thought no one could control them."

He flicked Branwen a sideways glance. "All men need a leader," he said. "The pirates are lawless but they have a code." He paused. "And they have a king."

Branwen furrowed her brow, a thousand questions swarming. It was true that she'd never given much thought to who the pirates were or how they lived when they weren't ravaging their neighbors' coastlines.

"In fact, they have a new king," Xandru continued blandly. "A man named Remus. He's risen up quickly, seems to have powerful backers."

"How do you know all of this?" she said in a whisper.

"Information is my trade."

"And I thought it was seeds," Branwen told him. Xandru released a solitary chuckle. "This Remus," she said. "You have orders to kill him?" It would not stun her to learn Xandru was an assassin as well as a spy.

"Not exactly."

"Marc can't mean to make an alliance with them?" Branwen's pitch grew high.

"No, my lady. But he wants Remus alive." As if divining her thoughts, Xandru said, "Marc didn't inform you of the details because I asked him not to. Secrets spread through court like a sieve."

She held her tongue. Xandru would never know all the dangerous secrets locked within Branwen's breast.

Sunrise skated over the Aquilan fortress, shadowy granite ramparts menacing. She stroked the thistle of her mother's brooch, which she'd fastened to her tunic. Alba had her medallion of Ankou; Captain Morgawr wore his antler shard. Her parents' memory was what Branwen held most sacred.

"When we arrive," she said to Xandru, "how will we find this pirate king?"

One corner of his mouth tilted upward. "We have a guide."

From the *Mawort*'s position at the edge of the formation, Branwen could now spot the *Dragon Rising*. As it sailed into the harbor where the pirate ships were docked, sails tied up, appearing deceptively harmless, a teeth-rattling boom echoed across the water. Across the world.

Branwen shuddered at the ripping, almost crunching noise, but she couldn't see what had caused it. The prow of the *Dragon Rising* tipped violently skyward. The next two ships in the convoy—one Kernyvak, the other Armorican—glided into line with *Dragon Rising*. Two more booms resounded. Her knees quaked.

All three ships were stopped dead at the entrance to the harbor, thrashing like wild stallions.

Alba rushed toward the helm, gripping her sword. Her expression was murderous.

The front four rows of the combined fleet began to collide, bobbing and weaving too close to one another. Branwen couldn't help but think of apples in a barrel. When Eseult was a girl, she would challenge both Branwen and Dubthach to see how many they could grasp using only their teeth. Branwen had always let her cousin win.

"It's a chain!" Alba spat, talking to Xandru.

"I can see that." His casual stance stiffened, barely, the only sign of his alarm.

Fear dissolved Branwen's memory. "A chain?" she said.

"Across the harbor, beneath the water," Alba told her, terse, as if it were obvious. "To prevent ships from entering." Branwen didn't know such things existed. Doubtless more Aquilan technology. To Xandru, Alba said, "Were we aware of the chain? Why didn't we account for it?"

The captain rounded on his cousin. "We were aware. It should have been down during the festival."

"Someone warned them we were coming!" Alba swiped at the deck with her *kladiwos*.

"Don't damage my ship." Xandru rolled his shoulders. The sign of agitation alarmed Branwen almost more than the continued noise of hulls being shredded.

"In battle, things rarely go according to plan," he said. "Which you well know, cousin." He gave Alba a long look. As Xandru barked orders at his crew in languages Branwen didn't understand, a sense of dread pervaded her. The ships farther back in the formation began lowering their sails, attempting an about-face. Chaos ensued.

Someone had betrayed their plan to the pirates. The element of surprise was lost.

On the battlements of the fortress, Branwen saw great fires being lit. They glowed like angry eyes—like the deathless eyes of the Shades. Her magic simmered beneath her skin, destruction calling to her, a sister.

Then the fire took flight. Enormous balls of flame were flung at the *Dragon Rising*. Branwen gasped. The fort was armed with five catapults.

The first fireball hit squarely on the mast of the *Dragon Rising*, slicing it in two. The top half crashed to the deck, burning. The second fireball, thankfully, landed just short of the prow, plunging into the water with a tremendous splash.

The remaining three shots hit their mark, crashing through the hull of the vessel.

The crippled ship burned as it sank.

Branwen bit down on her knuckles to stifle a scream. There would be no repairing the *Dragon Rising* this time. Her chest heaved. Would it be possible for any man to survive in the wreckage?

There was a temporary respite before the catapults were reloaded and began to assail the fleet once more.

An unexpected hand touched Branwen's shoulder and she batted it away.

"Captain Morgawr brought you from Iveriu," said Alba. Branwen nodded. Tristan must have told her. "I'm sorry."

"We still have a mission to carry out," said Xandru. Branwen swallowed. She couldn't mourn yet. Sorrow was for later.

Alba jutted out her chin. "Someone needs to get the chain down."

"Not us."

"What could be more important?" she retorted. Branwen saw panic in her eyes, and guilt. Alba had led men to slaughter herself; she would never abandon them to their fates.

"Finding out who sent the pirates to Karaez," Xandru answered. He exchanged a glance with Branwen. That was why Marc wanted the pirate king alive. "The peace will always be endangered if we don't know who started the war."

Alba's eyes widened. She parted her lips, but no protest came.

"Let's give the wheel of fortune a spin," said Xandru.

The *Mawort* broke farther away from the convoy. A good wind fanned its sail as full morning broke, illuminating the carnage at the harbor. The pirates continued to lob fireballs from their catapults. Another row of ships started to sink.

A golden lion followed the *Mawort*. Lord Diarmuid's ship. Ivernic vessels were smaller than those of the royal Kernyvak and Armorican fleets. While its design wasn't as ingenious as the *Mawort*'s, Diarmuid's ship managed to pursue at a fair clip.

Alba paced the bow as the island drew closer. Branwen stayed near Xandru. That was where she'd promised Marc she would be. Xandru was navigating them east along the coast, behind the fortress, toward a rocky beach. The water was shallower, a crystalline blue, and treacherous.

Tension closed like a vise around the *Mawort* as the captain dropped anchor. Behind them, Branwen glimpsed Diarmuid's ship come to a halt.

"Is Lord Diarmuid part of the plan?" Branwen asked. Xandru shook his head.

The crew started preparing a rowboat to take them to shore. Xandru called out various names. Branwen followed Xandru to the boat, and Alba joined them.

"You're staying here," Xandru told his cousin.

"Try to make me." Alba rested one hand on her hip while lifting her sword with the other. Eyeing Branwen, she said, "Why would you take the healer and not me?" Suspicion flared in her gaze.

"I'm not the heir to a kingdom," said Branwen, as Xandru snapped, "I don't have time to argue with you, Alba."

"No," she agreed. "You don't."

Xandru looked from Alba to the five men waiting to board the boat. He made a lightning judgment.

"You and Branwen stay together."

Her nostrils flared. "Fine."

He pointed at the men, naming each one for the women's benefit, although Branwen scarcely took them in. The sounds of the battle carried on the wind, and her heart thundered.

"This is Otho," Xandru said, directing a gaze at a short man of forty summers, skin pale and weather-beaten, gray at his temples, snaggle-toothed, with a bulbous nose. "Otho is not a supporter of the current pirate king. He will be our guide into the fort."

"We can't trust him!" Alba exclaimed. She stared at the pirate as if she were vivisecting him. Slowly.

"I don't need trust," said Xandru. "I have gold."

"He might have already betrayed us!"

"I've taken precautions." His voice was so cold that Branwen didn't want to know what those precautions might be.

Branwen, Alba, Xandru, Otho, and four other crewmembers crammed themselves into the rowboat. The remaining men lowered the boat into the water. They would protect the *Mawort* until their captain returned, prepared to make a speedy escape.

Another rowboat splashed against the choppy waters from Diarmuid's ship. Xandru grimaced as he spotted it. He didn't trust anyone but his own men. Given the trap the pirates had laid for the fleet, he had good reason.

Their boat reached shore first. Xandru ordered everyone out as two of the crew—a wiry man from the Melita Isles and a broad-shouldered Mílesian—dragged the boat onto the pebbled beach. Seawater permeated Branwen's calfskin boots.

As Diarmuid's rowboat reached the shallows, she saw Ruan sitting beside him. Her stomach clenched, although she was relieved to see he was unharmed. Six other men dressed in uniforms bearing the lion standard filled out the benches of the boat.

Diarmuid hopped out into the surf first. Morning light gleamed on his shorn head, the blue eye patch cutting across his face like a shadow.

He strode across the beach to meet the crew of *Mawort*, filled with purpose. He was utterly unrecognizable as the egotistical lord who had filched kisses from Branwen's cousin behind his king's back.

"Why did you follow us?" Xandru asked in crisp Aquilan, like a serrated blade.

Diarmuid raised an eyebrow at the interrogation. "Your reputation as a navigator precedes you, Captain Manduca," he said. "We need to get

219

to the chain tower and lower it. I presumed you would find a safe place to drop anchor—and I was right."

His gaze skipped to Alba, then Branwen. His lips pursed at the swords in their hands.

"Shouldn't you wait for the wounded on the ship?" he appealed to Branwen in Ivernic.

"Lady Branwen fights quite well," Ruan said, coming shoulder to shoulder with Diarmuid. Glancing at Alba, he switched to Aquilan and noted, "Unless I'm very lost, this isn't Armorica. Shouldn't you be on your way there with your husband?"

Alba snorted. "I must have boarded the wrong ship."

Xandru's men pressed in closer as the Ivermen surrounded Diarmuid and Ruan.

"Follow the coast, perhaps half an hour down the beach, and you'll see the chain tower," Xandru told Diarmuid.

"Where will *you* be going, Captain?" asked Ruan, glancing between Xandru and Branwen. He worried his knuckle against his lower lip.

"On an errand for your king."

Screams could be heard from the direction of the harbor. Diarmuid nodded at his men. There was no time to lose. People were dying. Every second mattered.

"Good luck, Captain Manduca," said Diarmuid, and he took off running.

Ruan held Branwen with his eyes. She saw fear—fear for her—in his amber gaze. Stepping into her, he said, "Battle lust suits you, Branwen," with a smile that spoke of other kinds of lust.

"Try not to get yourself killed," she replied hotly.

"*Comnaíde.*" *Always.*

He sprinted down the shore after the Ivermen.

Branwen touched her mother's brooch, praying for their safekeeping—all of them. Fighting their way into the chain tower was a suicide mission, but the only chance to change the tide of the battle. Otherwise the war for peace would be over before it began.

"We go," said Xandru. He nudged Otho into the lead.

Alba and Branwen followed immediately behind the captain and the turncoat, the four *Mawort* crewmembers at their backs. Branwen shared Alba's misgivings about following a pirate, who was also a traitor to his king, into a fortress teeming with cutthroats.

The eight of them moved like a pack inland, up the beach.

"They can see us coming," Alba muttered to Xandru.

He glanced at her over his shoulder. "We were supposed to use the chaos of our own attack on the harbor as cover." He gave an elegant shrug. "Adapt or die."

Branwen tightened her grip on her *kladíwos*, relieved it wasn't her only weapon.

Alba caught her eye. "Tristan would miss you if you died," she said. She gave Branwen a smile that was half snarl, brandishing her sword. "Let's avoid that."

A LIFE IN A MOMENT

THUNDER REVERBERATED AROUND BRANWEN AND the others, except it wasn't thunder.

Otho led the hunting party, for that is what they were, through dune grasses up a hill from the beach into a small wood. Branwen licked a salty bead of sweat from her upper lip; her leather trousers started to cling to her thighs, and she envied Alba her short hair as the temperature continued to rise.

The pirate was taking them on an indirect route, climbing the promontory on which the fortress was built, using the branches of alder and blackthorn trees as camouflage. Their nondescript clothing shouldn't mark them as foreigners when they reached their destination. Hopefully.

Branwen listened attentively for the shriek of a Death-Teller, but she only heard the song of a lark. Alba marked several trees with her sword.

"We may need to find our own way back," she said quietly to Branwen. Branwen gave a single nod.

Twigs crunched underfoot. This side of the island was strangely serene save for the booms of the fireballs raining down on the royal forces. Branwen watched as a coral-winged butterfly drifted from wildflower to wildflower, almost disoriented. Her magic fizzed in her veins, suspense mounting until it became unbearable.

"Eseult is your given name," Branwen said to Alba. "Kahedrin told me you didn't like it."

Alba pitched her a quizzical stare. "I have more given names than are worth counting, like most princesses," she said. "Eseult never fit. Alba did."

"No, I can't see you as an Eseult," Branwen agreed. Alba was as different from her cousin as a person could be.

"Although I imagine the court gossips across the southern continent will delight in the knowledge that Tristan was accused of an affair with one Eseult, and ended up married to another." Her laugh was brittle as she slashed the trunk of an alder.

"You danced well together at your wedding feast."

"He's quick on his feet." She smirked. "Just not as quick as me."

The trees thinned before them. A road stretched up the hillside to the fort, the impressions of wagon wheels well-trodden in the grass.

"Are we planning to knock on the front door?" Alba demanded to know. Xandru's posture was taut, ready to pounce.

"Otho will get us inside, little cousin," he said.

The hill grew steeper as they followed the road. A sharp drop on one side revealed a quarry. Granite had been in high demand at the peak of the Aquilan Empire and the pirates' ancestors had been sentenced to hard labor in the Veneti Isles. Men had been exiled from across Albion, as well as the southern continent. The prisoners must have quarried the stone to build the fortress themselves.

Sunlight glittered on the rectangular structure. Branwen spied four gatehouses, each in the center of the walls surrounding the fort to the north, south, east, and west. Clouds scudded above a further four watch-towers that loomed at the corners where the walls met. Master Bécc had always praised Aquilan architecture while lamenting their emperors.

A network of ramshackle dwellings extended outward from the shadows of the fortress. Some made of brick; others not much more than tents. It reminded Branwen of a rabbit warren.

"Who lives there?" she asked.

"The pirates have long since outgrown the fort," Xandru replied. "There are more and more families every year."

Branwen exhaled shortly. *Families.* The pirates had inhabited the Veneti Isles for a century. Of course there would be families. Still, her palms grew sweaty.

Xandru and Otho exchanged a few words. The pirate seemed to speak a version of Aquilan that Branwen could only half understand.

Pointing at the eastern gatehouse, Xandru said, "The man at the gate has been bribed. The catapults are mounted on the southern ramparts—most of the fighting men will be there."

"Won't the king be with them?" said Alba.

"Otho says no, he'll be in the old warden's villa."

"He could be leading us straight into a trap."

"Which is why I told you not to come. No more questions," Xandru commanded.

"Follow my lead and I won't have to explain your death to Queen Yedra." With a glance at Branwen, he told Alba, "Translate when I speak in Melitan."

She shrugged at Branwen. "I speak my mother's language."

Otho directed them through the encampment beyond the wall, and Branwen caught the scent of frying meat. Someone was cooking. A goat tied up outside a wooden hut bleated. Branwen hadn't expected to encounter signs of normalcy as a battle raged.

"Don't let your mind wander," Alba said, watching her from the corner of her eye. "Focus on your next breath."

A trench had been dug around the fortress but the moat was dry. The shouts of men rose from behind the walls.

Xandru turned to the four *Mawort* crewmembers, giving an order. The men fanned out around Branwen and Alba as they approached the east gatehouse.

A gangly boy, around Andred's age, but exceptionally tall, nodded at Otho. He had light brown hair and blue eyes.

The boy opened a small door cut into the gate to let them pass without raising the gate itself.

"Now the fun begins," said Xandru.

Inside, tens of dozens of men hurried back and forth, frenzied, running across an enormous open space, carrying supplies to the pirates on the battlements. Like Monwiku, the fortress was a small city, and the north and south sides were further divided into a grid pattern. Otho led the hunting party past a granary, stables, and many other buildings made from brick, including what looked like an Aquilan temple.

From above, Branwen heard cheers. Her stomach roiled. Not quite an hour had passed since Diarmuid and Ruan had headed in search of the chain tower. Yet the chain must still be in place.

Xandru raised his voice, speaking in Melitan. "The villa where the pirate king lives is located in the north quadrant," Alba translated for Branwen.

Two main thoroughfares—one running from the east gate to the west, the other from north to south—bisected the huge quadrangle, delineated by white cobblestones. They walked with purpose, but they didn't jog, trying not to draw attention to themselves, turning right where the avenues intersected. Branwen spotted women scattered amidst the men hauling supplies to the south-facing ramparts. Some wore trousers, some skirts. Neither she nor Alba looked out of place.

"Do you think all the women were pillaged in raids?" Branwen whispered.

"Some, probably," said Alba. "Some of the men, too. Others were doubtless born here."

The idea was chilling. "Then why don't they leave?"

"Maybe they have nowhere to go."

A portico supported by granite pillars surrounded the square villa; its roof of terracotta tiles glowed in the morning sun, the color of Mílesian spirits. Dotting the roof were painted statues of Aquilan gods. Branwen recognized Jana, the huntress with her bow and arrow.

As they passed through a rounded arch to the internal courtyard of the villa, Branwen's eyes brushed the mosaic at her feet: a three-headed dog with a snake for a tail. When the warden lived here he must have wanted to inspire fear in his prisoners. The pirate king must desire the same. How sadistic was he that Otho would risk his life to deliver the man to his enemies?

In the middle of the courtyard was a rectangular, sunken pool. For bathing, perhaps, although Branwen had never seen anything like it. The bottom was tiled with another mosaic of a woman emerging naked from a conch shell. Branwen was awed by the wealth of an empire that would construct something so lavish at a prison.

"Otho!" someone called out. A thickly muscled man, a head taller than Branwen, strode toward them. His face was a combination of hard lines, his skin tanned and leathery.

Otho didn't stop. Xandru followed their guide, and the rest of the party followed their captain. Next to Branwen, Alba tightened her grip on her *kladiwos*. "I should have given you more fighting lessons," she said from one side of her mouth. Infiltrating the fortress had thus far been too easy.

The other man broke into a sprint. He headed them off in front of the bathing pool.

Otho showed him an edgy grin. The two men traded what appeared to be pleasantries, again speaking a dialect of Aquilan that Branwen couldn't quite follow. She breathed in and out through her nose, jamming her lips into a line. She shifted her gaze to the Mílesian crewmember at her side. His eyes were pinned on this new friend of Otho's.

The smile slipped from the second pirate's face as he tipped his chin at Xandru.

Branwen held her breath as Xandru extended a hand, as if in friendship. Before she could exhale, the hard-faced man had started to shake Xandru's hand and Xandru pulled him in close. The pirate's eyes bulged.

Xandru spun on his heel, like he was dancing with the other man, and withdrew his dagger as he pushed him into the pool.

There was a splash and then a blossom of blood exploded in the water.

The pirate was dead before he could scream. Iron coated Branwen's tongue.

Someone else screamed.

Xandru cursed. Two more men launched themselves from another rounded archway, running toward them at a diagonal.

"Dwardu! Cherles!" Xandru shouted. The Mílesian and one of the Melitan Islanders ran straight for the pirates, raising their swords. A muscle flickered in Xandru's neck. "We find the king," he said in Aquilan.

Branwen jogged beside Alba, following Xandru and Otho into a second courtyard that contained an overgrown garden. The garden was lined with pillars in another portico. A man's grunt came very close to Branwen's ear, and her heart leapt into her mouth.

Steel clashed against steel as a crewmember Xandru called Iermu swung his sword toward the pirate who had drawn first blood. The fragrance of sweetbriar roses teased Branwen's nose, lush and incongruous.

"In there!" Otho yelled, the words simple enough for Branwen and Alba to comprehend. He pointed at an archway at the far end of the garden.

Otho sprinted ahead, lifting his sword, which was short and thick. The last crewmember of the *Mawort*, a man with a hawkish nose named Spiru, kept pace with the pirate. Xandru ran shoulder to shoulder with Branwen, Alba just behind.

"If there's any truth to the rumors about how Monwiku was saved," Xandru said as they neared the archway, "now is the time for a demonstration."

The air strained in Branwen's lungs. There was no way to call the Shades on land.

Xandru passed beneath the archway first. Branwen was halfway across the threshold when she head Alba cry out.

She whipped around. A female pirate with orange hair had grabbed the back of Alba's tunic. Branwen blinked. For less than a heartbeat, she saw Kahedrin dueling with King Marc in the castle gardens.

Alba turned on her heel like a whirlwind, leaving the other woman holding a scrap of fabric. Branwen watched the women fight, torn between her promise to Marc to keep Xandru safe and her need to balance the scales.

The orange-haired pirate wielded a curved sword, closer in shape to a *fálkr*. She swiped at Alba's thigh, landing a blow. Alba hissed. She charged the pirate woman, slashing at her forearm.

Branwen ran back to Alba as Alba shouted, "Go! Help Xandru!"

Branwen's appearance momentarily distracted the pirate and Alba sliced the meaty part of the other woman's shoulder. Rushing from the opposite direction of the garden, the male pirate who had attacked Iermu crashed through the rosebushes. There was no sign of Iermu.

Alba roared as the orange-haired pirate took another swipe at her midsection but failed to land the blow. She twirled around, kicking out the other woman's ankle. The woman fell to the tile, hitting her head. Her eyes rolled back in her skull.

The man who had bested Iermu was bald, and blood smeared both his lips and teeth. He let out a battle cry as he ran at them headlong, a broadsword above his head.

Branwen didn't make a decision. She let impulse guide her.

She switched her *kladíwos* to her left hand. A small black flame erupted along the mark of Dhusnos, burning through the lace covering her palm.

The wail of a Death-Teller echoed in Branwen's mind. Alba shoved her to one side, showing the pirate a vicious smile. She taunted him with her weapon.

Branwen launched herself at their attacker, running toward him at an angle. She lashed out at him with her flaming hand, managing to make contact with his spine just before he could bring the sword down on Alba's neck.

The bullish man seized. He stumbled backward.

Euphoria swept through Branwen. The pirate's grip on his sword loosened as he staggered to his knees. His complexion grew whiter than a sail.

"Stay back!" Alba hollered at Branwen, rushing toward the pirate, her *kladíwos* aloft. Branwen ignored her. Panting, she took two steps toward the pirate from behind, placing her right hand on his shoulder.

Fire surged through Branwen. She laughed as memories coursed through her. Memories of a life she hadn't lived. A scared boy hiding in the loft of a barn. A callous man who derided the women he used for sex.

Alba's eyes shone with horror. She clasped the medallion of Ankou.

When Branwen removed her hand, the big man fell flat on his face.

His cheeks were sunken and he looked as if he'd been dead for weeks. Branwen felt as if she were floating. She'd consumed his life in a moment. She'd savored it.

Cherles, one of the Melitan Islanders, loped into the garden from the first courtyard. Dwardu wasn't with him. He looked from Branwen to Alba.

Branwen pointed toward the archway. Cherles nodded. He gave the pirate facedown on the stone only the briefest of glances. If somehow they all managed to make it out of the fortress alive, Branwen and Alba would have to have a very uncomfortable conversation.

The princess clutched her *kladíwos* and stabbed the orange-haired pirate in the gut for good measure as she and Branwen ran after Cherles.

Masculine voices in even tones could be heard from inside the room where Otho had led Xandru.

Cherles stalked in first. Alba and Branwen entered together. Alba maintained several handsbreadth of distance between herself and Branwen.

Just inside the doorway, the hawk-nosed Melitan Islander, Spiru, stood with a knife at his throat.

A pirate with one eye lay dead at the feet of a man who lounged on a reclining chair carved from marble that resembled a bed. Otho brandished his short sword at the man.

Xandru maintained his own sword aloft, though he managed to make it seem casual. A stocky man holding a battle-ax had positioned himself between Xandru and the lounging man.

"So glad you could join us," Xandru said to Branwen, shocking her by speaking Ivernic. Yet another language the spy knew, apparently.

The lounging man lifted his eyebrows.

"An Iverwoman?" he said. His face was rounder, more childlike, than Branwen would have expected from a pirate. He was slim, and his hair was so blond it was nearly white.

"This is Remus," Xandru announced as if there were nothing peculiar about the introduction.

Outrage lit Branwen. *No.* It was impossible. The pirate king, the man responsible for so much destruction in Iveriu, could not be her countryman.

"Remus is not an Ivernic name," Branwen said to the lounging man.

His eyes became slits. "I was brought to the Veneti Isles when I was six years old. No one cared about my name. No one from Iveriu came looking for me." He sat up. "I have no kingdom. I am free. When I realized that, I chose my own name."

Branwen's chin trembled, anger overwhelming her.

"But now I am a king myself," boasted Remus. He was no more than thirty summers, yet he had risen from a plundered boy to king of the pirates. He must be savage indeed, and pragmatic.

"We were just negotiating the terms of King Remus's surrender," Xandru said blithely.

"I don't think that's entirely accurate," Remus countered. "Your

231

fleet is being torn to pieces by my catapults. And you won't make it out of this fortress alive." To emphasize his point, he nodded at the pirate holding Spiru at knifepoint.

The man slit Spiru's throat.

Branwen's heart kicked but she suppressed a scream.

Xandru betrayed no emotion as his crewmember slumped to the floor, blood gushing down his tunic. Branwen didn't know whether it was because the captain truly felt nothing, or because showing allegiance to anyone or anything besides his objective would be a sign of weakness.

"I believe we still have the numbers," said Xandru, panning his gaze over Otho, Cherles, Alba, and Branwen.

"Inside this room, yes," Remus acknowledged. Above his lounge chair hung a threadbare tapestry of some Aquilan feast. "Outside?" He raised his shoulders. "Not so much."

"King Marc wishes to speak with you, but he didn't say you had to be in excellent condition."

The pirate king laughed, and the sound reminded Branwen of the goat she'd heard earlier.

"I don't think we have many common interests," said Remus. "Aside from comely Iverwomen." He leered at Branwen. "Isn't there an Ivernic queen on the throne of Kernyv these days?"

"There is. But no, King Marc wishes to know who's been staking your raids."

"Ah. Well, I'm afraid I'm not inclined to tell him."

The man with an ax took a step closer to Xandru, and Branwen moved closer to the captain.

"I would very much appreciate it if you came with us," Branwen said to the pirate king. She showed him a placid smile. Feeling a rush of power, she stepped in front of Xandru.

"As much as I would enjoy your appreciation," said Remus, "I cannot oblige."

Branwen lowered her sword, raising her right hand to the cheek of the ax-wielding man. He startled, then laughed. He said something she didn't understand to Remus, but which she inferred to be lascivious.

The ax rattled as it fell to the tiled floor.

A different villa, on a lush green coastline, flashed through Branwen's mind. She saw a boy with a gray cat, caring for its kittens.

Xandru tugged her hand away from the pirate. It was too late. There was no more light in his eyes.

Remus jumped to his feet. "By the Old Ones, what was that?" Fear pulled his features into a sneer.

Though shock washed over him, Cherles wasted no time in dispatching the pirate who had slit Spiru's throat.

A shout could be heard from the garden. A few moments later, a stocky man, chest heaving, rushed into the room. Scrambling for breath, the newly arrived man forced out his message for the pirate king.

"The chain is down," said Xandru. "The chain is down."

Alba stabbed the stocky newcomer in the heart.

To Remus, Xandru said, "Would you like to reconsider your position?"

The pirate king's eyes hadn't left Branwen. Otho hit his temple with the pommel of his sword.

"I believe that qualifies as a yes," said Xandru, and this time his smile wasn't careless at all.

THE POETRY OF LOSS

PIRATES STREAMED OUT OF THE fortress, racing for the harbor to get to their ships. All of the gates were raised. The moored ships had been dangled like bait to lure in the royal fleets, but the pirate king had been overconfident that the chain would protect them.

In the chaos, Otho procured a wheelbarrow, loading Remus into it unceremoniously and covering him with a woolen tarp. Branwen walked next to Xandru as they wheeled the pirate king straight out the east gate.

Alba kept her distance as they hustled through the encampment on the other side of the trench. People were dashing from their tents, down the south side of the promontory toward the harbor. Cherles pushed the wheelbarrow along the road at a steady clip, and the pirates were too panicked to notice that he and his companions were headed in the opposite direction from the battle.

Before they started to descend the hill, the vantage point allowed

Branwen to glimpse the royal ships that had retreated now changing tack again to rejoin the fight. Diarmuid and Ruan had done it. They'd given the fleet a chance of success.

She hoped they were still alive.

When the hunting party, returning with their prize, reached the wood without being followed, some of the tension left Branwen's shoulders. She noticed a subtle shift in Xandru's gait as well. Otho scratched his nose, his expression brooding despite the captive beneath the tarp. She wondered again what Otho's motives were and whether he would be returning to Kernyv on the *Mawort*.

Alba eyed Branwen warily. She flicked the tip of her sword against the trunks of the trees she had marked on their way to the fort. The sun beat down on them from directly overhead, the leafy branches dappling their faces with cool spots of shade. Branwen tasted salt on the breeze as they neared the shore.

The wheelbarrow bounced as Cherles navigated it through the dune grasses toward the pebbled beach, jostling the unconscious pirate king within.

"Look!" said Alba. "They're coming." Excitement lifted her voice. Branwen spotted them, too, farther along the beach: Ruan, Diarmuid, and two of the Ivermen.

Her relief was fleeting. "They're not alone," said Xandru. Branwen looked again. Five men were pursuing them, and they were gaining ground.

"We get Remus to the ship," Xandru commanded.

"We can't leave them," said Branwen. Her heart twisted. She hadn't been able to save Endelyn, and she cared for Ruan—even if she couldn't love him back in the way he wanted.

"They're not part of the mission, Branwen. They knew the risks."

"*I'm* not leaving them."

"Do what you must," Xandru told her. "I'm taking Remus to the *Mawort*."

Magic flaring, Branwen bolted in the direction of Diarmuid and Ruan, the dune grasses giving way to rocks as she descended the slope. Her ankles ached as she sped over the uneven ground. Exhilaration spurred her on and for a ghastly moment, Branwen thought she saw the bullish pirate and the ax-wielding man running beside her. She didn't know their names, yet she'd witnessed the most intimate details of their lives.

She had stolen them.

Something solid banged against Branwen's shoulder. "I don't leave anyone behind," said Alba. The other woman burst forward, shouting at Ruan in Aquilan and lifting her *kladíwos*.

Alba and Branwen converged on the band of Ivermen just a breath before the pirates. Diarmuid's shirt was sprayed with blood and he'd lost his eye patch.

One of the Ivernic sailors, his dark hair thick and frizzy, had a huge gash on his thigh. He was limping, leaning on his crewmate, a man with russet-colored hair and features like cut glass.

"I count five!" Branwen yelled in Ivernic.

Ruan ran to her side. He had a wound on his shoulder but it didn't look deep. They exchanged a sideways glance. "Not dead yet," he said. "As promised."

Alba clashed swords with a pirate whose mouth glinted gold as he bared his teeth. Diarmuid dueled with a long-haired pirate who looked no more than fifteen. Branwen couldn't keep track of who was fighting whom, because her *kladíwos* sang as another sword struck it.

The man at the other end of the blade was Branwen's height and he wore a silver hoop through either ear. His face was sunburned, and his expression ugly.

Branwen retreated a pace. The pirate pursued. He spit blood onto the black and white pebbles. She searched for Ruan with her gaze, but he was now engaged in his own sword fight.

The pirate targeting Branwen circled his curved blade in the air. He thrust and she jumped back into the surf. The tide was coming in and sea foam covered the rocks. Branwen's breath came in pants.

She was no match for the pirate physically, yet she felt a surge of strength. Maybe from the life force she had absorbed. She'd been lucky not to kill Alba the day she'd tried to escape.

The man snarled as he edged Branwen farther back into the water. At his feet, the skeletal fox prowled out of the tide. The creature shrieked at Branwen, red eyes burning. It wanted her to drain the pirate of life. She felt the fox's desire.

Or, perhaps it was her own.

She lowered her sword, and confusion crinkled the pirate's brow. Then he bellowed a laugh. He thought Branwen wanted to surrender.

He lunged closer; her pulse pounded, acid sloshing in her stomach.

The pirate stopped dead. The tip of a sword sliced through his tunic from behind.

Stunned, he fell onto the rocks with a thud. Blood spurted from his mouth, covered his front.

Diarmuid's *kladíwos* dripped crimson as he removed it from the pirate's back.

"Are you all right, Branwen?" he asked.

She nodded, grateful yet frustrated. The fox yowled and vanished into the surf. Diarmuid gave a tight smile, satisfied, spun around, and ran toward Ruan.

Branwen spied the long-haired pirate dead on the ground. So too was the Iverman who had already been wounded. Alba danced around the man with golden teeth, though she was clearly tiring.

Diarmuid and Ruan fought an ogre of a man together. The russet-haired Iverman had been chased into the dunes by a pirate Branwen realized was a woman, and the Iverman was losing.

Branwen sprinted past Ruan to help her countryman. To her surprise, from the direction of the moored ships, she saw Xandru tearing down the beach.

Pebbles became sand, tall grasses whipping against Branwen's knees. Xandru caught up to her right before she reached the Iverman dueling with the pirate woman.

"Gods curse you," Xandru said. "I won't be the one to tell Marc you're dead."

"I'm already cursed, Xandru." And part of her wanted another taste of life.

He clenched his jaw, eyebrows drawing together, then attacked the female pirate before she could hear his approach. Xandru was a blur of motion and instantaneously the woman was in his arms, almost as if she had swooned.

He laid her down gently in the grasses and closed her eyes.

"Thank you," sputtered the Iverman.

Jerking his head at Branwen, Xandru replied, "Thank her."

"Thank you," the man repeated, still in shock. He clutched at a wound on his hip. "I'm Bearach."

As the three of them jogged back down the dune, Branwen saw Alba finally land a killing blow on the golden-toothed pirate.

Ruan had fallen sideways onto the beach. Diarmuid continued to battle the enormous pirate alone, reminding Branwen of how he'd fought the Reykir Islander at the Champions Tournament.

"Ruan!" Branwen called out. He didn't seem to be moving.

Somehow Diarmuid knocked the sword from the pirate's grasp. With a guttural shout, he struck the pirate in the chest and the other man fell backward.

Diarmuid turned to Ruan, crouching down beside his companion-at-arms. Branwen ran faster than she knew she was capable, scanning his body for injuries.

"Look out!" cried Alba.

It was too late.

While Diarmuid was kneeling next to Ruan, the giant pirate got to his feet. He swung his sword down on Diarmuid's neck. Blood spurted violently from the artery like a fountain.

"No!" Branwen shouted.

The pirate stumbled back a pace from the force of his own blow, then teetered face-first into the sand. Before she could blink, Alba had parted the pirate from his head.

Branwen crashed down beside Diarmuid. His blood was hot as it sprayed her face. She clasped his hand. There was nothing mortal that could repair such a wound, and her healing magic was gone.

"One Iveriu," Diarmuid rasped. They were his final words.

Tears scalded Branwen's eyes. As she crawled over to Ruan, she put two fingers to his neck. He was alive. She kissed him without thinking, her lips coated with another man's blood.

Xandru and Alba hovered above them, weapons still drawn.

Bearach bent down on one knee beside his fallen lord.

"We need to get back to the *Mawort*," said Xandru. "Now."

Ruan's eyelids quivered. He groaned. Branwen had never thought a groan so beautiful. She glanced at Diarmuid, his one eye staring up at the infinite sky.

"We need to bury him," she told Xandru.

He shook his head. "No time."

Ruan came around, rubbing his head. Sitting upright, his eyes focused on the man lying dead beside him. Genuine pain streaked his face.

"I'm sorry, Branwen," he said. "Diarmuid was a good man."

"Can you walk?" Xandru asked Ruan, switching to Aquilan. He nodded. "Then get up." Impatience striated his words.

"*Wait!*" Branwen's voice was high, almost hysterical. She wouldn't let Diarmuid become a Shade like Keane because his soul was unclaimed.

Swiveling her torso toward Bearach, she asked the Iverman, "Do you know the mourning prayer?"

"Do it quickly," said Xandru, exhaling in exasperation.

Branwen spied a chip of Rigani stone among the pebbles, gleaming green like the cliffs of Iveriu. Ivermen carried them for luck. It must have fallen from Diarmuid's pocket. Choking down a surge of emotion, Branwen kissed the stone and placed it on Diarmuid's mouth.

Bríga was invoked at Ivernic funerals because she inspired the poetry of loss. She helped people give voice to their grief. Branwen recited the prayer she had spoken at her parents' funerals so many years ago.

Goddess Ériu, she pleaded silently. *Do not abandon Diarmuid in this foreign land. Don't let Dhusnos claim him.*

Branwen and Bearach repeated the prayer to Bríga over the other fallen Iverman.

Ruan watched her as she collected Lord Diarmuid's sword from the rocks. Xandru strode ahead as they followed the beach back to the

Mawort. Alba stayed close to her cousin. The Rigani stone on the hilt of Diarmuid's *kladíwos* glittered in the midday sun. The northern lord had been bold, and he had been wise. If the fleet succeeded in taking the Veneti Isles, it would be because of his courage.

Branwen sidled next to Bearach, holding out Diarmuid's sword.

"When you return to Iveriu, take this to Talamu Castle. Give the *kladíwos* to Lady Fionnula."

"I will." He accepted the blade with reverence.

Branwen had never been particularly fond of Lady Fionnula, but the woman had lost both her husband and now her son in a matter of months. She wanted his mother to have this vestige of Diarmuid.

Ruan tugged at Branwen's sleeve, and Bearach walked on ahead.

"What happened at the fort?" he asked. He ran a hand through his hair, slick with sweat.

"We got what we came for," Branwen said.

"Whatever that is." He muttered something in Kernyvak.

Scanning his profile, she said, "Do you have spots in your vision? Do you need to vomit?"

Ruan laughed. "Always a healer first."

He didn't know how wrong he was. Branwen glanced at the mark of Dhusnos. Delivering the Dark One his Shade might not be as difficult as she'd once believed—and the realization terrified her.

"You didn't answer my question," she said shortly. "Are you seeing double?"

"No. No, I'm seeing fine. Ready for more action." Branwen looked at him in surprise. "The chain is down, but the fleet needs reinforcements," he said.

Her stomach lurched. "You were brave," she said.

Tenderness softened Ruan's features. "As were you. Like always."

Under his breath, he said, "Did you use your fire?" and concern brimmed from his eyes.

Branwen had used something worse. Bríga's fire was gifted to her for protection. Her withering power was a worse abomination than merely burning men alive. What rumors would circulate about Branwen now?

"I'm well enough," Branwen lied. She took Ruan's hand, and he shuddered a breath. "I'll see you in Monwiku," she told him sternly.

"You do love giving me orders." He raised her hand to his lips. "And I still don't mind."

Ruan and Branwen reached the rowboats. The *Mawort* and the Ivernic vessel cast long shadows on the waves. Bearach was waiting to row Ruan back to their ship.

"This is where we part," she said.

He walked Branwen to the waterline and cocked an eyebrow at the wheelbarrow.

"Get in!" Alba shouted at Branwen. The princess was seated at the back of their rowboat, Xandru in front; Cherles sat in the middle, holding the oars.

On the bench between Alba and Cherles sat Otho with the pirate king across his lap, a dagger tilted at his chest, ready to slide into Remus's heart.

Branwen watched Ruan as his eyes skidded across the faces of the passengers. His gaze settled on the pirate king and his jaw tensed.

If she hadn't known him so well, Ruan's reaction would have been imperceptible. But she couldn't lie to herself. Not now. Not after everything.

She knew what flashed in the eyes of her former lover when he spotted Remus.

Recognition.

"You kissed me just now," Ruan said to Branwen. "When you thought I was dead." He squeezed her hand. "If I make it back to Kernyv, I want to take you to my father's grave."

He released her and sprinted toward Bearach.

Branwen felt the wind blow through her as if she were made of straw.

Somehow, Ruan knew the pirate king. She thought he loved her, but he'd thought she loved him. Perhaps they'd never been more than two traitors.

Her heart overflowed with grief, but Bríga gave her no words.

LIVING LIGHT

THROUGH THE SPYGLASS, BRANWEN WATCHED the royal fleets sail into the pirates' harbor as the *Mawort* set a course for Kernyv.

The afternoon sun ripened from a buttery yellow to harvest orange and, finally, winter-rose. When the pirate king at last woke he found himself in restraints, and Branwen quenched his thirst with a waterskin laced with enough Clíodhna's dust to keep him asleep for the duration of the voyage to Kerynv. Otho sat with him belowdecks, in the captain's quarters, grim-faced. His knife ready.

Branwen dragged a crate to an empty section of the deck. She counted the crests of the waves. She should be as exhausted as the other members of the hunting party. *Slayer.* She pushed images of the men she'd killed from her mind. They weren't enough to fulfill her bargain with Dhusnos. She couldn't offer him a soul she had killed in self-defense or defending another.

The crew of the *Mawort* went about their activities in a somber manner. They had lost three of their own capturing the pirate king. Alba had climbed up the rigging with the fleet grace of a spider, and she stayed there.

Xandru approached Branwen, the sunset pink on his cheeks. He carried a tunic made from beige linen in his hand.

"I thought you might like a clean shirt," he said.

She lowered her gaze to her chest. Her tunic was crusted with Diarmuid's dried blood. With half a smile, she took the fresh tunic from him. Xandru sat down on the crate beside her. Leaning back on his hands, he said, "We lost friends today."

Branwen fidgeted with the fabric between her fingers. A few days ago, she wouldn't have called Diarmuid a friend. Now she did mourn his death. He would have been a strong leader for Uladztir.

"We might have lost more if not for you," said Xandru. He pried Branwen's right hand gently away from the balled cloth.

"If Marc didn't need you at Monwiku," he said, "I would offer you a place on my ship."

She pictured the wreckage of the *Dragon Rising* at the bottom of the harbor, Captain Morgawr in a watery grave. "I hope their sacrifices won't be in vain."

Could Dhusnos claim a soul devoted to a different god?

"You think you're cursed," Xandru said in a neutral tone. "Perhaps, so am I." He patted the sword at his hip. "We both use the weapons we have, and we do what must be done."

Branwen drew back her hand and intertwined her fingers.

"Do you think the pirate king will tell us who hired him to attack Karaez?" she said.

"With the proper motivation."

"Leaving him alone with Alba might suffice."

Xandru followed Branwen's gaze to the rigging. He gave one wry laugh. "I think Remus is far more afraid of you, my lady."

Her cheeks tingled. "Are you afraid of me, Captain?"

"I wouldn't want you as my enemy," he replied. "If I thought you were a threat to Marc, I'd promptly throw you overboard." Xandru said it lightly, as a joke, but Branwen knew it wasn't.

"How do you know Otho didn't betray our plans to the pirate king?" Branwen asked, changing the subject. Waves lapped against the hull.

"Otho's wife and daughter are being held in Kernyv—as collateral." Branwen flexed her interlocked knuckles. "He didn't want to live under Remus's regime, and he doesn't want to stay for the aftermath," said Xandru. "When we arrive in Marghas, he'll be given gold. He and his family can start a new life. He's half decent, I'd say."

If Xandru thought Otho was half decent, Branwen didn't want to meet anyone he considered to be craven. "Does Marc know?" she asked. She doubted he would approve of holding two women hostage to achieve his ends.

The captain gave her a canny look. "A king need not be bothered with the details of all the tasks he delegates."

Branwen had her answer and she decided not to press the matter.

"What will become of the Veneti Isles if we win?" she said. "There are women and children there."

Xandru shrugged. "The Veneti Isles belong to Kernyv. Armorica and Iveriu acknowledged Kernyv's claim in the treaty," he said. "The people will have to accept Kernyvak rule."

"I don't think that will be easy." And Otho was likely smart not to want to return.

"Governing never is." Xandru stretched his arms above his head. "One problem at a time, my lady. First we need to get the truth from Remus."

Branwen gazed down at her lap; she examined the tunic, which had a pattern of concentric squares meticulously embroidered around the collar. A swell of nausea rose from the pit of her stomach.

"How much do you know about the pirate king?" she said, unable to forget Ruan's reaction upon seeing him.

"Otho confirmed his story that Remus was captured in a raid on Iveriu as a boy."

"A raid authorized by King Merchion?"

"I'd assume so," Xandru replied. He leaned forward, tilting his head to give Branwen a level stare. "You should know, I thought Marc was wrong to stop staking the pirates' raids. I told him he would lose control of them—and he did."

"I'm glad he didn't take your advice." Though Branwen could hardly be shocked by the captain's expediency. She shifted her weight on the crate. "Has Remus ever visited Kernyv before?" she asked.

"It's possible." Xandru's eyes grew more intense. "Why?"

Branwen twisted the collar of the shirt, pulling the fabric taut. She didn't want to believe Ruan had been in league with the pirates this whole time. It didn't make sense. He loved Marc. Still, he knew Remus, Branwen was sure of it.

"What is it?" Xandru said low. Dangerous. "Have you seen him before?"

He pressed his hands over hers.

"No, it's just—on the beach . . ."

"What?" he demanded.

"When Ruan spotted Remus on the boat. The look he gave him . . . he seemed to recognize him." Branwen's chest caved as she exhaled. "That's all."

"Thank you."

"I don't know if it means anything."

"We'll find out," he said. "Marc is right to trust you." Xandru pushed to his feet. "You should take one of the hammocks, sleep a few hours."

"I'm not tired," said Branwen, dismissive.

"Your body will give out before your mind. It's always the way after a battle."

Branwen watched the sun drop below the sea, then made her way below deck. The crew gave her privacy in the main section to wash herself with a scratchy cloth. She slipped on the fresh tunic, pinning her mother's brooch to the collar. Crawling into a hammock, Branwen took a nip from the waterskin containing the remnants of the Clíodhna's dust.

She didn't want to think about what Xandru might do with information she'd provided him. She didn't want to think about Ruan fighting in another battle, of his warm lips or the many lies they had told each other.

Branwen closed her eyes and fell into a sleep that was far from dreamless.

Tutir and Bledros were there. The two pirates. Kahedrin. Nameless Armoricans.

And Keane.

Keane opened his arms, and Branwen went to him willingly.

He wrapped her green ribbon around her throat.

A woman after my own heart.

✛ ✛ ✛

Though she tossed and turned in the hammock, she didn't wake until just before dawn.

Eyes watched Branwen by lantern light.

"I suppose you think we're even," said Alba. She lazed in the hammock opposite Branwen's. How long had the other woman been watching her?

Branwen swung her legs to the floor, not wanting to remain prone.

"I don't expect you to change your opinion of me," she replied.

"Why didn't you use your—your power on Kahedrin?" Alba gripped the talisman of Ankou, the silver skeleton catching the light.

"Bríga gave me healing magic. Fire that could create and destroy. When you attacked Monwiku, I needed something else."

The princess squinted at her. "I don't understand."

Branwen took a long breath. The ship creaked as the waves rolled against it. Alba had seen her drain the life from two men—had already witnessed enough to betray her to the seers, to the court, to *everyone*. There was no hiding from the princess. And suddenly she didn't want to. Here, in the darkness of the hull, she wanted Alba to know how she had forced Branwen's hand.

"Your attack was brazen—and brilliant. We were losing," Branwen began, a strange urge, pressure building in her breast. "Iveriu has known war my entire life. I came with my cousin to Kernyv to protect the peace. I couldn't let it fall apart. I *wouldn't*."

She turned her right palm face up, and Alba flinched, drawing back in her hammock.

"Monwiku didn't have enough soldiers. It was going to fall," Branwen revealed to the other woman. The more she spoke, the greater the pressure grew to shrive herself, for Alba to understand what she'd sacrificed. "After I . . . after I killed Kahedrin, I threw myself on the mercy of the Dark One. The other Old Ones couldn't help me."

Alba's lips quivered as Branwen continued. "Dhusnos took my healing magic and replaced it with this." She stroked the outline of the mark.

"That's how you stopped my escape."

"Yes." Branwen nodded. "I didn't realize what was happening at first. I—I didn't intend to hurt you. I'm relieved I didn't kill you. Although you might not believe me." As the truth spilled from her, she grew dizzy. Unfettered.

Alba pulled at her gray strands of hair.

"Maybe Ankou saved me."

"Maybe she did."

The two women were so quiet Branwen thought she could hear the flame flicker inside the lantern. Yet part of her wanted to laugh or cry. Perhaps both.

"After I saw Kahedrin felled—" Alba swallowed. "I ran from the gardens. I wanted to find someone important to kill. Someone who would mean as much to King Marc as my brothers meant to me."

The words tumbled out as if they'd been held in too long, as if Branwen's confession had induced her own.

"I killed two members of the Royal Guard and it wasn't impersonal, like in war," she admitted. "I enjoyed it. I wanted them to suffer." Her breathing grew more shallow. "I returned to the gardens in time to see a tidal wave destroy all of my ships. My men being devoured."

Alba shook her head, revolted, a tremor in her hand. "I never took sailors' tales about the Sea of the Dead seriously. I thought I must be delirious with grief."

"The Shades are very real."

Disgust gripped her face. "You summoned them because of me," said Alba, her voice grainy. "You sacrificed your healing magic because

I attacked you—and I was wrong. Kernyv didn't kill Havelin. All of my men died for nothing. Kahedrin . . ."

The other woman's anguish moved Branwen, surprised her. "We'll get to the truth," she assured her.

A tear slid over the scar on Alba's cheek. Branwen wanted to comfort her, although she didn't know how.

"We're even," the princess declared. "I can't forgive you. But I doubt you can forgive me, either."

"I have lost count of the mistakes I've made in trying to protect the people I love," said Branwen. "I'm not counting yours, Captain."

Alba's lips twitched. "I have no ship, Healer Branwen." Branwen raised an eyebrow. "That's what the servants at Monwiku call you, and the guardsmen."

Branwen had thought it was only Seer Ogrin's name for her, one she chafed at.

"I am a healer with no magic," she said.

"Do you only use magic to heal people?" asked Alba.

"No. Tristan was the first." Branwen paused. "Ask him the story—tell him I told you to."

She nodded. "I will," said Alba. "And if you don't need magic, I'd like you to take a look at the wound on my thigh. It's throbbing."

"Of course. My satchel is on the deck."

Alba pushed to standing, ducking in the low clearance, and she winced as she put pressure on her injured leg.

"You stay here. I'll fetch it," Branwen offered.

"I want to see the dawn."

Branwen knew better than to try to argue with her. Alba climbed the rope ladder first, and Branwen emerged behind her just as the sun skimmed above the waves.

A brilliant green flash streaked across the horizon. It took Branwen's breath away.

"Living light," whispered Alba. "Sailors believe it's a portent."

"Good or bad?" Branwen asked.

"Auspicious."

RED RIGHT HAND

THE DOCKS SEEMED LONELY TO Branwen when the *Mawort* reached the Port of Marghas. Barren. A few fishing boats were moored along the pier, bobbing beside one Armorican vessel—the ship that should have been ferrying Alba and Tristan to Karaez.

The *Dragon Rising* would not be returning to port. Would Diarmuid's ship return without him? How many ships had been lost in the battle for the Veneti Isles?

Branwen descended the gangway, taking in the verdant cliffs that had made her heart pang with longing for Iveriu when she'd first arrived in Kernyv. Now her life was here, and her homeland seemed more distant with each passing day.

"Branwen!"

The afternoon was gray yet Tristan's brown skin glowed, his smile open. Whenever she looked at him, part of her would always see the beautiful stranger on the raft, feel that same sense of wonder. It had been true even when Branwen despised him, and she did not despise him now.

In the next moment, "Alba!" he called, waving frantically. His new wife returned his wave from the deck of the *Mawort*. Tristan sprinted down the dock, the tide splashing the wood.

Branwen touched her mother's brooch, biting the inside of her cheek, and forced the past back into the box where it belonged. *The right fight.* Captain Morgawr had given his life for peace, and it was closer than ever before.

Tristan couldn't stop himself from clasping Branwen's shoulders, nearly bowling her over, as if convincing himself she was real.

"You made it back," he said huskily. He glanced around the empty port. "Where are the others?"

"Still fighting. It was an ambush." The hazel flecks in Tristan's eyes glinted with enmity at her words. "Tristan, the *Dragon Rising* is gone." Branwen's tongue grew thick. "I'm so sorry. I know Morgawr sailed with your father."

"Who betrayed us?" Tristan barked.

"Hopefully the pirate king will tell us," said Alba. She strode down the gangway, limping slightly. Tristan released his hold on Branwen and rushed toward his wife.

Offering her a hand onto the dock, he said, "Are you injured?"

"Nothing serious," Alba told him, lifting a shoulder. "Healer Branwen patched me up." She tilted one corner of her mouth at Branwen, almost teasing.

Tristan looked to her for confirmation. "A few stitches," she said.

Relief crossed his features, followed by consternation. "I searched for you everywhere," he said to Alba, giving her hand a gentle squeeze. "It seems I'm no competition for a war."

"I had to be there, Tristan," she replied. He sighed as he studied his wife.

"I'm glad you're safe." Alba darted a glance at Branwen. "Both of you," Tristan said.

Heavier footsteps on the gangway attracted all of their attention. Xandru descended first, Otho and Cherles holding up the pirate king between them. Remus was upright, but still stumbling. Branwen might have been too liberal with the dose of Clíodhna's dust.

"I found something you lost," Xandru said to Tristan by way of greeting. The captain laughed as Alba glared at him. "Marc is at the castle?"

"He'll be happy to see you," Tristan replied. With a dubious look, he said, "This is the leader of the pirates?" and jutted his chin toward Remus. The other man's baby face and hair like dandelion fuzz didn't make him appear the most likely prospect.

Cherles and Otho half walked, half dragged the pirate king closer. Remus's hands and feet were both secured with manacles. He gazed up at Tristan drowsily, his pupils moon round.

"The Old Ones must love you, Prince Tristan," the pirate king slurred. Tristan startled at Remus's use of Ivernic. "The last time I saw you, you were slit from stem to stern, floating half dead in the Ivernic Sea."

Tristan cut a panicked look at Branwen. Alba pitched her gaze between the two of them. "What did he say?" the princess wanted to know, her tone a mixture of confusion and annoyance.

Remus bleated his goat-like chuckle. Xandru ordered Cherles and Otho to keep the pirate king moving down the pier.

Alba crossed her arms, waiting for an explanation. Xandru also looked at Tristan expectantly.

"Last year," Tristan began, addressing his wife in Aquilan, "I was aboard a vessel in the Royal Fleet, practicing evasive maneuvers, when we were attacked by pirates. I was injured and fell overboard."

"You told me it was a merchant ship," Branwen snapped, incensed, without thinking.

Tristan pivoted to face her. "We weren't on a raid, I swear it." His eyes were beseeching. "A storm blew us closer to Iveriu than we realized."

Branwen dropped her gaze to her hands. What was one more white lie among so many darker ones? Staring at her palms, her breath caught in her throat. She clutched at her chest as if she'd been struck.

She had seen it. Branwen had watched the attack on Tristan's ship in the waters, the first time the Wise Damsel had taught her to scry.

In the vision, she'd been aboard a pirate ship with black sails, chasing a Kernyvak vessel with a sea-wolf on its sail, and she'd sighted Castle Rigani in the distance.

Tristan stared at Branwen but she wasn't seeing him at all.

"I'm sorry, Branwen," he said. He took her hand in his, and once more her right hand sparkled with blood.

She had asked the Old Ones to tell her who was the greatest threat to peace—and they had.

A red hand.

The red hand of House Whel.

The Old Ones had answered Branwen months ago. She wasn't listening. She'd only seen her own guilt.

Branwen pulled away from Tristan, feeling light-headed.

"It doesn't matter," she whispered. "None of it matters now."

"You were missing for weeks before we found you," Xandru said to Tristan, and Branwen couldn't even feign surprise that the *Mawort* would have been among the ships Queen Verica sent to retrieve her grandson from Iveriu. "You never did reveal how you survived your injuries. Or stayed hidden for so long."

"The Old Ones must love me," Tristan replied. He'd never told anyone save Queen Verica that Branwen had pulled him from the waves, but Branwen no longer saw saving Tristan as betraying her cousin, or her people.

This was one secret—just one—that she no longer had to keep.

"I found him," said Branwen. Tristan sucked down a breath. "I saved his life before I knew he was my enemy."

"It seemed a shame to let me die on the shore when you'd rescued me from the waves." He grinned, repeating her words from so long ago.

"You assured me you were a poet and not a pirate."

Xandru coughed in a dramatic fashion. "Let's get the actual pirate to the castle—sooner rather than later. Branwen, ride with me," he said, taking her arm in a genteel but firm fashion. "I'm sure Tristan and Alba have much to discuss."

Branwen matched Xandru's brisk pace toward the market square.

"Remus didn't attack Tristan's ship at random," she said quietly.

"No. He didn't."

✢ ✢ ✢

The castle was abnormally still, caught in a state of suspense, like in tales of Old Ones enchanting mortals to sleep for hundreds of years.

Xandru and Branwen entered the king's study first. Marc started, spinning on his heel toward the door.

"Xan!" he said, joy on his face, his relief so great that his kingly mask dissolved. Only for a moment. Clearing his throat, Marc shifted his eyes to Branwen.

"Sister," he said. The love that underscored his voice was of a different hue, but no less profound.

"Branwen," exclaimed Andred. He beamed at her from the other side of a *fidkwelsa* board, his game with the king interrupted by their arrival. Branwen felt an excruciating pinch in her chest. The boy's mother was a traitor and, perhaps, his siblings as well.

"We obtained the package," Xandru announced. He locked eyes with King Marc, then cast Andred a cagey glance.

King Marc nodded. "I also discovered Princess Alba aboard the *Mawort*. She has been safely returned," Xandru went on. Marc brought the antler shard around his neck to his lips. "She and Tristan are in the West Tower now."

"Thank you," Marc told him in a deep voice. He rubbed his beard, which had a few days' growth.

"Lady Branwen was a great asset," said Xandru.

"She always is." Marc met her gaze. "Thank you, too."

"Would you like to see the package?" Xandru asked.

The king's kindly demeanor transformed into a scowl. "I would," he said, and Xandru clicked his fingers. Otho and Cherles hauled Remus into the study. The sneer on his face was foul.

"Andred," said Xandru. "Do you recognize this man?" He pointed at the pirate king.

Marc furrowed his brow at Xandru's question. He looked at the boy.

"Answer him, Andred," said the king.

The boy toyed with one of the pieces on the *fidkwelsa* board. A squire.

"Yes," he told Marc. "Before my father died, I saw this man a few times at Villa Illogan." Andred swallowed. "I don't know if he's visited since you brought me to Monwiku, my Lord King."

Hearing the formality in her apprentice's address of Marc touched a nerve in Branwen. Ruan had confided in her that Prince Edern reviled Andred because of his clubfoot, and Marc had asked him to serve as his cupbearer to get him away from his abusive father. Fortunately Andred wasn't present on the night when Prince Edern struck Endelyn, and so he was unaware that Ruan had been the one to kill him.

"Thank you, Andred," said King Marc. He traded a glance with Xandru. "We'll finish our game later," he told the boy. "Why don't you see whether Lowenek and the queen have returned from the moors?"

"Of course, my Lord King." The boy got to his feet and performed a small bow. Branwen smiled at him as he walked toward the door, favoring his left. His answering smile was tinged with apprehension.

As he closed the door to the study behind him, Branwen peered at the game board. Andred was winning.

Cherles and Otho forced the pirate king to his knees; then Xandru told them to wait outside. Otho was obviously loath to let Remus out of his sight until he'd been remunerated and reunited with his family. Still, he did as the captain commanded.

"You'll never be able to control the Veneti Isles without me," boasted Remus. He spoke in Ivernic, then repeated himself in Aquilan at the obvious lack of comprehension on King Marc's face.

"No wonder you can't control your wife," said the pirate king. "You don't even speak her language."

Xandru socked him on the jaw so fast he didn't see it coming. He spat a tooth onto the floor and it rattled against the stone.

Marc gave the captain one curt shake of the head.

"If you would like to leave the castle with your throat intact, you'll tell the king what he wants to know," said Xandru, dispassionate, although Branwen noticed tightness in the tendons of his own neck.

"I was dead the minute I woke aboard your ship, Captain. Why should I tell you anything?"

"I can make your final hours spectacularly miserable."

"Perhaps." The pirate king directed a glance at Branwen. "But you're not half as terrifying as her. I've never seen such a pretty monster."

Xandru punched Remus again. Marc didn't dissuade him.

"You're not wrong," Branwen told the pirate king. She raised her right hand in the air, and he noticeably shivered.

Marc hurried to Branwen's side. "You don't have to do this," he whispered.

But she did. Furthermore, she wanted to. Her pulse raced, excited. Like so many others, the pirate king looked at Branwen and saw the face of his own death.

"You were raised in Iveriu," she said to Remus. "You know who Dhusnos is. I'm a favorite of his."

The heels of her boots clicked against the stone as she moved closer.

"You should fear me," she told him. "You disgust me. You've visited untold atrocities upon our people."

"The Iverni are *not* my people." The pirate king ran a tongue across his teeth, which were coated with blood. "If I'd lived my life as a swineherd in Conaktir, like my father before me, I never would have amounted to anything. The pirates did me a favor when they burned my village. In the Veneti Isles, we can at least make our own fate."

To King Marc, Remus said, "You may win the war. You won't keep the peace. My people are not sheep—unlike yours. They won't live penniless simply because they were born poor."

"Tell me about your agreement with House Whel," Branwen said to Remus, and Marc dashed her a sideways glance.

"Just kill me, pretty monster."

"I can—and I will. But, as I drain the life from you, I will see your memories. I will learn what I need to know regardless."

The pirate king snarled a laugh. "I don't believe you."

"The man with the ax—the one I killed at the fort," she started. From the corner of her eye, Branwen saw King Marc go rigid. "He grew up on a leafy coastline. In a villa by the sea."

"An easy guess," Remus said, unimpressed. "We have many fortune-tellers who peddle speculation and call it prophecy."

"He loved cats. Especially gray ones." All color bled from the pirate king. "You've heard of the Shades," said Branwen. "How they drain their victims to sustain their afterlife. They also receive their memories. And so do I." She leaned into him. "Once I've taken who you are, you will become a Shade yourself."

Revulsion swept across Remus's face. "Keep her away from me, and I'll tell you everything I know."

"Go on," said Xandru. Branwen lowered her hand. She smiled at the pirate king, and he shivered once more.

"Prince Edern approached me when your father died," he said to Marc. "House Whel has wanted the crown for a long time. After Edern died, the countess continued our arrangement."

"Kensa will never sit on the throne," said the king.

"No, not her. Ruan."

Branwen advanced toward him. "That's why you attacked Tristan's ship last spring."

Remus nodded, grudgingly. "With Tristan dead, Ruan would be a logical heir."

"But then I got married," said Marc. He tugged at the hairs on his chin. "Did you arrange the assassination attempt?"

"That was Bledros." He let the information sink in. Ruan had told Branwen that Bledros was first commissioned by House Whel. "Bledros was born in the Veneti Isles," added Remus.

"Bledros is dead," Branwen informed him. "And I killed him." Remus simply shrugged at the news. "What was Ruan's part in the conspiracy?" she asked.

The pirate king showed her a lecherous smile, blood dripping from the gum above his missing tooth.

"Your heart is torn, isn't it? I can hear it in your voice." He sniggered.

"Answer me."

Remus spread his hands. "I never dealt with him. As to what his mother told him?" Another shrug. "Drain my memories from me if you want, pretty monster, you won't get a further answer."

Branwen could barely restrain herself from slapping him. She and Marc exchanged a glance. He stroked his beard, then, "Why did you attack Karaez?" the king asked without emotion.

"Wars can be profitable. But you have no stomach for it," replied Remus. "The barons would have demanded a stronger king."

And hadn't Ruan argued for war at every turn. Branwen felt sick. "Who warned you of our assault on the fortress?" she said, wanting blood—anyone's blood.

"A message arrived by raven. By white raven."

Chills erupted down Branwen's spine. "From a temple," said Marc. Anguish stitched his brow. "What did Kensa promise you?"

"Liones. And to make me a duke of Kernyv."

"I thought you had no kingdom," said Branwen, ferocious.

"I planned to make my own."

Marc took a step toward the pirate king.

"If you repeat all that you have told me before the assembly of barons, I will let you leave Monwiku with your life." Remus canted his head, disbelieving.

"You have my word," Marc swore, and though it was a mistake Branwen knew he would keep it.

"Agreed. I'll take a dozen jugs of your best wine. I want to get good and drunk before I die."

"You will not die within my castle walls." King Marc stared at Branwen, then Xandru. They both nodded. "Xandru, would you escort the prisoner to Ruan's—to the bedroom below. I want to keep him close." He paused. "And safe."

Xandru pulled the pirate roughly to his feet.

"You despise me," said Remus to Branwen. "But I have no regrets. Can you say the same, pretty monster?"

"You don't need your teeth to speak," warned the captain and shoved the other man across the threshold. The door slammed closed with a bang.

Branwen shook where she stood. Marc rested a hand on her shoulder, and she recoiled.

"Sister," he said. His tone was gravelly. "I fear I've asked too much of you." Tears began to leak from her eyes, and Marc drew Branwen into him. "I won't ask you to use your power again. I was selfish— forgive me."

"You didn't ask me. Xandru and I protected each other." She licked the tears that fell onto her lips. "We needed the truth to protect the peace." Her voice quaked. "But Ruan—despite how it looks, he loves you. He went back to the fight. He might already be dead. I—I don't want to believe he's a traitor."

"I don't either." Pain shone in Marc's eyes. "Endelyn could have stolen the queen's seal ring for Countess Kensa without his knowledge. He loves you, too, Branwen. I can't believe he'd harm you." Branwen nodded against the king's chest, still hoping, despite all of the bloodshed she'd witnessed, that it was true.

"The men that House Whel sent to reinforce the Royal Guard after the attack—we should send them home," she said, struggling to regain her composure.

"Yes, that would be prudent." He wiped a tear from Branwen's cheek. "How did you know about the attack on Tristan's ship?" Marc asked her.

"I was the one who pulled him from his raft. It was me. I'm sorry I never told you."

Marc planted a kiss between her eyes.

"You are no monster, Branwen. You are my family."

TWILIGHT CALM

BRANWEN RETURNED TO HER CHAMBER in the West Tower and stripped out of her clothes, unsteady on her feet, as if she were being buffeted by the waves. She filled a shallow tub with soapy water, scouring her limbs, trying to wash away the past few days. Her heartbeat wouldn't slow.

Countess Kensa's ambition was far greater than she had imagined. The countess had tried to frame Eseult for Branwen's murder to discredit her with King Marc, with the court. How much had Ruan known? Had he worked so doggedly to expose Tristan and Eseult's affair at the behest of his mother?

Branwen stared at her naked body in the looking glass. She missed her scars. Her scars had made Branwen human. She looked at her palm. The white line from the blade of binding was gone, too.

Pretty monster. That was what she had become. What she had made herself.

Her lip curled. She turned from the mirror, twilight casting a violet glow on the walls. She picked a linen dress from the wardrobe and it felt like a disguise, like she was concealing her true nature: a woman after Keane's heart.

She slumped onto her bed, fully clothed, and closed her eyes. She slid her hand beneath her pillow, fingers curving around the parchment scroll. She could suck the life from men, but she was too much of a coward to read her aunt's letter.

The white raven from her vision circled in her mind. Had it been a forewarning, after all? Branwen hadn't been aware that the temples of the Horned One sent their messages by air. What exactly did the *kordweyd* have to gain by helping the pirates? Why had Casek allied himself with Kensa?

A knock came at the door.

"Come in," she said, sitting up with a huff.

"Branny!" Eseult enthused, smiling brightly. "Andred told me you were home!" She rushed toward the bed and threw her arms around Branwen. "I couldn't rest while you were gone."

Her cousin held her a long moment. Branwen allowed herself to bask in the queen's warmth, feel the beat of the heart rabbiting in her chest. It was both familiar, and not. A song to which she only knew half the words.

"Others aren't coming home," said Branwen, drawing back. "Captain Morgawr." She took a breath. "Diarmuid—I'm sorry, Eseult. He's gone."

The queen's lips parted, regret creasing her brow.

"How did it happen?"

"The pirates had been warned. A vast chain was strewn across the harbor. Our ships were caught on it. The pirates launched fireballs from their fortress. The *Dragon Rising* was destroyed." The words came out in a rush.

"Diarmuid, Ruan, and other Ivermen brought the chain down,"

Branwen went on. "But at great cost." She remembered Ruan saying the countess had tried to forbid him from going to the Veneti Isles. Why would she let him sail into an ambush? And why would he go if he was party to her schemes?

"Branny," said Eseult softly, after Branwen had trailed off, lost in her thoughts. "It must have been horrible to witness," said her cousin. She stroked Branwen's cheek.

"Diarmuid died a hero," she said. "For Iveriu." Branwen wet her lips. "You always saw the best in him. He was a better man than I'd allowed."

"We should toast him."

Branwen glanced toward the bookshelves. "I have elderberry wine," she said.

Her cousin went to retrieve the waterskin from where it lay beside the wooden sword. "Didn't Uncle Morholt give this to you?" She lifted it from the shelf. Branwen nodded. "Do you ever wonder what might have happened if our uncle had won?"

The queen set down the child-size weapon and returned to Branwen with the waterskin.

"No," Branwen replied. "I can't rewind the ribbon of time."

If their uncle had bested Tristan—fairly—in the Final Combat, Branwen would never have been gifted the Hand of Bríga. She wouldn't have conjured the Loving Cup. She wouldn't have made a deal with Dhusnos.

There would also be no peace.

Eseult uncorked the wine. "When I first saw Diarmuid, we were children. He was still scrawny," she said. "He didn't hold my interest." She lowered her nose to inhale the scent of elderberries. "When we met again, he was handsome. Charming."

The queen sighed. "Each letter he sent me was a rebellion. Thrilling.

I treasured them, but . . . it was all about me." The look she gave Branwen was doleful. "I wish I'd known Diarmuid better—truly *known* him. Not merely craved his sweet nothings."

She touched the antler shard that rested against her chest.

"Perhaps we never know people as well as we should," said Branwen. "But Diarmuid believed peace was worth fighting for, and he gave his life so that we might know it. He died with honor."

Eseult sighed, raising the waterskin. "To Lord Diarmuid Parthalán of Uladztir, a true Ivernic hero." She put the metal lip to her mouth and took a substantial swallow.

"To Diarmuid," Branwen said, taking the waterskin from her cousin. "May he find his way back to Kerwindos's Cauldron to be reborn with his father in his next life."

She drank, the wine tart and sweet. Treva adamantly refused to share her recipe, and no other wine tasted as good. Memories of her cousin's harmless pranks and the confidences they'd once shared flickered through her mind. She took a bigger sip.

The cousins sat together in the twilight calm. Eseult's cheeks grew rosy, as they always did, and she hiccupped as she stole another swallow.

"I've been thinking about a gift for Dubthach and Saoirse," she said. "Maybe a baby blanket?"

"That would be nice," Branwen replied. She found it hard to think about celebrating a new life in the wake of all the carnage she'd seen.

Smiling mischievously, Eseult said, "I could embroider a trim of chickens and eggs on it!" She winked, and Branwen laughed, heartier than she'd expected.

Dubthach couldn't stand the sight of eggs or chickens, since her cousin had convinced him hard-boiled eggs were eyeballs and forced him to touch them.

"I also want to send Gráinne a new doll's dress," said the queen. "When the Ivernic ships return." Branwen hoped the Ivernic ships did return. And she hoped Ruan would be with them. Although she didn't know what fate would await him.

"I wonder how much she's grown?" Eseult mused. "I might not even recognize Gráinne now." She had always loved children, delighted in telling them stories, and she had taken a particular shine to an orphan she'd met on the Rock Road. "Lowenek reminds me of her. She has spirit. She's teaching me Kernyvak—I think she's rather clever." Her cousin spoke quickly, nervously, filling the quiet.

Branwen placed her left hand over Eseult's. "You would be a good mother," she said. "You'll get another chance. If you want one."

Her eyes grew shiny. Looking at Branwen's gloveless right hand, she said, "I'll sew you a new one."

"I lost it during the fight. I'm sorry."

"Don't be silly." Eseult's words were hushed. "Do you want to talk about what happened?"

"Not tonight."

The queen nodded. "Whatever you need, Branny. Just tell me and it's yours." Eseult offered Branwen the waterskin, but she shook her head. The queen recorked the wine and laid it atop the coverlet.

"When you're feeling rested, I'd like to take you to the infirmary site. See our progress—see if there's anything you'd like changed."

"I will," Branwen promised. "You seem to be enjoying the project."

"I feel useful." Eseult pursed her lips, a determined look on her face. "I didn't think I had any talent. I've never been a healer like you, or Mother. But this infirmary will help our people, and I can make it happen. I want to open it by the end of summer."

"You've always had a talent for bossing people around," Branwen said lightly.

"I suppose I have."

"I'm teasing, Essy." Her cousin stared at her. Branwen hadn't used her childhood name for months. Maybe it was the effect of the elderberry wine.

There was a quick rap on the door, and Branwen shot up to answer it. Her nerves buzzed, wondering whether the fleet was putting into port.

"Tristan," she said. "Is there news?"

"Not as yet." He scratched the scar on his eyebrow. Noticing Eseult over Branwen's shoulder, he said, "*Nosmatis*, Lady Queen. I didn't mean to intrude."

Branwen opened the door wider, glancing back at her cousin.

"It's no intrusion," said Eseult. "I was just leaving." She stood, crossing toward them. "I'll see you both at dinner."

Eseult smiled tentatively at Tristan, and gave Branwen a kiss on the cheek as she left. Tristan glanced after the queen, then back at Branwen, brow pinched.

"You two seem to be getting along better," he said.

"We're . . . trying. Eseult has known me my whole life." Branwen heaved a sigh. "Does Alba need me? Is her wound inflamed?"

"No." Tristan stepped farther into the room, but he left the door open.

Branwen retreated toward the window. She lit a candle in a sconce on the wall as the evening thickened.

"I didn't think I'd see you again after the wedding," Branwen said, turning back toward Tristan. "Not for some time, at least."

"It would have been easier."

"Yes."

"Alba told me you saved her life," he said, and Branwen's chest constricted.

"She has the heart of a Champion," she told him. "Alba is kind and strong. She will be a magnanimous queen." Branwen rubbed her thumb against the sole scar that remained—the mark of Dhusnos. "I—I think you will be happy. I hope so. You deserve a wife like her."

Tristan took several strides closer. "Yours is the heart of a Champion, too, Branwen."

"Maybe once. Not anymore." She shook her head. "When I created the antidote—I lost a part of myself. I created a crack, and let darkness seep in."

"Oh, Branwen."

"I don't want your pity," she snapped. "It's what I deserve."

"It's not." There was anger in his voice as well.

"I enjoy killing, Tristan. I drained the life from a pirate to save Alba, but it was intoxicating. I wanted more. I want it still."

She released a harsh exhale, clenching her fists. "I'm afraid," she said. Branwen's voice had grown hoarse, barely audible.

Tristan framed her face with his hands.

"From the moment I opened my eyes and saw you, I knew you were Otherworld-sent. I still believe it."

Branwen's eyes grew wet with tears. "You shouldn't."

He brushed his thumb across her lips, smearing the tears that had dripped down. Branwen trembled as warmth curled through her.

"Tristan," she said, his name a plea. "The bargain I made with Dhusnos, there was another condition." His eyes bored into hers. "I have to deliver him a Shade by Samonios. I have to kill of my own volition—*murder*. Not because I'm in danger, not to save someone else. Because I *desire* it." And a growing part of Branwen *did* desire death.

She broke his gaze. "If I don't, Dhusnos will steal the soul of someone I love."

Tristan hissed a curse and dragged Branwen against his chest. His lips tickled the shell of her ear as he said, "Let it be me."

Branwen pushed against him in horror. He held her firm.

"You're always too willing to throw away your own life," she told him, fury stirring. "I could never wish you dead."

Tristan rested his chin on top of her head, squeezing her tight.

"I should have died in the Champions Tournament. Without your magic, I would have. This is how I repay you," he said in a low voice. "This is fate."

"No," Branwen said through gritted teeth. She broke free of his embrace. "You will sail to Armorica with your new wife, and you will live. It's where Kernyv needs you to be. Where Iveriu needs you."

"I will send for you before Samonios."

"I won't come!" she roared.

"Why are you so willing to save everyone but yourself?"

"I'm beyond saving, Tristan."

"Then you don't see what I see." He closed the small space between them. "I see a woman whose heart is fierce, yet open enough to turn her enemies into friends—to love them. We all have darkness inside us."

Tristan gathered a loose curl between his fingertips.

"*Odai eti ama.* You hate and you love, Branwen. As do we all." She felt his breath on her face as he spoke. "There's another verse by the same Aquilan poet that makes me think of you. *En vos meos mortis, en vos meos vita.*"

"In you my death," she whispered. "In you my life."

"It was true the day we met. It's true now."

"Alba will be wondering where you are," Branwen said.

Tristan took her right hand in his, raised her palm to his lips, and kissed the mark of Dhusnos.

Branwen shivered, and watched him walk away.

WASHER AT THE FORD

WISHES FLITTED IN THE BRANCHES above Branwen, colorful slivers of desire in the fog.

She followed the stream to the healing well. The way Tristan had looked at her last night, his faith in her despite how she'd wronged him— it gave Branwen hope.

As she came upon the Wise Damsel's cottage, she saw Ailleann kneeling on the bank of the stream, washing a green woolen cloak. The silver strands amidst her loose, deep garnet hair caught the hazy light. She radiated power, and no one would dare mistake her for a simple old woman doing her laundry.

Branwen kneeled down at the ford, beside the Wise Damsel, who had yet to glance at her. The stream gurgled.

"You were right," Branwen began. "We found the True Queen by the river."

Ailleann made no response. She scrubbed her cloak beneath the bubbling waters. The fabric flowed like seaweed.

Steeling herself, Branwen said, "I think I know what I lost." Her words were hesitant. "My cousin, the True Queen—I lost the love that bound me to her."

She exhaled a thin breath. "We made a vow when we were children, stitched each other into our hearts. I cut the threads."

Branwen leaned back on her heels, hugging herself. If not for the spell, would she have believed that Eseult had tried to have her murdered?

"Can the bond be repaired?" she asked.

The Wise Damsel tilted her head in Branwen's direction for the first time.

"The memory will not return," she told her. "But your heart is yours, *enigena*. If you want to let your cousin shelter within it, that is your choice."

Branwen nodded. The devotion that had driven her to conjure the Loving Cup, that had fueled the Hand of Bríga, was gone. Maybe such devotion had obscured her understanding of who Eseult truly was. Branwen would have to get to know her cousin as she was now.

With a small swallow, she said, "I told the queen the true source of her pain, and her suffering has abated, even without the spell. How can primordial magic be so easily undone?"

The Wise Damsel glanced at Branwen sharply. "I told you that magic requires honesty." The hairs on the back of Branwen's neck lifted. "Truth can be a weapon or it can be a balm. Its force is as potent as any magic."

The bells tinkled in the trees, a harbinger.

"My magic . . . it's changed, and it's changing me," said Branwen. She extended her hand, palm up, toward the other woman. "Slayer." She choked on the word. "I can no longer heal. I cannot create. Only destroy. I can steal the life from men and see their memories."

Branwen lifted her hand closer. "This is the Hand of Dhusnos now. It craves power and it sickens me."

Ailleann continued scrubbing her cloak.

"When you consume life," she said, "you will lose a part of yourself, Branwen of Iveriu." Soap foamed against the rocks. "The power will hollow you out. Old Ones, as you call them, who sustain themselves in this way become vicious creatures."

Branwen expelled a tremulous breath. "How do I stop it? How do I stop myself from being a monster?"

"You took the hand of darkness, yet there is light all around you." She glanced up at the rays of sun piercing the fog. "I told you not to return until you had regained your balance."

"I want to find the balance, I do," Branwen protested. She dropped her hand to her lap. "I don't know how." Her voice cracked. "You offered to help me tame my magic. I wasn't ready. Teach me now."

"I am not a god, *enigena*. There is no escaping the bargain you made with Dhusnos."

"You *are* an Old One," she said, only half in question.

"I am the guardian at the well."

"If I don't take a life of my own volition, the Dark One will claim the soul of someone I love. How do I condemn someone to an eternity as a Shade?" Branwen was growing agitated. "How could my magic find balance after that?"

Ailleann lifted the cloak from the water and spread it onto a rock to dry.

"Kings come and go. Many arms will hold you. What is it in *you*, Branwen, that is constant?" The Wise Damsel touched her wet fingers to Branwen's heart, and the linen of her dress grew damp.

"When you find what is constant, you will see the light in the darkness. I do not envy you the choices that lie before you, *enigena*. I cannot make them for you."

Anger flared and fizzled. "I believe in peace," she said.

"And yet, you have none." The other woman tapped a finger against Branwen's chest. Branwen bowed her head.

The Wise Damsel pushed to her feet.

"The healing you need won't be found at the well. You must heal yourself."

✢ ✢ ✢

As Senara trotted back toward Monwiku, a fog rolled in from the sea that was so thick Branwen could hardly make out the path in front of her.

She'd gone to the White Moor with hope; she was leaving with resignation.

Every day, Samonios grew closer. The Old Ones could not—or would not—help her. She had asked for godlike powers, and now she alone must bear the consequences.

Branwen reached the stables and was feeding her mount extra oats when a lean figure slipped into the stall beside her. Xandru stroked Senara's muzzle and the mare nickered, delighted. The captain's charm extended to animals, it seemed.

"You were looking for me?" Branwen surmised.

"The queen said you'd gone for a ride." He patted Senara's neck. "If you were anyone else, my lady, I would think you'd be worried about traveling alone through the same forest where you'd been attacked."

Xandru laughed. "The fort has fallen," he reported, abruptly changing the subject.

Relief and apprehension wound through Branwen at the news.

"How many ships did we lose?" she asked.

"At least twelve." His posture was relaxed, but Branwen knew better than to trust his demeanor. "King Marc has ordered a contingent of the Royal Fleet to remain in the Veneti Isles to establish order."

A knot formed in her stomach. "And the Ivernic ships?" she said.

"Four have been sighted making their way to Marghas." Xandru held her expectant stare. "Lord Diarmuid's ship is among them."

Branwen sighed heavily, the knot tightening. "Good news," she managed.

"Indeed. The King's Council has also been sent for. When Countess Kensa arrives, she will be arrested," said Xandru, tone casual, as if he were talking about the weather. "Remus is enjoying his stupor in Ruan's old apartment. I can't say that I blame him."

Senara whinnied, and Branwen pacified the mare with another handful of oats.

Xandru's eyes narrowed ever so slightly.

"I know Ruan means something to you," he said. "He means something to Marc, too." The captain stepped close to Branwen. "Go to him, persuade Ruan to confess his involvement to the king before he is formally arrested. Marc is too forgiving for his own good."

"Why would you risk giving Ruan the opportunity to warn the countess? Or to run away?"

Xandru sighed. "Because I don't want Marc to be forced to watch one of his closest friends burned as a traitor. It would break his heart."

For a moment his eyes were unguarded.

"Marc is not like us," he added.

Branwen grazed her mother's brooch with her fingertips.

"If you leave now, you should be able to catch Ruan at the port," said Xandru.

"Very well," she agreed. Whatever they were to each other, whatever they had been, Branwen did not wish to see Ruan executed.

She made her apologies to the mare, promising Senara apples as well as oats, and swung herself back into the saddle.

"Be persuasive," Xandru told her.

He gave her a silent salute as Branwen set out for Marghas. From the coastal path, she could glimpse four golden lions upon green sails. Two were already docked. She urged Senara faster. Villa Illogan lay in the opposite direction from the port as well as Monwiku, and she needed to catch Ruan—assuming he'd survived the battle—before he left Marghas.

The rock pools glittered like black pearls. The earlier fog had evaporated, although Branwen still felt a chill.

Branwen was rounding the last bend in the road toward Marghas when Senara's front legs flew into the air. Another rider was coming at them at high speed. The mare released an enraged neigh, her hooves sending small pebbles over the edge of the cliff as she found purchase.

"Ruan!" said Branwen. Her heart leapt into her throat. He pulled back on the reins of his stallion, showing Branwen a rakish, if tired, smile.

"You saw the green sails," he said. Something tender passed over his face. "You were coming to see if I was alive."

Ruan walked his horse closer. "I thought you might return to Illogan," she said. "If you were alive." Branwen's response was short, her pulse skittering.

"You told me you'd see me at Monwiku, so that's where I was headed." His smile deepened. "I wouldn't dare disobey you."

"The pirates' fortress is secured?" Branwen asked.

"It's ours. For now, at least. We burned their ships." Branwen watched him intently, trying to detect any hint of remorse. He sidled his mount next to hers.

"*Karid*," Ruan said, and the timbre of his voice conjured memories of lying in his arms, legs intertwined. "I survived the battle because I wanted to see you again."

"We have the pirate king," she told him. A ripple of confusion spread across Ruan's brow. "But you already know that."

"*What?*" he exclaimed. "How would I know that?" His surprise and irritation appeared genuine, but Branwen didn't trust her instincts in this moment.

"You recognized him. The man in the rowboat."

Ruan worried a knuckle against his lower lip. "I thought I'd seen him before. I couldn't remember where." He leaned across his mount, reaching for Branwen, and she lurched backward in her own saddle, out of his grasp. "What are you accusing me of?" he demanded.

"The pirate king has been working for House Whel," she said. "He's admitted it. You are the one fond of accusations, but this is not an accusation. It's a fact."

"No, Branwen." Ruan's eyes widened, horrified. "He's a pirate! He's full of lies!"

"Andred saw him at Villa Illogan on several occasions. With Prince Edern."

Ruan let out a string of Kernyvak curses, then dragged a hand through his wind-knotted locks.

"Branwen," he said, pleading. "Let us go somewhere we can talk properly." She cast him a skeptical look. "Just there." He pointed back toward Monwiku. "By the rock pools."

She acquiesced with a curt nod. Even if he was a traitor, Branwen didn't believe he would ever harm her.

Letting Ruan take the lead, they dismounted farther along the road. Below, waves crashed against the cliffs, a dull turquoise. To Branwen's surprise, a wooden bench decorated with sea glass had been erected between the rock pools.

"After you," said Ruan, gesturing for Branwen to be seated. "A resting place for travelers."

He lowered himself next to her, careful not to brush against her. Branwen traced her forefinger around the bits of sea glass: green, blue, and crimson.

"If you think I'm a traitor," Ruan began. "Why have you come to warn me?"

"Because I care about you. Because I don't want it to be true."

"What lies has this pirate king told you?" He gripped the edge of the bench tightly between his fists.

"Prince Edern wanted the throne for himself. He staked the pirate raids to undermine Marc's authority as a young king," said Branwen. "When Edern *died*—" Ruan flicked her a sidelong glance. "Afterward," she started again, "Countess Kensa continued the arrangement with the aim of making you king."

Ruan shook his head, half laughing. "I could believe anything of Edern," he said, voice forlorn. "But I have never coveted the throne. Even if I truly were of royal blood."

"Only your mother and Endelyn know—*knew* that you're not."

"And you."

Branwen started, realization creeping over her. "Did you tell your mother I know?"

His amber eyes flashed. "The night of Queen Verica's funeral, after you went to bed . . . I got myself drunker. My mother and I had an argument. I may have told her I love you and that I wanted you to know who I really was."

She gulped. "Don't you see?" Branwen said, putting together the pieces. "Endelyn stole the queen's seal ring for the countess, and the countess sent Tutir and Bledros to kill me—because I could expose *you*."

Ruan shook his head more violently, and Branwen could practically hear his wrestling thoughts. The guardsmen had tried to silence her not because she knew the queen's secret, but because she knew the countess's. Framing Eseult was merely a bonus.

"The pirate king admitted that Bledros came from the Veneti Isles. And Bledros hired the Armorican assassin—most likely poisoned him, too."

"And where is this pirate king now?"

"At the castle. Being held in *your*—in the King's Tower, until he can testify before the barons."

Ruan's knuckles bulged white against the bench.

"Go to Marc," Branwen entreated. "Tell him you had no part in this."

"I can't believe my mother would resort to murder," he said. "She's conniving and ambitious, but murder is something else. She wept for months after my true father died." His eyes had grown glossy. "She wouldn't take you away from me, Branwen. She wouldn't."

"She ordered the attack on Tristan's ship—the one last spring that landed him in Iveriu. With Tristan dead, you would have been the obvious heir."

"Even if what you're saying were true, I would *never* take the throne from Marc, and my mother knows it." The words were nearly a growl.

"But you wanted to wage war against Armorica, and so did the barons. King Marc has been losing their support for some time. People are unhappy about freeing the prisoners, about the peace with Iveriu," Branwen pointed out. "Your accusations against Tristan and the queen only served to further undermine Marc's reign, make him look like a weak leader."

"The countess had nothing to do with that." Ruan pummeled the sea glass with his fist. "I was dishonored, Branwen! And my mother has been inconsolable since Endelyn's death. She blames me for that, too!"

"Ruan," said Branwen, iron in her voice. "You told me yourself that your mother forbade you from going to the Veneti Isles. She knew it was an ambush. The pirate king received a warning by white raven."

Ruan's head lifted involuntarily. He jammed his lips together. Branwen slipped a hand behind his neck, and he shuddered a sigh.

"We don't always see the truth about the people we love," she said quietly.

His gaze grew pained. "No, we don't. When I saw you on the road just now, I was fool enough to think you might have realized you loved me."

Branwen broke his stare, letting her eyes wander to a serpent star crawling on the bottom of a rock pool. She continued to stroke the back of his neck.

"My father gave me his knife the last time I saw him alive," Ruan began. "A few of the miners had escaped the week before, and Prince Edern was behaving even more . . . unreasonably than usual."

He scoffed. "When I learned of the prisoners' escape, I was afraid my father had left me. He gave me his knife as a promise that he never would."

Branwen's heart cramped. "His name was Conchobar, wasn't it?" Ruan nodded. "There's an Ivernic hero by that name—a legendary king, married to the warrior queen Medhua. It's said he was so wise that he was made High King of Iveriu when he was only seven years old."

A smile flickered on Ruan's lips. "My father wasn't wise. He should have left with the others." He shook his head. "Edern saw Conchobar giving me the knife, embracing me—and he finally noticed that I resembled the miner more than I did him."

"That wasn't your fault," Branwen said in a whisper.

"I don't know what you want from me, *karid*."

"I want you to go to Marc—or to flee. I *don't* want you to die."

Ruan stared at her. "And condemn my mother?"

Branwen unpinned the brooch from her shawl. "This belonged to my mother, Lady Alana. She was wearing it the day she died." She turned it over so the light glimmered on the silver inscription.

"The ancient Ivernic language of trees," she said.

"What does it say?"

"*The right fight*."

Branwen pierced the collar of Ruan's tunic with the needle. "I believe you will make the right choice."

"I can't accept this."

She finished hooking the clasp. "You gave me your father's knife." Part of her ached as she gifted the brooch to him, but "I want you to have this," she said firmly, and she prayed it would be enough to convince Ruan to save himself.

"You will never not fascinate me," he said. The surf surged up against the cliffs. "I need time to think."

Branwen rose to standing. "Will you warn the countess?"

He shook his head. "My mother would never flee," Ruan said. "But, no. Besides, there's no way to outrun the Royal Guard. When will she be arrested?"

"At the King's Council meeting."

He nodded. "Thank you."

She started to skirt between the rock pools when Ruan called out, "Is a life at Monwiku really what you want?"

"My queen is here."

"That's not an answer."

"It's the only one I have."

Branwen smelled rain on the salty air, a tang on her lips, as she left her former lover on the cliffs.

YOU HAD TIME

BRANWEN GLANCED AROUND THE GREAT Hall. There were Royal Guardsmen posted at every exit, and those who had been sent by House Whel had been relieved of duty. King Marc and Queen Eseult were ensconced on their thrones in the middle of the raised dais as members of the King's Council entered the hall. Sir Goron stood behind them.

Afternoon light gleamed off Marc's golden crown; diamonds winked from Eseult's. For the first time, the monarchs appeared unified. Formidable.

Andred stood beside Branwen to the left of the dais. Xandru and the pirate king would remain just out of view, beneath a shrouded archway to the right of the king until they were summoned. Xandru had choreographed the council meeting so as not to arouse Countess Kensa's suspicions.

Ruan didn't believe his mother would flee, but Branwen thought her to be a survivor above all else. When Countess Kensa strode into the

Great Hall, chin raised, Branwen released a breath. Ruan hadn't warned her. It had been two days since their conversation on the cliffs above Marghas. She hadn't seen him at Monwiku, and she presumed he'd returned to Villa Illogan.

Branwen looked past Countess Kensa, but there was no sign of Ruan. Her stomach dropped.

King Marc's face remained impassive as the barons stopped before the dais. Baron Julyan leaned harder on his cane than usual, and Branwen noted that his face was thinner beneath his beard. Baron Chyanhal also regarded the elderly baron with concern.

Seer Casek trailed behind the countess, and Branwen exchanged a lightning quick glance with Tristan. He and Alba stood on the other side of Andred. The king had asked them to delay their departure for Karaez until after the council meeting without furnishing all of the details.

Barons Gwyk and Dynyon positioned themselves beside Countess Kensa, both of their faces creased, no doubt wondering why they had been directed to the Great Hall rather than the king's study. Baron Kerdu took his place next to Baron Julyan.

Once everyone was assembled before the king and queen, King Marc let them wait another minute in taut silence. A summer wind blew through the cavernous space, and Branwen's throat grew parched. The vast hall became stuffy, too small.

With a cough, Baron Gwyk was the first to speak. "*Dymatis*, my Lord King," he said, bowing his head. "What news of the Veneti Isles?"

King Marc's rib cage expanded as he drew down a breath. Tension slithered among the barons like a snake.

"The Veneti Isles are once more under Kernyvak control," the king said, voice deep, with no satisfaction. "The pirates had been warned, but the combined fleet prevailed."

Baron Kerdu clapped. *"Kernyv bosta vyken!"*

The others followed suit with an eruption of applause. Branwen watched Countess Kensa, who had pasted on a pleasant smile. The ruby combs holding back her plaits glittered.

Marc pushed to his feet, expression drawn.

"I have summoned you all here today not to relish our victory," he said. "But to inform you of a defeat—a betrayal that cuts this kingdom to the quick."

The countess stilled, but her smile faltered only a fraction. Branwen rubbed her gloved right hand against the skirt of her linen dress. Baron Julyan inhaled a short breath at the king's pronouncement.

"What betrayal is this?" Seer Casek asked. He fidgeted with his jewel-encased antler shard.

"Captain Xandru!" the king said, raising his voice.

Branwen's eyes darted to where she knew he was waiting. The forms of two men emerged from the shadows. As light from the oil lamps spread over the men's faces, Branwen sucked in a painful breath.

"What is the meaning of this?" Countess Kensa exclaimed. Outrage lit her blue eyes.

Ruan walked toward the dais, his hands in chains. The skin around his left eye was puce-colored, swollen. He wore the same clothes as when Branwen had last seen him. Lady Alana's brooch was pinned to his tunic. His eyes traced the stone floor, chest concave.

What had Ruan done?

Andred stiffened at Branwen's side. Fear and sympathy welled. Her gaze roved, frantic, from Ruan to Eseult to the king. Eseult seemed as surprised as Branwen. Marc remained stoic as he nodded at Xandru. Branwen peered at Tristan, who balled his hands into fists. Alba curled her lip.

One hand clenched around Ruan's upper arm, Xandru was the one to answer the countess.

"Prince Ruan was apprehended the night before last attempting to murder Remus—the pirate king," he announced to the barons. Xandru called out something in the dialect of the Veneti Isles, and Otho pushed Remus forward from beneath another darkened archway.

Murmurs escaped the barons. Branwen's heart seized.

Remus was dressed in a fresh tunic and breeches. His hands were also bound, and there was a vulgar smile on his baby face. His eyes were large, perhaps from being half drunk.

"What reason would Prince Ruan have for wanting the pirate king dead?" asked Baron Julyan.

"Prince Ruan was informed that the pirate king had confessed House Whel paid the pirates to attack Karaez, to ambush Prince Tristan's ship last spring, and to assassinate the king."

"Lies!" Countess Kensa declared, thrusting out a hand.

"Your son, Prince Andred, has confirmed that Remus met with the late Prince Edern at Villa Illogan on several occasions," reported Xandru.

The countess spun toward Andred, expression venomous. The boy reeled backward.

"Prince Ruan wanted to prevent the pirate king from testifying to his family's treason before the council," the captain continued.

Baron Dynyon cleared his throat. "Precisely who informed Prince Ruan of the pirate king's allegations, and how was he apprehended?"

Branwen swallowed. Ruan looked at her for the first time.

"The allegations are true, Baron Dynyon," said Ruan. Branwen's throat burned. "Lady Branwen asked me to confess my crimes to King Marc, ask for forgiveness. She told me where the pirate king was being held. When I arrived, however, he was nowhere to be found." His tone was a mixture of remorse and acquiescence.

"Alas, no," said Xandru. "Ruan discovered me in the pirate king's bed when he put a knife to my throat."

Anger seared Branwen, and now she understood how Ruan had obtained his black eye. Xandru had wagered that Ruan would kill to protect his family. He had used Branwen to bait the trap because of Ruan's feelings for her.

She wanted to tell Ruan that she didn't know, but she bit her tongue. What did it matter? She clumped her skirts in her hands.

"The treason is mine and mine alone," Ruan told the barons, then pitched his gaze at Marc. "Please spare my mother and brother."

"The pirate king says otherwise," declared King Marc.

"The pirate king lies," Ruan countered. His tone was curt but his shoulders sagged, a man who had accepted his fate.

Baron Chyanhal planted his feet, his generally placid demeanor tinged with menace. "The punishment for treason is death by burning."

"I'm aware," said Ruan, almost as if he were bored, slipping into the role of the caddish nobleman who had first greeted Branwen when she arrived in Kernyv. He was willing to burn for his mother's crimes.

"I would like to hear the pirate king's testimony," pronounced Baron Julyan. He wheezed, and Branwen detected the phlegmy rattle of a chest infection.

Xandru inclined his head at Otho, who shoved Remus forward.

"He speaks Aquilan," Xandru said to the baron. "Ask him your questions."

"Remus? That is your name?" said Baron Julyan.

"King Remus," he replied, puffing out his chest.

"A king no longer," said Alba, voice full of spite. Her hand felt reflexively for her sword, but she was unarmed.

"Remus," Baron Julyan repeated. "Did Prince Ruan warn you of the impending attack?"

"The warning was delivered by white raven," the pirate king said. He looked directly at Seer Casek. "The temple in Marghas often stakes our raids."

Branwen's lungs burned with hatred. This man who had tried to suppress her gods, to make her cousin bleed, was a traitor to the crown all along.

"That's preposterous!" Seer Casek spluttered. "The temples teach the mercy of the Horned One. I am his servant."

Remus shrugged, disinterested. Baron Kerdu glanced at Casek askance. Branwen glimpsed several guardsmen approaching from the back of the hall.

"And did Ruan instruct you to carry out the attack on Karaez? On Prince Tristan?" Baron Chyanhal pressed him. "And the king?"

Baron Gwyk and Baron Dynyon traded a glance, both paling considerably. They had allied themselves with the wrong House.

The pirate king smiled, running his tongue across his jagged teeth.

"Instructions for the raid on Karaez came directly from Countess Kensa after the assassination attempt failed. Payment for the attack on Prince Tristan came from the temple." Remus shifted his eyes to Tristan. "If I were a honest man, I suppose I should refund their money." His laugh was empty.

Seer Casek took several aggressive strides toward the dais. Xandru blocked his path. Alba moved toward the countess, fists white with rage, and Tristan held her back. Countess Kensa remained uncharacteristically quiet; she visibly swallowed.

"Are you going to take the word of a pirate over that of a *kordweyd*?" the seer challenged the king. "I would have thought that your faith was strong, my Lord King."

"I am," he answered coldly. "I recall that neither you nor the countess was present when I was attacked in the Morrois Forest. You both departed separately from the festival."

Marc targeted Ruan with his gaze. "And Branwen had to prevent my Champion from killing the assassin. Although he made sure he was poisoned afterward."

Ruan hung his head, but he didn't protest his innocence. Branwen's breathing grew shallow. Had he truly fooled her so thoroughly for so long?

To the guardsman, King Marc said, "Arrest Countess Kensa and Seer Casek."

Branwen watched as true fear gripped the other woman's features.

"Wait," said the countess. Her voice trembled. She pressed a hand to the bodice of her dress. "My Lord King," the countess began again. "My son is only guilty of trying to protect me."

Kensa looked from Ruan to Andred. Her expression was not soft, yet something akin to love tinted her eyes.

"Neither of my sons was involved in my schemes."

King Marc folded his arms. "Who were your co-conspirators?"

"Seer Casek," she replied. "And Baron Gwyk."

To Branwen's surprise, much as she disliked him, it seemed Baron Dynyon was not a traitor.

"Duplicitous whore!" the *kordweyd* burst out, at the same time as Baron Gwyk shouted, "She's a wrecker! She's just trying to save her own hide!"

"Prince Ruan isn't even a prince!" Seer Casek yelled, continuing his rant. "Kensa spread her legs for some Ivernic prisoner!"

Marc startled at the rebuke. A few gasps were emitted from around the hall. Branwen saw a flush crawl down Ruan's neck as Casek revealed the secret he'd concealed his entire life. She was no supporter of the countess, but she would not shame her for finding kindness where she could.

Baron Gwyk rounded on Kensa. "You would put half-Ivernic scum on the throne of Kernyv?" He spat at her feet.

"Arrest him as well," the king instructed his guards tonelessly.

There were no tears in Countess Kensa's eyes, only steel, as she told Baron Gwyk, "Ruan is the son of a man who loved me. Andred is the son of Prince Edern."

She raised her head, undaunted, meeting the king with a leveling gaze.

"I suffered Edern's attacks and humiliations for years while the entire court pretended not to notice. Why shouldn't *my* son wear the crown?" she charged. "Are you so much more deserving because you were born to King Merchion?"

The countess screwed up her lips like she might spit. "Edern whipped Ruan to punish me—because he enjoyed seeing him in pain. For years. Seer Casek treated his wounds in secret, and we decided that one day Ruan would sit on the throne."

"Did Prince Edern know of your plan?" asked King Marc.

Countess Kensa laughed scornfully. "Edern wanted the crown for himself. When he died," she said, shifting her gaze to Ruan, "it was a simple matter to continue his arrangement with the pirates."

"You wanted me eliminated because I was next in line," Tristan said to the Countess.

She turned to him. "Yes. And Baron Gwyk was easy enough to convince with the promise of land, and his hatred of anyone who isn't of pure Kernyvak blood."

The baron made to spit at the countess again, when one of the guards pulled him back, pressing a sword to his middle.

"Those who hate are easily manipulated," she added.

Nostrils flaring, Alba said, "Why attack Karaez?"

"Peace is an illusion. Power is what matters." Countess Kensa drew in a heavy breath. "My nephew has always been too tenderhearted to rule."

Ruan shook his head. He had once told Branwen that Marc was the kindest ruler Kernyv was ever likely to know.

"Why should we believe that Ruan was unaware of your plots?" Baron Kerdu said, impaling the countess with his gaze.

"Because Ruan has always been too loyal to Marc for his own good."

Alba released an incredulous laugh. "By accusing the True Queen of treason with Prince Tristan?"

Before the countess could reply, Eseult stood and walked to the end of the dais. Her blond hair shimmered around her, and her wrath was magnificent.

"You had Endelyn steal my seal ring, and then tried to frame me for ordering my cousin's murder," she asserted, words growing shrill.

"Bledros was loyal to me, but Tutir was loyal to the crown. He needed proof he was on the queen's orders," Kensa told her, unrepentant. "If they had succeeded in their mission, they would have been able to testify that you'd had Branwen killed."

"To jeopardize the alliance."

"Precisely."

"And you chose Ériu's Comfort to poison the Armorican assassin to frame Lady Branwen. To make me think she wanted to harm me."

The countess nodded. "Why?" Eseult demanded.

"Because your cousin is far cleverer than you, Lady Queen. Without her at your side, you would never have held the throne on your own."

"Insulting the True Queen is no way to obtain leniency!" roared King Marc.

"I don't expect any for myself," she said. "I'm only being honest." Countess Kensa clasped her hands together as if she were praying. "My Lord King, please believe me that neither Andred nor Ruan had knowledge of my plans."

"Why should we believe a word that comes out of your mouth?" said Baron Chyanhal, his eyes wide, stunned.

The pirate king watched the drama play out with an amused smile. Branwen wished that Marc hadn't given Remus his word to let him live. Most avidly.

"I have already lost one of my children, Baron Chyanhal," stated the countess. "I do not want to lose another. My sons are innocent."

Ruan tilted his head toward her. "Mother," he said. A ragged word.

"I'm sorry, Ruan."

At Branwen's side, she heard Andred gulp. Kensa didn't look at her younger son.

"Baron Gwyk and Seer Casek," said King Marc, stepping down from the dais. "I sentence you both to death."

"You aren't half the king your father was," said the baron, disgust filling the edges of his words.

Seer Casek sneered. "The Horned One will embrace me. Resurrect me. What I did was for him—to bring his truth to the people of Kernyv."

He looked between Marc and Xandru. "You are too weak to know his mercy, my Lord King." The seer spoke his title with disdain. "You are not pure of heart, or strong of flesh. You are corrupted. I pity your kingdom."

Xandru's hand grazed the hilt of his dagger, his expression serene and eyes murderous.

"My kingdom does not need your pity," said King Marc, his voice dangerously reserved. "You have no authority over my faith. You have allowed your desire for power to corrupt *you*, Seer Casek. My god and yours are not the same."

"At the moment of your death, you will know I'm right," countered the seer.

"Take him away," the king told his guards. The Royal Guardsmen marched Seer Casek and Baron Gwyk toward the side exit.

Marc returned his attention to Countess Kensa. He sighed and glanced sideways at Eseult.

"You have admitted your treason, Countess Kensa. Kernyvak law says you should die by fire. And yet, I find that my heart rails against the idea of executing a woman—my own aunt."

Branwen exchanged a quick look with Xandru. Clemency now would be a mistake. No doubt Marc was recalling a different noblewoman whose death he'd failed to prevent, but Branwen believed even her mother would have seen the countess executed.

"I believe in the Horned One's compassion." Marc paused. "Which is why I will allow you to live out the remainder of your days as a prisoner at Villa Illogan. The territory that House Whel received as a blood price for the death of Princess Endelyn will be returned to the crown."

The countess bowed her head as the king pronounced her sentence.

"Furthermore, the other lands and holdings belonging to House Whel will be transferred to Prince Andred, true heir of Prince Edern," King Marc continued. "House Whel was created by my grandfather when he elevated the status of your family."

Another pause. "Today, I unmake it."

Baron Dynyon couldn't suppress a shocked intake of breath.

"You are a countess no more," the king intoned. A bleak look crossed

Kensa's face, and Branwen wondered if she wouldn't have preferred death.

To Ruan, Marc said, "I do not believe that you sought my throne or that you were party to your mother's crimes. However, you did attempt to assassinate the pirate king to protect your mother, and to obstruct justice."

"Yes, my Lord King," rasped Ruan. The sadness in his eyes was fathomless.

"I trusted you with my life," Marc told him. "I loved you."

Ruan could only make a rumbling noise at the back of his throat. His eyes shone.

"You are banished from Kernyv from this day forward," the king pronounced. "I will allow you a horse and the clothes on your back. If you ever set foot in my kingdom again, your life will be forfeit."

"*Mormerkti.*" Ruan bowed from the waist. "I am indebted to your mercy, *Ríx.*"

"Xandru," said King Marc. "You will escort Countess Kensa to Villa Illogan." He said the words like a command, but Branwen saw the look that passed between the men. The trust. The supplication.

With feline stealth, Alba crossed toward Kensa and smacked her, open palmed, across the face.

"Be glad I'm not your queen," she said.

"Be glad you were born with power," spat the countess.

Kensa's cheek beamed a vibrant red, nearly as scarlet as her combs, but she made no move to soothe herself.

Tristan walked to his wife, touching Alba gently on the elbow.

"She's not worth your anger," he said.

"King Marc," said Branwen. "I would be happy to ensure Ruan is escorted to the causeway."

Their eyes met in understanding. He nodded. Xandru unlocked Ruan's manacles, and he shook his wrists free. Andred hurried toward his older brother.

"Hello there, scamp," said Ruan. Andred's shoulders heaved, and Branwen could tell the boy was trying not to sob.

Branwen retreated toward the front of the hall, giving the brothers space for their goodbyes. She knew Ruan would follow. He had no other choice. She turned toward the gathering dusk in the courtyard as Ruan embraced his mother. He would never see her again.

The chimes tinkled in the hot air. Eventually another shoulder pressed against Branwen's, familiar and warm. Guards walked behind them as Ruan and Branwen strolled toward the stables in silence. His stallion neighed at him in greeting.

Branwen's heart thudded in her throat. Ruan scarcely looked at her as he led the horse by the reins down the hill of Monwiku for the last time.

They stopped at the edge of the causeway, the tide beginning to rush in. Branwen motioned the guardsmen back with her hand.

"You had time to think," she said.

"I did."

Ruan unpinned Lady Alana's brooch and offered it back to Branwen. She looked from the brilliant silver to his muted, honeyed eyes.

"Endelyn's death was my fault," he said. "I couldn't watch my mother die, too."

She understood. She did. In the end, Ruan had chosen the right fight for him—his family. Yet they were now on opposite sides of an impassable ravine.

Branwen nodded, crouching down, and retrieved his father's knife from his boot. She held it out to him.

"You could go to Iveriu," she suggested. "Find Conchobar's family."

"Iveriu isn't my home." Ruan lifted his gaze from the knife to Branwen's eyes. "I once thought it might be you."

Her heart wrenched violently. "I'm sorry." She offered him the knife again. "Take it."

"You're the only woman I'd ever want to have it."

"And I don't want you to be without it," Branwen insisted.

After a beat, reluctantly, Ruan traded her mother's brooch for his father's knife.

"Knife or no knife, you will always have my heart," he said. "Remember that. *Comnaide*."

He tucked the knife into the waistband of his breeches and swung one leg over his stallion. Gripping the mane with two hands, he hoisted himself up.

"Take care of Andred for me."

"*Comnaide*," she echoed.

Ruan quirked his lips. "Farewell, *karid*."

He kicked his horse into a gallop, and Branwen watched until he was nothing more than a speck against the evenfall. Black against mauve.

She fastened her mother's brooch to her collar, and exhaled.

A SECOND SUN

THE EYES OF THE RED owl pierced Branwen as the sail billowed in the breeze.

Alba stood at the helm, speaking with the captain of the Armorican vessel, although Branwen had little doubt who would truly be captaining the ship back to Karaez. The crew lugged the final crates, filled with bottles of Kernyvak wine, up the gangway—a wedding present from King Marc.

Branwen proceeded slowly down the pier toward the ship, her eyes roaming the port. Marghas was bustling once more. After dismounting from Senara, she'd dawdled in the marketplace. Her heart was restless, and she'd already said too many goodbyes.

She spied Eseult speaking with King Marc and Tristan, the king clasping his nephew's hands. Branwen wasn't close enough to hear the words they exchanged, but the emotion was written on their faces.

With the revelation that his own nobles had plotted against him, King Marc's alliance with Armorica and Iveriu was essential to the stability of his kingdom. Tristan would serve Kernyv, and his uncle, because he loved him. Glancing back at Alba, her feelings muddled, Branwen stroked the fingerless leather glove she'd fashioned to cover her palm.

From nowhere, Xandru appeared at Branwen's side, moving with catlike precision. She acknowledged him with a tight smile.

"Back from Illogan already?" she said, slowing her pace further.

"Yesterday." The wind teased the dark hair tied at the nape of his neck. He waited a beat before saying, "I wouldn't think you'd expect an apology."

Branwen snorted, tilting her gaze at him sidelong. "No."

"No," Xandru repeated. One corner of his mouth lifted. "We needed a confession. Marc needed to be certain all of the conspirators were ferreted out."

"And you reasoned that if anyone could lead Ruan into a trap, it would be me."

"For Marc's sake, I had hoped he wouldn't come," said Xandru. "The other traitors will be executed tomorrow at dawn, and the kingdom can begin to heal."

"I fear that Remus will only return to the Veneti Isles and rile up the pirates, bide his time, and take up arms against us again," Branwen said. "He's a dangerous man. Cunning."

She traced the outline of Dhusnos's mark on her disguised palm, a new habit, and Xandru's gaze followed her forefinger.

"King Marc promised Remus that he would leave Monwiku alive, and he left last night." Xandru gave Branwen a long look. "He will not be returning to the Veneti Isles."

She nodded, relief loosening her shoulders even as coldness oozed into her belly. Death was a currency in which she now traded too easily.

"You could have left with Ruan," said Xandru.

"My place isn't with him." She gave a shake of the head. "And you, Captain, will you be staying at Monwiku now that the pirates have been quelled?"

His lips twitched. Eseult waved at Branwen as she neared. "My place isn't here, either," said Xandru so only Branwen could hear. "He needs peace more."

King Marc squeezed Branwen's shoulder with affection as she came to stand beside him, and Xandru melted into the busy port.

Tristan coughed. "*Dymatis*, Lady Branwen," he said, stilted.

She met his gaze, and the hazel flecks in his eyes intensified. Her chest constricted. Branwen had avoided him for the past few days since the plot was exposed. She had thought it would be better to grow accustomed to his absence, and now she regretted it.

"*Dymatis*, Prince Tristan," she choked out.

"We will leave you to say your farewells," Eseult told Tristan. She embraced him warmly, as old friends might. Drawing back, she said, "You served me faithfully as my Champion, and I will always be grateful. I will never forget."

Tristan bowed from the waist.

"It was my honor."

King Marc pulled in a labored breath. He placed a hand on Tristan's shoulder, staring at him with a severe expression, mastering his grief.

"We will see each other again, brother."

Tristan responded with a determined nod. The queen tugged discreetly at her husband's arm and, as they brushed past Branwen, the din of the docks faded away.

"I regret what happened with Ruan," Tristan started, a roughness to his voice. "Although you may not believe me."

"We have peace now." Branwen swallowed. "For now."

"We do." Tristan reached for her gloved hand and she let him take it, his fingers gentle on her skin, on the leather. "I will send for you. Before Samonios. I won't let you face Dhusnos alone."

Her mouth grew dry. Their fingers intertwined.

"But you must, Tristan. You have made enough hero's sacrifices," she told him. "I stitched this back together once." With her other hand, Branwen traced the line of love-knots just beneath his tunic, across his heart.

Tristan shuddered a breath.

"More than once," he said.

"Branwen!" called Alba as she raced down the gangway. Branwen released Tristan's hand, an ache in her chest. The princess was dressed in black leather trousers and an olive-colored tunic. Her short black hair was iridescent in the sunlight; the one gray streak tucked behind her ear.

She glanced from Branwen to Tristan, eyebrow quirked, not unaware she'd interrupted something. To her husband Alba said, "We're ready to hoist anchor."

Tristan wet his lips. "Until we meet again," he said to Branwen. He turned toward the ship, and Branwen studied his profile for the last time.

The surf sprayed the dock. "The weather is fair," Branwen said, forcing herself to look at Alba. "You must be eager to return home."

"I am, and I'm not. I have a lot to answer for."

"We all do." She couldn't prevent her eyes from drifting in Tristan's direction as he reached the deck of the ship. "I wish you happiness," Branwen told Alba, and she meant it. "Both of you."

Her magic had brought Tristan so much despair, she wanted only good things for him now.

"I don't hate you," said Alba. "I wanted you to know that before I left."

Branwen flattened her lips against the threat of tears.

"Under different circumstances, I would have been honored to call you a friend, Captain Alba."

"And I you, Healer Branwen."

She held Branwen's gaze. The two women did not embrace, but they shared a smile. Gratitude, and a strange kinship, knit itself between them.

Then Alba joined Tristan on the bow of the ship that would carry them to their new life together, and Branwen walked back toward hers.

✠ ✠ ✠

As they traveled the coastal path back to Monwiku, Eseult sidled her mare beside Senara. "When we reach the castle, we should finish the elderberry wine," she declared.

Branwen flicked her cousin a half smile. "Is that an order?"

"If you like."

The red-and-yellow sail of the Armorican ship was bright against the blue sky, like a second sun.

The queen glanced around them. Marc and Xandru rode in front, farther along the path, and Sir Goron trailed several horse lengths behind.

Lowering her voice, Eseult told her, "You were right when you said Tristan would never love me if he knew me as well as you did, Branny."

Frost-hot panic swept over Branwen. "I was speaking from anger," she said.

"You know me best. I always wanted someone to love me for me— and you did. I've been selfish, and I've been horrid to you. But my whole life, you've loved me best, even when I did nothing to deserve it."

Tears speckled the queen's lashes. "I'm sorry I took Tristan away from you," she said in a rushed whisper. "If I'd been strong enough to let him go, he wouldn't be married to Alba. Ruan wouldn't be—"

Branwen cut her off. "We can't know what might have happened. Tristan still might have had to marry Alba—or someone else—for peace. For Kernyv. A prince's life is not his own."

Eseult blinked, a few tears falling upon her cheeks, which were pinking under the glare of the cloudless afternoon. Branwen blew out a breath, too exhausted to cry.

"There's a ship leaving for Blackford Harbor in a few days' time," said her cousin. "Do you want to go home, Branny? Marc would understand. I don't want you to stay here for me any longer. I want you to do as you wish."

Branwen inhaled the sea air, glancing from the yellow sail gliding toward Armorica like a fin, to the sun arcing westward toward Iveriu. Her life at Castle Rigani had revolved around her younger cousin, and she was still too cowardly to read the letter from her aunt. She feared she wouldn't be welcomed back after the way she'd endangered the peace.

Branwen's place wasn't with Ruan or Tristan, but it was also not on Ivernic shores.

"I promised Ruan I would watch over Andred," she said, after a few quiet moments. "I am the Royal Healer, and I want to see Queen Verica's legacy established in Kernyv."

Eseult dried her eyes. "I'm so glad. I have other news," she said with a hint of mischief, "but I didn't want to color your decision."

Frowning, Branwen said, "What is it?"

"Marc is bequeathing you Castle Wragh for services to the crown. And the other lands that comprised Endelyn's blood price."

"Liones?" she gasped.

"You will be made Duchess of Liones, which will make you the highest ranking noblewoman in Kernyv—after me, of course." Her cousin winked. "I suggested it," Eseult said, a tad prideful. "I would give you more if I could."

Branwen stared at the queen, mouth agape. "It's too much."

"The title also comes with a permanent seat on the King's Council," Eseult continued.

"Baron Dynyon won't like it," Branwen cautioned, and she worried how the other barons would react as well.

"After tomorrow, I doubt Baron Dynyon will dare complain."

The executions of Baron Gwyk and Seer Casek were to be a very public affair. Branwen knew the grisly nature of their deaths would turn King Marc's stomach, but he couldn't afford to balk. He had already shown perhaps more mercy than was wise.

The turrets of Monwiku Castle came into view as Branwen lost sight of Tristan and Alba's ship.

"I don't think I deserve the honor of such a title," she told her cousin, throat growing hoarse. She held up her right hand. "I have a darkness in me. I think I always have."

Eseult folded her hand over Branwen's as their palfreys walked side by side.

"And for that, I am to blame," she said.

"I can't blame you, Essy. I won't. I've made my own choices."

"The Belotnia Eve when we carved our names into the hazel tree, we declared we'd never need lovers," the queen said, expression becoming wistful. "Not as long as we had each other." She sighed. "Sometimes I wish we could have stayed girls forever."

"Sometimes I do, too." Branwen surprised herself by pecking her cousin on the cheek, warmth unfurling in her chest.

"Please consider accepting Marc's offer," urged Eseult. "The king needs you. He needs allies on the council. He's lost too many."

Realization dawned. "You care for him," said Branwen.

"You told me he could become a steadfast friend—if I let him."

A smile flitted across her face, relenting. "I'll consider the offer."

"Can I ask you another favor?" said Eseult. Her cousin wouldn't be her cousin if she didn't press her luck. Branwen arched an eyebrow in question.

"I'd like to learn to suture wounds," said the queen. "Would you let me apprentice with you?"

Branwen hadn't thought she could receive any further shocks today.

"Really?" she said. "Why would you want to?"

Her cousin drew her shoulders back, lifting the reins of her horse.

"It's time I learned how to heal for myself."

FAITH

THE DUNGEON WAS DANK, A musty odor filling Branwen's nostrils. After she'd returned from Marghas, she declined the king's invitation to dinner, retreating instead to the West Tower. She fell asleep, still dressed, atop her bed. The hour was late when she woke with a start. Heart hammering, she began walking toward the barracks of the Royal Guard—and the dungeon below.

Drops of moisture slid down the stone walls, pooling at her feet, making the steps slippery as she descended. The guardsmen posted at the entrance hadn't questioned why the Royal Healer wanted to visit the prisoners. In truth, she could not discern what precisely compelled her.

Branwen had dreamed of the raven, its wings winter-bitten. The Wise Damsel had told her that the Fire of Inspiration no longer gave Branwen access to the world of the living. Could she only dream of death?

Her path through the gloom of the dungeon was lit by oil lamps and, although the night was mild aboveground, she shivered. She could well believe she was traveling through a *ráithana*, the hills belonging to the Old Ones, to the Otherworld beneath the earth.

At the bottom of the stairs, three cells lay on either side of a spindly corridor. Baron Gwyk occupied the cell closest to the stairwell. The flickering flame from the oil lamp reflected in his glass eye. He had lost the eye in raids on Iveriu. A year ago, the nothingness Branwen felt at the prospect of this man's death would have alarmed her.

"*Nosmatis,*" she said, voice staccato.

The baron's lips twisted in a ferocious expression and he cursed at her in Kernyvak.

His eldest son would take the baron's place on the King's Council as the new head of House Gwyk, and Branwen could only presume that he would be hostile toward the king who had ordered his father's execution. Branwen schooled her features, refusing to give him the satisfaction of provoking her, and continued walking toward the last cell.

Seer Casek rose to his feet as Branwen approached. The diamond-encrusted antler shard twinkled, disconcerting. He ran a hand over his bald head, flecked with grime from the squalid cell.

He smiled one of his terribly pleasant smiles.

"Lady Branwen," he said, tone snide. "Have you come to pray with me in my final hours?"

"Why does the temple use white ravens as messengers?" she replied.

The seer canted his head, intrigued. "Temples of the Horned One have always used white ravens." Branwen glared at him and he continued, "Our god is the Lord of Wild Things. After Carnonos was impaled by the stag, his father left him in the forest, running to their village for aid."

Seer Casek paused, regarding Branwen as if she were a dim-witted child.

"Carnonos died alone, with only a white raven who alighted upon his chest as company. When other carrion birds circled his body, the white raven fought them off, prevented them from defiling his flesh."

Branwen crossed her arms, her right thumb stroking the bend of her elbow.

"As the truth of the Horned One began to spread across the Aquilan Empire, the emperor persecuted his followers. They were forced to meet in secret. A white raven painted on a house indicated a place of safety." The *kordweyd* sighed dramatically.

"But why is this of interest to you, my lady? You cling tightly to your false gods."

Her temper flared, but the man before her no longer posed any danger to Branwen or the True Queen. His eyes were haggard despite his sneer. She traced the inside of her right palm, almost wishing her gods were false.

"You committed treason in the name of your god," Branwen told Casek. "Your actions will not help spread his truth."

"On the contrary." The seer stepped to the front of the cell, gripping the iron bars. "I will die a martyr. Word will carry among the anointed of the tyrant king who burned a *kordweyd* because he tried to show him the true path."

Branwen laughed. "No one will believe such lies."

"Won't they? The Kernyveu who adhere to the Cult—including many of the nobles—will not be happy that I was executed like a common criminal."

He leaned closer, pressing his face against the bars. "The king's foreign bride still has not produced an heir. Perhaps the True Queen is barren as punishment for the king's lack of faith?"

"That's ridiculous," Branwen hissed. "Nature is not cruel."

"Human nature is, and people believe what they must. Everyone needs forgiveness, Lady Branwen. The peasants whose crops fail, the women whose children die in their cots—the Horned One gives them hope. The promise of resurrection is more powerful than any king can ever be."

Branwen's magic stirred at the *kordweyd*'s words, afraid that there was truth to them.

"I was born on the southern continent, in what is now Langazbardaz," Seer Casek continued. "I was born a slave." His eyes narrowed as Branwen inhaled. "Ruan's wounds were not the first lacerations from a whip that I'd treated."

He pulled up one sleeve of his sumptuous robes. In the low light, Branwen saw that his forearms were crisscrossed by white scars.

"For twenty years, I was considered less than human. When my master was close to death, he freed me because he believed the act would assure his resurrection. He did not regret my beatings. He was not a changed man. He freed me because he feared his own mortality."

Casek laughed bitterly. "I left my master's farm and found the nearest temple. I became consecrated as a *kordweyd* the very next day. Faith is power, and I vowed never to be powerless again."

"Queen Verica said you loved your own power more than you loved your god."

"They are one and the same, Lady Branwen. If King Marc were a wiser man, he would see that."

Gesturing at the bars, Branwen said, "Look where you are now, Seer Casek. Powerless once more."

"My legacy will be ensured, my lady. Mark my words."

Branwen turned to go. "I see the guilt in your eyes," said the seer. "You are Artume. A false woman. You will lead many men to ruin."

A hunger rose up in Branwen, nearly uncontrollable. The desire to steal this man's life. To drain him dry. Savor it.

"I might be Artume, but King Marc believes!" she shouted, pivoting back toward the *kordweyd*. "His faith in the Horned One is pure. Why would you seek to depose him?"

"Because he is weak. He is not my king."

"He is *my* king, and when morning comes *you* will burn." Composing herself, she told him, "And I will watch."

Branwen rushed from the dungeon before she did something else she'd regret, before she acted on the need humming in her veins. She ran through the barracks and up the hill.

A man's shape filled the path before her. "Branwen?" said Marc.

She met the king beneath a lantern that swung from a spear-leafed tree. "Brother," she said. "*Nosmatis*. Or, perhaps, *dymatis*."

"Dawn approaches," he said grimly.

"You couldn't sleep."

Marc sighed. "I did not want to rule like my father did."

Branwen stepped closer, her breath steadying. She rested a hand against the king's elbow. "You mourn the men who conspired against you. You showed Ruan mercy. You do not rule as he did."

He shifted his jaw, uncertain. In the lantern light, she noticed that his beard was precisely trimmed and she wondered if Xandru had been his barber.

"What keeps you from your bed?" Marc asked, sympathy shading his voice.

"I—I had a disturbing dream."

The king peered past Branwen toward the barracks. "Did your dream lead you to the dungeon?"

"I suppose it did. A white raven appeared to me."

Inhaling through his nose, Marc said, "A white raven transported Carnonos to his rebirth."

Smoke shimmered in Branwen's mind. The white raven seemed to be leading her to her end.

"You went to see Seer Casek," deduced the king. His expression was inscrutable.

Branwen nodded. "Your mother told me she didn't want Matrona to be forgotten in Kernyv. Men like Casek would suppress anything that threatens their own power. You don't owe him anything," she said, voice rising. "Visiting the traitors will bring you no solace."

Marc gave her a sad smile. "Sometimes I feel like I've known you my whole life, sister."

"We've been bound together without knowing it."

Regret tensed the corners of his mouth. "We have."

"Eseult relayed your offer to me," said Branwen. "I worry that making me—a foreigner, a woman—a duchess of Kernyv will not serve the best interests of the kingdom after such . . . turmoil."

He took her hand. "It is your concern for the kingdom that only makes me more confident. You have already put my people above yourself." Marc rubbed the leather covering her palm. "I will never have cause to doubt your loyalty."

Branwen choked down a sob. She had been the cause of a deeper betrayal, a deeper treason, and yet this man trusted her, considered her family.

"I'm still a monster," she said in a strained voice.

"A monster cannot forgive, and your forgiveness makes me a better man."

Tears sprang to her eyes that she couldn't hold back.

"You have become the best of men," Branwen told him, "and that is not my doing."

"Sister, if you want to leave my court, you have my blessing." He squeezed her hand. "I am sorry for Ruan."

"I know you are," she said. "He told me of his true parentage—and I kept his secret. I kept it secret from you."

"And you have kept mine." Marc's silver eyes flashed as the night began to thin. "You don't need to divulge all of your secrets for me to consider you my sister, Branwen."

Her tears flowed freely now. "I will accept a seat on your council," she said. "On one condition."

"Which is?"

"One Royal Infirmary is not enough. I believe Liones is rich in white lead. I want to use it to fund the creation of infirmaries across Kernyv. Perhaps elsewhere in Albion."

"The lands are yours to do with as you please." Marc gave her a knowing look. "Tristan will be heartened by the news."

The king brushed the tears from Branwen's cheeks. She hiccuped.

"Will you escort me back to my rooms?" she said.

Holding her gaze, Marc ducked his head. "I did come in search of solace. And I've found it." He kissed the top of Branwen's head and offered her his arm.

✢ ✢ ✢

The white raven skimmed the edges of her consciousness as Branwen returned to the West Tower. Perhaps it was a warning—or an entreaty. Once she fulfilled her bargain with Dhusnos, she would no longer be who she was.

In a few hours, Seer Casek would burn. Branwen's relief that she had saved Eseult from that fate—saved Iveriu—was all encompassing. She could no longer pretend that she was a good person, but she had done what was necessary. If her end was near, Branwen would spend her remaining days upholding the peace.

Tristan would send for her, she knew, but she would not come.

Summoning her courage, Branwen retrieved the letter from the Queen of Iveriu from beneath her pillow. She was ready to face her aunt's anger and disappointment. She could no longer act the part of cowering child.

The room was still save for the sound of parchment unscrolling.

My dearest Branwen,

I remember when you were a little girl and you would talk to the waves. I often wondered what they said that made you smile. Now there is a sea between us, and time is short as I write, but I want you to feel the love in these lines.

Alana was my younger sister, but I sought her advice more than I should admit. More than a queen should admit. Knowing the difficulties you have encountered in Kernyv, my heart aches. Like your mother, I know you will have found a way through the thorns, yet I dearly wish I could have helped you shoulder the burdens that I also know you will have taken onto yourself.

I have tried to impart the lessons you would need to be a woman in this world, like Alana would have, but I fear there is one that I have failed to teach you. The most important one.

Life's most closely guarded secret, my darling niece—my darling daughter—is that we fail more than we succeed. We must learn to love ourselves, and each other, in our failures. Watching you grow into a woman of conviction has been a privilege and I love you more than I can ever express, Branwen.

I want you to love yourself, too. As much as you have loved Essy. As much as you have loved Iveriu. Love yourself as much when you fail as when you succeed—more, even.

This is my last lesson for you. Please make it a promise.

Yours always, devoted,

Eseult

Parchment fell to stone. Every insult, every flaw, every word of loathing that Branwen had expected to see in ink would never have been authored by her aunt. She had feared the letter as if it would be a mirror, but Branwen was the author of her own self-hate. She had assumed the woman who raised her saw only what she saw.

A tremulous breath escaped Branwen's lips. Her aunt wanted only love for her. Only love. Yet she couldn't make that promise. The Queen of Iveriu didn't know the terrible choice that lay before her. Thorns still bit her deeply, crowded her path.

Branwen cried for who she had been, and for who she would become.

She slept a few restless hours on the wings of an ice-white raven.

PART III

THE END OF THE BEGINNING

RUDDERLESS

SUMMER LINGERED FOR SO LONG it seemed endless, and then it was gone.

Branwen and Eseult had held hands as they watched Seer Casek and Baron Gwyk burn at the stakes erected on the same beach where Tristan had fought Ruan for the queen's honor. The stench of singed flesh polluted the causeway for days.

Xandru made himself scarce immediately after the executions, the *Mawort* departing for the southern continent. King Marc spent his free hours replanting and reviving his gardens, seeds occasionally arriving from abroad, while Branwen and the queen started recruiting female students who were interested in healing.

The freckles that dotted Branwen's nose and forearms soon multiplied, and on nights the sky stayed shell-pink until midnight, she could almost let herself forget the deal she had struck with the Dark One. But Laelugus, the Festival of Peace, had taken place two moons ago. A year had passed since the Champions Tournament, and now only three weeks remained until Samonios.

By the next moon, Branwen must take a life, or condemn someone she loved.

A nip was in the air that teased the hem of her cloak as she skulked beside the Stone of Waiting, surveying the crowd assembled for the official opening of the Royal Infirmary. Maroon snakestone glistened in the mist of the moors.

The True Queen had ensured the infirmary was larger—and grander—than anything attached to the temples, although she was now never without the antler shard around her neck. Built in the Aquilan style, the square, two-story structure was constructed around a central courtyard and divided into four wards: surgery, maternity, wasting sickness, and a clinic for minor injuries. After various delays, the infirmary had begun receiving patients in midsummer, although this afternoon was its dedication to Matrona in accordance with Queen Verica's wishes.

Branwen scanned the faces of the villagers, both Kernyveu and Iverni, who had come to celebrate the dedication. Laughter echoed across the moor as they enjoyed the spiced wine, Stargazy pies and apple tarts laid on two long tables, offered by the king and queen. Eseult always loved to organize a feast, and she was greeting her subjects in Kernyvak, Lowenek at her side, paying particular attention to the boys and girls.

Branwen exchanged a smile with Talorc from a distance, the elderly Iverman also hovering near Lowenek. He had taken up a post as a custodian at the infirmary to be close to the girl who had become his family. Queen Verica had been right about Lowenek's skillful fingers, and Branwen suspected she would soon surpass her own talent with a needle.

The day she'd met the Wise Damsel at the mining disaster, Branwen had been told by Ailleann that healers were all sister, daughter, and mother to each other in turn, and she now felt the truth of those words. When Branwen instructed Lowenek how to prepare a poultice or clean an infected wound, she experienced a new kind of pride, a different sense of contentment.

Her eyes found her other apprentice in the crowd, sticking close to King Marc. When not given a specific task, it was nearly impossible to coax Andred from his rooms. He devoted all of his time to his flowering box experiments and to compiling a compendium of the medicinal properties of Kernyvak plants for use in the infirmary.

"*Dymatis*, Healer Branwen," said Seer Ogrin as he wandered over to her. He held a goblet fashioned from white lead, filled with spiced wine. "Normally, I abstain," he said, glancing at the dark liquid. "But it is a celebration, and we have worked hard." His jolly face parted in a smile.

His brown robes were plain, cinched with a belt of wooden beads from which dangled an antler shard. Dull sunlight illuminated his shorn head, a smattering of gray hairs closely shaven.

"Today is for celebrating," Branwen agreed, although her stomach clenched at how few nobles were in attendance. The *kordweyd* raised an eyebrow at her empty hands. "I haven't eaten yet," she explained. Her appetite diminished with each day that Samonios neared.

Seer Ogrin never asked Branwen about the fingerless glove that had become like a second skin.

His eyes crinkled as he took another sip of wine. "Have I ever told you how I came to Kernyv?" he said, and Branwen shook her head. "In a rowboat."

"From where?" she asked, curiosity piqued.

"The Kingdom of Míl."

Branwen shot Ogrin a disbelieving look. "You crossed the sea in a rowboat?" she said. Alba had managed the Southern Channel in a din-ghy, but the kingdom of Míl was much farther.

"I didn't say it was an easy journey." He tilted his head at her, laughing in his childlike manner. "After my Consecration, I chose to wander. I climbed aboard a boat—oarless, rudderless—and trusted the Horned One would lead me where I needed to be."

Branwen gasped. "That's sheer folly."

"We're all rudderless sometimes," he said with a shrug.

Eseult waved at the seer from beneath the entrance to the infirmary. It was time to begin. A linen sheet covered the statue of Matrona that was to be unveiled as part of the dedication. Ogrin raised his glass to Branwen and walked toward the queen. The smile beaming from her cousin's face elicited a small one from Branwen. She had never seen Eseult so confident.

Several births had taken place at the infirmary in recent weeks and her cousin was becoming a diligent midwife. She wasn't as capable with sutures and stitches as Lowenek, but the queen took great joy in delivering babies. Branwen chided herself for her own astonishment, and she wished her aunt could see the patience and kindness that Eseult lavished on expectant mothers or hear the lullabies she sang to newborns.

The murmurings of the crowd dimmed as King Marc began his address. Sir Goron stood behind the two monarchs, ever watchful.

Branwen slipped between the guests in the direction of the banquet tables. Sea-wolves and lions were embroidered on the tablecloths, the backdrop white, black, and green. A shallow breath became trapped in Branwen's chest as she recalled the tricolor bracelet Tristan had given her aboard the *Dragon Rising*.

Pilfering an apple tart, she began to nibble. The crust was not as light as those prepared by Treva at Castle Rigani, and yet when Baron

Chyanhal appeared at Branwen's side, startling her, she discreetly brushed the crumbs from her lips.

"*Dymatis*, Duchess Branwen," he said. Branwen returned his greeting, yet she was coming to prefer the title of Healer. The baron's slender frame cast a long shadow across the grassy moor.

Branwen's eyes circled those assembled and she said, "I only see Baron Kerdu and yourself from the King's Council in attendance. Do the other barons have more pressing obligations?"

"Baron Julyan has grown too ill to leave his manor," replied Baron Chyanhal. "He's sent his eldest daughter, Lady Neala, in his stead." The baron pointed toward a short woman who had seen at least forty summers, her light brown hair coiled atop her head, fine lines streaking her pale forehead.

"I am sorry to hear of his illness," Branwen said. "I would be happy to visit him."

Baron Chyanhal nodded, making a noncommittal noise. Keeping his voice low, he said, "The dissolution of House Whel has raised concerns among the other Houses, Duchess."

As well as her own elevation to duchess, she surmised. Branwen skewered him with a glance. "Kensa committed treason against the crown. All ranks—and lands—are bestowed at the king's pleasure."

"True, but we all have relatives whom we cannot control," said Baron Chyanhal mildly, features composed in a mask of calm. "Prince Andred is of royal blood, yet he no longer has a House. To be stripped of our lands without notice, without any protections—it makes the nobles uneasy."

"Are you making a threat?" Branwen demanded in a quiet, but harsh, voice.

The crowd cheered and clapped as King Marc finished his speech, motioning at the True Queen.

"I'm making an observation, Duchess," replied the baron. "My ancestors were once foreigners in Kernyv, too, and I supported the peace with Iveriu. House Gwyk waits each day for news of its own dissolution, and their new head, Doane, is an impulsive man. Quick to draw a sword."

Branwen tugged at the hem of her cloak, stomach twisting, as Eseult addressed the crowd in Kernyvak, thanking them for coming. The queen had taken pains this summer to become proficient in the language of her subjects. A diadem of white lead winked atop her head. She looked like the True Queen she was always meant to be.

"Why are you telling me this?" Branwen whispered to Baron Chyanhal.

"Because I believe you to be pragmatic, my lady. Prince Tristan belongs to Armorica now; Ruan is banished. Andred's status is muddy. There is no obvious heir should both the king and queen perish before their time."

He paused, considering his next words. The baron's brown skin glimmered in the luminous afternoon, intensifying his impassive features. "Reassure the barons that the kingdom is stable—and that their Houses are secure."

"*Mormerkti*," Branwen said shortly. "I will consider your counsel."

She walked toward the front of the crowd as Seer Ogrin intoned a blessing of the Horned One. When the *kordweyd* had finished the prayer, he spoke in Kernyvak, then Aquilan.

He met Branwen's stare as he said, "Matrona, the mother of Carnonos, was herself a healer. She understood the Mysteries of life and death. All healers are beloved of the Horned One, and all those who seek consolation are welcome here."

Eseult pulled on a rope and the sheet covering the frieze above the rounded archway rippled to the ground. Boisterous applause erupted from the onlookers.

While the infirmary building had been constructed from snake-stone, the relief of Matrona was carved from a cream-colored marble. A master stonemason had brought the sorrow of Matrona to life—her downturned lips, tears in her eyes, and bowed head—as she cradled her son's slack, prone body. Branwen could almost hear the woman's weeping on the wind. The Land, too, wept for her children, and Branwen's throat grew tight.

Behind Matrona a stag kneeled, offering Carnonos his antlers—the implements of the god's death—in apology, the creature shriving itself. This was the moment before the Horned One was reborn as a god. When he was still a man.

Perched on his mother's shoulder was a raven. Its stone eyes fixed on Branwen, and they blinked.

✝ ✝ ✝

Branwen dawdled in the king's study after supper. Eseult retired to the Queen's Tower for a bath, her muscles sore from the exertions of the day, as Andred and Lowenek disappeared to his rooms across the hall to continue with his experiments.

"The days grow shorter," remarked King Marc. He lit another candle on the dining table. Glancing at the *fidkwelsa* board in the room, he said, "Could I tempt you with another game?"

This summer Branwen and the king had finally found time to play. She had currently won two more matches than Marc in their running tally. A comfortable routine had been established during the hot months: dinners with Eseult, Marc, Andred, and Lowenek—a new family of sorts; games of *fidkwelsa* with the king afterward. Branwen had allowed herself to be lulled into the false belief it could last forever.

Marc leaned forward in his chair, resting his elbows on the table.

"What occupies your mind, sister?" he said. A line appeared on the bridge of his nose.

"Did you notice how few nobles attended the ceremony today?" asked Branwen.

The king stroked his beard, candlelight accentuating the sorrel bristles. "Lady Neala told me that Baron Julyan is unwell."

Branwen nodded. "He has seen many summers." She waited a beat. "Baron Dynyon has no such excuse. Neither does the new head of House Gwyk."

"No." A weighted word.

"The barons are in need of reassurance that their Houses will not be destroyed."

"If they don't commit treason, they have nothing to fear." Marc's voice was gruff, loud, not like himself. He sighed. "What kind of reassurance would you propose?"

Branwen plucked the bronze goblet from next to her plate. She swirled it, observing the sediment drift in the wine.

"Perhaps a treaty?" she said. "An alliance."

"With my own barons?"

She took a sip. "A document that enumerates the rights of the barons—and their duties to the crown."

Marc rubbed his hand over his forearm, over the sea-wolf tattoo that was inked beneath. The tattoo he'd received before his first raid.

"It's an intriguing idea," he allowed, after a minute or two. "Does Iveiru have such an agreement between the High King and his retainers?"

"Not as such."

"But a king's subjects keep him in power," said Marc, grabbing

Branwen's gaze, as if he had lifted the thought from her head. He rubbed his forearm with more force.

"Baron Dynyon's wife is a fervent follower of the Horned One," said the king. "She was dismayed at Seer Casek's death."

Branwen swallowed, throat burning from the wine. If her time on this side of the Veil was drawing to a close, she would not let Casek's predictions be proved true. She wasn't content to leave her adopted kingdom rudderless.

"You need an heir," she told the king.

Marc gave a small cough. "Sister, I will not press that issue. Your cousin is beginning to embrace her life here." His statement was firm.

"Could you not designate someone else?" she said. "Until such time as you and Eseult . . . until the queen is once again with child?"

Candlelight wavered between them. The sea lashed the rocks at the base of the island. Marc stroked his beard, considering, but made no reply.

"There is also the matter of Andred." The king raised his brow at Branwen's words. "He is Prince Edern's son, and you have given him the holdings that once belonged to House Whel. But his official status is unclear. Perhaps . . . perhaps it would pacify the barons if you were to create a new House, with Andred at its head?"

King Marc leaned back in his chair. "He has always spoken the truth. Even when it implicated his own family."

"He is young, but he is just. He is not to blame for the actions of his mother or siblings."

Marc held Branwen's gaze. "I agree. Let's play another round of *fidkwelsa*. Perhaps this time I might win."

WATCHFIRES

FIVE DAYS HAD PASSED SINCE the opening of the infirmary. Each sunrise chiseled another chip from Branwen's heart. The dread that coursed through her at the thought of Samonios was a constant companion. If she could still scry, Branwen would have searched the kingdom for someone whose pain she could end as Queen Verica had decided to end her own.

She draped her cloak over the chair beside the hearth in the Queen Mother's apartment—which now belonged to Branwen. Eseult insisted that she needed a suite fit for a duchess. The bright yellow curtains did nothing to cheer her, however. She stretched her arms above her head, weary from the day and the long ride home from the Royal Infirmary.

Slumping into the chair, Branwen flicked the alabaster dice that rested upon the table. Queen Verica had adored games of chance, but Branwen had made a wager with a god, and a god played with loaded dice.

A knock came at the door, jarring Branwen from her thoughts. She called out leave for them to enter in Kernyvak.

"*Nosmatis*," replied a familiar, if unexpected, voice as a lithe figure appeared in the doorway.

"I didn't know you had returned," said Branwen.

Xandru closed the door behind him. He looked handsome in a tunic of deep blue velvet that complemented his golden-brown skin. Dust motes floated in the shafts of twilight that striped the room.

"Just this morning," he told her. His stride was fluid, gliding toward her from the doorway and taking the seat opposite hers.

He glanced around the suite; embers crackled in the hearth.

"You have risen high, Duchess Branwen."

"It was never my ambition."

Xandru relaxed into his chair. "I know," he said. "Which is why I'm glad Marc has had you by his side these past months."

"And where have you been?" she asked.

"Here and there." He picked up one of the dice, tossing it in the air and catching it one-handed. "I've been keeping an eye on the Veneti Isles, and other matters."

"Tending the watchfires," Branwen said as her nerves prickled. Xandru nodded. "How do things fare?"

"Not well. Food shortages. Riots," he answered, shrugging in his casual fashion. "Pirating was their only source of income. There are few farms. The terrain is rocky."

Xandru leaned closer, fiddling with the dice.

"If Kernyv is to maintain control, the islands will need a governor. And revenue. The Manduca family is interested in exporting the granite from the abandoned quarries."

Branwen stroked her gloved hand, taking in the news. The shrewd look in Xandru's eye undercut his placid demeanor.

"Family business brings you back to Monwiku, then," she said.

"One is a Manduca for life." Xandru's laugh was resigned. "But that is not the reason I've sought you out." His gaze skimmed her gloved hand and Branwen dropped it to her lap, tingles rushing down her spine.

"What is it I can do for you, Captain?"

"Marc has told me of your proposal—a treaty with the barons, and the creation of a new House for Andred. It's not a bad suggestion."

Xandru collected both of the dice, shook them, and watched as they spun; the table creaked.

"The former countess is still a threat." He met Branwen's gaze. "As long as she has a living son."

"Andred won't even visit her," said Branwen. Noble prisoners were often allowed visitors and the king had given him permission, but he refused to go.

"Ruan was also unaware of her schemes."

A valid point but, "Kensa is isolated at Villa Illogan," she protested.

"Do you remember our pirate friend, Otho?" Branwen raised an eyebrow, tension coiling in her chest, as Xandru went on, "He has found employment at Villa Illogan as a guard; his wife and daughter as maids."

The soldiers who had been sworn to House Whel had been disbanded, and Kensa's jailors handpicked by the king—and Xandru.

"They're spying for you," Branwen said, and she should have realized sooner. Xandru would never leave Kensa to her own devices, without eyes and ears on her. He loved Marc too much. A sliver of a laugh escaped her.

"Information is your trade," she said. "What do they report?"

He cocked his head at her, his smile cold. Dusk shone on his sleek black hair.

"A man matching Baron Dynyon's description has visited Villa Illogan twice in recent months."

Branwen inhaled sharply. "I don't understand. Why would she risk her life with another plot?"

Xandru answered her question with a question. "Have you ever watched a man drown?" he said, and she nodded, thinking of the horrible moment Eseult was thrown over the side of the *Dragon Rising*.

"Desperation makes a man clamor—hasten his own death," continued Xandru. "Kensa is already drowning."

And she would pull Kernyv down with her. "But would she really endanger her last living child in Kernyv?" Branwen wondered aloud.

"I think that woman would do anything for power. To put Andred on the throne—and rule in his stead as regent until he comes of age." Xandru's lip curled.

The possibility of Kensa acting as regent for her young son hadn't occurred to Branwen, but of course it was a gambit the countess would consider.

As Branwen's lips parted in dismay, Xandru noted, "You know I'm right."

She did. Kensa could do untold damage to Kernyv in a matter of months, never mind years as a regent. "Does Marc know?" Branwen said, fear lacing her words.

"The countess didn't name Baron Dynyon among her co-conspirators, and the king is loath to execute the head of another House without substantial proof."

She clasped her hands together, rubbing one thumb over the other. "The barons are already . . . agitated," she agreed.

"Even when a king is in the right, there is a fine line between enforcing the law and being seen to be a despot." Xandru paused. "Despots are often overthrown."

Although they were alone, Branwen whispered, "What are you suggesting?"

"Baron Dynyon is a pompous man, easily enticed by the right incentives. Prisoner or not, Kensa wields considerable influence. She lost Endelyn and Ruan because of your cousin and the king. She is not a woman who forgives."

Xandru held Branwen with a level gaze. "Kensa is a threat to Marc—and Kernyv—as long as she draws breath."

"He'll never have the stomach to kill her."

"He is too good." The captain's eyes gleamed. "Sometimes threats must be removed so that a king does not become a tyrant."

Branwen went utterly still. Her heart beat painfully. Dark murmurings filled the back of her mind, both the taunts of Dhusnos and the threats of Seer Casek.

Xandru pushed to his feet. "There have been reports of black lung near Illogan. Perhaps you should visit and see if Kensa is in good health? I fear she may have already caught the sickness."

He held her with a look. "No one will question the Royal Healer if she succumbs to an illness under your care."

Branwen nodded again, more slowly, realizing the truth of his words. It had to be her.

"Also, I trust you to protect Marc as I do."

His admission was no small thing, and she swallowed with sudden emotion.

"And where will you be?" Branwen asked him.

"I will be helping Marc to draft a new charter. The heads of the

Houses have too much power. Surely it would be fairer if we were to create an assembly with more representatives from the noble families. Don't you agree, Duchess?"

"Also more likely that they will fight among themselves."

Xandru grinned. "Precisely."

✠ ✠ ✠

Sleep did not come that night. Or the next. At dawn of the following day, Branwen saddled Senara and crossed the causeway, the White Moor her destination.

She felt each passing minute like grains of sand sliding through an hourglass. Fifteen days remained until Samonios.

Branwen rode her palfrey hard through the Morrois Forest, sweat forming on her brow as she reached the Royal Infirmary. Following the tip of the Stone of Waiting northwest for a league, she plunged into a shroud of fog.

Senara whinnied as the same doe with a missing tip of its ear, whose reddish coat was snow-flaked with bright spots, followed them into the thicket. The animal hadn't grown at all since the spring.

Bells tinkled from the branches overhead. The mare stomped her hoof. They were in the presence of an Old One. Branwen urged Senara onward, looking for the copse by the stream that led to the Wise Damsel's dwelling.

She heard no gurgling water.

Branwen pulled back on the reins, turning her mount around. She walked Senara more slowly, wondering if she had missed the path when the doe distracted her.

She returned southward, then aimed northward again. The fog thickened. Panic bit deep beneath Branwen's skin, its fangs sharp.

The White Moor was protecting itself. She could not cross the Veil to the healing well or Ailleann's cottage.

Branwen choked down on a wail, chest heaving. Twigs crunched beneath the doe's hooves as it approached. Senara's eyes grew wide, frightened.

The young deer began to lope, and Branwen kicked her mount into a trot, giving chase, following the creature.

Wishes fluttered in the trees, flashes of color in the dense mist.

Soon enough, Branwen found herself at the edge of the White Moor. The doe—the Old One—had guided them out, but the message was clear.

Branwen was no longer welcome.

✠ ✠ ✠

Dejected, she let the mare carry her back toward the Royal Infirmary. There was work to be done, patients to be tended. Work would numb Branwen's mind.

Arthek barked as she tied Senara to a wooden post near the Stone of Waiting. Andred had brought the pup to the infirmary to entertain the patients, although it hadn't lifted his spirits much. If Branwen did what Xandru had proposed, the weight on the young prince's shoulders would only increase.

Her eyes were drawn to the statue of Matrona above the entrance. Was Branwen truly the white raven? Taking Kensa's life would not lead her to rebirth.

"Branny?"

Branwen's gaze dropped from Matrona's mournful visage to the queen.

"I didn't expect to see you so early," said her cousin, drawing closer.

"I couldn't sleep," she replied, still in a daze. "What are you doing here?"

"Lamorna went into labor yesterday afternoon, and I didn't want to leave her. I stayed the night." Branwen's lips creased into a smile. "It's been a difficult delivery so far," said Eseult. "Her contractions are finally growing closer together."

She raked her cousin with her gaze: bruise-like smudges beneath the queen's eyes, blond plaits skewed, her gown soiled. And she looked happy. Genuinely happy.

Branwen's knees grew weak. She struggled for breath. The sob she had suppressed overwhelmed her. Eseult's mouth pinched in concern. "Branny, what is it?"

She couldn't find the words.

Eseult embraced Branwen, holding her up as her rib cage quaked. Her cousin drew circles on Branwen's back as Branwen had done for her on so many occasions. Branwen's cheeks grew so wet it was as if she'd cried the entire Ivernic Sea. The queen held her firm against her slight frame.

Sir Goron came running at the sound of a woman's distress. Embarrassment heated Branwen's face. Eseult shooed her Champion away and led Branwen into an empty room that opened onto the central courtyard. King Marc had sent the castle gardeners to plant it with spike-leafed trees and other foliage. Branwen shivered as wind stirred the chimes.

The queen sent Lowenek to brew some tea, and seated herself beside Branwen on a thin cot, stroking her spine in silence. The close quarters reminded Branwen of their cabin on the *Dragon Rising*, before everything had gone wrong.

Lowenek returned with the tea, the girl's gaze pensive as she handed Branwen a ceramic cup. Branwen sipped.

"What happened?" Eseult prodded, tender, once the girl had gone. Her cousin's green eyes were pained, filled with love, so like Lady Alana's.

"I'm afraid what my parents must think of me. If they can still see me from the Otherworld."

When the Armoricans had attacked Monwiku, Branwen had believed one life for many was a fair trade. Choosing that life was a slow form of torture.

Eseult stroked Branwen's brow, fingers cool, touch gentle.

"I fear what my parents think of me, too," said the queen. "Maybe we always do."

Branwen shook her head. "You don't understand. *I* . . . there is something I must do. A darkness that must be appeased."

She'd been a fool to think death had saved her. Branwen had saved the castle, and lost herself.

"You've done enough for peace," her cousin declared.

Branwen turned the cup between her fingers. She saw no choice but to become more lost.

"I've never told you the full truth."

Eseult swallowed. "I know, and I know why. You don't have to tell me now."

"I want to," said Branwen, and for the first time in their entire lives it was true.

"Then I want to listen."

She breathed in and out. "When Monwiku was besieged, I offered myself to Dhusnos. In exchange for his assistance in defending the castle, I—" Branwen rushed the next words, "I agreed to provide him with another Shade by Samonios." The queen touched her throat. "If I don't, Dhusnos will claim the soul of someone I love."

Eseult pried the mug from Branwen's hands, setting it on the floor. With a deliberate motion she intertwined their fingers.

Voice strained near to breaking, Branwen confessed, "And, Essy, part of me *wants* to—the rush when I take a life . . . not even love feels as good."

Her cousin pulled Branwen closer on the bed, wrapping her other arm around Branwen's back. "What can I do to help you?" Her voice was hushed, resolute.

"Tristan already offered me his life," said Branwen, leaning back, meeting Eseult's gaze. "I won't condemn him that way."

Her cousin opened her mouth. "Or you," Branwen preempted her.

"There must be something."

Branwen's shoulders rose and fell, fresh tears welling. "I have no choice but to fulfill my end of the bargain. I don't know how it will change me," she said. "I need you to remember me—remember who I am."

"Nothing will change my love for you." Eseult traced the honeysuckle and the hazel atop Branwen's leather glove. "You have one last battle," said the queen, lifting her chin. "And I will be waiting when you return. You will always be the sister of my heart."

Who Branwen would be when she returned she did not know. She only knew that it would not be the woman she was now.

VILLA ILLOGAN

BRANWEN RODE ALONE ACROSS THE peninsula.

She forded the River Heyl where it was shallowest, near Sir Goron's home, then continued south toward Illogan, which was located on the tip of a jagged cape. She stayed a night at the same inn where she had rested together with the king and queen during Eseult's welcome tour last winter.

Sheer physical exhaustion had forced a few hours of sleep on Branwen, but she woke before the sparrows.

Villa Illogan was perched on a clifftop, ferocious waves assaulting the cape below. Branwen spotted its silhouette from several leagues away. Derelict mines lay on either side of the road. She remembered Ruan telling her that his ancestors had grown wealthy selling white lead to the Aquilan legions, but the land around Illogan was now depleted of minerals. Ruan's true father must have been pressed into labor in one of the mines that Branwen now passed.

The day was blustery as Senara carried her steadily toward the villa, a heavy inevitability closing in on her. Her cloak fanned around her. It was unadorned.

Branwen had left her mother's brooch at Monwiku. This was not the right fight, yet it was the fight she had chosen. Despite knowing her destination, she felt as rudderless as when Seer Ogrin had abandoned himself to the will of his god and a rowboat.

Twelve days. Twelve days until Samonios. Branwen could let the former countess live a little longer. She could. But this was the road she traveled.

Five days from now, King Marc would announce the new Crown Charter to all of the noble Houses. His invitation to attend a feast at the castle made crystal clear that apologies could not be sent. Nor could anything—anyone—be allowed to interfere with the implementation of the new laws.

Yellow gorse sprinkled the loam, sprouting stubbornly in the ruined earth. The road tapered as Branwen approached the villa. She had never visited Ruan's home with him. The remnants of the vinegary tea and stale bread she'd eaten for breakfast rose in Branwen's throat. If fortune were kind, Ruan would never learn the details of his mother's death.

The façade of Villa Illogan was not dissimilar to the late pirate king's residence in the Veneti Isles. Six snakestone columns supported the triangular roof of the building in the center of a rectangular complex. Behind the Aquilan structure, set farther back, loomed three rounded towers made from granite in the Kernyvak style. Perhaps they'd been added later, when House Whel required more fortification. The overall impression of Ruan's childhood home was daunting.

In addition to the soldiers who had been in the employ of the countess, the servants had also been dismissed and replaced with a skeleton staff. Now, as Branwen's mount beat the dirt road toward the portico of the villa, there was no one to be seen.

She inhaled shortly. It was as if the villa already belonged to the dead.

Wind whistled between the pillars of the portico as Branwen brought Senara to a halt. "*Dymatís!*" she called out. She received no response.

After a few minutes, Branwen tried again.

Finally, Otho appeared at the top of the steps that led to the portico. He rubbed his substantial nose and waved. He did not look surprised to see Branwen.

He wore a black uniform with the crest of House Whel embroidered in red thread on his tunic. Kensa had dressed her jailer in her colors. Xandru's assessment was correct. The former countess would not so easily accept the destruction of her House. She was still clamoring.

Branwen jumped down from her mount, boots squelching in the soft ground. It had rained overnight and the air was thick, presaging another storm.

As Otho took Senara's reins from Branwen, he thinned his lips into a not quite smile, revealing his snaggled teeth. He was careful not to make contact with her. He had already witnessed the power of Branwen's touch.

"*Mormerkti,*" she told him, and she patted her mare's shoulder. "Kensa?"

A woman appeared between the pillars above them. Otho slanted his gaze in her direction. Her white skin was tanned, and her shoulders were broad. She looked younger than Otho, perhaps thirty summers.

"My wife, Petra," said Otho in the Aquilan dialect spoken by the pirates. Branwen nodded. "Petra will take you."

Branwen forced a skittish smile, grateful to understand the simple phrases, another wash of acid rinsing her throat.

She ascended the stone steps toward Otho's wife. The woman was grim-faced, her eyes watchful. She also seemed to have expected Branwen's arrival.

Petra walked briskly through the central building, and Branwen kept pace silently at her side. They passed into another courtyard that contained an elaborate fountain in the middle: a sea-wolf spitting water onto terraced levels of crimson marble. She could picture Ruan playing here as a boy, splashing around in the fountain on a sweltering summer's afternoon—except that his childhood had not been filled with frolicking.

The courtyard led to another building and out again. With each step she took, Branwen grew more nauseated. Sickened by the craving she could not deny.

She clamped her left hand over her gloved one, willing her shoulders not to tremble as Otho's wife steered her through the outer ward hemmed by the three towers.

The pirates had died almost instantly by the Hand of Dhusnos, Branwen tried to convince herself. It would be more merciful than death by burning. She bit the inside of her cheek. An appealing lie. Eternity as a Shade was no kind of mercy.

At the entrance to the northernmost tower, Branwen spotted several men. They were dressed in the same uniform as Otho, and yet she suspected their true allegiance was also to Xandru. *Kladiwos* blades jangled at their hips.

"I am Duchess Branwen, the Royal Healer," she said to the guards, words lodging in her throat, as she stopped in front of them. "I am here to see the prisoner."

The guard closest to the door exchanged a glance with Otho's wife.

"Welcome, Duchess," said a man only slightly older than Branwen. He turned a large iron key.

Branwen crossed the threshold into the tower first, timid. Petra was close behind her, tutting. The other woman directed Branwen up a flight of winding stairs. Pressure mounted beneath her skin.

Petra knocked on the first door on the second landing, bumping Branwen's shoulder. Otho's wife didn't wait for a response before pushing into the room.

Kensa turned her head toward the intruders. She sat on a stool before a looking glass, a girl of fifteen summers in the midst of braiding Kensa's caramel locks, which hung like a curtain about her shoulders, nearly reaching her waist. Even stripped of her rank, Kensa was allowed by King Marc to have the trappings of a countess.

She afforded Branwen a languorous smile. "I had been expecting Captain Manduca," she said.

Petra spoke crisply to the girl, whom Branwen recognized immediately as the woman's daughter. The girl scurried toward her mother.

Kensa stood. The half-woven plaits came apart, falling haphazardly on either side of her face. Branwen had not once seen Kensa with bare skin, free of rouge or tints. She looked younger and sadder, and more beautiful. Her smile deepened, the slope of her mouth the same as Ruan's. Branwen swallowed hard.

Looking between Kensa and Branwen, Petra said, "We go." She pressed a hand to her daughter's elbow and marched her from the room.

"Greetings, Kensa," said Branwen, hoping her voice wouldn't crack.

"I am no longer a countess. Although it would seem you are a duchess." Her smile wilted to a grimace. Baron Dynyon must be the source of her information.

"I would like to visit Endelyn's grave," Kensa stated. "It lies just beyond the perimeter wall."

"As does Conchobar's."

342

Kensa's blue eyes flashed. "Ruan trusted you too much. He wanted me to like you—he said we were cut from the same cloth."

"He told me the same."

Drizzle began to mull against the window. "And here you are," said Kensa. "So it would seem he was right."

"You've killed for your ambition."

"I've done what was necessary to survive in a world of cruel men."

"Marc is not cruel."

"Ah, and therein lies his weakness. There will always be someone more ruthless who wants to wear the crown more." Kensa took a step toward Branwen. "You are ruthless enough, Duchess."

Branwen didn't reply, because the other woman was not wrong, and that was precisely why she had come.

"Grant me permission to walk outside the wall?" said Kensa, voice cloying. "I would like to feel the rain on my face one last time."

She spread her hands. "I have no weapons. I have nowhere to run."

"After you," said Branwen. She should not delay, and yet she found herself telling the guards that she and the prisoner were taking the air. They didn't dare question a duchess, although their gazes were wary. Petra and her daughter had vanished.

Kensa shut her eyes as the light rain dappled her lids. She took Branwen's arm. They strolled through a small gate in the perimeter wall as if they were friends. Branwen's skin crawled.

Kensa came to a halt when they neared the edge of the cliff. Hedges of thorns trailed down to the sea, clinging to variegated rock.

A mound of earth, recently packed, had been planted with blush roses. Raindrops sprinkled the blooms like tears. The petals were beginning to brown as autumn spread across Kernyv.

Kensa released her hold on Branwen and sank to her knees before the burial mound. "You seem anxious, Duchess," she said, glancing over her shoulder. Again her tone was saccharine. The wind harangued Kensa's dark blond tresses.

"We are just two women." She spread her lips into a viper's smile. "What is there to fear?"

"I asked the Old Ones what was the greatest threat to peace," Branwen replied. "They told me it was you."

"I'm flattered." The other woman snorted. She closed her fist around a dead rose and tore it from the bush. "Conchobar told me of the Old Ones. He said the rain was the tears of Goddess Ériu." Kensa canted her head at Branwen.

"Does she still give you succor?"

Branwen shifted her weight. Her heart hammered. She had forsaken Ériu's succor when she'd bargained with Dhusnos.

Kensa heard an answer in Branwen's silence.

"No, I don't think Conchobar's goddess comforted him at the end, either, when Edern forced Conchobar's friends to tear him limb from limb."

She plunged her nails into the dirt. "I could not protect my children. I could not protect myself." A sigh racked Kensa's frame. "Gods—if they do exist—do not care about us. We must help ourselves. Especially us women."

"Do you think Seer Casek would have let you hold on to power?" said Branwen in disbelief. "He thought very little of us."

"Seer Casek was a means to an end. The Cult of the Horned One will dominate all of Albion soon enough—if Ruan had been the king to bring it about, so be it. I cannot save all women. I tried to save myself. My daughter."

Kensa brushed her hand from Endelyn's grave to the flattened earth beside it.

"I met Conchobar when I was seventeen. When I still believed love could change the world." She lifted her eyes to Branwen. "I was a fool, but for a short time I was free." She clumped a bit of earth in her fist, and kissed it.

"Do it here," Kensa told Branwen. "I looked at you today and saw my death. Maybe I've always known."

Branwen's eyes stung, and not from the wind. The sea roared. It sounded like the hungry beaks that covered the Shades' hideous bodies.

"You could have chosen a different path," said Branwen.

"No. I couldn't. I *wouldn't*. I've been the prisoner of one man or another my entire life. Why should I be content to live out my days under lock and key?" Kensa raked Branwen with her eyes. "Don't fool yourself that your ambition is any less great than mine, Duchess. We merely desire different things—and I am an obstacle to what you want."

"Yes," she choked out.

"Then don't disrespect me by indulging your guilt. You are making this choice. Guilt changes nothing."

Branwen sank to the earth beside her. "Is there anything you want me to tell Andred?"

Kensa sighed. "He is my greatest regret. I wish I could have loved him." She stared Branwen in the eye, resolved. "You might think it's because of his clubfoot, but you would be wrong. When I look at Andred, I see the violence of his conception. I see the years Edern terrorized me to produce a rightful heir."

"I am sorry for you," said Branwen, guttural. Her sympathy was a dagger in her own heart.

"Perhaps you are." Kensa lifted her chin. "How will I die?"

Branwen slipped the leather glove from her right hand.

"Quickly," she said.

"I do not believe in the Otherworld. For me, this is the end."

How Branwen wished it were true. She gulped down the last breath she would take as this version of herself.

"Take my hand," she entreated Kensa.

The other woman closed her eyes as she extended her hand, regal and composed in the face of death. Branwen watched her for a suspended moment, the rain dripping onto the bow of Kensa's mouth.

The instant Branwen clasped her hand, Kensa convulsed.

Euphoria streamed through Branwen. She gripped the other woman's hand tighter. A hysterical noise escaped from her lips, a shriek or a peal of laughter she couldn't tell. Branwen floated far, far away from herself.

She saw a younger Kensa embrace a fair-haired man. Joy bled through her.

She watched Endelyn's birth, and fear pricked her, combined with the ferocious need to protect.

Time grew sticky around Branwen. Ruan beat Edern bloody, and she experienced both relief and pride. All of Kensa's anger, all of her affection emptied from her heart, feeding Branwen, making her strong. Vitality—she knew its flavor, mineral and constantly shifting like the tide.

The force of absorbing Kensa's life—her unbecoming—laid Branwen on the ground beside the woman she had killed. Her own limbs twitched.

Rolling onto her side, a scream died in her throat. A desiccated corpse with blond hair stared up at the sinister sky.

Lips quivering, Branwen relinquished Kensa's hand, the other woman's fingers covered with rot.

Thunder rumbled across the cape. White bolts pierced the clouds.

346

The sea rushed in, scaling the cliff in an impossible manner. Branwen's mind filled with the whispers of the surf, the hungry surf, until she could scarcely hear the chattering of her own teeth.

Branwen cradled Kensa's corpse in her arms, like Matrona with Carnonos, and lifted her body with stolen strength. She tiptoed toward the edge. The obsidian tidal wave reached out, tickling Branwen's forearms as it accepted her offering.

A vortex opened, a gobbling beak, Kensa's body falling into its center. The Sea of the Dead consumed her, and Branwen felt its yearning.

She stepped back from the edge of the cliff, fighting the temptation to swan dive after the other woman.

Branwen of Iveriu. The Dark One's voice slid over her like the caress of a lover. *You fulfilled our bargain, as I knew you would,* said the god. *You understand the power of death. It gives you the life you want.*

No, said Branwen, but her protest sounded feeble.

You served me a most delicious Shade. You tasted her for yourself. Thank you.

Our deal is done. You will not claim the soul of anyone I love.

Dhusnos laughed. *Your heart is darker than the abyss. Do not fight me. You will want my aid again. Soon.*

I won't. Restore my healing magic. The Hand of Bríga.

That is not within my power to grant. Lightning streaked the sky, and Branwen felt the rain on her face like a wet tongue.

Then leave me be, she told him.

I have always been inside you, Branwen of Iveriu, the Dark One chided her. *I helped you when the Land could not, and yet you would repudiate me? Cast me out like Ériu did?* The Sea of the Dead roared, freezing the blood in her veins.

Branwen's right hand began to smolder. Her scream rent the air. The black mark drained of color. Tears of agony rushed down her cheeks.

You will crave life as I do, but you will be unable to take it unless you join my House,

347

pronounced Dhusnos, as if it were a curse. *You will no longer be able to summon fire against my Shades.*

Through her blurred vision, Branwen saw the mark become a hateful red welt, a brand. *Slayer.* She would never be able to forget what she had done.

But I will *restore the Fire of Inspiration to you*, the Dark One taunted her. *You will see death and destruction on the horizon, yet you will be powerless to prevent it.*

Tristan glimmered behind Branwen's eyes as if she were scrying. He lay on a battlefield, bleeding heavily. His flesh began to decay.

Farewell, Branwen of Iveriu.

The Dark One's laughter was earsplitting as the unnatural wave evaporated, drenching Branwen with the salt of the sea.

Dhusnos could not frighten her with visions of the past. She already knew the outcome of Tristan's duel with Uncle Morholt. She'd witnessed the destiny snake's venom burning its way through his veins—and she had saved him.

Her thighs quaked and Branwen fell backward onto the rosebushes. Thorns bit into her palms.

Killer. Branwen had wanted to take Kensa's life and she had received all of it. She had snatched mere glimpses from the pirates.

The woman she had murdered was the only person whom she understood completely. More than her cousin. More than the man she'd loved, or the man she'd taken to her bed. Now she knew Kensa as well as she knew herself. Better.

A place in Branwen's heart, in her soul, had been carved out and Kensa had been interred there—all of who she was. She understood the Wise Damsel's admonition: with each life she took, she would lose a piece of herself, something even more essential than the memory she had sacrificed for the forgetting spell. If she followed Dhusnos's path, she would become nothing but a collection of stolen souls, her heart a Sea of the Dead.

Kensa did not want her guilt. This was Branwen's burden, her punishment. She would have to reconstruct who she was—who she would be, who she would love—with the weight of another life inside her. Empathy would be Kensa's revenge on her, and she had no choice but to let herself be haunted.

In the distance, she saw the skeletal fox prance across the waves.

ALMOST FOUND

ANDRED WAS WORKING IN THE gardens with King Marc when Branwen returned to Monwiku. The afternoon was bright, autumn sun showering the island. Xandru stood beside them, observing, a wry smile on his face. For a fleeting, unguarded moment, devotion softened the captain's features as he watched Marc. The king was absorbed with pruning weeds from his flower beds.

Xandru's shoulders drew back as he sensed Branwen treading the path toward them. He pivoted as she emerged from behind a spear-leafed tree. She had not smiled since she'd left Villa Illogan and she could not conjure one now.

His calculating eyes latched onto hers. Before Branwen could speak, Xandru gave her a nod. The small movement conveyed not so much relief as appreciation, as if she were a member of his crew who had obeyed an order. But Branwen had taken Kensa's life because she was both an obstacle and a solution. The fresh welt on Branwen's palm stung. She would not cover it. This was who she was now.

Andred crouched in the dirt beside Marc, and Branwen saw his mother kneeling on the clifftop. Branwen had failed to see before just how much of Kensa lay in the aspect of Andred's face, the tilt of his forehead, his curly brown hair.

He smiled, less full than he had once, as he glimpsed Branwen over his shoulder, and her heart fractured.

"*Dymatis*. Marc and I are preparing the earth for the winter months."

The king angled his head toward Branwen, pushing to his feet. "Sister." He, too, smiled at her, and she could not return it. "Xandru tells me you went to investigate reports of black lung."

She shifted her eyes between the king and Xandru. Both Xandru and Branwen were willing to lie to Marc because they loved him.

Branwen nodded, wetting her lips. She had spoken the fewest possible words with Otho before departing the villa, and fewer still with the innkeeper last night. Her tongue was heavy, her throat cracked.

The king's brow stitched itself with concern. "Have you taken ill?" he asked, stepping toward her, touching a hand to Branwen's shoulder.

She shivered. The king's unthinking gesture, the need to console her without fear of contracting a sickness, confirmed what she already knew: his kingdom was blessed that Marc was not as ruthless as those who sought the crown. As she was.

"Branwen?" said Andred, levering himself to standing with his arm.

All attention was on her as she shook her head. "I—" Branwen started. She sucked on her tongue. "I'm afraid the reports of black lung were accurate," she said. "Andred, the sickness has spread to Illogan."

He rubbed his left hip. His gaze anchored somewhere in the mid-distance.

"I'm so sorry," Branwen told her apprentice. "Your mother was in the final throes of the illness when I arrived." The grief threading through her words was not feigned. She did grieve for this boy from whom so much had been taken.

Andred continued to stare at her blankly.

"The body needed to be burned," said Branwen, flicking her eyes at Xandru. "Villa Illogan and its inhabitants will be quarantined until further notice."

Marc rubbed a hand over his beard, creases forming at the corners of his eyes in sympathy. "This is sad news," said the king. He betrayed no hint of relief that the woman who'd plotted his death was gone. Perhaps he didn't feel any.

"Andred—" Marc began, dropping a hand on his shoulder. Andred shrugged him off. Without a word, the boy broke away from him.

The king traded a look with Branwen. "Let me go," she said.

"*Mormerkti*," he replied in a hush. Xandru's eyes were steady on hers.

Branwen raced after her apprentice, lifting the hem of her skirt, small pebbles crunching beneath her boots. Sunlight warmed her face; incongruous, a perfect autumn day that made it seem like nothing bad could happen.

Andred stopped abruptly. He pressed one hand against the trunk of a reedy tree and let it take his weight. He doubled over and began to dry heave. Branwen had seen how shock affected people differently. She felt a compulsion to rock the boy in her arms, but she did not touch him.

Coming to stand beside the tree, she listened to Andred's shallow breathing. Branwen looked at him and saw herself the day her aunt found her on the beach, when her sandcastle was destroyed. The Branwen she would have become if her parents hadn't been killed had also died that day.

"I'm here," she whispered. Even without her promise to Ruan, Branwen would be here for Andred.

The curls atop his head vibrated. He clawed the bark of the tree with his fingernails. Branwen shoved down her guilt. Kensa was right. Guilt wouldn't change what she had done. She watched the pain she had caused and felt it acutely, as she should. Branwen had altered the course of Andred's life the way raiders had once altered hers.

Slowly, his breaths grew deeper and he raised his head, fixing Branwen with bloodshot eyes.

"I didn't visit her," Andred said in a rasp. Tears stained his cheeks. "I waited for her to send for me, and she didn't."

Branwen could hear the wound behind his words. "It's not your fault," she said. "Black lung is a swift death."

Andred lifted his shoulders, clinging to the tree, rising to his full height. He had also grown rapidly over the summer and he was now taller than Branwen. He hadn't wanted to celebrate his fifteenth birthday, but it had passed nonetheless, and soon he would not be a gangly boy.

"My mother never wanted me," he told Branwen, an emptiness in his voice that spread to his eyes. "At least I learned why when she was arrested."

Branwen shifted closer, reaching out to him. He heaved a sigh, allowing her to brush the curls from his face.

"I was there when she died," said Branwen. "Kensa loved you, Andred. She told me so."

Her apprentice cringed, suspicion filling his gaze.

"You're lying," Andred said. He released his grip on the tree. "She never said those words. Not once in my entire life."

"*Andred*—" she started to protest when he cut her off, saying, "I had a pet mouse once." Confused, Branwen tilted her head as he continued, resisting the urge to interrupt.

"He was my only friend at Illogan once Ruan left." The sadness with which he spoke squeezed the air from Branwen's lungs. "One day I came back to my room to find the mouse dead, between the jaws of a cat. My mother had let the cat into my room."

"I'm sorry."

Andred lifted a hand. "She told me it was for my own good. She said in a world full of cats, mice are dinner. She said better never to love a mouse, and she didn't."

He took another step back from Branwen. "Countess Kensa never loved me, and she certainly wouldn't tell you if she did. I don't know what really happened at Illogan, Duchess Branwen," he said, eyes hardening. "But I know you're lying to me. The advantage to being a mouse is that you recognize cats for the danger they pose."

Andred turned his back on Branwen and strode away, his gait deliberate.

Her heart kicked. She pressed a hand against the ache between her breasts, watching as the boy straightened his shoulders. With each step he took, he was leaving his boyhood behind. Branwen had ended it, and their friendship. One day, she was certain, he would make a strong, decisive leader. But they would not be friends.

✛ ✛ ✛

Night had wrapped itself around the castle when Eseult came to find Branwen in the West Tower. Queen Verica's apartment still didn't feel like it truly belonged to her.

Branwen sat up on her bed as the door creaked open.

"I didn't know you'd returned until I saw the light in your window," said her cousin, apologetic. "Did I wake you?"

Branwen huffed a laugh. She'd lain down on her bed hours ago, as soon as she left Marc and Xandru in the gardens, but sleep remained elusive. She had lost Andred and she deserved his wrath. His distrust. The boy saw her with clear eyes.

The queen's skirt made a shushing sound as she approached the canopy bed. Candlelight darkened her green eyes, which brimmed with questions. She sank into the thick quilt beside Branwen.

"Kensa is dead," she told Eseult.

"She tried to have you murdered. I won't mourn her, Branny."

"She did, and now I'm a murderer, too." Branwen's eyes were dry. Her pillow was already damp. "When I killed Keane, it was an accident. He found your letter to Diarmuid, he cornered me in the stairwell, and I thought he might . . . he seemed capable of anything in that moment."

Her shoulders hitched. "I didn't know Keane would become a Shade. I only half believed they existed. Yesterday, I knew. I acted with the power of a god."

Branwen turned her right palm face up and Eseult took it gently in her own. Her cousin traced the puckered flesh, then brushed a kiss upon it.

"My healing magic will not return," said Branwen.

"You don't need magic to heal, Branny."

"I needed magic to save you on the ship." Her tone was sharp. They peered at each other sidelong.

"I remember a field of white flames. Flames that almost looked like flowers," said Eseult, hushed. "Once when I stabbed myself, and once when I fell overboard."

Branwen nodded. "It was Bríga's fire," she explained. "Her fire that terrified the Shades. And now it's gone."

Not letting go of Branwen's hand, Eseult lifted her other to Branwen's temple.

"The Old Ones have demanded more of you than others."

"*I've* demanded more from them. And I've made terrible mistakes with the power they gave me."

"You've saved far more lives than you've taken," her cousin insisted. "Me. Tristan. Marc. You have saved *all* of us—more than once."

Branwen bit her lip. "When I stole Kensa's life, I received her memories," she replied. "If my life had been hers, I can't honestly say I wouldn't have done the same."

"Yes, you *can*. Everything you've done—even your mistakes—has been for peace." Eseult sighed. "Kernyv, Iveriu, Armorica—they should all be grateful you did what you did."

"Marc can't know," said Branwen with a start. "It's better if he doesn't. For him, and for Andred. I don't want to sour their bond." If Andred was to cast Branwen as the villain, let her be the only one.

Her cousin's expression grew earnest. "I won't break your trust," she said. "Not again. *Never* again."

"Will you stay?" Branwen asked. Her shoulders curled forward, her request—her need—making her shy.

"Of course." The queen's lips formed a small, contented smile. She unlaced her boots and stretched out beside Branwen on the bed, Branwen scooting to the far side.

"The Dark One said he would leave me my Otherworld sight so that I could see death coming without the power to stop it."

Eseult slipped her hand back into Branwen's, interlocking their fingers.

"Most people can't stop death, Branny. Most people wouldn't think to try."

Branwen blew out the candle on the bedside table. She screwed her eyes shut against the image of Tristan lying on the battlefield. That was in the past. The past couldn't hurt her any more than it already did.

"Your magic isn't why I love you," said her cousin into the murk-filled room. "You've always been my best friend. Your friendship is magic."

"Thank you, Essy."

She and her cousin were no longer girls. She did not love her in the same blind way she had a year ago, but the woman lying beside her was worthy of her respect, her trust, and a place in the heart she was reconstructing.

Branwen swooped over the starless tide, wings outstretched, teasing the whitecaps, searching—searching for something she'd found and lost, and almost found again.

FATE DELAYED

THE GREAT HALL TEEMED WITH people. An air of trepidation wove among the noble men and women, who did not know the reason they had been summoned to Monwiku, as they enjoyed the king's hospitality—dining on venison, lamb, trout, and harvest vegetables at the feasting tables that ran the length of the hall.

Branwen's thoughts coasted on the din of impatient chattering. Eseult had stayed close to her for the past few days, sleeping each night by her side like she had in the months after Branwen's parents died, when Branwen was too angry to share her blanket. Now it was not anger, but an amorphous grief that seeped through her.

Eseult had also insisted on preparing Branwen for the feast, combing her recalcitrant curls and painting her cheeks.

Her seat next to the queen at the king's table provided an excellent view of the courtiers. From the raised dais, Branwen's gaze skimmed the extended family members of the barons whose acquaintance she had made at various occasions since arriving in Kernyv, but whose names she struggled to remember.

She watched their expressions while she picked at her food, sipped the spiced wine. Andred sat on King Marc's left, a place of honor—the seat Ruan used to occupy—but he did not glance once in Branwen's direction. Doubtless news would be spreading through the hall that Kensa had died from black lung while a prisoner at Villa Illogan, and there was no way to prevent rumor or speculation.

Xandru had chosen to dine with the members of House Dynyon this evening. The baron touched his carmine moustache with increased frequency as Xandru engaged him in conversation, the captain's face a pleasant mask. Baron Dynyon's wife had a pallid complexion. She studied the lamb chop on her plate, eating quietly.

King Marc took a substantial swallow of wine, then pressed a hand to Eseult's shoulder. They both rose to standing. Eseult coughed. She spoke first, greeting her subjects in Kernyvak, and a hush fell over the hall.

Branwen leaned forward, catching Lowenek's eye. The girl was sitting next to Andred, at his request. Branwen winked at her, and her cheeks grew rosy with pride. Lowenek had been an excellent language tutor to the queen.

Her fiery hair was elegantly plaited for the feast by her own deft fingers, her face beginning to lose the fullness of girlhood. She had turned thirteen this summer, and Branwen had talked her through her first bleeding, just as the Queen of Iveriu had once done for Branwen. A language that only women could speak with one another, private and binding. Kensa and Endelyn had shared similar secrets, and now they were both dead.

King Marc smiled at Eseult and there was warmth in his eyes, yet it was not how he regarded Xandru.

Branwen clapped when the queen concluded her words of welcome, as did the rest of those assembled. In addition to the families that comprised Houses Gwyk, Julyan, Chyanhal, Kerdu, and Dynyon, the king had invited all of the petty Kernyvak lords. Men who ruled small pockets of land between the baronies—gifts from one Kernyvak king or another to their ancestors, usually for bravery in battle.

The king cleared his throat, and the tension tightened around the feasting hall.

"Friends," he began. "Thank you for joining me for this celebration. I hope you are enjoying the bounty of the autumn harvest."

Murmurs of appreciation and head nodding accompanied his statement. Branwen's Kernyvak had improved so that she understood what Marc was saying, even if she missed a word here or there.

"The past year has been tumultuous for Kernyv," said the king. "But now, thanks to all the gods—" Marc tipped a smile at Eseult. "We have peace with Iveriu, and peace with Armorica. The pirate threat has been quelled, and the Veneti Isles are under complete Kernyvak control for the first time since the Aquilan occupation."

Sir Goron lifted his voice in a cheer from where he sat on the other side of Branwen as she searched the crowd for the new head of House Gwyk. Doane. The man that Baron Chyanhal had warned her about. He was square-faced, his pale cheeks hollow, pitted. Branwen thought him to be the same age as King Marc. Doane was well muscled and he held himself as if braced for an attack.

King Marc pursed his lips. "In order to maintain this newfound peace, to ensure stability, the True Queen and I have drafted a Crown

Charter." Marc had consulted with Eseult on all of its minutiae, and Branwen could see how much his respect meant to her cousin.

He paused, surveying the faces of his nobles. "This document will enshrine the rights and responsibilities of the noble Houses and petty lords. As well as the crown's responsibilities to you, my friends and subjects."

Eseult lifted her chest and announced, "The Crown Charter will henceforth allow female heirs the right to ascend the throne, and the monarch to designate his or her heir—regardless of direct descent." Several intakes of breath rippled through the hall.

"One religion will also not be privileged above any other in the laws of the land," she stated firmly. Both the king and queen wore antler shards around their necks, but Eseult had not forgotten the Iverni who remained in Kernyv nor the Kernyveu who still cherished the Old Ones.

Branwen felt for her mother's brooch, but her fingers touched only velvet. She hadn't been able to put it on since she'd returned from Villa Illogan.

"We also believe there is a need for a Greater Council, in addition to the King's Council," King Marc continued. He and Eseult must have rehearsed the speech together.

"We want to hear the concerns and consult with more of our subjects," he said, his voice carrying through the silent hall. "The Greater Council will meet thrice annually and be composed of five members from each of the noble Houses, as well as all of the petty lords and their most direct heirs. The Houses may determine their representatives independently."

Foot stomping and thunderous applause rose to the ceiling, especially from the tables of petty lords. Branwen's shoulders sagged with relief.

The queen angled her body toward Andred, grabbing his gaze.

When the crowd had quieted down, "Prince Andred," she said. "You are the son of Prince Edern, of royal blood, and you have proven your loyalty to the crown. In recognition of your fealty, we bestow upon you the honor of your own House."

Eseult took a breath, looking out at the hall. "House Katwaladrus, after your ancestor, the great king."

"To House Katwaladrus!" said King Marc, raising his goblet.

Echoes of *House Katwaladrus!* bounced off the walls. The nobles all lifted their goblets and toasted to Andred.

Andred's face was drenched with shock. He squirmed slightly, unused to being the center of attention.

"*M-mormerkti,*" he stuttered.

"*Sekrev,*" replied King Marc, and he patted his cousin on the back. Shifting his gaze toward the table where Xandru sat among the members of House Dynyon, the king said, "Tonight I would like to honor another Kernyvman who has been a great asset to me on the King's Council."

The edges of Marc's mouth flickered.

"Baron Dynyon," he started, and the attention of the nobles trained on the baron. "You served my father faithfully for years, and you have served me well in recent months."

Branwen narrowed her eyes at Xandru and, even from a distance, she saw the laughter in his.

"For this reason, I am appointing you the Governor of the Veneti Isles. I know that a man of your acuity will bring them to order, and bring honor to your House."

King Marc lifted his glass again. "To Baron Dynyon, Governor of the Veneti Isles!"

The nobles cheered, although there were a few gasps mixed with the applause. Xandru nodded at Branwen as he drank deeply from his goblet.

Baron Dynyon's face took on a scarlet hue, but he could not refuse such an honor, and certainly not so publicly. He must see the exile for what it was, and yet Branwen hoped he was wise enough to show gratitude for King Marc's clemency.

"There is one final matter that I have assembled you all here to address," the king said. He took Eseult's hand. "The True Queen and I are determined that the future of Kernyv should not be marred by the strife we have seen this past year."

King Marc cast a pointed glance in the direction of House Gwyk.

"To this end, as Queen Eseult and myself have yet to be blessed with a child—" He gave his wife's hand a small squeeze, swallowing, and Branwen gripped her goblet tighter. He still believed that the child Eseult had lost had been his.

"Until such time as we have our own child," King Marc started again. "The True Queen and I have decided to designate an official heir, in accordance with the new Crown Charter. In the event that we should both succumb to illness or accident, we want the line of succession to be clear."

The sound of a hundred people holding their breaths throbbed in Branwen's ears.

"Prince Andred of House Katwaladrus, I have trusted you with my life as cupbearer, and I trust you with my kingdom," pronounced the king. The look on Marc's face was pure paternal pride.

"Prince Andred, will you consent to the honor of being our heir?" he said.

Another silence kept the hall in suspense.

"Yes, my Lord King," replied Andred, brow furrowed, and Branwen could see the gravity of what was being asked of him on his face. "It will be my greatest honor to serve my kingdom as your heir."

King Marc motioned for him to stand. He slid out of his chair sideways, and leaned against its back as he swung his feet under him.

"Raise your glasses to Crown Prince Andred!" urged the True Queen.

Xandru stood. Branwen followed his lead. All of the Kernyvak nobility leapt hastily to their feet. Branwen toasted her former apprentice, and her congratulations were heartfelt.

Andred was a good choice. A smart choice. No one could question his lineage, and no one had a bad word to say against him. His elevation would also dampen the fears of the other nobles.

Furthermore, he had chosen the truth, the good of his kingdom, even when it had cost him everything.

Eseult turned to Branwen, and they clinked glasses.

"Tonight you are a True Queen," Branwen told her.

Her cousin hesitated at the compliment, then kissed Branwen on the cheek.

✤ ✤ ✤

Once the meal concluded, the heads of the noble Houses—including Andred—and the petty lords were invited to sign the Crown Charter.

The king's table was cleared of dishes, and the elaborately decorated vellum was unfurled in its center.

Seer Ogrin had been the scribe. He'd learned calligraphy from the temple as a young *kordweyd*. Although he had little occasion to employ his skills now, he was a talented artist, evidenced by the capitals of the letters accentuated with delicate flowers and animals.

Eseult had trusted the seer to keep the terms of the charter secret.

Branwen was glad of the closeness that had developed between her cousin and Seer Ogrin, even though she realized her cousin's embrace of Matrona and the Horned One would soon leave no room in her heart for the Old Ones.

Branwen leaned against one of the snakestone pillars that supported the Great Hall, watching from beneath a shadowed archway as the Kernyvak nobles signed their names to the charter, reaffirming their loyalty to the crown, and receiving assurance that their rank and property could not be stripped from them without cause.

Lady Neala signed on behalf of House Julyan, her father still too ill to travel. Baron Doane of House Gwyk bowed before the king and queen, and yet Branwen sensed him chafing like a dog at his collar.

"A ruler always needs someone in the shadows," remarked Xandru, approaching her from behind. He lifted his goblet to Branwen.

"And how long will you remain in the shadows?" Branwen asked the captain.

"As long as he needs me." The reply was so sincere, so unlike Xandru's glib rejoinders, that Branwen didn't know how to respond.

Rearranging his features into an amiable smile, he added, "My next errand is to ensure that Baron Dynyon arrives in the Veneti Isles. I will transport him there personally."

Branwen listed her head, meeting Xandru's eyes. "Will Baron Dynyon arrive safely?"

Another laugh, darker. "I gave the king my word." Thrusting his chin toward the cluster of noblemen standing before the dais, Xandru said, "Have you signed the charter yet?"

"Me?" Branwen startled.

"Aren't you the Duchess of Liones, and a member of the King's Council?"

"I—I suppose I am."

Xandru gave one shake of the head, eyes crinkling.

Branwen left the captain and walked toward the dais. Andred—Crown Prince Andred—stood beside the king and queen.

Branwen joined the group of noblemen, and Baron Chyanhal drifted toward her. "My faith was not misplaced," he said into Branwen's ear.

"Thank you for your advice."

He ducked his head. "I look forward to working together."

Baron Chyanhal stepped before King Marc and Queen Eseult, bowing from the waist, and signed the Crown Charter. After they exchanged a few pleasantries, it was Branwen's turn. Her pulse unexpectedly began to accelerate.

Marc gave her a curious look. "I would have thought you'd be the first to sign, Duchess Branwen."

A flush spread down her neck.

"I forgot who I was," she said.

Eseult laughed, almost a giggle. "That makes you exactly who you are."

Branwen echoed her laughter, although her hands were clammy. Andred's face was a stone and he did not acknowledge her.

King Marc handed Branwen a feather quill. The nib was stained black from so many signatures. Her eyes traced them on the page before her. The swirls of ink were pledges, insubstantial in themselves, reliant on the honor of the individual behind the name.

She had been born Lady Branwen Cualand of Laiginztir, heir to Castle Bodwa. The Dark One called her Branwen of Iveriu.

The king's smile became a question as she continued to delay, the quill hovering above the parchment.

Here she was Branwen of Castle Wragh, Duchess of Liones.

She dipped the tip of the quill into the inkwell. Leaning forward, still uncertain which name to sign, Branwen spied a figure moving quickly toward the king and queen. For half a breath, she thought she saw the silhouette of a Death-Teller.

Sir Goron grabbed the man before he could reach the queen and pressed a *kladiwos* to his throat.

The nib of the quill skidded across the parchment.

"I—I come from Ar-Armorica," said the man, fear further whitening his pale face. "With a message from Crown Princess Alba." He spoke in Aquilan.

Sir Goron regarded the messenger, leery. The man wore a yellow tunic, a red owl embroidered on his chest.

"What is the message?" King Marc said curtly.

"It's for Healer Branwen."

She glanced up at her name—the name Alba would call her by.

"I am Healer Branwen," she said.

Glancing warily between Sir Goron and the blade of his sword, the messenger said, "The scroll is in my pocket."

King Marc nodded, and the Queen's Champion lowered his weapon. Xandru had deftly maneuvered himself just behind the Armorican messenger, placing his body between Marc and the stranger. The king needed a new Champion of his own, but he had thus far been unwilling to replace Ruan.

The messenger slowly removed the scroll from his pocket, and Xandru snatched it from the other man's fingertips, examining it.

"This is Alba's seal," he confirmed.

A chill skittered along Branwen's spine. Her first thought was that Tristan was sending for her before Samonios as he had promised. Yet she didn't think he would use his wife's seal. She accepted the scroll from Xandru, dread tensing her fingers, and broke the seal.

The red waxen owl fell to the stone floor. Many pairs of eyes bore into Branwen as she began to read.

Her breathing thinned. She recognized each of the words and yet, taken together, they didn't make sense. They began to swim across the page. Nonsensical.

Her hands trembled as if she'd plunged herself into an icy lake.

"Branny?"

Eseult's voice penetrated the water sloshing in Branwen's ears—just barely.

"It's Tristan," she said, rasping.

"Is he alive?"

Branwen swallowed, looking toward Marc, who had asked the question. She had never seen him look more capable of violence.

"He's wounded. Poisoned."

She heard Eseult gasp, but it still seemed very far away. Anger began to sear through Branwen's shock. Directing her gaze at the messenger, she said, "When did you depart from Karaez?"

"Five days ago," the man replied.

When Branwen was at Villa Illogan. The Dark One hadn't shown her a vision of the past, after all.

She choked on the bile that surged up her throat.

"Who poisoned him?" said King Marc, jaw stiff, looking between the Armorican messenger and Branwen.

Branwen wanted to cry, but she couldn't. She had nothing left.

"Ruan," she answered the king. "He challenged Tristan to a duel for Endelyn." Branwen forced herself to meet Andred's plaintive stare.

"Your brother is dead. I'm sorry," she said. "But he used a poisoned blade."

"Like Uncle Morholt," said Eseult. She covered her face with her hands.

"Like Uncle Morholt."

Had Branwen given Ruan the idea the night she showed him the wooden practice sword in her chamber? She swayed on her feet.

"Tristan wants me to come," she managed.

"Of course. You must go to him immediately," replied the king, terse. "If anyone can save him, it will be you, sister."

But Branwen had no more magic. Maybe she hadn't changed Tristan's fate at the Champions Tournament. Maybe she had only delayed it.

She exited the Great Hall to prepare a bag. Tristan had sworn to send for her, but Branwen had lied when she'd said she wouldn't come.

She would always come if he needed her.

She prayed she wouldn't be too late.

BLACK SAILS

THE *MAWORT* AND THE ARMORICAN vessel set out from Marghas at the same time, but by the end of the first day on the open water, Branwen had lost sight of the red owl and its all-seeing eyes. Xandru had offered to escort her to Karaez without being asked, and she could only hope that his ship truly was as fast as he claimed.

Four days passed in a haze of fear and snatched restless sleep. Whenever Branwen did catch a few minutes' rest, the white raven circled her in her mind.

She remembered Captain Morgawr telling her that all sailors were fate-tossed dreamers. Tristan, too, loved the Dreaming Sea.

Branwen's heart was not prepared for surrender. Not yet.

Now she and Eseult stood on the bow of the *Mawort* as the Armorican capital sprawled before them.

Eseult pushed back the flyaway hairs from Branwen's plaits, black as *kretarv* feathers. Branwen curved her mouth in the approximation of a smile. She'd questioned Eseult's desire to join her on this mission and her cousin had replied, "I owe Tristan my life. I want to help if I can, and I don't want you to be alone if we're too late."

Branwen believed her. To be able to trust her cousin, finally . . . to have spilled so much truth—it was a balm.

"That must be Castle Arausio," said the queen, pointing at the towers that rose from a hill just beyond the city. Stretching behind the hill was dense forest.

Branwen nodded absently, her attention focused on the maze of streets between the city walls. Karaez was vaster than anything she'd ever seen in Iveriu or Kernyv. The houses were brightly painted in yellows, reds, and blues.

Eseult took Branwen's hand. "We'll get there in time," she said stubbornly, as if willing it to be true. The cerulean cloak that Ruan had once said brought out the copper in Branwen's eyes flapped around her, taunting her.

How had he arrived in Armorica? When had he decided to avenge his sister? She shivered as she remembered Ruan's embrace, imagining it to be as cold as the grave. If Branwen had left Kernyv with Ruan, could she have stopped him?

Bitter tears stung her eyes.

Suddenly, the *Mawort* was gliding into a slip on the busy docks. Ships flying colors Branwen didn't recognize—from across the southern continent, possibly beyond—lined the port. Racing down the gangway, Xandru barked orders at his men and vanished into the bustling port.

A few minutes later he returned, shouting up from the dock at Cherles. The Melitan Islander immediately escorted Eseult off the ship, Sir Goron walking in front, and Branwen just behind. King Marc had insisted—the alliance notwithstanding—that Eseult be accompanied by her Champion in a foreign land.

Four horses waited at the end of the pier.

Xandru knew the quickest route to Castle Arausio, having visited many times, and Branwen rode out front with him. Eseult followed, with Sir Goron as the rear guard. Branwen's thighs burned as she gripped the saddle tight, urging her mount onward.

The traveling party followed the path of the sun. Samonios would be celebrated in three days' time, and afternoon was already being enveloped by evening.

Branwen's face was itchy with sweat despite the frigid breeze coming off the coast. The healing satchel slung across her chest bounced against her hip.

Between the city and the castle lay farmland. Castle Arausio dominated its environs, a strategic position from which to guard against siege. Orange light hit beige stone as the sun sunk behind its walls. The structure of the castle was square and its towers rectangular. Branwen glimpsed soldiers walking the perimeter of the curtain wall at the bottom of the hill.

Xandru was the first to cross the drawbridge, which had been lowered across the moat that ringed the hill. A soldier wearing an Armorican yellow tunic and leather trousers approached, hand on the hilt of his *kladiwos*.

Branwen strained to catch her breath as she slowed her stallion beside Xandru's. Her cousin joined them, her cheeks pink. Sir Goron guided his horse between the queen and the Armorican soldier. The man looked younger than Branwen, his pale face wind-chapped, brown hair clipped.

Xandru addressed the soldier in Armorican, and he seemed to recognize the captain. He looked from Xandru to Branwen, and then Eseult, ears perking up at something the captain had said.

The soldier bowed deeply before Eseult, saying something more anxiously to Xandru, and let them pass.

"What is it?" Branwen demanded of Xandru as their mounts trotted through the gate of the curtain wall.

"Tristan is in the East Tower."

"He lives?"

Xandru didn't reply, only gave her a heavy look, and she read his empathy for what it was. He kicked his mount and sailed past Branwen. Acid rising in her throat, she chased him up the threadlike trail that wound around the hill toward the main gate of the castle.

More soldiers, presumably members of the Armorican Royal Guard, were clustered outside it.

Branwen's patience was frayed. Before Xandru could address the guardsmen, she'd leapt from her horse and rushed toward the men.

"I am Healer Branwen," she told them in Aquilan, hoping someone would understand her. "Crown Princess Alba sent for me."

A tall woman of thirty summers stepped forward. She was dressed the same as the male guards except for a sash of red silk that cut a diagonal across her tunic.

"Alba has mentioned you to me," she said to Branwen. From her expression, what Alba had said wasn't all positive. The woman's complexion was the same golden-brown as Xandru's, her eyes several shades darker as she scrutinized Branwen.

"Take me to Alba," Branwen said, fear making her request a bark.

The woman gave a short laugh, her long black braid bouncing against her shoulder. "Greetings, Sofana," said Xandru, leading his own horse toward them by the reins. "This is Duchess Branwen and that—" he gestured behind him at Eseult, "is the True Queen of Kernyv."

Sofana arched an eyebrow as she bowed from the waist. This woman wasn't easily impressed, but she still had to bow before a queen. The diamonds winked from the tiara atop Eseult's head.

"Follow me," Sofana told Xandru, flicking another assessing glance at Branwen. Several of the other guardsmen approached to take charge of their horses.

"Sofana is the head of the Queen's Guard," Xandru explained to Branwen as they walked. Branwen clenched and unclenched her right fist.

She darted a glance at Eseult, who hurried to match her pace, and put a protective hand on her shoulder. Branwen shuddered a breath. She fidgeted with the strap of her leather satchel, heavy with every possible remedy.

Just before she'd set out from Monwiku, Lowenek had brought Branwen a vial of crushed gods' blood petals. The girl didn't need to tell her it was from Andred, and Branwen didn't need to ask why the prince hadn't brought it himself.

Sofana guided them through the inner bailey, but Branwen couldn't take in any of the details, the unfamiliar sights and sounds washing over her without leaving a mark.

Her only thoughts were for Tristan. The memory of the day they'd saved the fox together from one of the sandpits Keane had dug into the beach played in her mind. Tristan risked being discovered by his enemies to save a trapped animal, and that was the moment Branwen had realized that Tristan wasn't *her* enemy.

She had to stop herself from sprinting ahead of Sofana when they reached what appeared to be the East Tower. Branwen's entire life seemed to be composed of waiting and racing, with no middle ground, nothing in between.

Dusk filtered into a large room on the ground floor through long slit-like windows. Oil lamps had already been lit. From a cursory appraisal, Branwen could tell this room wasn't normally used as a bedchamber.

Her boots clicked on the stone floor as she rushed toward the bed at the far end of the room.

Alba roused at the sound. She was slumped in an armchair beside the bed, and Branwen thought she'd been dozing. She almost felt guilty for waking her. No doubt the other woman had slept little in recent days.

Their eyes met and Alba shook the man in the bed. "She's here," whispered the princess.

Branwen's legs halted without her permission when she reached the foot of the bed.

Tristan shivered beneath a pile of blankets and quilts. She could see only his face, his beautiful face, but he had the pallor of death, his brown skin nearly gray.

Branwen reached for the winter inside herself—the numbing calm. She could not let her patient see her fear. She was a healer, and a healer must always comfort even when she cannot cure. This summer, Branwen had repeated those words to Lowenek. The words she had learned from her aunt. She clung to them in this moment like a lifeline.

Summoning the last of her courage, Branwen took the remaining steps toward Alba.

"When was the last time he ate anything?" she asked his wife, and Alba immediately answered Branwen's question. "Three days ago."

"Will he take water?"

"Only a few sips."

Branwen nodded grimly. She extended a hand toward Tristan, then asked his wife, "May I?"

Alba stepped aside as Branwen perched on the edge of the mattress. From the corner of her eye, she glimpsed Eseult approaching the bed, hesitant.

Branwen stroked Tristan's forehead, which was slick with sweat. She traced the scar above his eyebrow—the first wound that Ruan had ever given him: the scar that betrayed Ruan's shame. Tristan's flesh burned, and he quivered from the burning.

With a somewhat violent motion, Branwen ripped the covers from him, tossed them to the floor.

Her eyes widened.

A skein of poison webbed across Tristan's chest from a festering wound to the right side of his belly button. If the poison had been as potent as that of a destiny snake, Tristan would have been dead within the first day. Even so, from the smell alone, Branwen knew that whatever poison Ruan had acquired was lethal.

She pulled her leather satchel over her head, and let it drop to the floor.

"Branny?" Eseult made her name a choked sound.

Branwen glanced at her, then at Alba. She knew that all her love, all her pain bled from her eyes.

"Branwen?"

This time her name was spoken by the same melodic voice that had once serenaded her, sung to her about the only jealousy of Emer.

"He's been waiting for you," said Alba, and there was no recrimination beneath her words. "Come, Queen Eseult," she said, wrapping one arm loosely around the queen's shoulders. "Let's give Branwen space to work."

Branwen's heart swelled with a gratitude that was pure, awestruck by the gift of one woman recognizing the love of another.

To her cousin, she said, "Tell him what you would have him know."

Tristan and Eseult had shared much, and there would not be another chance.

The queen nodded, eyes gleaming. Branwen rose from the bed as Eseult stepped forward, leaning over Tristan, and whispered in his ear. She did not hear her cousin's words and they were not hers to know. His eyes still shut, he half smiled and groaned as he squeezed Eseult's elbow in response.

Tears streaming down her face, the queen retreated toward Alba, making a small whimpering noise.

Finally, Tristan's eyelids fluttered open. He reached for Branwen and she sat back down on the bed. Branwen turned to him, only vaguely aware of the hushed footsteps as the room emptied of other people.

"You came," he rasped, tangling a finger in her knotty hair. "I've been dreaming of black sails. I feared you wouldn't come."

Branwen took his hand and kissed his knuckles. She would not sob. She would *not*.

"I'm here," she breathed against his skin, and he smiled. "The *Mawort*'s sail is white."

"I'm ready. It's not yet Samonios, is it? I've been trying to hold on."

His eyes opened fully, dark and bright like the night sky, and Branwen wanted to spend forever in his gaze.

"Take me, Emer. Branwen," he said. "Take my life."

She drew in a labored breath. "There's no need," she whispered.

"Why? What's happened?"

Branwen saw his mind clutching for reason through the fog of his pain. She pressed a finger to his lips. They were dry, cracked, bleeding— but she had never felt anything so soft.

"It doesn't matter. All is well. You can sleep, and I will be here—right by your side."

Tristan shook his head, as headstrong as ever, trying to raise himself onto his elbows. He was too weak.

"I'm sorry, Tristan. Tantris. My magic is spent."

Branwen pressed her scarred palm, her useless hand against his cheek.

"Your magic is your heart," said Tristan, sliding her hand from his cheek, down his neck, and resting it above the love-knots Branwen had stitched when things were simpler. He struggled for his next breath.

"The greatest joy in my life is that you entrusted it to me, for a little while."

Branwen touched his lips with her own.

"I will always come for you," she said, her voice breaking, suppressing another sob.

Tristan pulled her against his chest, resting her head against his scars, over his heart. "In you my death," he said. "In you my life."

His chest rose and fell, and Branwen kissed his heart, watered it with her tears, and then it rose no more.

LOVE-KNOTS

HIS BODY WAS STILL WARM.

Branwen began to sob now that Tristan could no longer hear her. This man who had burrowed into her heart, whom she had wronged so grievously, and who had forgiven her. This may have been the fate that was destined, but it wasn't the fate he deserved.

Time became an abyss of stars. Branwen clung to Tristan, not wanting to open her eyes. If she opened her eyes, she would have to face his death.

Her heart pounded so hard in her ears that she could almost fool herself into believing that the beat was coming from Tristan's chest.

A gentle hand stroked the length of her arm.

Branwen's head jerked toward the intruder, a predator ready to pounce, unwillingly opening her eyes.

Alba stared down at her. The room had grown dark save for the flames wavering above the oil lamps.

Slowly, Branwen raised herself from Tristan's chest. Alba sank down beside Branwen on the bed, next to her husband. The other woman's lips trembled. Exhaustion ringed her eyes.

"I'm sorry, Alba," said Branwen, voice croaky. She wiped her nose with the sleeve of her dress.

"Our healers said there was no cure," replied Alba in a bleak tone. "Tristan bade me send for you." She peered at Branwen sidelong. "I don't think it was because he thought you could save him."

Alba traced the back of Tristan's hand. "He's been happy these past months, I think," she said. "He charmed everyone at court. He's quite the bard. My mother was particularly fond of his ballads."

"Yes," Branwen rasped.

"Tristan and I—we . . . we enjoyed each other's company. But we didn't fall in love. We couldn't." Alba's gaze strayed back to Branwen. "The court gossips tittered that he was still in love with the other Eseult. I know the truth," she told her. "You are the one lodged deepest in Tristan's heart."

Branwen wet her lips. "I—" she started, and Alba interrupted, "I'm glad you were here with him, at the end."

"Thank you," said Branwen. "Thank you for sending for me."

"I regret not being with Kahedrin."

"I know."

Alba inhaled through her nose. "I told Tristan not to fight Ruan. I didn't trust the look in his eye."

The chasm inside Branwen yawned wider. "What happened?"

"Tristan was winning. He was a better swordsman." A tear leaked from Alba's eye as she spoke. "Then Ruan pulled this from his boot."

She withdrew Ruan's father's knife from the pocket of her trousers, her face a snarl. Firelight flickered on the golden lion's mane, and Branwen sucked in a painful breath.

"He cheated," spat Alba. "Ruan cheated like a coward."

Branwen had forced the knife back into his hand. "He knew he would lose," she said. Alba nodded. Ruan had come to avenge his sister knowing he couldn't beat Tristan in a fair fight. He'd been willing to die just to kill his cousin.

"We've already burned his body," Alba said more quietly. "His ashes were scattered to the sea." She extended the blade toward Branwen. "I kept the knife. Perhaps his mother will want it."

"Kensa is dead." Alba narrowed her eyes at Branwen in question as the words left her lips, but she only replied, "I will give Crown Prince Andred his brother's knife."

"*Crown* Prince Andred?"

"Many things have changed."

Alba shifted her gaze to Tristan. His eyes were closed. He looked as if he were sleeping. "They have," she said.

Branwen's ears pricked at the sound of new footsteps. The diamonds on Eseult's tiara sparkled dully. Branwen beckoned her cousin forward. Her skirts swept over the stone like whispers, and she lowered herself onto the opposite side of the bed.

Eseult did not need to be told that Tristan was gone. Her eyes were wet as she pressed a kiss to his cheek. The queen's grief was plain, and Branwen could not begrudge it to her. She had always wanted them to be friends.

Branwen trailed her gaze between her cousin and Tristan's wife— now his widow. The quiet thrummed with sorrow. Love knotted between the three of them, unexpected and delicate.

"We should bring him home," said Eseult, after several minutes. "King Marc would want Tristan laid to rest with the kings and queens of Kernyv."

"Armorica will also mourn him," Alba replied, a tinge of protest to her voice.

"Of course."

Alba exhaled. "But Tristan should be with his family in death. With those he loved most."

In you my death, in you my life.

Branwen ran her finger across his chest. Could Tristan's life possibly lie within her? In Kerwindos's Cauldron, Branwen had offered the Mother of Creation her love for peace. Could she offer the one thing she had left?

Brushing the tears from her cheeks, Branwen said to Alba, "Do you have somewhere very cold to store his body for the voyage?"

Tristan's soul now lay on the other side of the Veil, traveling back to the cauldron of rebirth. Branwen glimpsed the white raven in her mind. Maybe, just maybe, she could find him there. Would the Old Ones accept one final sacrifice? Would they accept her heart?

Hope—like a bud in the snow—sprouted amidst Branwen's grief.

She would *make* them accept it.

"We will bring him to the icehouse," Alba told her, nodding. The princess drew her shoulders back, composing herself. She looked regal.

"We will hold our own funeral for my husband before you depart for Kernyv."

"As you wish," said Branwen. She gave Alba's hand a squeeze, and the other woman listed her head, giving Branwen a canny look.

"A bedchamber has been prepared for both of you in the South Tower," Alba said, looking from Branwen to Eseult.

Catching Branwen's eye, her cousin said to Alba, "Branwen and I grew up together in the South Tower at Castle Rigani."

"We did," Branwen said, distracted.

"I will stay with the body and oversee its transport to the icehouse," Alba stated. "You should both rest."

Eseult stroked Tristan's lank curls. "Farewell, my Champion." She stood and rounded the bed, offering Branwen her arm.

Branwen didn't want to leave him. She glanced from her cousin to Alba. The other woman needed to mourn alone, and she had allowed Branwen to have the final goodbye.

Her feet tingled with pins and needles, but Branwen commanded herself to stand. She collected her satchel, shoving Ruan's knife to the bottom.

"*Odai eti ama*," she breathed, and let Eseult lead her away from Tristan.

There was no hate in Branwen's heart, only love—so much love.

✛ ✛ ✛

Xandru swept his gaze over the noblewomen as they exited.

He pressed a fist to his chest, a sign of condolence, as he realized their race to the castle had been for naught. Branwen knew his thoughts would be for Marc's loss.

Sir Goron's face creased with anguish for the boy whom he had mentored, taught to hold a sword.

Sofana showed Branwen and Eseult to the South Tower in silence. Nightclothes had been laid atop a bedspread of thick damask. Several fur blankets had also been provided. On a side table, Branwen noticed a jug of wine and a plate of cheeses.

The bedroom looked out over the inner bailey. The clang of a bell resounded through the courtyard.

"A call to Ankou," said Sofana, expression somber. "To collect the soul of Prince Tristan." The head of the Queen's Guard paused. "I am sorry," she said, looking between Branwen and Eseult. "The prince was well liked."

Branwen inclined her head, but could form no reply.

As the guardswoman left them, Branwen glimpsed Sir Goron standing watch outside the door. It clicked shut and Eseult helped Branwen to remove her cloak. She hadn't even taken it off.

She allowed Eseult to strip her clothes from her body, limbs as limp as a doll's, and to slip the nightdress over her head. Her mind whirled. The Veil between this world and the Otherworld was thinnest on Samonios. This year it would also be a Dark Moon.

The Loving Cup had been conjured on the Dark Moon because its magic would be most potent.

Your magic is your heart. Branwen would trade it for Tristan. Freely. Eagerly.

She watched her cousin rummage through her healing satchel. Would Eseult understand what she wanted—*needed* to do? To rebalance the scales? A life for a life. She was ready to cross the Veil and take his place.

The queen pried a glass vial from Branwen's bag. "This is Clíodhna's dust?" she said, seeking confirmation.

When Branwen nodded, Eseult pinched the powder into a silver goblet and filled it with wine from the jug on the side table.

"You need to sleep," she said to Branwen, maternal and firm.

Branwen accepted the drug-laced wine and drank it down. She crawled beneath the quilt, legs growing weak. Eseult slid into the bed beside her, covering them with another fur blanket against the draft.

"*Once on the island of Iveriu,*" her cousin sang softly, stroking the shell of her ear, "*there was a girl called Branwen of the Briars.*"

She kissed Branwen's temple. *"She did not care for balls or swoon-worthy lords, but of injured men and salves she never did tire!"*

Branwen intertwined their fingers and floated away.

✠ ✠ ✠

When she woke, it was yet dark. Eseult sat in an armchair beside the hearth, face glowing by the light of the embers, gazing into the fire. Branwen blinked, and for a moment she thought she saw the Queen of Iveriu. But no, it was a glimpse of her cousin—older, fulfilled.

Branwen rubbed her eyes, slithering across the quilt toward the edge of the bed, closer to the hearth. Eseult stirred at the sound of rustling.

"I didn't mean to disturb you," she said.

"You didn't."

Drawing closer, Branwen saw that her cousin's cheeks were flecked with fresh tears. The queen dabbed at them with the hem of her nightgown.

"You have every right to weep for him, Essy," she said.

"I weep for Tristan, but not just for him." A sigh lifted Eseult's chest. "I love him as a friend—as family." She twisted a flaxen strand around her finger.

"Tristan never could have loved me for myself. Nor could Diarmuid. Because I didn't know who that was, Branny." Her cousin swallowed. "I told Tristan once that when I looked at him, I glimpsed the life I wanted. But I was wrong."

Eseult scooted forward in her seat. "I didn't know what I truly wanted. I only knew what I *didn't* want. Now, at the infirmary, I've found something I'm good at."

"You've always been good with children," said Branwen, an uneasy feeling dispelling the lingering effects of the Clíodhna's dust. "You have a gift for midwifery."

"I do," she said, eyes brightening. "I do, and I feel like I'm on the verge of finding out who I am."

"I'm happy for you, Essy."

"I've tried to make up for my selfishness, Branny. To be the queen dictated by my birth. And I've been more content at Monwiku than I'd thought possible," she said in a rush. "And yet . . ."

Eseult's expression sobered. "Marc will never love me, because he's in love with Xandru."

The air rushed from Branwen's lungs. "You *don't*—"

"He told me," said the queen. "He wanted to be honest." She paused, and Branwen gulped. Of course he did. That was who Marc was.

"He is a good man, and in the past months I've come to care for him as a dear friend," continued her cousin. "He should be with the man he loves, and I—I need to find out who I am before I can find someone who loves me."

"Essy, I don't know what to say."

"Our lives can be cut short at any time. We shouldn't spend them waiting," she said, tone becoming feverish, and for once Branwen couldn't disagree.

"Tristan is dead, but the Three Kingdom Alliance will endure," she continued. "I won't put my heart above the peace again, Branny. But . . . *but*—" Eseult sank to her knees, grabbing Branwen's hands, pulling her right to the edge of the bed.

"If I were dead, too, Iveriu would still be protected. Iveriu doesn't need me anymore—if it ever did."

Branwen inhaled. "Kernyv has an heir," said the queen. "It doesn't need me, either."

A thousand protests rushed up Branwen's throat and died on her tongue.

"Noblewomen rarely write the endings to their own stories," said Branwen.

"But we can. We *can*." She squeezed Branwen's hands tighter. "I came to Armorica for you—but I need to leave for me."

Tears glistened in her green eyes. "You were always better suited to ruling than me. In my heart, I know it's not who I was meant to be."

A regretful laugh shook Branwen's shoulders. "I've made far too many mistakes to rule."

"Rulers make mistakes. They're only human. You've always wanted to be perfect, Branny."

"Maybe I have." Branwen hesitated before saying, "I won't stop you. I have no right to force you to stay. Your heart is yours, Essy. I won't try to tame it—not again."

Eseult brought Branwen's scarred palm to her lips and kissed it.

"Will you help me? One last time? Help me rewrite my own history."

IN YOU MY DEATH

My dearest Branny,

Forgive me for leaving you. With Tristan gone, I find that I cannot be in this world without him. I wish you love and peace—and for King Marc, but I cannot stay.

Yours in love, always,

Eseult of Iveriu, True Queen of Kernyv

Branwen's voice shook as she read the missive aloud, translating from Ivernic to Aquilan. Sir Goron watched her intently. The sheen to her eyes wasn't feigned.

Pinching the queen's seal ring between her fingers, she held it up to the evening light. "The note has her seal," said Branwen in a hush.

The Queen's Champion stood at the foot of the bed and looked from the letter in Branwen's hand to the True Queen lying on the bed.

No breath lifted Eseult's chest. Her blond hair fell about her shoulders. She looked beautiful. Enchanted.

Branwen counted every second in her mind.

She had called first for Sir Goron, as had been planned. Sweeping her gaze around the bedchamber, speaking low even though they were alone, Branwen said, "I don't think that Kernyv needs to have the memory of its True Queen further tainted."

She gave Sir Goron an unwavering stare. Branwen had reasoned that the Queen's Champion would have to be convinced that Eseult's death was not the result of foul play, but also that he wouldn't shatter the peace his king so ardently needed. The letter was a risk to Iveriu, a final gamble. She kept counting the seconds.

Brow lined with consternation, the old sword master took the letter from Branwen's hand—and threw it in the fire.

"No," he agreed.

Tension momentarily leaving her shoulders, Branwen said, "Eseult has always had a weak heart." Branwen's gaze returned to the queen, to the antler shard hanging around her neck, atop a dress of heavy wool. A dress suitable for a long journey. "The Horned One called for the queen, and she answered," said Branwen to Sir Goron. She blinked and a tear trickled down her cheek.

"He did." Understanding filled his eyes.

Branwen fidgeted with the queen's seal ring: back and forth, back and forth. Every minute was precious. The charade could too easily prove real.

She wiped away another tear. "I will alert Princess Alba," she said. "We should move the True Queen's body to the icehouse directly." Branwen's words came out urgently, almost angrily. "I won't have my cousin be gawked at—become a spectacle."

Sir Goron took a stride toward her, placing his hands on Branwen's shoulders. She felt the strength of his grip.

"I am sorry for your loss, Duchess Branwen." His voice rumbled like thunder, yet it was kind. She was sorry to deceive him.

"*Mormerkti*," she muttered. Breaking away, Branwen exited the bed-chamber and broke into a sprint.

Alba waited beneath the entrance to the South Tower for Branwen's signal. Dusk cast shadows across her face, eyes alert.

"How much time do we have?" she asked as Branwen appeared.

Heart thumping, "Twenty minutes," she replied.

Alba whistled and a man appeared with a small cart. "It was good enough for the pirate king," she said, lifting a shoulder, almost smiling.

The next part of the plan was a race against the hourglass. Alba returned with Branwen to the bedchamber, and Sir Goron lifted the queen's lifeless body from the bed, carrying her down the stairs.

With reverence, the Queen's Champion laid Eseult into the straw-filled cart. The other man began to push it down the hill toward the ice-house. His name was Yannick, tall and muscular, his hair auburn. Alba had assured Branwen that she trusted Yannick with her life. Branwen was trusting Alba with her cousin's, and so she had to trust this stranger as well.

Alba walked in front of the cart, pace rapid, with Branwen at her side. The icehouse was located near the first perimeter wall. Anticipation tightened Branwen's chest. She and Alba exchanged several nervy glances.

Yesterday, Branwen had visited the princess alone in the North Tower—the tower she had shared with Tristan. A map of Armorica was painted across one wall in the sitting room.

"He still had so much of the kingdom left to see," Alba had said as Branwen entered, gesturing at the mural.

Branwen wasn't as skilled in making polite conversation as her aunt, or as Queen Verica had been, and so she'd come straight to the point.

"On our way back from the Veneti Isles," she'd started. "You told me we were even." Alba lifted an eyebrow. "I need to put myself in your debt."

The princess had pushed to her feet, folding her arms.

"What kind of debt?"

"You married Tristan for peace." Branwen crossed toward her, coming to stand just before the map. "When I killed Kahedrin, you lost the life you might have had. The life you wanted. The sea," she'd said, and Alba bristled.

"My cousin also married for peace. Her life has never been her own. She deserves the chance to make it so."

"We all do. But I don't see how."

"She could live the life she wanted if she were dead."

"Your magic?" Alba had said, eyes rounding.

"My magic is gone." Branwen had shown her her palm, the absence of the dark mark, and said, "There is a root that mimics death."

Bóand's tears. When they were girls, her aunt had warned both Branwen and Eseult never to play with it. Bóand was the Ivernic goddess of rivers, and the root was used to deeply anesthetize patients for long surgeries. It slowed your pulse, stole your breath from you as if you were drowning—just enough to give the illusion of death. Branwen had packed it in her satchel, and Eseult remembered its effects only too well.

Branwen and Alba continued to stare at each other. "I'll need another body," she told the princess matter-of-factly.

"And you think I know where to procure a dead body?"

"I do."

A small smirk. "I might know someone who does." Tilting her head, Alba had said, "Why would you do this? And why would you trust me to help?"

"I trust you because you sent for me when Tristan asked—when you didn't have to," said Branwen. "And I'm doing this because my cousin never wanted to be a queen, but I refused to listen. Now I hear her—I *see* her. I have many amends to make. Let this debt to you be mine."

Alba's expression had grown solemn. "I will help you, Healer Branwen, because a woman's life should be her own. There will be no debt to repay."

Now torches flickered outside the icehouse as night fell. Alba had needed today to make all of the necessary arrangements. Branwen glanced back at Yannick who pushed the True Queen in the cart behind them. He'd been tasked with finding another female body—no questions asked.

Several of the Armorican Royal Guard were keeping watch in front of the building where Prince Tristan's body was laid in advance of the funeral tomorrow.

Ten minutes, Branwen mouthed to Alba in Aquilan. Tension spread through her body.

Branwen had the antidote to Bóand's tears in the pocket of her dress. If she didn't administer it within an hour, however, the mask of death would become death itself.

She had poisoned her cousin to give her the chance to love. Perhaps the Aquilans were right to consider love and poison twin gods.

Alba spoke tersely to the guards and they stepped aside.

The icehouse was built from the same beige stone as Castle Arausio. Alba plucked one of the torches from beside the entryway, and Branwen followed her into the house, then down a darkened flight of stairs to where the ice was stored.

And, for now, where Tristan dwelled in eternal slumber.

The chill lifted the hairs all over Branwen's body as they descended.

Sir Goron lifted one end of the cart, and Yannick the other, carrying the True Queen carefully below.

Tristan was laid on a wooden table at the back of the room. Torchlight filled the confined space. Looking at him, Branwen felt a fist in her chest. His visage was waxy, his lips blue.

"I would like to be alone with my cousin," Branwen said as Yannick rolled the cart beside the table. First she must help Eseult. She looked from the Armorican to Sir Goron.

"Of course," said the Queen's Champion. He read the impatience in Branwen's eyes, although he didn't know its true source.

Yannick traded a charged glance with Alba, and headed for the stairs. Sir Goron followed while the princess lingered.

Once the men were out of sight, Branwen lowered her face above Eseult's. Heat from her shallow breath tickled Branwen's nose. Her cousin's heartbeat was faint enough to miss—but it was there.

Branwen positioned herself behind Eseult's head, dragging her cousin against her chest, cradling her. She withdrew the vial of antidote and uncorked it swiftly, with her teeth.

Forcing open her cousin's mouth, she poured the liquid down her throat. She kept Eseult propped against her chest so she would swallow it all.

For several awful moments, there was no change to her cousin's condition. Branwen looked from Tristan to Eseult, side by side in death: the former lovers too serene.

Then Eseult gasped, and it was a heartrending sound. She spluttered just as Tristan had on the raft, and Branwen kissed her forehead. Tears of relief rushed to her eyes.

Alba heaved a sigh. Branwen had almost forgotten she was there.

The princess hung the torch from a hook on the wall and then disappeared behind several large blocks of ice. Eseult blinked rapidly, regaining consciousness in Branwen's arms. "Branny?" she said.

"We're safe."

Alba reemerged from behind the ice, holding a thickly woven travel bag.

"Clothes," she explained. "Dried meat. Gold coins. The tiara." She walked toward the cousins. "Enough to start a new life."

Eseult coughed, rubbing her eyes, still disoriented. "Where are we?"

To Branwen, Alba said, "I'll invite Sir Goron back to the castle for supper." She pointed at a stone on the wall into which an owl had been carved.

"That's your way out," she said, and Branwen nodded.

The princess mounted the stairs speedily. A moment later, Branwen heard boots clicking above them as Alba escorted everyone from the ice-house. She might not want Branwen to be indebted, but Branwen felt what she owed her keenly.

"You don't have much time," she told her cousin. "We're in the ice-house. We need to leave."

By the mellow torchlight, Branwen could see her cousin's pupils remained dilated. She offered Eseult a hand as she found her feet, stepping down from the cart.

"Sir Goron?" asked her cousin, shaking her head, trying to gather her wits.

"He believed your note. Then he burned it."

Eseult nodded. "And Xandru?"

"No sign of him," Branwen answered. "I don't think he's returned from Karaez." By a stroke of luck, the captain had left that morning to visit with other merchants at the central city market.

Branwen collected the large traveling bag from the ground. "Alba prepared this for you," she said. "There's gold. Food. Your diamond tiara—you can sell it."

Her cousin gave a nod, taking the bag from her. "Thank her for me."

"I will." Branwen swallowed. "Have you chosen a new name?"

"Gráinne, I think."

"She would like that." The little girl they'd known in Iveriu had her whole life before her, and now so did her cousin. Branwen recovered the torch from where Alba had hung it.

She pressed on the owl engraved into the stone and a seam appeared in the wall. Alba had explained that this tunnel had been constructed so that the royal family could escape in the event of a siege.

"We should go," Branwen told her cousin. She held the torch aloft as she pushed open the hidden door.

Eseult hesitated a moment, eyes lingering on Tristan's face, before she hefted the traveling bag over her shoulder.

The stones were slick, wet, the tunnel no wider than the eye of a needle, and the sleeves of Branwen's dress grew damp as she brushed against them.

The last section of the tunnel became a cave, jagged stones dripping water onto the cousins from above. As they reached the mouth of the cave, which was cleverly concealed with hanging vines, Eseult took Branwen's hand.

"You must get as far away from the castle as you can before dawn," Branwen told her cousin. "Alba said to head west through the Brechliant Forest."

"Come with me," entreated Eseult. "*Not you without me, not me without you.*"

There was a time when Branwen would have followed her cousin anywhere.

"That is not my path," she told her, tongue growing thick.

Eseult nodded, tears welling in her eyes. "I'm sorry it took me so long to understand all the ways you loved me, Branny."

She pressed a hand to Branwen's chest. "Sister of my heart, always in my heart."

"Your future belongs to you now, Essy. Write your own ending."

Her cousin threw her arms around Branwen, and they clung to each other. Branwen shuddered a sigh. They would not meet again on this side of the Veil.

"Go," she whispered. She lifted the curtain of vines, brittle and brown in face of the coming winter.

A black mare was tied to the branch of a tree as Alba had promised, an unremarkable creature. Eseult was royalty no longer. She had no expectations on her, but also no security. She must travel far, far away from everything and everyone she'd ever known.

If she were to be recognized, it would mean a war.

That was the price of her freedom. Eseult was willing to pay it, and Branwen could only pray for her safekeeping.

Her own cheeks grew wet as she watched her cousin launch herself into the saddle. Eseult lifted the reins with poise.

Looking back over her shoulder, she held Branwen with her gaze.

Branwen felt the sting of every wound they'd inflicted on each other, and the joy of every confidence they'd shared—every laugh, every embrace. Her cousin had been first in her heart, and because she loved her she had to let her go.

A smile parted Eseult's lips. Even in the encroaching darkness, Branwen glimpsed the same thrill in her eyes as the day she'd leapt from the waterfall.

This was her choice. Whatever happened next, wherever she landed, Eseult was embracing the unknown.

Her cousin kicked her mount and vanished into the forest. Branwen had decided not to tell her about her plan for Samonios. She wanted Eseult to start her new life unburdened by the past—Branwen's final gift to her.

She watched until the sound of hoofbeats dwindled to nothing. Retreating back into the cave, Branwen retraced her steps through the tunnel.

Halfway down, the figure of a man blocked her path.

"Out for a stroll?" Xandru asked.

Each of Branwen's muscles tensed. She had no weapon. No magical advantage.

He prowled closer. She'd almost allowed herself to forget how dangerous the spy could be. They had become allies because they both loved Marc. Xandru regarded her now as a threat.

He stopped when they were toe-to-toe. "Word is spreading through the castle that the True Queen of Kernyv has died. A heart attack, said Sir Goron. Strange, Eseult being so young."

"My cousin has always been...temperamental. Nervous. Prone to...swooning." Which had been the truth once. "The heart is a mercurial organ. Hers simply gave out."

"Mercurial? Yes. But, stranger still, her heart seems to be missing along with her body. I did not see it laid out beside Prince Tristan's."

"You're mistaken, Captain Xandru. Her body is there."

"It is?" he replied, too casual.

"Marc wanted peace, and he has it. Marc needed an heir, and he has Andred." Branwen drew in a deep breath. "Why shouldn't Marc have love, too?"

Light from the torch glinted off the sword at Xandru's hip. Condensation dripped from above. Branwen remained utterly still, listening to the fire and the water.

Xandru's stare pinned her in place. Then, eventually, his stance relaxed.

"Kernyv will be plunged into grief by the loss of both Tristan and Eseult. Within a day of each other."

"It will," Branwen agreed, tentative.

"Are you ready to return?"

"Not yet."

✝ ✝ ✝

Past midnight, Branwen rapped on the door to Alba's bedchamber.

"I need another favor," she said as it opened.

IN YOU MY LIFE

S AMONIOS HAD ARRIVED, AND THE Dark Moon was rising over the Brechliant Forest.

Branwen followed Alba by starlight, pale and faint in the moonless night. The wood shivered with power. She sensed the thinning of the Veil.

"The shrine to Ankou is near," said Alba, wrapping her arms around herself. She must sense it, too.

"You sang beautifully," Branwen told her. The funeral of Prince Tristan of Kernyv and Armorica had taken place earlier this evening. As his widow, Alba sang his lament.

"I will miss him," she said. Twigs snapped beneath their boots. "But that was my goodbye. Tristan is dead to Armorica." Alba peered at Branwen sidelong, and she saw a warning there.

"You've arranged passage on a ship?"

"The *White Stag* is bound for the Bujan Empire. It departs the day after tomorrow," replied Alba, with a nod. "The voyage east will take half a year. Through the Saozone and North Seas."

"Thank you." Branwen's voice grew quiet.

"You only asked me to book a single passage?"

"That's all that's required."

The princess glanced from Branwen to the sickle-shaped blade in her hand. "Tristan told me how you saved him at the Champions Tournament," she said. "When he felt death upon him." Alba paused for a breath. "I thought your magic was gone?"

"It is."

Branwen couldn't say what had compelled her to pack the moon-catcher, which her aunt had gifted her, with her healing kit when she scrambled to collect her things for the journey to Armorica. She'd forgotten to pack any clothes. She walked through the forest in a dress of gray silk that she'd borrowed from Queen Yedra for the funeral. The queen was closer in height to Branwen than her daughter.

A mournful wind howled between the women.

Still eyeing the blade, Alba said, "Whatever you have planned, Tristan cannot return to the life he knew."

"I understand."

"Do you think he'll see the Bujan Empire?"

"I don't know." Branwen rolled the handle of the moon-catcher between her fingers, the mother-of-pearl cool to the touch. "I hope so."

The White Moor no longer welcomed her, but Branwen prayed that on this night of all nights, she could pierce the Veil. If the Old Ones were merciful, she would take Tristan's place on the other side.

Alba flattened her lips. "Tristan's body is being transported back to the icehouse from the funeral. If another . . . body is needed for Kernyv, Yannick will provide one."

"Yannick is resourceful," said Branwen.

"We've been sailing together for years. He saved my life once. He should have been with me when we attacked Monwiku, but he'd been injured in a tavern brawl." Alba laughed, although it was tinged with regret. Catching Branwen's eye, she said, "I'm glad Yannick wasn't there."

"So am I." Branwen swallowed. Her magic had wrought so much destruction. She didn't know whether the balance the Wise Damsel wanted her to find was possible.

An eerie clinking sound drew Branwen's attention. Not quite like a bell, almost more like creaking.

She looked up.

Bones.

Hundreds of tiny bones were tied from the branches above them. Hollow bird bones, and those of other small woodland creatures. Perhaps human fingers, or toes. Ribs.

Clink, creak.

The forest had thinned into a circular grove. "Wait!" said Alba, grabbing Branwen's elbow before she could step into the circle.

"This is the shrine to Ankou. Once you enter, you are in her world."

"The Otherworld—that's where I need to go," Branwen said, determined.

"In Armorica, we believe that the Old Ones will only let you return to our world if you give them what they want."

The concern for her that Branwen saw on Alba's face made a lump rise in her throat. "This is what I must do," she told her. "If you don't see me again, wait two days until you release Tristan's body to Kernyv."

"I will sit vigil myself." She gave Branwen's elbow one more squeeze. "Two horses will be waiting near the tunnel. The *White Stag* is docked two piers over from the *Mawort*. You'll recognize it by the stag on its prow."

The bones creaked overhead, a wistful refrain. From the corner of her eye, Branwen glimpsed a white raven circling the grove. She blinked and it was gone.

She would follow the creature to her end.

Laying a hand on Alba's shoulder, Branwen said. "I must go. Be safe. I see a Champion in you."

"You will always have a friend in Armorica, Healer Branwen."

Air rushed from her lungs. It was more forgiveness than she'd ever expected from the other woman.

"Farewell, Captain," she said, and squared her shoulders.

Walking toward the grove, Branwen understood the faith that Seer Ogrin had needed to step into a rudderless boat. Perhaps it was madness, but she had to believe—she had to believe in herself.

Keening filled her ears: lyrical moans, silent pleas, the wails of the Death-Tellers. Tingles inundated her body as she took her first step into the circle.

The tingles began to burn. Branwen gritted her teeth.

When she first crossed the Veil on Whitethorn Mound, she had been an innocent. A girl struck by love for the first time. When she'd plunged into the Sea of the Dead, Branwen had been lost, desperate.

The keening became shrieks, enough to make her ears bleed.

She continued to put one foot in front of the other. Branwen had killed and saved and loved. She would not be denied.

Let me in! she shrieked in her mind.

Battling the scorching wind, she lifted the moon-catcher. The Old Ones always wanted blood. Branwen would give them the very last of herself, of her love, of her life.

She sliced the crescent-shaped blade across the brand that Dhusnos had left her.

Slayer.

Her blood swelled to the surface, appearing black in the starlight.

It dropped from the silver blade to the forest floor.

The wild moon is high, my love. The shrieking in Branwen's ears transformed into a lullaby. *Come away with me.* A lullaby sung by a voice she'd thought she'd never hear again.

The wind ceased, and Branwen toppled to her knees from the lack of resistance. She shielded her eyes, squinting.

She inhaled the scent of rosemary. Eyelashes fluttering, she saw the silhouette of a woman approaching her, dark against the sun. Outside the grove, it was still night.

When the woman loomed over her, Branwen gasped.

"Mother?" she said.

In the fourteen years since Lady Alana's death, her features had become less distinct in Branwen's memory. And yet, she knew her at once.

"I am the goddess you call the Land," said the Otherworld woman— the *goddess.* "Your mother is one of my children. I am both her, and not. I thought you would like to see her face."

Tears scorched Branwen's cheeks. The love that radiated from Lady Alana's green eyes was too much. She'd forgotten that her mother had a dusting of freckles across her nose, just like Branwen did. She reached up, her hand bleeding, to touch the mahogany curls in which she'd buried her face as a girl.

"Ériu?" rasped Branwen.

"My children call me by many names in many kingdoms." The goddess's tone was mild.

"Your body is all kingdoms," Branwen realized, awe suffusing her. "Not only Iveriu."

Ériu offered Branwen a hand, and she pushed to standing. The goddess kept ahold of Branwen's right hand, examining her bleeding palm.

"Prince Tristan of Kernyv is dead," said Branwen, struggling for the right words. "My magic has wronged him. I offer my life for his."

"You have made mistakes in your quest for peace, Branwen of Iveriu."

Shame scalded her, and she dropped her eyes to the forest floor. Wildflowers peeked out from the moss. In the Otherworld, it was spring. Perhaps that was why the Iverni called it the Land of Youth.

"Make me a Shade," Branwen said. "If that is what's required. I accept my fate."

The goddess relinquished her grip on Branwen's hand.

"I am not the Dark One."

A hint of danger underscored the statement, and Branwen trembled. It was because Dhusnos had slighted Ériu that she'd cast him out. The goddess had a temper.

"No, but you also deal in death," Branwen said, not knowing if she was brave or foolish. "And I have, too." She held out her palm. "I have tried to keep the peace for Iveriu—for Kernyv. I have bled for it."

Ériu's face—Lady Alana's face—softened.

"Peace is not a destination, *enigena*. Nor is happiness," she said. "It is a journey that you must begin anew each day."

Branwen blinked as more tears leaked from her eyes. "I want Tristan to have the chance at happiness." Inhaling deeply, she asked, "What can I offer you?"

"Your blood is my blood. You are a natural healer, like your mother," said the goddess. Branwen's throat constricted at hearing Lady Alana's voice speak the words. "Magic comes from the Land and it is not gifted— it is loaned."

"I don't understand."

"The power you call the Hand of Bríga? You no longer have need of it. It has returned to the Land."

Branwen pressed her bleeding palm to her heart, vivid red staining the gray silk beneath the glare of the Otherworld sun.

"Then take this," she said, pounding her hand against her chest. "Take my heart."

"You have already lost pieces when you stole life." The goddess shook her head, and Branwen felt her mother's scolding as if she were six years old again.

"I will not take more," said Ériu. "The mistakes you've made have been for love, from love, and there is still much healing for you to do on your side of the Veil."

Branwen opened her mouth to protest, and the goddess of the Land silenced her as her eyes flashed with the fury that only a goddess could summon.

"You must ask Prince Tristan if he would like to return to the mortal realm," Ériu went on. "If he agrees, you will be stripped of the lives you stole—of the death magic still corrupting your blood. You will die several times over, Branwen of Iveriu."

"Where do I find him?"

The goddess lifted a hand to the sky. A white raven cawed.

When Branwen glanced back to Ériu, she was gone.

"Goodbye, Mother," she whispered.

The raven cawed again, flying toward the sun, and Branwen started to run.

✠ ✠ ✠

Sweat darkened the silk of her dress beneath the blood.

Sunlight streaked Branwen's face between the trees as she ran through the Otherworld. She pursued the raven. The leaves were lush, intensely green. Maybe this was how Brechliant Forest looked in springtime—or maybe this was a different part of the Otherworld entirely. She didn't care. She just kept running.

Her legs quivered, rebelling, and her shoulders strained as she wheezed.

The sun didn't move across the sky in the same way as it did in the mortal world, so she lost all sense of time. Eventually—maybe hours later, maybe minutes—Branwen found herself in a field of whitethorn blossoms. Bushes of thorns and buds surrounded her like a maze.

The heat became more oppressive. The gray silk was now black. In her exhaustion, under the haze of the sun, Branwen saw the petals of the whitethorn blossoms dance like flames.

Throat parched, Branwen kept her eyes pinned to the wings of the raven. She was so focused on the bird that she didn't see what—or who— was right in front of her.

"Branwen."

She stopped just before she slammed into him. "*Tristan,*" she breathed.

The raven cawed and flew away. Tristan and Branwen stood at the center of a maze, alone in the Otherworld.

"I've been here before," he said. Tristan was dressed in the clothes in which his body had been prepared for the funeral. He wore a tunic of Armorican yellow and black leather trousers, but he hadn't broken a sweat.

"I found this," said Tristan, tugging something from beneath the collar of his tunic.

Branwen's lips parted. It was the chip of Rigani stone that she'd given him that day on the beach when the pirates were scouring Ivernic shores for the lost prince—when she and Tristan had shared their first kiss.

"I thought I'd lost it on the pitch of the Champions Tournament," he said. Branwen remembered. "It's brought me back to you—again."

His grin captured her heart like it had when she gave him the first kiss of life.

"But why are you here?" Tristan asked.

"What do you remember?" said Branwen carefully, daring to touch his arm, wanting to make sure it was really him.

A crease formed on the bridge of Tristan's nose and he arched an eyebrow, accentuating the scar she so adored.

"I know I'm dead," he told her.

"I'm sorry—I didn't reach you in time." Branwen raised her hand from his arm to his cheek. "But you were right, Tristan. My heart is my magic."

He traced Branwen's hairline, and her whole body sighed.

"Why are you here?" he repeated in a whisper.

"I'm here to offer you a way back to the mortal realm—if you want it."

A scowl gripped Tristan's face, which wasn't what Branwen had anticipated.

"*How*, Branwen? What did it cost you this time?" He wrapped one arm around her waist, pressing her closer. "I won't take any more from you."

"From me?" She startled. "*I'm* the one who took everything from *you*."

Tristan gave one shake of the head. "And yet your face was the only one I wanted to see before I took my last breath."

His lips were near enough that Branwen felt his breath on her lips—and it was cold. No wonder he didn't feel the heat.

"Tristan, your life was cut short—because of *me*. Because of my magic. If not for the Loving Cup . . . Endelyn would be alive, and Ruan never would have wanted you dead."

"Ruan made his own choices," said Tristan.

"Yes, and I've made mine." Branwen stepped back. "*This* was my choice to come here—to offer you another chance at mortal life. But it won't be the life you've known."

Her chest rose and fell. "We held your funeral at Castle Arausio. You are dead to Armorica. To Kernyv. To everyone you've ever known."

She wiped the salty sweat from her eyelids. The smell of the whitethorn blossoms was intoxicating.

"Do you remember, aboard the *Dragon Rising*, when I asked you what you would do if you weren't a prince?"

"Explore," said Tristan.

"Yes." Branwen exhaled. "Alba has arranged passage for you east—to the Bujan Empire."

He shook his head, a chagrined smile on his face. "I think she's the one who wants to see the Bujan Empire."

"Maybe." Branwen swiped her right hand across her face, tracking blood.

"What happened?" Tristan said, sucking in a breath, taking her hand.

"Nothing."

"No, Branwen. No more lies." His voice was hard.

Branwen's shoulders deflated. "No more lies," she echoed.

She tore a length of silk from the hem of her dress and wrapped it around her palm. Tying a knot, she said to Tristan, "Walk with me?"

He offered her an arm. They walked through the maze with no particular destination.

"The first night I hid you in the cave near Castle Rigani, when you attacked me—I thought I'd been the worst kind of fool to help you," said Branwen.

"I *did* apologize. I felt terrible."

"I know," she said. "I told you I was Emer because I was afraid you would kidnap me. Hold me for ransom."

Tristan peered down at her. "I know."

"You said no more lies. I'm telling you every lie I ever told you."

"*Every* lie?"

"The important ones."

His expression sobered. "Tell me, and I will tell you."

Branwen's stomach dropped. Truth was far more terrifying than lies. She clutched Tristan closer.

"When you returned to Iveriu, I was furious with you—for endangering my countrymen, for not telling me your name. And I was furious with myself because despite all of it—I wanted to kiss you. *Hard*." Tristan chuckled at her emphasis.

"That's why I gave my ribbon to Keane at the Champions Tournament," she added.

He didn't laugh.

"Afterward, I hid Eseult's relationship with Diarmuid from you because I believed in peace above all," said Branwen. "But also because I knew if our kingdoms were at war, we would never get the chance to love each other."

"Branwen," said Tristan in a deep voice, stroking her cheek.

"I didn't tell you about the Loving Cup because I didn't want to ask you to commit treason against your king. If I had . . . everything could have been different."

Tristan halted. His dark eyes held her with a look of understanding, of pity, of love.

"You should know I didn't sleep with King Marc," Branwen told him. His eyes grew wide with surprise. "I drugged him," she continued. "I cut my hand and sprinkled blood on the sheets to satisfy Seer Casek."

Timidly, she met Tristan's gaze. "I know it was wrong. I didn't see any other way to keep the peace. To protect you and Eseult."

Tristan lifted Branwen's chin. "I don't blame you," he said. "I'm sorry I couldn't help you. I'm sorry you've been so alone."

"I didn't want Eseult to keep the baby," she said, the words rushing out of her. "I didn't poison her, but I told her not to tell you. I was afraid you might get yourself killed."

Tristan shut his eyes for a long moment.

"You weren't wrong," he said. A sad smile. "It seems I did anyway."

"I cared for Ruan," Branwen admitted. "I cared for Ruan, and he loved me."

Tristan nodded. "Is that all?"

"Isn't that enough?" He framed her face with his hands as Branwen told him, "I killed Kensa. To fulfill the bargain with Dhusnos. I'm a murderer."

Tristan rested his forehead against hers. It was cold, clammy.

"I lied when I said I hated you. I never hated you, Branwen." He ran his fingers through his curls. "You should know, I consummated my marriage with Alba. More than once."

"She was your wife."

"Yes," he said. "My vows were until death, and I am dead." His chilly breath tickled Branwen's face. "You're the only woman I've ever wanted to ask to share my life with me."

Stepping back slightly, Branwen lifted her eyes to his. "If you return," she said, "it can't be for me. Our paths are not the same. I must return to Kernyv to finish what I've started."

Tristan wrapped his hand behind Branwen's neck.

"You're the strongest person I've ever met." He lowered his mouth to hers, seeking, asking, demanding, giving her his answer. Branwen embraced him, opened herself to him fully.

Life. *This* was life. *This* was love. She sucked his wintry lip between her own, wanting him, wanting all of him. Willing life back into him.

Pain sheared Branwen's consciousness like she had never known.

Agony became her entire existence.

Her body convulsed. This was her unbinding. Her unbecoming.

Branwen screamed until she could scream no more, and day became night.

IF ONLY FOR A NIGHT

DARKNESS SURROUNDED HER, BUT BRANWEN was unafraid.

Warm arms held her and she heard the crackling of twigs in the fire pit. She was dreaming of the man in her cave—the Kernyvman. The poet. She shouldn't be dreaming of sleeping in the arms of her enemy. She should open her eyes, rouse Essy for the day, but the dark was so warm, so inviting.

"Branwen," whispered the man's voice. Her body tensed. How did he know her true name?

Her eyes flipped open: she was in a cave. Her gaze darted around the rocky interior—it wasn't veiny green Rigani stone. Nor could she hear the Ivernic Sea lapping against the shore.

Heart frantic, Branwen's eyes latched onto the man who held her.

"Tristan," she said. The hazelnut flecks in his eyes glowed. A sob burst from her chest as she read their entire brutal history in the spaces between them.

"*Shh*," murmured Tristan, stroking her hair, holding her close against his chest.

Branwen wept. She had forgotten. For a brief respite, everything that had happened once Emer and Tantris had left their cave was blotted from her mind. And yet somehow they had returned.

Glancing around them, vision still blurred, she said, "Where are we now?"

"In the forest, near Castle Arausio," Tristan replied. He brushed his lips against her temple. They were warm.

Joy penetrated her sorrow. "You're *alive*."

He kissed her again. "I'm alive," he said. "But I watched you die." His voice was rough.

"It was the price." Branwen wriggled around in Tristan's arms to face him. "The Old Ones took back the lives I stole. I had to experience their deaths."

"You didn't tell me."

"I wanted it, Tristan. I wanted to be purged of the death magic, but I needed you to make your choice unburdened," she said, pleading. "It was a kindness, ridding me of it."

He quirked his lips—his soft, tempting lips—unconvinced. "It didn't seem like a kindness. I lost count of how many times your heart stopped."

Tristan pressed his palm flat against hers. "I held you in my arms, and suddenly we were in a grove of trees. I carried you here—barely breathing."

"I'm sorry. I didn't mean to scare you." Branwen placed her hand over his. "It's beating now." She dared to brush her lips against his. "How long was I . . ."

"It was night when I found the cave. The day has come and gone, and evening has fallen."

Relief spread through her. "Your ship departs tomorrow from Karaez," Branwen told him, urgent. "Alba was to leave horses and supplies just outside the curtain wall."

She moved to stand, but Tristan stopped her, drawing Branwen more securely onto his lap. "*Rest,*" he said. "We have the night." He wove his fingers through her long curls, holding them out to her.

Branwen gasped. *White.* She gathered another thatch in her hand. All of it.

A heavier breath lifted Branwen's chest. The unnatural life force that had sustained her was gone. The Old Ones had taken back all of the magic that had been loaned.

"It's beautiful," Tristan assured her. "Like moonlight." He twiddled a strand between his fingers. "Although I'll have to change the verse again."

Branwen pinched her brows together, confused, as he began to sing.
The Hound of Uladztir bites and hisses,
Longing for Lady Emer's sweet kisses.

She took his hand and pressed her lips to Tristan's fingertips. "*Hair like a raven's wing,*" he continued to serenade her. "*Only for her does he sing.*"

Branwen's chest constricted. She had always been the raven—somehow she had forgotten.

Tristan paused, rubbing his eyebrow with his knuckle. "Hmm, maybe, *Hair like the wing of a dove,*" he suggested, his baritone washing over her. "*Only she does he love.*"

"No," said Branwen, with a soft laugh. "I've seen a white raven. Bright raven skies led me back to you."

Tristan gripped her tighter and kissed the spot where her jaw met her ear, nibbling the lobe. Branwen moaned. He continued trailing kisses down the length of her neck; he hesitated at the nape.

"The Shades did this to you," he whispered, breath hot, with a trace of anger. Branwen's scars had vanished when she'd withered the pirates in the Veneti Isles.

She lifted her hand to the spot. Touching the soft lump of scar tissue, a laugh bubbled up in her throat.

"Yes," she said. "Yes." A smile ripened on her face. She had missed her scars. They were part of her—her mistakes, her battles. They told the story of who Branwen was. She wanted to see them all.

"Unlace my dress," she said to Tristan, and it came out like a command.

He laughed, deep and mellow. "You can't imagine the number of times I've dreamed of doing just that."

"I can." Branwen leaned down, tracing her nose lightly across Tristan's cheek. "I've dreamed of it, too."

Tristan emitted a raw, masculine growl. "I've always imagined it taking a long, long time." He untied the knot at the top of the dress, the silk making a smooth sound in the quiet of the cave.

"Not too long," said Branwen, but this was where Tantris and Emer had always existed—outside time and place. Branwen scratched him lightly as Tristan teased her, loosening one lace at a time down her back.

She slid her finger beneath the gold chain that held the Rigani stone, and he sighed. "You said fate needed a push," Branwen recalled. "The night you returned to Iveriu."

"If anyone can give fate a push, it's you." Tristan's eyes were round with desire as he taunted her with another smile, another pull of the silk.

"I think I've pushed too much."

The cave pulsed with memory, remorse—acceptance.

"We're here now," Tristan said. He pulled free the final lace and the bodice of her dress slid down Branwen's shoulders.

Actual moonlight filtered through the mouth of the cave, illuminating her pale skin. The Dark Moon had passed. Tonight the magic between Tristan and Branwen belonged entirely to them.

Reverently, Tristan tugged the dress farther down. He stroked the back of his hand over the swell of Branwen's breast, across the dip, and she trembled. His touch was like the promise of rain.

Branwen whipped his tunic over his head. Tristan's skin was once more a rich, healthy brown. No shadow of death was upon him. She teased love-knots across his heart with her tongue, nipping at them.

Tristan surged up, lifting Branwen so he could trail his own kisses from the crease of her breasts to her belly button. He kissed each scar made by the Shades, and she had never felt more beautiful.

Holding her firm, he laid Branwen gently against the floor of the cave. It was smooth and she barely noticed the chill.

"I wish we hadn't waited so long," Tristan said. He lowered his chest to hers, skin to skin, and it became nearly impossible to formulate a thought.

Branwen shook her head, driving her fingers through his curls, tugging him closer.

"We didn't know each other in Iveriu. You didn't know what I was capable of," she said. "Neither did I."

"I know you now, Branwen. And you're miraculous."

She kissed him with tongue and teeth, his face no longer untouchable. She reached for the drawstring of his trousers. "I'm still taking the Ériu's Comfort," she whispered in his ear, reassuring Tristan that he would not father a child he'd never know.

Tristan had been first in Branwen's heart, although he was second to lie in her arms. She didn't feel the same trepidation she had with Ruan, she knew what to expect, but even so, as they shed their final garments, Tristan laying his naked body against hers, Branwen grew shy.

Their love had changed kingdoms, left carnage in its wake.

"Branwen?" said Tristan, worried. He held himself above her, the muscles of his arms flexed. "Is something wrong?"

"No," she breathed. "I just don't know if I deserve this—*you*—to share myself with you, after everything I've done."

"I take back what I said—sharing myself with you now is better. My love deeper," he told her, voice husky.

"If only for a night?" Branwen ran her hand down the length of Tristan's naked spine, and he groaned.

"Let's make tonight last forever."

Forever would never be long enough, but Branwen grinned, pulling Tristan on top of her, crashing her mouth into his. He tasted like the sea, like hope. As she guided him into her, pure pleasure rippled through Branwen. She shed her fears and regrets like a snakeskin.

Their bodies rocked together, their hearts joined. The fire began to burn very low.

Her hair like starlight draped across Tristan's face as they rolled onto their sides, never letting go. "*Odai eti ama*," Tristan whispered as Branwen cried out, sweating and trembling. He panted against her face, and she let her hands roam his thighs, his chest, the curve of his hip.

Tristan buried his head between her breasts, the muscles of his back taut beneath Branwen's fingers. His cry followed, and she shuddered with his release.

They lay together, legs tangled, counting each other's heartbeats. Neither of them wanted to sleep.

At some point, Tristan struck a small stone against the floor of the cave, restarting the fire. Dawn would soon be approaching.

"You made us a shelter," Branwen whispered. Tristan wrapped his arms around her, using her dress to cover them like a blanket.

Kissing her cheek, he said, "You were the one to shelter me first."

Branwen breathed deeply. She would always remember this: how he smelled, the sweat from their lovemaking, the hazy glow of the fire.

"You could come with me," Tristan said. "We could explore the world together."

"I can't."

He propped himself on an elbow so that he could peer down at Branwen. The radiance of the moon accentuated the troubled look on his face.

"Because of your cousin?" he asked.

"Eseult is gone," replied Branwen, and Tristan's brows shot skyward. "She is dead to the world—like you. It's what she wanted."

Nodding, he said, "She always wanted her freedom." He stroked Branwen's face. "If not for Eseult, why can't you join me?"

"Marc made me Duchess of Liones. I'm using the white lead to finance more Royal Infirmaries. Many changes are afoot in Kernyv, and I—I need to see them through."

"I have never truly envied Marc before this moment."

"He is the brother I never had," said Branwen. "But I'm not returning to Kernyv for him." Tristan's gaze grew more intense, probing. "On the *Dragon Rising*, you told me you'd explore if you could," she said.

"You asked me who I would be, and I didn't have an answer. Ruan, too, asked me if a life at Monwiku was what I wanted. I didn't have an answer for him, either."

"Now you do?" said Tristan.

"I am a natural healer. My blood is the blood of the Land—of all the lands," she told him, confidence rising. "I want to ensure the Old Ways are not forgotten. That women always have a place to learn."

Tristan inhaled a sharp breath. "You saved me the day we met. I won't ask you not to save others."

"This is how I save myself." Branwen lifted a hand to brush the tears from beneath his eyes. Extending her right palm, "Look," she said.

The brand of Dhusnos was gone. Tristan narrowed his eyes at her flesh.

"This scar is from the blade of binding at Marc and Eseult's wedding," she said, tapping it with her left forefinger. Next to it, she traced a second line.

"From the Champions Tournament." Branwen trailed her finger to the next ridge, explaining, "From the siege of Monwiku. And this—"

She touched the freshest wound. "This is from last night."

"You have bled enough," Tristan told her, taking her hand in his, curling his fingers around her open palm, protective.

Branwen smiled. "Willow," she said. "The four marks form the letter in the Ivernic language of trees."

"Eseult told me about the vow you made: the honeysuckle and the hazel."

Her smile wobbled as she said, "Willow is the symbol of renewal. Plant a healthy branch in the ground, and a new tree takes root."

This was her chance to make amends for all the lies and all the blood—to heal the land by training one woman at a time, spreading knowledge, and tending peace like Marc did his garden.

Tristan kissed Branwen's palm, teased each line with his tongue, and tingles radiated from the spot.

"I saw us once—in the in-between. You an old warrior, and me your wife, sitting by a fire," Branwen admitted. Her voice quavered. "But that was only one possibility. The paths our lives might take are infinite. Somewhere between fate and chance."

Tristan toyed with one of her bleached curls. "I will plant a willow for you, Branwen. Everywhere I go. And I will write you a song. I will send it to Castle Wragh, and you will know that I live."

"Even without my magic, I will know." She kissed him long. "But you must promise me something else," she said when she was starved for breath.

"Anything."

"You were my first love—" she started.

Interrupting, he said, "And you were mine."

"I don't want to be your last, Tristan."

"Branwen, I—"

She silenced him by pressing his lips to his. "*Promise.*"

"You've given me a second chance at life, and I won't squander it. My life will be long—this time. I will live long enough to make you my last."

"Maybe, but Tristan, I'm done waiting. I don't want you to wait, either. I want you to love someone who can cut you deeply."

"Like you did."

"*Promise.*"

The first fingers of dawn crept across the mouth of the cave. "I would promise you anything," Tristan told her. Their time together was growing short. Branwen drank in the sight of his body, unmasked: the tightly packed muscles of his abdomen, the hard lines of his thighs.

"To seal the promise," she said.

Branwen merged their bodies, crying with pleasure and the knowledge that as close as Tristan was in this moment, he would soon be across the sea, exploring lands full of strangers she hoped would welcome him into their hearts. She hoped he would find shelter there.

✛ ✛ ✛

Birds trilled from all the branches, calling to one another throughout the Brechliant Forest, celebrating the new day.

Branwen and Tristan walked hand in hand, mourning the loss of an endless night.

The horses waited precisely where Alba had said they would be. In the saddlebags of a sable-colored stallion, Tristan found provisions, clothes, gold. He gave a sad smile as he inspected it.

"I hope Alba finds someone to cut her deeply, too," he said.

Attempting to stifle another sob, Branwen said, "I can't watch you sail away from me again. I will leave you here."

Tristan scrunched his lips together, a sigh expanding his rib cage. "The *White Stag*?" he said, and Branwen nodded.

"The passage is booked in the name of Tantris," she said, and he made a guttural noise. "Tristan is dead, but Tantris lives. Tantris the explorer."

Tristan swept Branwen into an embrace, transporting her back to their first goodbye on the beach below Castle Rigani. His first kiss had transformed Branwen into a sea of flames. His last kiss, their last goodbye—unmade, and remade her again. They loved while they burned, and they burned while they loved.

"Possibility is everything," said Tristan, when he at last tore himself away. He mounted his horse swiftly.

"I wish you love," Branwen replied.

Her eyes strained until his outline converged with the trees, just as she had watched her cousin. The lovers who had nearly destroyed two kingdoms were no more.

She wiped the tears from her cheeks, but they overwhelmed her. She didn't notice the tread of the spy's footsteps until Xandru stood at her side.

"You've changed your hair," he said.

Branwen barked a laugh that was too loud in the quiet forest. "Always so observant," she said.

"I understand from Alba that you ordered the bodies of both Tristan and the True Queen to be burned."

"He was a prince of Armorica, after all." Branwen met Xandru's watchful gaze. "Marc will understand. We can still hold a funeral."

Xandru withdrew a handkerchief from his pocket and offered it to her.

"Are you ready now? To return?"

"I am."

THE SONG OF BRÍGA

BRANWEN WORE A BLACK CLOAK, although no bodies would be buried today. It billowed around her like a sail as she rode Senara up the headland toward the final resting place of the kings and queens of Kernyv.

Thousands of black and white stones covered the circular burial mound, dazzling from a distance. Nearly as many mourners dotted the surrounding cliffs.

The wind was fierce on Branwen's face, and her long white braid slapped against her back. Almost a year to the day that the *Dragon Rising* had landed at the port of Marghas carrying the Princess of Iveriu, nothing but ashes remained of Prince Tristan or True Queen Eseult.

Branwen had asked King Marc to let her be the one to write to her aunt with the sad tidings. Iveriu had the peace with Kernyv that it had so desperately needed—it only looked different from how they'd thought it would. Branwen promised the Queen of Iveriu that she would learn to love herself in her failures, too.

She tilted a half smile at Lowenek, whose eyes she felt on her cheek, as the girl rode Lí Ban at Branwen's side. She hadn't asked Branwen why her hair was now white, but she studied her carefully with intelligent eyes, absorbing everything around her. Branwen thought Eseult would want the girl to have the mare, and Lowenek would need a mount as Branwen's new full-time apprentice.

Arthek had chosen Andred as his new master, and the Crown Prince was rarely seen without the dog at his heels.

But not today. The young prince was already dismounting his steed closer to the burial mound. Sir Goron stood beside him, watching the crowd. Andred was now King Marc's sole heir, and the old sword master had been convinced to delay returning to his retirement for a little while longer.

Andred's grim expression brightened for a second when his gaze landed on Lowenek, then clouded over again as it skipped to Branwen.

She slowed Senara, walking the mare toward the prince, and Lowenek followed.

"*Dymatis*, Prince Andred," said Branwen. "Sir Goron." She dismounted and Lowenek was quick to jump to the ground, taking the reins of Branwen's horse.

Sir Goron met Branwen's gaze with a knowing look.

"*Dymatis*, Duchess Branwen," he said.

Rumors swirled that the affair between Tristan and Eseult must have been real, and that Eseult had died of a broken heart when Tristan was felled. Only Sir Goron had seen the false evidence of its truth—a secret he believed that he and Branwen were keeping for the good of the kingdom.

Andred nodded curtly at Branwen in acknowledgment of her

presence. Lowenek tied their horses to the sturdy branch of a thorny gorse bush. The prince held himself more rigid, the weight of being heir already changing his countenance.

"King Marc has arrived," Andred said, nodding toward the entrance of the burial mound. He wanted Branwen to leave. He extended a hand toward Lowenek, whose cheeks reddened as she glanced between the prince and her teacher.

"I would speak with you a moment," Branwen said to Andred. "Escort me?"

He frowned, but he complied. However much he now distrusted her, she was still a duchess. As she and Andred walked ahead of Sir Goron and Lowenek, the young prince demanded, "What did you need to talk to me about?"

Branwen swallowed, her gaze drifting over the faces of the mourners. The heads of all the Houses, the petty lords, and many commoners had come bearing small white stones—an ancient Kernyvak tradition to wish the dead peace in the afterlife.

"I am sorry there was no funeral for Ruan," said Branwen in a quiet voice.

"Nor my mother." Andred's glance was sharp.

She made no comment. She stopped, withdrawing a knife from her boot. Behind her, Branwen sensed Sir Goron's alarm, his steps growing nearer.

"This belonged to Ruan's father—his true father." The late autumn sun burnished the blade. "His named was Conchobar. Ruan gave me this knife once, but you are his brother and it should be yours."

Sorrow fractured Andred's face. "Ruan wasn't who I believed he was." There was gravel in the prince's voice. "He lost his honor."

Branwen's heart panged for her former apprentice. "Ruan was a good brother. All of us are capable of losing our honor when we're pushed too far," she said. She pressed the knife into Andred's hand. "Keep it."

"You don't hate him?"

"In Iveriu, a man's closest male relative drinks his Final Toast for him. We believe it's the first drink the departed will take in the Otherworld," Branwen replied to Andred. "I would like to share Ruan's Final Toast with you."

Andred gripped the knife. He nodded, scrubbing a hand across his eyes. Branwen let him walk away as he composed himself.

King Marc waited for Branwen together with Xandru and Seer Ogrin. He held a golden urn in either hand.

Branwen accepted murmurs of condolence for her cousin as she moved through the crowd. Baron Kerdu and Baron Chyanhal seemed genuinely grieved at Tristan's loss. Baroness Neala, now head of House Julyan, wore black to honor Tristan and Eseult, but also her father who had passed beyond the Veil while Branwen was in Armorica.

Doane, the restless head of House Gwyk, stood beside Baron Dynyon—whom Xandru would be escorting directly to the Veneti Isles tomorrow morning.

Lowenek shadowed Branwen until she reached the king, when the girl sought out Talorc. The elderly Iverman caught Branwen's eye, pressing a fist to his chest, his mouth forming the words, "One Iveriu."

"Sister," said King Marc, leaning forward and kissing Branwen lightly on the cheek. His beard was longer. He wore a suit of black velvet, a white sash across his chest. His eyes were red from lack of sleep.

"Healer Branwen," Seer Ogrin greeted her. He took her right hand, patting it. "We have lost a great queen."

The edges of Branwen's mouth flickered. Eseult might have been a great queen if that had been what she had wanted. Only Branwen knew that Eseult was in the process of becoming an extraordinary woman. And an extraordinary woman was worth as much as any queen.

Before she could reply, Xandru said, "The True Queen's legacy will be one of peace, and she gave her heart for it," as he stared Branwen straight in the eye.

They hadn't spoken of what Xandru knew, or suspected, during the return voyage from Armorica. He had suggested a blackthorn dye for Branwen's hair—spycraft, she supposed. But Branwen had demurred.

The white raven had led her to her end—and her beginning.

"Peace will be the legacy of both Tristan and Eseult," Branwen said, looking from Xandru to Marc.

The king audibly swallowed. He held out one of the urns to Branwen. Delicate ivy leaves had been etched into the gold, the vines overlapping from one urn to the other.

"Sister," said King Marc. "Would you do me the honor of laying the True Queen to rest?"

A small breath escaped from Branwen. "But I'm not a member of the royal family." Only the descendants of the ancient Kernyvak monarchs were permitted to enter the burial mound.

"You *are*." The king's tone brooked no compromise. Andred had joined them in silence, and Marc looked between his heir and Branwen. "You will always be my family," he told her. "Both of you."

Branwen's throat grew so dry it was painful. She took the urn, tears rushing to the surface. King Marc believed that his wife was contained within, and Branwen's heart twisted at the betrayal. She hadn't asked

Alba whose ashes they were, but in all the ways that mattered Eseult *was* dead; it was Graínne who had mounted the horse in Brechliant Forest to take her chances in the world. Branwen's longing for her cousin was outmatched only by her pride.

Seer Ogrin lifted his hands toward the clouds and began to chant. The mourners fell silent.

When the *kordweyd* had finished, King Marc stepped forward.

"Today we lay to rest my nephew, Prince Tristan of Kernyv and Armorica. The most honorable man I have ever known. Tristan put his kingdom and his family above his heart. Above any desires of his own."

The king's voice boomed over the clifftop. "The Horned One blessed me to have such a man, a true brother in my life—even if it wasn't for nearly long enough."

The surf broke against the rocks. Tristan had always been wed to the sea in Branwen's mind, and now whenever she heard the waves, she would know he was somewhere upon them—exploring.

Slanting his gaze at Branwen, King Marc said, "We must also bid farewell to the first True Queen of Kernyv, Eseult of Iveriu. But the love and peace she has brought to our kingdom will never be forgotten."

He paused, and Branwen clutched the urn to her chest.

"*Kernyv bosta vyken!*" declared the king. Then, to her surprise, he added in Ivernic, "One Iveriu!"

Seer Ogrin began to chant once more. The king pivoted on his heel, processing into the burial mound. Branwen followed just behind him. She glanced back over her shoulder, but Andred remained with Xandru.

Branwen had expected the inside of the burial chamber to be pitch black, like the long night of death that graced the Kernyvak flag.

Instead, sunlight showered the interior from a hole at the top of the mound that was invisible from outside. The bones of King Marc's ancestors lined the walls, interred into the dirt, reinforcing the structure.

At the far end of the cavern was an altar, piled high with colorless quartz pebbles, their edges jagged.

Marc stopped before it, holding the urn of what he believed to be Tristan's ashes. His knuckles grew white around the gold.

Alba sat vigil just as she'd promised and when his body vanished, another was found. Branwen asked no details.

"My forbearers came here to commune with their ancestors," said Marc, grief leaking from the words. He set the urn atop the altar. "I believe in the Horned One's resurrection, and yet I would also like to believe I can find my family here."

"I'm sorry I couldn't save him, brother," said Branwen. Marc's shoulders quaked and he wiped tears from his eyes.

Branwen hadn't arrived in time to save Tristan. She could only save Tantris.

"You have lost your sister, and I have lost my brother," said the king. He traced a finger along the filigreed ivy on the urn between Branwen's hands.

"I comfort myself with the knowledge that they both knew great love, and that they were well loved."

Branwen's heart stuttered, unable to decipher the emotion in Marc's silver eyes.

He unsheathed the blade of binding, which adorned his belt.

"I gave this to Eseult on our wedding night," he said. "I told her she was the keeper of my honor. But I was never able to give her the love she deserved."

The king placed the blade on the altar beside Tristan's urn. "I hope Eseult will find love in the Otherworld, if that's where she is."

Again, his expression was inscrutable.

Branwen nodded, not trusting herself to speak. She touched her lips to the urn. The metal was cold.

Sister of my heart, always in my heart. Branwen would always miss Eseult, but she would never be without her—not truly.

She set the urn on the altar, the blade of binding resting between the ashes of Tristan and Eseult.

"My cousin would want you to be with someone you love," said Branwen, finding her voice. Marc's eyes shone.

"*Mormerkti,* sister." He cleared his throat.

Branwen reached a hand into her pocket, turning over a smooth stone between her fingers.

"My rule has been divisive," said King Marc. He glanced from one urn to the other.

"We have the Crown Charter," she said.

"We do. But the kingdom needs more than that. It needs a leader who all of the people can love."

She clenched the stone in her pocket. "Peace is a constant battle. Circumstances shift like sands. You have reacted as best you can—it's all anyone can demand of a king."

Marc placed a firm hand on Branwen's shoulder.

"In a few years, when Andred comes of age, I will step aside. It's what I believe will be best for Kernyv, and for the alliance."

The news came as a shock but, after a moment, Branwen realized it was exactly what Marc would do. One of Kensa's sons would sit on the throne of Kernyv, although she had not lived to see it, and Branwen wouldn't regret that.

"You have always loved your kingdom more than yourself, brother. I will support you however I can."

His gaze was level. "You signed the Crown Charter this morning," he said. "Healer Branwen."

"That is who I am."

"Yes, it is."

King Marc kissed the crown of Branwen's snow-white head. As he offered her an arm, she took the stone from her pocket—the stone she'd discovered there as she retreated from the Brechliant Forest—and laid it on the altar. A speck of gray amidst the white. Three words carved with a crude knife.

Odai etí ama.

✢ ✢ ✢

Branwen remained on the clifftop long after the other mourners had departed for Monwiku to celebrate the Feast of the Dead. Every now and then, the ageless doe skittered into her peripheral vision.

She stared west toward Iveriu, alone as twilight purpled the sky, stars beginning to appear. She breathed in and out, on the precipice between the land and the sea. They would always exist together, inside her: the starless tide and the spring's promise of renewal.

She smelled the salt of the sea and the sweetness of honeysuckle.

"You found your balance."

Branwen's cloak slapped the breeze as she turned. The Wise Damsel surveyed her, creases forming around her eyes.

"You have accepted your gift," she said.

Lifting her bleached braid, Branwen shook her head. "My magic has returned to its source. I have no more."

Ailleann threw her head back in a laugh. "You know who you are now, Healer Branwen. Your true purpose." She took a step closer. "That is the greatest magic of all."

Branwen brushed her fingers along her mother's brooch. She'd pinned it to her cloak today for the first time.

The Wise Damsel smiled. "Safe travels, *enigena*."

She opened her mouth to protest that she was staying in Kernyv, but the words didn't come. She didn't know what her future might hold.

A ferocious wind rolled across the cliffs, whipping Branwen's cloak over her eyes. When she beat it back, the Wise Damsel was gone.

She looked out at the Dreaming Sea, and she knew that somewhere under the jeweled sky, Tristan and Eseult were alive.

They were dead to the world so that they might live in it as they chose.

The song of Branwen's heart was the song of Bríga, and it would be for seasons to come, but not forever. Her losses were deep—and so was her hope.

ACKNOWLEDGMENTS

Dear Reader, thank you for coming on Branwen's journey with me and for wanting to know how it ends. Your support means everything to me. As you now know, Branwen's story is only at its beginning and she can live a thousand different lives—the only limit is your own imagination. I'm excited to leave her in your hands.

My heart is full of gratitude for the many people who have worked tirelessly to bring this trilogy to its conclusion. Once again, it was a joy to work with my brilliant editor, Nicole Otto, who championed both me and Branwen in telling a dark, unflinching story about women trying to claim power for themselves in a world dominated by men. I couldn't have asked for a better home than Imprint for my trilogy. Profound thanks to Erin Stein, Brittany Pearlman, Jo Kirby, and Katie Halata. Thanks to Linda Minton and Ilana Worrell for their eagle eyes. A round of applause for Devin Luna, Kara Warschausky, and the entire international sales team. On this side of the Atlantic, I'm buying champagne for Jamie-Lee Nardone and Laura Dodd.

A thousand thanks to my early readers: Carlie Sorosiak, Lucy Hounsom, and Kelly deVos. For sending out a zillion ARCs, always giving me a place to stay, and making sure my parties have panache, I couldn't do any of this without you: Deborah McCandless, the Harvey Family (Kitty, Kazie, and John), Ame Igharo, Brooke Edwards-Plant,

Suzanne Lynch, and Georgina Cullman. Love to my parents and extended family for spreading the word on three continents.

There are now so many wonderful writer friends in my life that I can't possible list them all and for that I feel eternally grateful. This past year has been one of transition and I want to give a special shout-out to everyone who has lent me an ear: Kamilla Benko, Rhoda Belleza, Annie Stone, Sarah Gerton, Romina Garber, Stacey Lee, Amy McCulloch, Ashley Poston, Susan Dennard, Jen Cervantes, Karen M. McManus, Elizabeth Lim, Marieke Nijkamp, Ali Standish, Rebecca Schaeffer, Beth Revis, Natasha Ngan, Mia García, Bree Barton, Joy McCullough, Chelsea Mueller, Rosalyn Eves, Nonieqa Ramos, Katya de Becerra, Sara Faring, Rena Rossner, Corrie Wang, Nisha Sharma, Mary Watson.

And, Jack: *En vus ma mort, en vus ma vie.*

GLOSSARY

A NOTE ON LANGUAGES AND NAMES

The languages used in the Sweet Black Waves Trilogy are based, fairly loosely, on ancient and medieval languages. As I have adapted the Tristan legends for my retelling, Ireland has become Iveriu, Cornwall has become Kernyv, and the Roman Empire has become the Aquilan Empire. I have taken liberties with history and linguistic accuracy while trying to postulate how the political realities of my world might influence the development of its languages.

Today, nearly half the world's population speaks what are known as Indo-European languages. This group includes English, most of the European languages, but also Sanskrit and Persian. One branch is the Celtic languages, which are now spoken primarily in northwestern Europe: Ireland, Cornwall, Scotland, Wales, Brittany, and the Isle of Man (as well as small diaspora communities), but during the first millennium BCE these languages were spoken as far afield as the Iberian Peninsula, the Black Sea, and Asia Minor. The Celtic languages are further divided into two groups: the Goidelic (Irish, Manx, and Scottish Gaelic) and the Brittonic (Cornish, Welsh, and Breton).

Since the nineteenth century, scholars have been working to recreate the Proto-Indo-European language—the hypothesized common ancestor to all Indo-European languages. Celtic linguists have also made significant headway in the reconstruction of Proto-Celtic, the language from which all Celtic languages derive.

Therefore, my fabricated Ivernic language is based on Old Irish and Proto-Celtic, whereas my Kernyvak language is based on Proto-Celtic and the Brittonic languages. For the Aquilan language words I have looked to Proto-Italic—the forbearer of Latin—for inspiration. Given that the Aquilan Empire occupied the island of Albion for hundreds of years before Branwen's story begins, I have also allowed for there to be some linguistic influence of the Aquilan language on Kernyvak. Since the Aquilan Empire never invaded Iveriu, their languages would have remained quite separate. Although, of course, Branwen and the rest of the Ivernic nobility speak Aquilan as a second language.

In creating the place names for Branwen's world, I have tried to incorporate relevant aspects of the Celtic tradition. For example, rīganī is the reconstructed Proto-Celtic word for "queen," and since the Land is a female goddess in Iveriu, it made sense for me to name the seat of power Castle Rigani. Likewise, bodwā is the Proto-Celtic word for "fight," which is fitting as the name of Branwen's family castle given that their motto is *The Right Fight*.

The ancient language of trees that Branwen calls the first Ivernic writing is a reference to the Irish Ogham alphabet. It was devised between the first and fourth centuries CE to transfer the Irish language to written form and is possibly based on the Latin alphabet. Ogham is found in approximately four hundred surviving stone inscriptions and is read from the bottom up. In addition to representing a sound, the letters of the Ogham alphabet have the names of trees and shrubs. The Ogham letter *coll* translates as "hazel" and represents the /k/ sound as in *kitten*. The Ogham letter *uillenn* translates as "honeysuckle" and represents the /ll/ sound as in *shell*.

Hence, when Branwen and Essy trace their private symbol, they are only writing two letters rather than a whole word.

The legend of Tristan and Isolt has been retold so many times in so many languages that simply choosing which form of the character names to use also poses somewhat of a challenge. Two possible origins for Tristan's name include Drustanus, son of Cunomorus, who is mentioned on a sixth-century stone inscription found in Cornwall, or a man named Drust, son of King Talorc of the Picts, who ruled in late eighth-century Scotland.

In the early Welsh versions of the legend, Drust becomes Tristan or Drystan. Tristan was the name propagated by the French poets, who employed its similar sound to the French word *tristesse* ("sadness") for dramatic effect. Another consistent feature of the legends is Tristan's disguising his identity by calling himself Tantris—an anagram of his name—and I therefore decided to do the same.

While the name Isolt is probably the most easily recognized, it is in fact derived from the Welsh name Essyllt. The French poets translated her name as Yso(lt) or Yseu(l)t(e). I have therefore synthesized the two for my Eseult.

In the Continental versions of the story, Isolt's lady's maid is usually called Brangien or Brangain. However, this is a borrowing from the Old Welsh name Branwen (br.n "raven" + (g)wen "fair"). This choice was also inspired by another Branwen from the Middle Welsh *Mabinogion*, the earliest prose stories in British literature. The Second Branch of the Mabinogi is called *Branwen uerch Lyr* ("Branwen, daughter of Llŷr"), the meaning of the patronym *ap Llŷr* being "Son of the Sea," and the connection that the Branwen of the Sweet Black Waves Trilogy feels for the sea was inspired by this forerunner.

The Branwen of the *Mabinogion* is a member of a Welsh royal family who is given in marriage to the King of Ireland to prevent a war after one of her brothers has offended him. When Branwen arrives at the Irish court, the vassals of the King of Ireland turn him against his new queen and she is forced to submit to many humiliations. Her brothers then declare war on Ireland, and Branwen is the cause of the war her marriage was meant to prevent.

Several prominent Celtic scholars have made the case that the Welsh Branwen can trace her roots to Irish Sovereignty Goddesses or that both the Welsh and Irish material derive from the same, earlier source. Particular evidence of this is that Branwen's dowry to the King of Ireland included the Cauldron of Regeneration, which could bring slain men back to life, and which served as the inspiration for Kerwindos's Cauldron in my own work.

While there is no evidence of a direct connection between the Branwen of the *Mabinogion* and the Branwen of the Tristan legends, I find the possibility enticing and so I have merged the two into my Branwen as a forceful female protagonist with magical abilities and a strong connection to the Land.

In the conclusion to the trilogy, I have introduced Princess Eseult Alba of Armorica, and the process of her naming reflects the ways in which my portrayal of her character deviates from the medieval legend. Now an integral part of the story, Tristan's marriage to a second woman also named Isolt was a later addition to the tale. This double for the woman he loves is known as Isolt of Brittany or Isolt of the White Hands (*Blanches Mains* in Old French). For the purposes of my world building, I decided to supplement the actual Roman place name for the Brittany Peninsula and parts of Gaul: Armorica. I also wanted to keep a hint of the epithet "of the White Hands" while reinventing the princess's relationship with the other women in the novel.

Scholars have suggested that the "White Hands" moniker might derive from the Welsh name *Essylt vynwen*, which is a variant of *meinwen* ("slender fair"), but that a French redactor could have misinterpreted the *mein* as *main* ("hand" in French) and then combined it with the correct translation of *(g)wen*, which, as we saw above, means "fair/white" in Welsh. Throughout the many variations of the Tristan legends, the association of the color white remains ambivalent: sometimes it alludes to beauty and purity; other times, it signifies danger and death.

The medieval Isolt of the White Hands that we've inherited is a flat, two-dimensional personage, cast as either a sniveling, unloved wife or a vengeful shrew. Her primary purpose is to serve as a foil for Isolt of Ireland. Tristan marries the second Isolt out of duty, but he does not desire her and their marriage is often unconsummated. American poet Dorothy Parker noted with her habitual acerbic wit: "How long these lovely hands have been/A bitterness to me!"

In Thomas d'Angleterre's twelfth-century verse romance, while Tristan lies dying from a poisoned wound, he sends for Isolt of Ireland to heal him. Enraged, Isolt of the White Hands exacts her retribution. She lies and tells her husband that the returning ship bears black sails, meaning that his true love has not come for him. Tristan dies in anguish, and when Isolt of Ireland arrives she, too, dies of a broken heart.

From the outset, I knew that I didn't want to perpetuate the narrative that pits one woman against the other: the inevitable "cat fight" that we see daily in literature and pop-culture. I wanted my Isolt of the White Hands to be a strong leader in her own right and to form friendships with her rivals based on mutual respect. Accordingly, I decided that she would prefer her middle name, Alba, which is entirely my own invention. However, *alba* is the feminine form of the Latin *albus* ("white"), and so I did not completely abandon her roots.

Albus may also be the origin of Albion: the oldest recorded name for the island of Britain. Geoffrey of Monmouth, among other chroniclers, noted that Albion was once populated by giants, hence my invented Kernyvak tale about the giantess Alba who carved out the island of Monwiku. I think it's a much better assignation for the independent, brave, and loyal Armorican princess, and I hope that readers will agree.

IVERNIC FESTIVALS

Imbolgos—Spring Festival of the Goddess Bríga

Belotnia—the Festival of Lovers

Laelugus—the Festival of Peace

Samonios—New Year Festival

IVERNIC LANGUAGE VOCABULARY

comnaide—always

derew—a pain-relieving herb

enigena—daughter

fidkwelsa—a strategy board game

Iverman/Ivermen—a person or persons from Iveriu

Iverni—the people of Iveriu

Ivernic—something of or relating to Iveriu

kelyos—a traditional Ivernic musical band

kladiwos—an Ivernic type of sword

kridyom—heart-companion

krotto—an Ivernic type of harp

lesana—ring-forts belonging to the Old Ones

ráithana—hills belonging to the Old Ones

sílomleie—an Ivernic type of cudgel made from blackthorn wood

skeakh—a whitethorn bush or tree

KERNYVAK FESTIVALS

Long Night—the shortest day of the year

Hunt of the Rixula—takes place the day before Long Night

Blessing of the Sea—a festival to mark the beginning of spring

KERNYVAK LANGUAGE VOCABULARY

dagos—better/good

damawinn—grandmother

dolos—pain

dymatis—"hello"/"good day"

karid—beloved

Kernyv Bosta Vyken—"Kernyv Forever"

Kernyvak—something of or relating to Kernyv

Kernyveu—the people of Kernyv

Kernyvman/Kernyvmen—a person or persons from Kernyv

kordweyd—a seer of the Cult of the Horned One

kretarv—carnivorous seabird

menantus—an apology/a deep brook

mormerkti—"thank you"

nosmatis—"good evening"

penaxta—prince

rix—king

rixina—queen

rixula—"little queen"/a red-breasted bird

sekrev—"you're welcome"

AQUILAN LANGUAGE VOCABULARY

ama—"I love"

amar—love

amare—bitter

de—of

en—in

est—"is"

eti—and

fálkr—a broad, curved sword

la—the

meos—my

misrokord—a thin dagger; literally means "mercy"

mortis—death

odai—"I hate"

vita—life

vos—you

SOURCES, LITERARY TRANSMISSION, AND WORLD-BUILDING

The legend of Tristan and Isolt is one of the best-known myths in Western culture, and arguably the most popular throughout the Middle Ages. The star-crossed lovers have become synonymous with passion and romance itself.

When I first decided to write Branwen's story, I put on my scholarly hat and reacquainted myself with the most influential versions of the Tristan tales, then followed their motifs and principle episodes backward in time before arranging them into a frame, a loom onto which Branwen's story could come to life. Despite the numerous retellings of Tristan and Isolt throughout the medieval period, the structure remains remarkably consistent.

The names of the main characters can be traced to post-Roman Britain (sixth or seventh century CE). There was no real Tristan or King Arthur, but there are tantalizing stone inscriptions in the British Isles that suggest local folk heroes whose names became attached to a much older body of tales, some mythological in genesis. And while there is evidence that some motifs may have been borrowed from Hellenic, Persian, or Arabic sources, the vast majority are Celtic. Rather than viewing these Celtic stories as direct sources for the Tristan and Isolt narratives, however, most scholars agree the medieval Irish and Welsh material should be viewed as analogues that presumably stem from the same, now lost, pan-Celtic source.

These oral tales were probably preserved by the druids, and our earliest surviving versions were written down by Christian clerics in Ireland between the seventh and ninth centuries, and in twelfth-century Wales. Because Ireland was never conquered by the Roman Empire, it didn't experience the same "Dark Age" as elsewhere in Europe. Women in early medieval Ireland also had many more rights and protections under the law, enshrined in *Cáin Adomnáin* (Law of Adomán), *ca.* 679-704 CE, than their Continental counterparts—which is echoed in the strong female protagonists of its literature.

There are three Old Irish tale-types that feed into the Tristan legend: 1. *aítheda* (or, elopement tales), in which a young woman runs away from her older husband with a younger man; 2. *tochmarca* (or, courtship tales), in which a woman takes an active part in negotiating a relationship with a man of her choosing that results in marriage; and 3. *immrama* (or, voyage tales), in which the hero takes a sea voyage to the Otherworld.

The Old Irish tales that share the most in common with Tristan and Isolt's doomed affair are *Tochmarc Emire* ("The Wooing of Emer"), a tenth-century *aíthed;* and *Tóraigheacht Dhiarmada agus Ghráinne* ("The Pursuit of Diarmuid and Gráinne"), an *aíthed* whose earliest text dates to the Early Modern Irish period but whose plot and characters can be traced to the tenth century. In these stories, the female characters wield tremendous power and are closer to their mythological roots as goddesses. Other tales that are reminiscent of Branwen's complicated relationship with Isolt include the ninth- or tenth-century *Tochmarc Becfhola* ("The Wooing of Becfhola") and the twelfth-century *Fingal Rónain* ("Rónán's act of kinslaying").

When the Romans withdrew from Britain in the fifth century, many residents from the south of the island immigrated to northern France. For the next five centuries, trade and communication was maintained between Cornwall, Wales, and Brittany. The Bretons spoke a language similar to Welsh and Cornish, which facilitated the sharing of the Arthurian legends, to which they added their own folktales. By the twelfth century, the professional Breton *conteurs* (storytellers) had become the most popular court entertainers in Europe, and it was these wandering minstrels who brought the Tristan legends to the royal French and Anglo-Norman courts—including that of Henry II of England and Eleanor of Aquitaine, famed for her patronage of the troubadours in the south of France.

The Breton songs of Tristan's exploits were soon recorded as verse romances by the Anglo-Norman poets Béroul, Thomas d'Angleterre, and Marie de France (notably, the only woman), as well as the German Eilhart von Oberge. Béroul's and Eilhart's retellings belong to what is often called the *version commune* (primitive version), meaning they are closer to their folkloric heritage. Thomas's Tristan forms part of the *version courtoise* (courtly version), which is influenced by the courtly love ideal.

The twelfth century is often credited with the birth of romance, and Tristan is at least partially responsible. Which is not to say that people didn't fall in love before then, of course (!), but rather that for the first time, the sexual love between a man and a woman, usually forbidden, became a central concern of literature. The first consumers of this new genre in which a knight pledges fealty to a distant, unobtainable (often married) lady were royal and aristocratic women and, like romance readers today, their appetite was voracious. While the audience was female, the poets and authors were male, often clerics in the service of noblewomen. The poetry produced at the behest of female aristocratic patrons might therefore be considered the first fan fiction.

However, while the courtly lady may have appeared to have the power over her besotted knight, in reality noblewomen were rapidly losing property and inheritance rights as the aristocracy became a closed class ruled by strict patrilinear descent. Legends like that of Tristan and Isolt provided a means of escape for noblewomen who were undoubtedly in less than physically and emotionally satisfying marriages of their own, while also reinforcing women's increasingly objectified status. The portrayal of women in the Tristan legends therefore exemplifies the conflict between the forceful protagonists of its Celtic origins and the new idealized but dehumanized courtly lady.

It is this conflict that particularly interests me as a storyteller and which I explore through my own female characters. Because the legend as I have inherited it is a mix of concerns from different historical epochs, I decided to set my retelling in a more fantastical context that allowed me to pick and choose the aspects of the tradition that best suited Branwen's story. In this way, I also followed in the footsteps of the medieval authors who, while they might make references to real places or kings, weren't particularly concerned with accuracy. The stories they produced weren't so much historical fiction as we think of it today but more akin to fantasy.

During the nineteenth century, the German composer Richard Wagner drew on his countryman Gottfried von Strassburg's celebrated thirteenth-century verse romance of Tristan as inspiration for his now ubiquitous opera. Gottfried had, in turn, used the Anglo-Norman version of Thomas d'Angleterre as his source material, demonstrating the unending cycle of inspiration and adaption. The Tristan legends started as distinct traditions that were grafted onto the Arthurian corpus (possibly in Wales, possibly on the Continent) and became forever intertwined with the thirteenth-century prose romances.

Concurrently with Gottfried, there was a complete Old Norse adaption by Brother Róbert, a Norwegian cleric, and the Tristan legends gained popularity not only throughout Scandinavia but on the Iberian Peninsula and in Italy. There were also early Czech and Belarusian versions, and it was later translated into Polish and Russian. Dante also references the ill-fated lovers in his fourteenth-century *Inferno*, and Sir Thomas Malory devoted an entire book to Tristan in his fifteenth-century *Le Morte d'Arthur*, one of the most famous works in the English language.

The popularity of Tristan and Isolt fell off abruptly during the Renaissance but was revived by the Romantic poets of the late eighteenth and early nineteenth centuries, who sought an antidote to the changes enacted by the Industrial Revolution—although they viewed their medieval past through very rose-tinted glasses. Nevertheless, the preoccupation with Tristan and Isolt, as well as their supporting characters, has persisted for more than a millennium and it would be surprising if it did not persist for another.